IRON GUARD

Hool made a more ostentatious assault on the enemy position, stepping out into the alleyway and launching a wide volley of las-fire down the alley. When he stopped firing, he lingered out of cover for a couple of seconds.

Tempted by the open target, an armoured figure leaned around the corner of the building, a slim, squared-off rifle with a wickedly sharp blade beneath the barrel carried in both hands. The creature's armour was polished black with dashes of red, the curved helmet topped by a plume of long red hair. It had the bladed rifle raised, pointed directly at Hool's head.

Three shots from Smoker's hellgun caught the thing square in the chest and it reeled back, gracelessly keeling face first into the ground.

More Imperial Guard from Black Library

BANEBLADE
Guy Haley

• THE MACHARIAN CRUSADE •
William King
Book 1: ANGEL OF FIRE
Book 2: FIST OF DEMETRIUS
Book 3: FALL OF MACHARIUS (2014)

• GAUNT'S GHOSTS •
Dan Abnett

THE FOUNDING
Contains books 1-3 in the series: First and Only,
Ghostmaker and Necropolis

THE SAINT
Contains books 4-7 in the series: Honour Guard, The Guns of Tanith,
Straight Silver and Sabbat Martyr

THE LOST
Contains books 8-11 in the series: Traitor General, His Last
Command, The Armour of Contempt and Only in Death

Book 12: BLOOD PACT
Book 13: SALVATION'S REACH

SABBAT WORLDS
Anthology edited by Dan Abnett

A WARHAMMER 40,000 NOVEL

IRON GUARD

MARK CLAPHAM

BLACK LIBRARY

To Georgina, who blew my deadline by being born partway through the writing of this book.

A BLACK LIBRARY PUBLICATION

First published in Great Britain in 2013 by
Black Library,
Games Workshop Ltd.,
Willow Road, Nottingham,
NG7 2WS, UK.

10 9 8 7 6 5 4 3 2 1

Cover illustration by Stefan Kopinski.

A CIP record for this book is available from the British Library.

UK ISBN: 978 1 84970 498 4
US ISBN: 978 1 84970 499 1

See Black Library on the internet at
www.blacklibrary.com

Find out more about Games Workshop
and the world of Warhammer 40,000 at
www.games-workshop.com

Printed and bound by CPI Group (UK) Ltd, Croydon, CR0 4YY

It is the 41st millennium. For more than a hundred centuries
the Emperor has sat immobile on the Golden Throne of Earth.
He is the master of mankind by the will of the gods, and master
of a million worlds by the might of his inexhaustible armies. He
is a rotting carcass writhing invisibly with power from the Dark
Age of Technology. He is the Carrion Lord of the Imperium for
whom a thousand souls are sacrificed every day, so that he may
never truly die.

Yet even in his deathless state, the Emperor continues his
eternal vigilance. Mighty battlefleets cross the daemon-infested
miasma of the warp, the only route between distant stars, their
way lit by the Astronomican, the psychic manifestation of the
Emperor's will. Vast armies give battle in His name on uncounted
worlds. Greatest amongst his soldiers are the Adeptus Astartes,
the Space Marines, bio-engineered super-warriors. Their comrades
in arms are legion: the Imperial Guard and countless Planetary
Defence Forces, the ever-vigilant Inquisition and the tech-priests of
the Adeptus Mechanicus to name only a few. But for all their
multitudes, they are barely enough to hold off the ever-present
threat from aliens, heretics, mutants - and worse.

To be a man in such times is to be one amongst untold
billions. It is to live in the cruellest and most bloody
regime imaginable. These are the tales of those times.
Forget the power of technology and science, for so much has
been forgotten, never to be re-learned. Forget the promise of
progress and understanding, for in the grim dark future
there is only war. There is no peace amongst the stars,
only an eternity of carnage and slaughter, and the
laughter of thirsting gods.

I, General Wharris, commend the 114th Mordian Iron Guard for their supreme valour in holding the line at the Siege of Defure. In acknowledgement of the 114th's unique achievement on this day I make the following commitment, and request that any successor to my command position honour it as I have:

That, should the 114th be anything less than totally annihilated in battle, if even a single Guardsman of the 114th still lives, then the regiment will be permitted to rebuild and recruit, and its surviving men and resources will not be merged with or seconded to any other regiment.

While soldiers of that regiment still stand, the 114th Mordian Iron Guard will also stand, in honour of how they stood today: fearless, unbreakable.

PROLOGUE

Only yesterday, Hool had been told that in a hostile universe, for a boy to reach manhood was a victory in itself. The day you turned eighteen, you could count yourself lucky to have got that far, knowing that so many children of the Imperium would never make it to such an age, having fallen to disease or accident or act of violence.

Eighteen years, they said. He should feel proud. It was an achievement.

Happy birthday, welcome to the world of men.

A day later, and those first eighteen years seemed relatively easy. Reaching eighteen years and one day old – at this point *that* seemed like it was going to be the real achievement.

Hool ran down a corridor, much like the corridors Hool had crawled, walked and run around his entire life. It echoed with the sound of shouts and swearing from behind him, his pursuers' voices reaching him when their physical grasp couldn't.

Hool ran harder, faster. It was a long corridor, and he didn't know where he was running to, other than away from his pursuers. This wasn't his lev, the horizontal where he'd been born and raised, the old 199.

That he had strayed from his own lev was the cause of all his current problems, the first mistake that had led him into danger. Celebrating that brief couple of weeks between the rigorous education all Mordian citizens lived through, and the beginning of an adult life of toil, he'd allowed himself to be led astray, ending up on a different lev, 226.

226 and 199. The tensions between these two levels ran deep and old, so deep no one quite knew where they had started. None of the many floors of the hab-pyramid in between those two levs had anything like the same rivalry.

199 and 226. Just numbers. Even by the standards of Mordian gang culture, it was arbitrary warfare. Now Hool was going to die for it, for wandering into an illegal drinking den on the wrong floor of his own damn hab.

Trust his luck to get recognised by two of the handful of 226ers he'd ever met in his entire schooling: Hervl and Rebek, who had been in the same compulsory weapons test as him a month before, down on one of the hab firing ranges.

The two boys from 226 had been cocky, overconfident, determined that their gang savvy and whatever shots they'd fired before would make them masters of a standard lasrifle.

Hool had scored higher than either Hervl or Rebek, who

had barely hit the outer rim of the targets. The instructor, a stocky woman in a light grey uniform, had noted Hool's marks but not given any indication his shots were remarkable. Hool had forgotten the experience the moment he'd left the range – just another bureaucratic ritual you had to go through as a Mordian youth coming of age.

It seemed that Hervl and Rebek remembered what had happened, and were determined to get payback for their humiliation.

The corridor was drab and grey, with only one in three of the lumens working. To Hool it was a dingy blur as he ran, motes of grit coughed out by ancient air processors causing his eyes to tear up. The main guidelines he had to follow as he ran were the markings on either side of him, thick stripes of rich blue paint, edged with thinner lines of red, that ran across every level in the hab.

Where everything else was poorly maintained, these lines of blue paint were fresh and unchipped, regularly repainted. It was a matter of respect that this blue line be marked for every citizen to see, proud and perfect.

It was Mordian blue. A deep, warm shade, an ideal of a dark, open sky that the Mordians themselves could only imagine, growing up within the lightless habs. Mordians prized colour and flair like no other society in the Imperium, a reaction to the dark, enclosed lives they led, and that blue was the most prestigious colour of all.

Hool had never seen outside the hab-pyramid. He'd lived his whole life deep within, his family never rich enough to even visit the edge, where shielded windows ran around the exterior of the hab, and look out into the dark of Mordian's endless night. Hool had seen picts, but he knew it wasn't the same.

He had held some hope of getting a transfer out of the hab, of being work-assigned to the Administratum, or even being sent off-world. Great Emperor, even one of the outer manufactorums would have been preferable to slaving away in the depths of the hab. His results from his last tests were good, and were currently chewing their way through a series of cogitators. Within the week his role would be assigned, and he would know how the rest of his adult life would be spent.

Of course, for that to happen he had to survive the day. Reaching the end of the corridor, Hool dropped to his knees, almost tumbling headfirst with his own forward momentum. He was relying on the layout of each lev being the same, and that knowledge didn't let him down – to his right was a busted-up maintenance hatch, and as on every floor of the hab it wasn't just unlocked, it was barely fastened.

There were few kids in the hab so timid that they hadn't crawled through one of these hatches a hundred times before, to climb the pipes in an atrium.

Ignoring the screams of abuse from the juves on his heels, not even daring to look back, Hool lifted the hatch and slithered through the hole beneath.

The bright yellow shirt Hool was wearing, an expensive silken garment that he saved for special occasions and lovingly hand-cleaned with a Mordian's pride in appearance, snagged on the rim of the hatch, briefly pulling him backwards.

Hool didn't stop to unhook it, instead forcing himself onwards, letting the fabric tear, pulling himself free and out through the hatch.

On the other side of the wall, Hool dropped a short distance onto a pipe that crossed the great atrium, grabbing one of the thick braces that held the sections of the pipe together. It was easy enough to stabilise himself – the pipe was far wider than he was, the curve so gentle as to be almost flat. He began to scurry on all fours, trying not to look down.

The atria were supposed to be inaccessible to residents of the habs, airwells sunk through the middle of the hab, crisscrossed with pipes, girders and splinted power cables. However, as some of the few open spaces in the habs, their lure had proven irresistible, access hatches constantly being broken open so that Mordians could crawl along the pipes and cables, enjoying the relative space and the free flow of air.

In the early days people had fallen, their screams echoing through every airwell in the hab as they plummeted to their demise, occasionally punctuated by a metallic *clang* as they bounced off an obstruction in mid-descent.

At some point the Tetrarchy, a government not known for yielding to the public will, had consented to the placement of atrium-wide grilles every ten floors, which had become unofficial, but sanctioned, meeting places. People still climbed the pipes, still fell, still died – but at least now they wouldn't fall as far, and the screams were relatively brief.

All this was hab history, as well drilled into Hool as any formal lesson.

Halfway across the pipe, he leaned over. One floor down, another pipe crossed the atrium at ninety degrees to the one he was crossing. It was a long drop, but not impossible. If he landed properly, he should be able to avoid falling off, while preventing himself from dropping all the way to the grille at 220.

Six floors to the grille, then out through the big hatch on the other side. Hool would then be enough turns and distance ahead of Hervl and Rebek to get himself lost in the intersection, then find his way back down to his own lev.

All he had to do was find a safe, quick way down through six floors' worth of criss-crossing pipes, cables and gantries without falling to his death.

A metallic tap rang out behind Hool. He turned around to see Hervl squatting on the same pipe as him, knocking his knuckles against the metal. Having got Hool's attention, Hervl stood up straight and began to walk across the pipe, slowly but with perfect balance. He was showing off, a smug grimace across his wide, pink face.

Hervl held his arms level at his sides, hands slightly spread. Hool could see the dark weight of a folded knife in Hervl's right hand, sharply contrasting with his light green jacket, his 226 colours.

No way back. Hool rolled off one pipe, falling towards the one below.

Hool fell straight down, hitting the pipe below shoulder first, rolling with his momentum as he made contact with the hard surface. The shock jolted through his upper body, but he managed to roll over onto his front and get a handhold before he slid off the pipe.

Ignoring the ache from his arm, Hool pulled himself to his feet and ran across the second pipe, hands dangling forwards just in case he slipped and needed to grab anything. It was only a dozen paces before he was level with a thick cable rig, only a slightly bigger drop away than Hool's own height, relatively level with his position on the pipe. Hundreds of cables were bundled together in the rig, braced with plasteel splints that kept them rigid.

Hool shimmied sideways off the edge of the pipe, until he was hanging by his fingertips, then dropped the rest of the way. He landed well, quickly balancing himself as he found his footing on the rig.

There was a heavy smack above as Hervl dropped onto the second pipe, following Hool's example. Hool heard a laugh from across the atrium, and saw Rebek shimmying down a series of vertical pipes on the atrium wall, moving down faster than Hool could.

He needed to move quick, or be trapped by their pincer movement. The next few steps down were easy enough: a series of relatively short drops from rig to pipe to rig, with small shuffles back and forth to line up with the next level. Landing on the top of a creaking, thin waste pipe, Hool was halfway there – only three levels to go and he would be at the grille.

His next jump was a difficult one, an awkward leap across a wide gap to a narrow maintenance gantry a level below. With a run-up, it would have been easy, but the narrowness of the pipe, and its angle compared to the gantry, made it more difficult.

Hool froze, intimidated by the jump he had to make, his eyes fixed between where he was and the gantry he needed to reach. Halfway there, but it was still a long way down.

Something very small and very fast hit Hool in the forehead, snapping him out of his haze of indecision and nearly causing him to lose his balance. It was a missile from Rebek. He looked across to see Rebek, hanging from a pipe on the wall, laughing at him. The laughter was echoed from above by Hervl.

Retreat wasn't an option. Hool steadied himself, ran a few paces along the pipe, then with all his strength jumped forwards and to the right, pushing himself away with his heel. He twisted through the air in an ungainly fashion, falling towards the gantry.

For a second, it seemed like he wouldn't make it, that he would fall short, and far. He stretched out his fingers, as if that would make any difference.

Hool hit the railing of the gantry with another bruising thump, the lateral bar catching under his armpits, his legs kicking thin air. He felt something give in his ribcage, but scrabbled to grip the railing tightly between his arms and body, rather than slip straight off.

Hool took a second to manage the pain, to take a deep breath, then attempted to swing himself up onto the gantry. His first attempt failed, his foot failing to gain purchase on the base of the gantry, but second time around he managed it. Hool pulled himself upright, rolled over the railing and onto the gantry proper.

Another missile hit him, bouncing off his chest and

landing on the gantry. It was a small coin, virtually value-less. Hool felt a brief surge of rage. It was bad enough having coins thrown at him by rich edger bastards when he was a little kid – he wasn't taking it from 226ers. He was going to shake them off, come back with a gang from his own level, and show them.

With a brief glance over the edge, and ignoring the grow-ing number of bruises that smarted all over his body, Hool leapt off the gantry, dropping to another immediately below. He landed on his feet, dropping to one knee to cushion the impact. He ran across the gantry to where it met the wall, climbed on the left railing, and leapt across to grab a vertical pipe that ran nearly all the way down to the grille.

His grip failed him. Hands slipping off the well-oiled pipe, he fell straight down, landing on the grille with an agonis-ing crunch. Pain seared up his right leg as it crumpled under him, and his right arm twisted out of his shoulder socket. He rolled over onto his front, his face pressing against the cold metal mesh of the grille.

Hool must have passed out, because the next thing he was aware of was being struck across the back of the head, hard. He tried to push himself up with his bad arm, and cried out in agony. Pain caused him to instinctively let himself go, dropping back to the floor, but a kick to the ribs brought him back up again.

As another blow struck him on the back, Hool forced himself up with his good left arm, trying to push himself away from the source of the blows. Through watering eyes, he could see that Hervl was raising a length of thin metal, presumably pulled from the wall of the atrium or torn from one of the gantries, ready to bring it crashing down on Hool. Rebek was standing back, maybe preparing for another kick.

Hool weakly shuffled backwards across the grille, feebly raising his broken arm in his own defence. There was little else he could do.

Happy birthday, welcome to the world of men.

'Mordians, present!'

The voice was deep and loud, the order bouncing back off the walls of the atrium, like the screams of falling Mordians all those centuries ago.

Those two words hit both Hool and his assailants and triggered an instant reaction, one so deeply instilled through their short lives that it was barely conscious.

Hervl dropped his weapon and spun on his heels, Rebek also turning and stepping next to his friend, so that the 226ers were in perfect line. Hool used his unbroken arm to pull himself onto the knee of his unbroken leg then, gripping the grille with that good hand, managed to pull himself onto one foot.

While his assailants stood stiffly next to him Hool unfolded himself, centimetre by agonising centimetre, until he was standing next to them. He was shaky on one leg, but he stood to attention nonetheless, tear-stung eyes staring forwards.

The man who had given the order walked briskly across the grille to inspect them. He wore a sergeant's uniform, as well-pressed and cleaned as would be expected, but a little worn around the edges. The blue of his coat was slightly faded, the brass of his epaulettes dented from combat. The front of his coat had the rigidity that indicated he was wearing battle armour underneath, and displayed a proud iron aquila.

The sergeant took off his peaked hat, better to inspect the three young men before him. He was, to Hool's eyes, middle-aged, with weathered skin and close-cropped hair. A thin scar ran across the top of his head, a white-pink line through the stubble.

His face had a colour that Hool had only seen in picts, the reddish tinge that only those who had travelled off-world possessed. In the habs even Mordians who, like Hool, were born with naturally dark skin had a pallid sheen to them, a side effect of lives spent without natural light.

The sergeant looked each of them up and down, his brown eyes passive and expressionless. When he came to Hool his glance flicked downwards briefly, to the crippled leg Hool was keeping off the ground. When his glance met Hool's, there was an odd expression, something Hool couldn't quite read.

'I am Sergeant Polk of the 114th Iron Guard,' the sergeant said, producing a small, aged device and raising it to Hervl's right eye. The device flashed, causing Hervl to flinch. 'You may have heard of us. The Unbreakables.'

Polk looked at Hervl witheringly, then repeated the process with Rebek and Hool. Hool tried not to react, but found the light left his vision even more blurred than before, coloured spots swimming before him.

'You boys clearly have some youthful energy to work off,' said Polk. 'And this is your lucky day, citizens...' Polk examined his device, reading off a small pict-screen. '...citizens

Raif Hervl, Thurt Rebek and Fernand Hool. None of you are assigned reserved occupations, all of you are of fighting age and today the glorious 114th has new orders, and requires a spontaneous raising to fill its ranks.'

Polk looked all three of them straight in the eye, one after another.

'Congratulations, you've just been recruited. I had some doors to knock on, but you've saved me three of those.'

'Report to station six in two cycles' time,' Polk shouted back to them as he marched away. Halfway across the atrium, he turned around.

'Oh, and Hervl, Rebek – get Hool to the nearest infirmary and make sure he's fixed up. Any of you three turn up dead or go missing before you report for duty, the ones who survive will be fighting in a penal platoon. Front line, no guns.'

Polk's parting words barely registered with Hool. Cramp had crawled up his good leg, and he was beginning to shake. His broken limbs were numb. As Hervl and Rebek, muttering and swearing to each other, moved to grab him by the shoulders and carry him away, darkness crept into Hool's peripheral vision, and his leg finally gave way beneath him.

Fernand Hool, newest recruit to the Imperial Guard, fell.

ONE

Hool fell.

He tumbled through the air in a cloud of splintered wood and plaster dust, landing awkwardly on a hard floor covered with broken junk and trash. He rolled on impact, the knee pads of his uniform absorbing most of the initial impact, allowing his body to roll out the momentum rather than jerk to a halt.

Broken roof tiles and chunks of plaster clattered around Hool, debris from the ceiling that had collapsed beneath him. He lay on his back, letting his vision settle. If he had broken anything, the worst thing to do would be to try and stand without checking.

He tried to blink dust out of his eyes, but it kept falling, so he closed them. Hool very gently stretched the muscles in his arms and legs, and felt no resistance except for a slight ache.

Good – nothing broken. He rubbed his eyes with the fingers of his right hand, then held the palm over them at an angle, keeping the rain of dust away.

Hool blinked a couple of times, adjusting to the light within the room he had fallen into. It wasn't much to take in: a standard workspace, narrow and dimly lit with rows of cogitators on plain desks. Small, high-set windows allowed shafts of orange dusk-light to fall into the centre of the room, providing some faint illumination.

That light was cut off by a shadow falling over Hool. He instinctively reached down for the lasrifle he could feel resting on his chest, its shoulder strap half-stuck under his left elbow. His hand was kicked away and an instruction barked into his face.

'Hands up!'

Hool felt something cold under his chin, not sharp enough to cut on contact but probably jagged enough to gouge his windpipe open if enough pressure were applied. Whatever it was jabbing into his flesh, it was being held unsteadily, the cold edge shifting against his skin.

He gently lifted his hands level with his head, wishing that he had at least had the chance to push himself up onto his elbows before getting caught.

The dust seemed to have settled, and Hool's eyes had fully adjusted to the dark. He looked at the man standing over him: stripped to the waste, head shaved, face and upper body covered with a crude tattoo of an inverted aquila, the eagle's twin heads curving down beneath his ribcage.

A rebel, a *usurperist* to be precise. Exactly who Hool was

expecting, but that was hardly a comfort, especially when this one seemed to be in the grip of some kind of mania: eyes wild, teeth clenched, shaking with some internal tension.

From the angle Hool was looking up from, he couldn't quite make out the weapon being held under his chin, but previous experience, and the angle of his captor's arms, suggested a looted lasrifle with a makeshift bayonet welded to the barrel.

Hool gulped involuntarily – a side-effect of breathing in so much dust – and the bayonet gouged into his chin. He tried not to flinch further, and stayed still and calm. For some reason, the rebel hadn't fired yet, which meant that there was a slim hope of Hool getting out of this alive, provided he didn't startle his captor. Judging by the man's slim build, he had probably been some form of administratum drone before falling in with the heretical followers of one of the usurpers, the false Emperors. The usurpers had that effect, their presence turning nobodies into fanatics through the mania of the crowd.

The rebel licked his lips, then spoke.

'Kell, get in here!' he shouted, not taking his eyes off Hool. 'We've got a visitor.'

Hool was gripped by a chill, not just by the confident tone of voice, but by the presence of another rebel so close. One might not have the nerve to shoot an incumbent man through the head, or jab a twisted piece of metal through his skull – but two would encourage each other. The same group hysteria that had drawn these people into worshipping a false god would have them happily decorating themselves with Hool's guts in a couple of minutes.

He had to act now, grab the barrel of the lasrifle and thrust it back as hard as he could into the rebel's face, then hope that the rebel didn't squeeze the trigger, or at least that he paused long enough to give Hool time to force it to one side.

It wasn't the best plan, but it was all Hool had. He stretched his fingers gently within his glove, hopefully not enough to be noticeable.

A door somewhere to Hool's right creaked open, beyond his field of vision, and the rebel glanced in that direction.

Hool took his chance, and made a grab for the gun barrel he couldn't even see, his arm seeming to move painfully slowly.

As Hool made his move, the rebel looked back at him, a murderous intensity in his eyes.

Hool had the vertiginous feeling of not being quick enough, of a trigger finger faster than his own, of everything coming to an end–

The rebel jerked back as an explosion echoed around the room, his head reduced to a red mist.

Hool didn't question the source of this miracle, but followed through on his grab, seizing the barrel of the rebel's gun and forcing it back and upwards, a ragged scrap of metal sweeping perilously close to the tip of Hool's nose. His other hand reached instinctively for where he knew the butt of the gun must be and clasped it. Before the rebel could even drop to the floor Hool was kicking his knee, pushing him away.

It was a standard lasrifle, and Hool swivelled it around in his grasp, finding the trigger and raising the barrel as he rolled towards the sound of the opening door. His thumb swept the area above the trigger where the safety catch lay, and found it was already off.

The words *near miss* flashed through Hool's mind, but he ignored them, raising and aiming the weapon before he even had a clear look at the target. Hool landed on his side, lasrifle aimed.

Another rebel stood in the open doorway, his own gun rising, the beginnings of a shout on his open mouth.

Hool squeezed the trigger on his stolen lasrifle three times in quick succession, three rapid shots hitting his target in the torso. Hool watched the body drop to the floor, and held his lasrifle steady in case of further movement.

The door flapped shut with another creak. Hool paused, taking a deep breath. There was no sign of any further usurperists arriving to avenge their fallen brothers.

Only then did Hool allow himself to look up, towards the hole in the roof he had fallen through, and the only place that the shot that killed the first rebel could have come from.

Sergeant Polk, Hool's immediate superior, grinned down through the hole. His combat shotgun was poking downwards, the fat barrel still smoking from the short-range shot that had taken the first rebel's head clean off.

Polk coughed and touched the side of his neck, activating the vox-bead in his collar.

'Sergeant Essler? Guardsman Hool has found a way into the compound. North-west corner of the roof.' There was a pause as Polk received a brief reply. 'Yes, a couple of rebels but they're dealt with, no problems. We'll secure and hold.'

Polk gave Hool a look that said *and that's all he needs to know.*

Hool nodded gratefully, and hurriedly pulled himself to his feet, dusting himself down. Polk was doing Hool a favour by not reporting Hool's fall through the roof, and Hool wouldn't forget that. Hool also suspected that this wasn't just leniency, but an acknowledgement that mistakes would be made in the heat of the moment, especially by Guardsmen going into a combat situation totally unprepared.

It was no one's fault. Time was against them, and there was no opportunity to plan or prepare or obtain proper resource. Either they succeeded by nightfall, or... The alternative wasn't worth even considering.

It had been nearly a year since Hool's conscription, a year that had taken him from the habs of Mordian to a different hive world: Elisenda.

Elisenda was a beautiful name for an ugly world, an industrial planet of strategic importance, manufacturing supplies that shipped across the Imperium.

Once, it may have lived up to the delicacy of its name, but millennia of heavy industry and over-habitation had wrecked Elisenda's environment.

Manufactorum complexes had sprawled across the landscape, and as the hab-blocks couldn't be built fast enough to house the working population, makeshift slum habs grew in the spaces between the industrial sites.

Elisenda had no shortage of habitable land, and so when one factory or foundry became obsolete, the entire site was abandoned and a new factory sprung up on virgin territory, the population shifting to the new centre of activity.

While ever greater manufactories expelled poison into the skies and rivers, the deserted sites were partially claimed by lifeless sands that had once been fertile ground, dunes of dust and filth consuming them until only broken smoke-stacks piercing the sky indicated that these deserts had ever been inhabited land.

The people of Elisenda laboured on production lines and in furnaces, crawling back to the hovels they had made themselves for a brief rest before the next day of servicing the endless demands for components and materials across the Imperium. As humanity waged war on the alien and the heretic, the demands for supplies never let up, and all other matters were secondary.

The resentments of Elisenda's population, sweating beneath a smoke-stained sky, were an ideal breeding ground for dissent. When a heretical idea – that the God-Emperor of Mankind was dead, and would be reborn somewhere on Elisenda – began to spread throughout Elisenda's hierarchies, official and unofficial, no one in the Administratum had sufficient oversight to understand what was happening. The highest echelons of planetary authority had fallen to this peculiar heresy first, in secret, waiting as the local magisterium and planetary defence force came under their influence.

When various individuals emerged claiming to be the reborn Emperor, they gathered supporters and attempted to seize power from the legitimate authorities and each other, slaughtering loyalists and the followers of rival usurpers alike. While pockets of loyal resistance remained, most had already been corrupted or neutralised.

Only intervention from outside could drive the stain of heresy from Elisenda and restore order so that the supply ships could run once more. Not only was the loss of Elisenda a logistical one, but the absence of the true faith, and the worshipping of unchecked psykers claiming to be the Emperor reborn, made Elisenda a potential breeding ground for Chaos. While some of the false Emperors were mere opportunists with no psychic power, the mad psykers needed to be put down quickly before they grew so powerful that they brought daemons to Elisenda, and the whole system fell to Chaos.

Among the forces dispatched to Elisenda were the 114th Mordian Iron Guard regiment, the so-called Unbreakables, and among their number the newly recruited Guardsman Hool.

Hool, along with the rest of the regiment, had been on Elisenda for the best part of a year.

Less than an hour before he had fallen through the roof into a near-death encounter with two rebels, Polk's squad had been receiving what passed for a briefing. The slim information provided was rendered even less helpful by the location of the briefing – a moving Chimera, heading towards the target at the maximum speed attainable for a troop carrier.

It was a very bumpy ride as the Chimera negotiated the junk-strewn streets of one of Elisenda's largest city-slums, the sides of the vehicle throwing up sparks as it clipped the enclosing walls of the narrow alleyways.

Jostled from side to side within the Chimera were a driver, and Polk's squad. Aside from the sergeant and Hool there were eight other men. Corporal Midj was Polk's right-hand man, a few years older but lower in rank. Midj wasn't much of a shot, but he had a reputation for being able to set exactly the right quantity of explosive and the perfect charge for any job.

Hool had heard a rumour that Midj had once, long before joining Polk's squad, won a bet by blasting the badge from the front of his cap with a spot of high explosive, while wearing the cap, without scorching a hair on his own head. The money Midj won had been enough to make the month of night duties imposed by his sergeant for vandalising his uniform worthwhile.

The rest of the rank were common Guardsmen, like Hool: Dall, a heavy-set man with a carefully waxed moustache who, in spite of his bulk, could run without making a sound; Nauk and Keller, veterans of a number of previous campaigns, who spoke in unintelligible gang-slang learned growing up in a different hive to Hool; Okre, a softly spoken Guardsman recruited from a ravaged agri-world, who maintained his equipment carefully and frequently compared them to the tools he used to till the harsh ground of his lost home world; the hulking Blant, tall and gruff, half his face covered with red burns from an explosion that had destroyed the regiment's Chimera depot, taking most of the vehicles with it; and finally Treston and Gobu, recruits from the same press-gang as Hool.

The voice of Lieutenant Munez squawked out of the Chimera's internal vox from every corner of the vehicle but was still intermittently inaudible, drowned out by the grinding of gears and brakes as they took a corner, or some chunk of debris clattered or crunched beneath the hefty treads.

The basics had been explained to them before the Chimera had arrived to take them away from their previous assignment, a raid on one of the makeshift hab-slums that had grown up between the working factories and facilities of Elisenda. It was supposed to be a standard raid, undertaken either just before dawn or after dark. This one was due to take place in a couple of hours, at nightfall.

As their vox-operator had been hastily told, something more important had come up: intelligence suggested that the power complex at city sector Z-20-Q had fallen into rebel hands and that they intended to overload the main generator stacks. If overload occurred, not only would manufactories vital to the Imperium be deprived of power for months, cutting off the production of supplies, but half the continent would be left polluted, possibly uninhabitable for unaugmented humans, for years to come.

Without really wanting to, Hool had picked up a working knowledge of Elisendan beliefs during the campaign, many of which were shared by both usurperists and those still loyal to the Emperor. Due to Elisenda's ancient history as an agricultural colony, the dusk signified a propitious time for any ritual seeking the favour of the Emperor, as a successful rite during that period would bring a great harvest at the next dawn – even if that harvest were one of bodies and blight, a scourge that poisoned the land.

In line with these beliefs, Munez's intelligence stated that the rebels intended to detonate the main reactor at nightfall. This left precious few hours to avert a disaster.

Those were the basics; that, and the fact that only two squads, Polk's and Sergeant Essler's squad of veterans, a mere twenty men in all, were the nearest to the sector, and should proceed there as soon as possible. How they were supposed to deal with the situation, only Munez could say.

'Reinforcements are being gathered, and will be on location within the hour,' squeaked Munez's voice through the vox.

Hool could feel a major caveat to this supportive statement coming.

'However, we do not have time to wait for the full force to arrive before taking action,' Munez continued, leaving another pause for the inevitable grunts of protest from around the Chimera. 'The defences at the power complex are substantial, and any attempt to break through the main gates with explosives or lascutters could lead to the rebels deciding to detonate early.

'We have no access to detailed plans of the facility, but there is a north-side administration block adjacent to the Colup slum-hab. Enter the admin block through the adjacent hab, then proceed through the complex to the main dome. Security control will be in a prominent position with direct views of the generatoria and the entry gates.'

'Gain access to the security data-stacks and unlock the place. Prevent any attempt to detonate. I know this is a challenge, but you are all we have for now. Open those gates, and we *will* be there to provide support. Until then, I'm afraid you're on your own. Sergeant Polk, I'm giving Sergeant Essler operational command on this one – convene with him on arrival.'

Munez cut off communications. A short while later the Chimera tore to a halt in a rancid back alley, and Hool and his fellow Guardsmen stepped out of the hot tin box of the Chimera into the even less comfortable muggy heat outside. Essler and his squad were already waiting for them.

They had proceeded on foot through the corridors and stairwells of the slums to the roof of the administration block, where a search had begun to find an access point.

Spreading out across the sweating expanse of chem-sealed recycled panelling they had lost sight of each other, disappearing behind the extractor pipes, air processors, and all the other junk that kept an administration building of this size running.

The ugly metal blocks and tubes reminded Hool of Elisenda's buildings, the grim functionality of factories and generatoria. Looking across at his fellow Guardsmen searching the rooftop, they had looked like giants walking among hab-blocks, the heat haze lifting off the sun-curdled rooftop a miniature replica of the smog clouds that clogged the sky.

Hool had blinked sweat from his eyelids. His mind was wandering, he knew that. This realisation was too late for him to avoid clumsily stepping on a badly patched section of roof and falling right through it.

* * *

After Hool had opened up a route into the building, the rest of the men quickly convened on that position and dropped, with greater dignity and precision, into the room below. They were just twenty men, a mere two squads to deal with an indeterminate number of rebels. Polk's men were in a secondary position to the veterans, led by Sergeant Essler, known to anyone below the rank of major as 'Smoker'.

While Polk's men were line infantry, wearing the traditional Mordian blue, Smoker's men were veterans, their charcoal jackets indicating their role as raiders and marksmen. Mordians were known for their boldness: wearing bright colours into battle, standing fearless in rigid lines of attack.

But even a Mordian regiment couldn't entirely neglect the occasional need for stealth and precision, for soldiers who could be unseen until the moment of attack, and disappear before the enemy had time to retaliate.

Smoker and his squad were those men. Until they had been brought together by Munez's orders, Hool had never really spoken to any of the veterans, and he didn't know their names. They were quiet men, used to long hours waiting to strike, days spent preparing in silence.

But Hool knew Smoker. Everyone in the regiment knew Smoker. In spite of having a reputation for stealth on the battlefield, in other ways he was very, very hard to miss.

Polk had told Hool the story, but had omitted the details, to avoid the memories as much as anything: of a battlefield many years before, of the medicae dragging young Corporal Essler past on a gurney, the contents of an acid shell eating through his face, of a scream that suddenly died as he lost the ability to make the noise.

Hool had watched Polk lapse into silence, chewing on a thumbnail as he recounted the incident. One of the Adeptus Mechanicus attached to the regiment, Magos Gilham, had assisted the medicaes in saving Essler's life, using the Cult of Mars's knowledge of bodily augmentation to replace damaged flesh and bone with mechanical equivalents.

A rebreather sat where his mouth and nose had been, with built-in filters that could screen out poisons and pollutants behind vertical slashes in a surface of polished black metal. Nozzle holes at the side of the mouth allowed Smoker to plug in his food supply, bypassing his airways to run down thin tubes straight to his stomach. His synthesised voice could channel straight into an inbuilt vox, allowing him to communicate long-distance without anyone nearby hearing, should he wish.

Then, connected to his optic nerves, complex picters ran beyond the visible spectrum, with two adjustable lenses that ran on whirring, automated motors, retracting and extending as the user looked closely, or into the distance.

All of these augmentations had, in the end, made Essler into a better soldier, able to enter dangerous environments without recourse to additional rebreathers or goggles, making him a finer marksman than any unaugmented Guardsman.

But they didn't make him the Essler he had been before. From that day onwards he was Smoker.

Smoker led the way as they progressed through the administration block, moving from room to room, corridor to corridor, Smoker and his men in the lead, Polk's squad taking the rear.

Smoker's weapon of choice was the hellgun. As they made their way through the building, Smoker would occasionally raise a hand to pause the men behind him, raise his hellgun and let off a shot – sometimes at a figure down a corridor that he had spotted ahead, at other times seemingly at a blank wall.

In the case of the former, Hool would see a body as the Guard continued on their way. In the case of the mysterious shots to the wall, the high-powered las-shot would tear through the cheap interior walls and disappear, but no doubt there was a body, somewhere out of sight: a rebel unseen by Hool and the rest of the men, but a thermal target vulnerable to a predator that the heretic would never see coming.

Hool had been a Guardsman for less than a year, but he already knew his steady aim was one of his better skills – Smoker's targeting made Hool look like a kid throwing half a brick.

Once, this must have been another drab building where Administratum bureaucrats spent long shifts working at rows of cogitators, a miserable but unthreatening place. Now it had been unutterably changed by the presence of the heretics: walls had been smashed through, seemingly without logic or practicality. Some rooms were wrecked, daubed with blood and graffiti. Others were left untouched.

They passed a pristine bathroom, and a few doors later an office that had been turned into a crude cesspit. Hool had fought these rebels for the best part of a year, and he still had little understanding of how they thought.

A winding stairwell took them down to ground level, each man covering a different potential point of entry as they descended. No attack came.

Approaching a set of double doors, Smoker stopped the squad with a raised finger, and they dropped back into a waiting position. The sergeant communicated a quick set of instructions to two of his men with a series of hand gestures.

Squads often had their own odd shorthand language, refined between fighting men down the years, but the meaning of these gestures was clear:

Two enemies ahead. Go around. Eliminate quietly.

The two Guardsmen gave their superior a curt nod, and disappeared down a side corridor. When they had gone, Smoker gave the rest of the squad a patting direction, indicating they should drop back to the previous room.

'Two sentries ahead,' said Smoker, after the door had closed behind them. His voice was metallic and emotionless, a slight whine of electronic feedback at the end of every sentence. It made the hairs on Hool's forearm twitch, like a sting of static.

'Hellick and Katz will deal,' Smoker continued. Each phrase came out as a harshly modulated burst of words: 'Sentries guard conduit between here and dome.' Smoker checked his chronometer. 'Not much time. Move quickly, find cover in dome. Stay low. I assess situation, then orders.'

He turned to Polk. 'Sergeant Polk, once we ID security control, move to capture. Stay hidden. If you are exposed, we will provide covering fire, distraction.'

Polk began to protest: 'But–'

Smoker silenced him with a sharp hand gesture. 'Yes, my men are good in the shadows, stalking ahead, but we also have the longer range of fire. Better for you to run while we provide cover. Better chance of success. We are experts in stealth, but also experts in causing confusion. Get to security control, open the gates. We will draw enemy fire. Trust me, we will hold their attention.'

Polk gave a brisk, respectful nod.

Hellick entered the room. 'Sentries down, sir. We have a clear route through to the main dome. Katz is keeping watch.'

Smoker nodded. He turned to the rest of the men. 'You have your orders. Succeed, or don't live long enough to know failure.'

With that odd motivational speech, he turned and led the way.

Polk passed close to Hool as they followed.

'Cheery one, ain't he?' Polk whispered.

It was a short run to reach the main dome, and a series of battered equipment banks provided convenient cover once the Guard were in.

Peering around the edge of one of the blocks of equipment, Hool thought that the positioning of this cover was really the only positive aspect of the situation. Cover aside, it was all bad: Hool didn't need to be a strategist or senior officer to work that out.

At the centre of the dome stood four great generatorium stacks, broad columns of equipment that almost reached the surface of the rockcrete dome. The stacks showed no sign of the huge amounts of energy coursing through them, with the exception of the teeth-rattling background hum that filled the entire dome. Insulated maintenance rigs allowed access to the stacks, which were placed a short distance apart.

In the centre of the dome, equidistant between the generatoria, was the main reactor, a semi-translucent sphere clasped in four great fingers of rockcrete, illuminated by the terrible energies within. Thick knots of cables ran between the reactor and the stacks. Occasionally a stream of untamed power would burst out from the globe's surface, only to be captured by the nearest stack and disappear. These discharges lit up the entire dome, streaking the vision of anyone unfortunate enough to look straight at the blazing streams of energy.

Hool turned his attention to the maintenance platform that had been rigged between two of the stacks. It had been decorated with drapes adorning the inverted aquila to create some kind of altar piece. A bank of equipment had been installed on the platform, which trailed thin cables to a series of canisters placed around the reactor. If – and it wasn't a great leap of logic to make – these were explosives, with a detonator at the altar, then the intelligence that had caused Munez to order them here had been right.

It wasn't the mechanics of the scene that caused Hool's stomach to knot so much as the players. Three rebels stood on the altar platform, two dressed in ragged white robes while a central man wore far more elaborate garb. Stripped to the waist like most of the rebels they had seen, his tattoos and scars were accompanied by an extraordinary ceremonial rigging, a structure of bone and steel that started at the base of his spine. It was attached to his torso with straps that ran around his chest, then exploded at shoulder height into an ornate head-dress that rose like a banner above him, a grotesque industrial approximation of a wheat sheaf.

One of the false emperors, a usurper who had indoctrinated his followers in a twisted version of their old beliefs in the Emperor as bringer of sun and rain, father of the harvest. Eliminate him, and a whole front in the war on Elisenda would collapse, leaderless.

This false emperor addressed a crowd of followers, over a hundred strong, gathered before the generatorium stacks. His every utterance was greeted with shouts and manic gibbering. Ritual fires were burning, the tinder at their core looking suspiciously like human bones. Were those the remains of the power complex's non-heretical workers, Pool wondered?

Many of the rebels still wore the rough-cut trousers of workers, and had crafted weapons and ceremonial staffs from industrial tools. A few had lasguns, but not many.

Still, the numbers were the threat: in the long campaign against the Elisendan heretics, Hool had been involved in confrontations of all scales, from small hab-raids to massed battles in courtyards and squares. But on every occasion the numbers had been even or in the Guard's favour. Untrained and undisciplined, the rebels' only chance of gaining a strategic advantage was to vastly outnumber the Guardsmen, an advantage they were scrupulously denied.

Now, twenty Mordians faced over a hundred rebels, with

little time until their leader detonated the reactor, and the risk that he could do so earlier if the Guard's presence were detected.

The scale of the conflict ahead would have left him frozen if Polk hadn't slapped him on the shoulder to get his attention.

The squad gathered around Polk for instruction.

'Our target is on the other side of the dome, about three storeys up, accessible by an open stairwell. The most covered route will be around the back of the stacks, but we won't stay unseen for long, so we need to move fast. One of us needs to get to that control centre, so don't let anything slow you down. If one of us falls or gets swamped, leave them behind; don't pause to provide fire support or stop to help.'

They nodded, and Polk gestured to Smoker that they were ready.

Smoker raised his hellgun. 'Distraction. One minute. Go.'

Hool ran, keeping as low and discreet as he could. Polk took the lead, dashing between cover as they ran between banks of equipment, avoiding the open as much as possible and, where line of sight between the Guardsmen and the horde of rebels was unavoidable, veering towards the shadows.

The air in the dome was thick with strange fumes and the foul scent of burning flesh, and Hool felt his lungs burn. The traitors had taken up a rhythmic chant that echoed around the dome, which combined with Hool's own racing heartbeat and the pounding of his boots on the hard floor to form an oppressive drumbeat in his ears.

Polk's squad were halfway around the curve of the dome when Smoker provided his 'distraction'. A shot rang out, audible even over the din of the rebels, and was quickly followed by screams of anger. Hool glanced around – he had direct line of sight between two of the stacks, and caught a glimpse of a headless figure falling from the altar platform.

Smoker had taken out the false emperor. A volley of shots rang out, presumably tearing into the other rebels on the platform.

Hool and the rest of the squad kept running. The chanting was now a discordant, angry babble. Hool risked another glance – the rebels were surging in the direction of Smoker and his men with murderous intent.

Polk's squad were now in sight of the stairway that wound up towards the control chamber: it was a flimsy metal structure with low handrails, which would leave their ascent exposed. But not as exposed as reaching the bottom of the staircase, which required a dash across a completely open, well-lit area with no equipment banks or other detritus to hide behind.

There was no time to consider the dangers, or even to pause. They broke into the open, leaving behind all shadow and shelter. For a few precious seconds they went unnoticed, but halfway to the stairway cries rang out.

Not stopping or slowing, Hool looked for the source of the jeers. He now had a direct view across the dome to the position they had started from, where the main body of rebels had surrounded Smoker's position. The equipment banks the Guardsmen had used as cover seemed to have been knocked over or destroyed, and all Hool could see was a mass of violent humanity, a mob of traitors.

Hool couldn't see any sign of Smoker's squad, but that wasn't the immediate problem. A few rebels had broken away from the main group, and were shouting for support as they ran to intercept Polk and his men. One had a lasrifle and fired wildly ahead: Hool ducked as he ran, las-shots zipping overhead. Dall was less lucky, catching a glancing shot to the ribs and falling.

Polk shouted orders to Treston and Keller and they peeled away from the rest of the squad, dragging the downed Dall to cover while firing on the approaching rebels. Hool and the others kept running.

Further trouble lay ahead, where the call for assistance had found a response – more heretics were emerging from above, their footsteps clattering on each metal step as they descended.

Polk was nearly at the bottom of the stairs, and turned to his men and shouted.

'Nauk, Hool – with me. The rest of you – hold this last step. I don't want anyone following us until this is done.'

Polk didn't stop to check whether his orders were being followed, taking the first three steps in one leap. Nauk and Hool were right behind him, and Hool looked back to see the others standing shoulder to shoulder, forming a perimeter around the bottom of the stairs, lasrifles raised and firing.

Hool didn't have the opportunity to see whether those shots hit their targets. Polk was slowing ahead as he turned the first bend in the stairway, dropping to one knee and raising his combat shotgun as the first rebels rounded the next bend on their way down. Hool and Nauk dropped in behind him, shoulder to shoulder, aiming over Polk's head.

Together, the three Mordians formed a line across the stairway, greeting the descending rebels with a hail of fire-power, the rapid las-fire from Hool and Nauk punctuating the slower blasts from Polk's combat shotgun.

Hool's rifle jerked back in his grip as he fired, slamming into his shoulder. His first shot caught a rebel square in the torso, leaving a blackened entry wound at the centre of the heretic's naked chest. The dead rebel jerked backwards with his last spasm of life, reeling into those behind him. One grabbed the corpse to stop it from falling, and surged forwards using the dead rebel as a shield.

'Cease fire,' snapped Polk, and as Hool and Nauk lowered their weapons he lunged towards the rebel with the body, sweeping his shotgun round to thrust the butt of the weapon forwards. Polk slammed the butt into the head of the dead rebel so hard that the neck snapped back, the corpse's skull crashing into the head of the very-much-alive heretic carrying it. The second man, stunned, staggered backwards.

'At 'em!' ordered Polk, and Hool and Nauk charged into the fray.

The rebels were mainly wielding tools and pieces of pipe, edges and ends sharpened to make them into better weapons. A tall rebel with long, blood-matted hair was swinging a wrench overarm, down towards Polk's head. Hool stepped between the rebel and his sergeant, raising his lasrifle to block the wrench's descent. The impact vibrated down Hool's arms but he held firm, kicking the renegade in the knee. The man buckled, dropping the wrench as he fell forwards, his scraggy mass of hair falling over his face.

Hool swung his lasrifle around, aimed right at the man's crown, and pulled the trigger. Polk and Nauk were ahead of him, firing up the next flight of the stairwell. Hool stepped over the bodies as quickly as he could to follow them.

A cry of warning came from below. Hool looked down through the fine grille of the stairs to see rebels below: the men holding the stairwell had been overwhelmed and pushed aside. Okre and Blant, had been at the centre of the stairway and had been driven down rather than aside, trampled to the floor with six or seven rebels surrounding them, arms rising and falling as crude weapons crushed and slashed at the two prone Guardsmen, a trail of gore flitting through the air as each weapon was raised again before descending to deliver another blow.

'Incoming from below,' Hool warned, smacking his rifle butt into the face of an incoming heretic as he joined Polk and Nauk. There must have been fewer than a dozen rebels ahead of them, but fighting on the stairs was even worse than fighting on the level sections, a struggle with unsure footing as much as the enemy, and the constant threat of falling over the low railings.

They turned another corner, onto the last flight. Two dozen steps led to a narrow platform straight ahead, to the right of which was the open door to a control chamber. Half a dozen rebels crowded down the steps, thrusting sharpened objects towards the Guardsmen.

Polk and Nauk were engaged with the enemy above, so Hool turned around and leaned over the railing, firing a couple of shots into the rebels running up from below. Bodies dropped in the path of more rebels, disrupting their attack.

Hool hoped it would stall them long enough. His breath was rapid and frantic as he looked up to see Polk and Nauk facing off against the last four rebels between them and security control. It was a tight brawl, with no room for either Guardsman to level their weapon enough to fire. Hool ran up behind, raising his own lasrifle, hoping to get a shot, but his two comrades were blocking his line of sight to any of the remaining rebels.

As Hool watched, Polk received a blow to the side of the head from a rebel's elbow, causing him to drop to the floor. This enraged Nauk, who thrust forwards with his whole body, ramming himself shoulder-first into the two rebels he was wrestling with. The two heretics lost their footing and tumbled backwards over the railing to their deaths. Nauk stumbled forwards with his own momentum, but fell short of the edge of the platform, landing on his side.

By now Hool had a clear shot of the rebel who had floored Polk, and took it. He began to turn his aim to the final rebel, only to see the heretic bringing a fiercely sharpened spear down into Nauk's side as the Guardsman tried to stand. Hool shot the rebel in the head but it was too late – the spear gouged into Nauk's body with a nauseating crunch. The body of Nauk's attacker fell forwards onto the spear, pushing it in deeper, and Nauk cried out.

Polk and Nauk were both down, but Hool didn't have time

to check whether they were alive or dead. The sound of footsteps from below meant more rebels were nearly on him.

Hool reeled into security control. It was a narrow gallery of a room, equipment decks overlooking the entirety of the dome. The layout of the control panels was simple enough, mainly colour-coded but with simple descriptions etched in white on the black surface above certain buttons. Hool found the lockdown release, a once-shiny lever tarnished from years of constant use.

Hool grabbed the lever and pulled it forwards. An alarm began to blare.

Beneath the siren, Hool could hear a huge roar of collective las-fire, the sound of Mordians pouring in through the open gates and setting about the rabble. The dome echoed with disciplined bursts of fire, the sound of ranked men working together to sweep into a building, cleaning it of heretics.

Hool closed his eyes, allowing himself a brief second of calm before running out to rejoin the fray.

After the energy and human cost of getting the gates to the power complex open, the business of fully securing it took no time at all.

By the time Hool had helped the injured Polk down the stairs, there were no rebels left standing. The action had already moved on, squads dispersing back into the administratum block and across the rest of the complex, determined to hunt down and kill any remaining heretics.

Under the dome, there was nothing but bodies. A couple of Guardsmen walked among the corpses, checking them with a kick, firing the odd point-blank headshot where there was some sign of life or uncertainty.

Okre and Blant were dead, not that Hool needed confirmation. There was satisfaction in seeing the number of dead enemies scattered around them, and the thought that the two Guardsmen had not gone down quietly – but not much. Their bloodied corpses, hacked at repeatedly by the mob, didn't look to Hool like a glorious death. The others, including the wounded Dall, were battered but alive.

Of Smoker's squad, who had attracted the full fury of the rebels to give Polk's men the chance to complete the mission, only Sergeant Essler himself remained alive.

Hool saw Smoker from a distance, shrugging off a medicae as he walked away from a site of carnage, the odd grey jacket visible among a blast pattern of dead rebels.

Smoker flexed his shoulders, and even from a distance Hool could see a thick rip in the back of his jacket, the edge stained with blood where some enemy weapon had torn into the sergeant's flesh.

Smoker rolled his shoulders again, as if shaking off the wound. He reached one hand into his jacket, produced a lho-stick, and inserted it into the grille of his rebreather.

Smoker lit the lho-stick, and the artificial airflow of his rebreather caused it to flare into life.

Covered in the blood of his enemies, his own men, and even himself, Smoker walked away, a trail of lho-smoke in his wake, hanging in the battlefield air.

TWO

It had been a year.

A year since belief in the Emperor's death, and his rebirth on Elisenda, had caused the planet's society to collapse into warfare.

A year since the 114th Mordian had been ordered to raise as many Guardsmen as they needed from their home world, and set out to reclaim Elisenda.

A year since Hool had been swept up in Polk's press-gang.

To Hool, it seemed like half his lifetime. A year ago, he had entered adulthood and not only left childhood behind, but every aspect of his former life. Delirious from the painkiller implant numbing the ache of his broken leg, he had said goodbye to his family and reported for duty.

He had barely stepped outside the hab-block that had been his entire world before he was on a transport ship for

Elisenda, leaving a home world that he had never properly known.

Too disorientated to know whether he was experiencing the wrench of separation or the joy of escape, Hool had been thrown into a fierce routine of compressed training: discipline, weapons, hand-to-hand combat, endurance, more discipline.

In spite of having rehabilitation for his injuries alongside the accelerated training programme, Hool had adapted well to the regime of the 114th, to the extent that he felt prepared for what waited on Elisenda.

He was wrong. Although he had travelled far, Hool had still not stepped outside corridors of hardened plasteel, illuminated by artificial light. All the new recruits from Mordian had been instructed to rub a thick paste into their skin the morning they landed on Elisenda. Hool hadn't understood why, and Polk had smirked at him.

Stepping down the ramp and out onto the dusty surface of Elisenda, Hool had been overloaded with sensations, each less pleasant than the next: unfiltered air in his lungs, loaded with particles and unfamiliar scents; the beating sun, stinging his skin and eyes; the vertiginous, endless space above.

It had taken him the best part of three months to fully adjust to the sky, to be able to look up without suppressing an instinctive, rising fear of the void.

On the ground, Hool had learned fast. The 114th's orders were to scourge the planet of the rebels, but to do so with minimal damage to the manufactories considered so vital to the Imperium: heavy weaponry was only to be used in non-vital areas such as habs or public spaces. The manufactories themselves were to be reclaimed by a precise elimination of the heretics. Hool had spent the best part of a year fighting the rebels in corridors and underpasses, breaking through walls and storming enginaria.

Steadily, over the months, further territory had been reclaimed. Manufactories were retaken, enginseers sweeping in with armies of servitors to restore damaged equipment and machinery, before new workers were shipped in to begin work.

But with every city block and manufactory brought back under the Emperor's gaze, another fell as rebel activity flared up elsewhere. It was a fire that seemed impossible to extinguish, suppressed in one spot only to ignite again in the distance, just out of reach.

The tide had turned though, albeit slowly. The taking of the power plant had been the most significant rebel action in weeks. Most of the false emperors were dead. Although the work wasn't over yet, the Mordians' campaign on Elisenda did seem to be near completion.

The end was in sight.

For his role in averting the disaster, and for being one of the few survivors from the previous day's action, Hool was rewarded with a rare privilege – a single day of rest and recovery before reporting back for regular details.

The 114th were based in a series of abandoned hangars and warehouses near one of the main spaceports. Some previous owner of the site had surrounded it with a high fence and watchtowers, making it a relatively secure base for the Guard during the early weeks on Elisenda when it seemed like half the population were launching strikes against them. A burnt-out shell near the edge of the site was the result of an early attack that had destroyed most of the regiment's Chimeras, killing several enginseers and drivers in the process. Twisted prongs of blackened metal still towered over most of the other buildings, a reminder that their enemies were everywhere.

The barracks were little more than a long, narrow shed with a flat roof and rows of windows at the top of the thin metal walls, most of them broken. A hundred men slept there in basic military cots, fifty lined on each side of the long shed, their few belongings stashed beneath in standard-issue foot lockers.

The 114th being a Mordian regiment, where presentation was everything, highly polished pieces of metal and battered mirrors were propped against the rusty walls so that the Guardsmen could check that their uniforms were immaculate.

On the morning of his rest day, Hool allowed himself to sleep late, the deep, long sleep that arrives in the lull after a period of tension and physical exertion. He woke to find himself alone in the barracks.

At the end of Hool's cot was propped a piece of rough board, with a crudely scrawled message telling anyone passing that Hool had earned his rest day in battle, and making some graphic suggestions as to what would happen to anyone who woke him. Hool recognised the handwriting as Polk's.

Hool's head was fuzzy from oversleeping, but a shower shook most of the torpor from his skull. He dressed quickly in a clean uniform from his locker – the servitors clunked through the barracks at night, picking up dirty, ripped or otherwise battle-scarred uniforms, returning them repaired and pressed a day later – and looked at himself in one of the long mirrors.

A year ago, he had still resembled a boy, but a year at war had changed all that: he was still thin, but had filled out around the shoulders as his muscles toned. The merciless sun had brought out the tone of his skin, and flecks of light in his dark brown, tightly curled hair. The puppy fat had gone from his cheeks, revealing a long, narrow face, and months of near-exhaustion had added lines around his deep brown eyes.

Hool looked closer at his reflection, into those eyes. He saw something there that he had never seen before, something he didn't entirely like…

He snapped out of the thought and stood back, checking the line of his jacket, squeezing his cap over his close-cropped curls. He looked entirely respectable, as a Mordian in uniform should. Dressed soberly for a solemn task.

Hool removed his cap, and tossed it back on his cot. There was no further reason to delay a job that needed doing.

He walked down the line of cots until he got to Okre's. Dropping into a squat, he reached under the bed and slid out the foot locker.

Alone in the barracks, Hool began the grim task of sorting through his late comrade's possessions.

* * *

To all outward appearances Major Halvern Geiss was a man in his late thirties. Many presumed from his demeanour and his rank that he was much older, and had maintained his youth via juvenat treatments. To many, his thick red-brown hair and square jawline were a little too good to be true, the signs of an older officer trying to cling on to their youth.

In fact, Geiss was slightly younger than he looked, and the hair and jawline were entirely unenhanced. At thirty-six he was precociously young to be leading a large force of men, effectively only a couple of steps down the regimental pecking order from the colonel himself. He had earned that rank through his own efforts and a gift for tactical thinking.

Geiss was not, however, one to brag about his precocious advancement: if representatives of other regiments or civilian authorities wished to presume he was a two hundred year-old who had plodded up the ranks in a long career, he let them.

Summoned to report to Colonel Ruscin, Geiss arrived at the lavishly appointed palace that the colonel had requisitioned as his command centre, and was nodded through the main gates.

The palace had belonged to a local family who had prospered from the many centuries of successful industry on Elisenda, and had been first up against the wall when rebellion broke out. The decor was arch high-gothic, closer to an Ecclesiarchy cathedral than a private residence, with high arched ceilings and stained-glass windows bearing images of the family's ancestors performing various great acts of piety.

The decor still bore the scars of the uprising, and the

Guard's retaking: las-fire had scorched the tapestries, windows were smashed and statues decapitated.

When ordered to report to Colonel Ruscin, Geiss presumed it was for a progress report, and as such he carried a sheaf of papers as he walked down a corridor lined with tapestries of the seventeen martyrdoms. Geiss knew what he was going to say to the colonel: a laundry list of the recent territory gained, the outstanding pockets of resistance, and so forth. Geiss also intended to praise the actions of Lieutenant Munez, whose rapid improvisation had averted disaster in the previous day's power-complex incident.

However, when Geiss entered the colonel's war room, he realised it was not the meeting he thought it was at all.

The war room had been the palace's main hall, with gilded mirrors on every wall and a floor of polished, jet-black stone. At least half the mirrors in the war room were cracked or shattered, and it was impossible to look around without catching sight of a fragmented reflection. The floor had been cleared of all previous furnishings and replaced with the ephemera of strategy: maps and battle plans laid out on every surface, vox-relay stations for forwarding reports.

Usually when summoned to the war room, Geiss found Colonel Ruscin poring over regional maps of Elisenda, or architectural plans of specific facilities, but today a fragile-looking star chart had been rolled out.

But it wasn't the map itself that caught Geiss's attention so much as the company the colonel was keeping. The first Geiss recognised: Gillick, an ancient woman who represented the interests of the Lord Governor of the subsector.

Gillick's small frame was swamped within the layers of ceremonial furs that came with her office, the furs in turn draped with obscure badges and medals representing a long lifetime of ruthless service.

The other visitor was not someone Geiss recognised individually, but it was impossible to not know what he was. A towering, red-cloaked figure, his hood thrown back to reveal a head that was a mass of brass augmentations – ornate pistons pumped in and out of the sides of his face, and an orange glow was visible behind two dark lenses, as if he had hot coals in place of eyes. He held a metallic staff from which chunks of circuitry hung on wires, and a heavy brass cog lay around his neck, the signs of his faith and his office as a tech-priest of the Adeptus Mechanicus, the Machine Cult of Mars.

All three – the colonel, the official and the tech-priest – were examining the star chart as Geiss approached. Colonel Ruscin, the 114th's commanding officer, looked up and nodded at Geiss, who gave a sharp salute in reply. Ruscin was silver-haired and lean, wearing his age as a badge of experience.

'At ease, major,' Ruscin said. He stood back to politely gesture to his two guests. 'I am sure you and Senior Administrator Gillick remember each other.'

The old woman gave Geiss a curt nod of acknowledgement, which Geiss returned politely.

'Lord-Adept Brassfell, this is Major Geiss, one of our most promising officers. Geiss, Lord-Adept Brassfell is here on behalf of the Adeptus Mechanicus, and represents their interests in this sector.'

Brassfell nodded, wisps of steam expelling from vents around his cheeks. When he spoke, it was in a surprisingly human, almost musical voice.

'It is a pleasure to make your acquaintance, Major Geiss. The Adeptus Mechanicus thank you for your part in reclaiming the great machines of these, our most sacred manufactories, and hope that you will be similarly successful in this new matter.'

'Thank you, my lord,' said Geiss, but behind his polite facade his mind was racing.

The Adeptus Mechanicus were responsible for the maintenance of all machines within the Imperium, and there was no shortage of those on Elisenda. Their forge worlds were also dependent on the flow of supplies from worlds like Elisenda for components and the like, but there was something unusual about a tech-priest of Brassfell's obvious seniority taking a direct interest in what were, after all, matters of procurement.

And what was this 'new matter'?

That, at least, did not remain a mystery for long.

'We have received new orders,' stated Ruscin briskly, tapping a point on the star chart. 'Belmos VII is a Munitorum world with a single city-factory built around a mining complex that supplies raw minerals to this and many other manufacturing hives. Not very interesting, barren apart from that one city-factory, and the only active world in its system, but a key supply resource, sufficiently significant for the facility there to receive a recent inspection from a senior Munitorum official. An urgent report was received from said official and, well, perhaps it's best if you see for yourself.'

Ruscin clicked his fingers and a servitor activated the large pict viewer set up near the map table. The image it displayed was of a murky resolution, which looked even worse blown up to such a large size. The fuzzy monochrome image showed a pudgy male face close to the camera, the light so poor that the eyes were invisible, cloaked by shadows beneath the brow.

The sound quality was poor, dominated by white noise and crackles that could be either interference on the recording or distant gunfire, but some words were audible as the man on-screen babbled:

'Harmless during the day, it's at night that they–' The next section of the recording was inaudible beneath a burst of static. 'Rescue needed urgently, caution advised. You can't tell in the light.' At this point the face suddenly became smaller, as if the man had been dragged backwards, away from the screen. He was shouting now. 'You can't tell in the daylight–' His face rushed forwards, filling then obscuring the screen before the image cut out, the screen blank apart from an Imperial reference number in the centre of the screen.

Someone, or something, had killed two birds with one stone, slamming the man's head through the picter to silence both him and the device. It was an act of very precise ferocity.

There was an uncomfortable silence, which the colonel broke with a cough before providing further explanation:

'That was transmitted some time ago. The pict may be poor quality, but the Munitorum confirm that the man in the recording is Recorder Gellwood Jenk, a senior auditor,' said

Ruscin. 'Leaving aside the valuable raw materials supplied by Belmos VII, the Munitorum consider an assault on such a senior official to be entirely unacceptable.'

Geiss stopped himself from raising an eyebrow at the use of the word 'assault'. He very much doubted that Jenk had survived such an attack.

'Has there been any further communication from Belmos VII?' Geiss asked.

Brassfell made a low whistling sound which could have been his equivalent of a cough, a laugh, or something else altogether.

'The Belmos System is highly unstable, full of turbulent gases and radiation fields,' said the tech-priest. 'Even our most advanced and sacred long-range communication systems find it hard to breach the fog of interference, and it is not unknown for Belmos VII to fall out of contact for decades on end, with the exception of hand-delivered messages couriered by the heavy transport ships. The system is a void, and it is, frankly, an Omnissiah-granted miracle that Recorder Jenk's message was received at all, even in such a partial state.'

'Unfortunately we are in no position to measure the severity of the situation,' said Ruscin. 'Your orders, major, are to take a strike force to Belmos VII and respond accordingly to whatever threat you find. It could be that this is no more than a local uprising that has already been dealt with by the local PDF, in which case the Munitorum has requested the decimation of the non-essential population in response to the attack on their man.'

'A strike force, sir?' queried Geiss. 'Not the entire regiment?'

The colonel didn't answer, but Gillick did:

'The 114th's mission on Elisenda is not yet complete, major,' said Gillick, an implicit criticism beneath her banally polite tone. 'The Lord Governor has requested that both matters be attended to, but neither neglected.'

'Thank you, Mamzel Gillick,' said the colonel drily. 'Command has granted the Lord Governor's request, and as such I will remain here on Elisenda with half our complement to deal with the rest of these fanatics. Ideally, the 114th would move as one, but with two threats within our auspices and no other regiment within range to assist, for now we are required to deal with both fronts at once. However, major, as these heretics are a known quantity while the threat on Belmos VII is not, I am assigning our best assets to your strike force.'

Gillick seemed to be about to protest at this, but the colonel silenced her with a glance.

'Rest assured, Mamzel Gillick, that we are entirely capable of dealing with the rest of this filth with a few infantry platoons alone.' Ruscin turned his attention back to Geiss. 'Major, you will have lieutenants Hossk, Deaz and Munez, and their full platoons at your disposal. The population of Belmos VII is small: just the mining workforce, the local planetary defence force, and representatives of both the Munitorum and the Adeptus Mechanicus. Nothing your force shouldn't be able to handle. Unfortunately the Munitorum has yet to supply further Chimeras, so you will only have a small number of vehicles for command purposes, but the small size of the Belmos VII city-factory should mean this isn't a problem.'

'Thank you, sir, I'm sure the men will appreciate the exercise,' said Geiss drily.

'I'm sure they will equally appreciate that Commissar Tordez has decided to accompany your force,' added Ruscin.

This was less welcome news to Geiss. He would rather the old commissar stayed here on Elisenda, lecturing the men on the threat of heresy. Did Tordez suspect that Geiss wasn't up to this command, and would crack under pressure? If so he was out of luck. Geiss had no intention of ending this mission – and his career – with a shot from the commissar's pistol.

Brassfell made his whistling noise again, snapping Geiss out of his distracted chain of thought. 'I understand that the enginseer assigned to your regiment will also accompany your strike force, major. I would like to brief him before you depart.'

'Of course,' said Geiss. There was something very wrong here, a lord of the Adeptus Mechanicus taking an interest in a regimental enginseer. Whatever had happened on Belmos VII, there was clearly a potential advantage for the Adeptus Mechanicus in it. Unfortunately, Geiss was in no position to fathom what that could be.

'Prepare your men, major. You depart as soon as the navigators can chart a course,' said Ruscin. He looked between Brassfell and Gillick. 'If we're all agreed, then this meeting is over.'

There was general agreement, and Gillick and Brassfell departed. Geiss saluted, and turned to follow them. He was halfway across the room before Ruscin called out to him.

'One more thing, major,' said Ruscin. 'The Imperium will not allow Belmos VII to fall from the Emperor's sight. If the threat is greater than you can manage, then reinforcements are already being requested from further afield. They'll take longer to get there, but they'll get there all right.'

Geiss looked back at Ruscin blankly. Why had the colonel waited until they were alone to tell him?

'Let's not get into a position where the 114th require a helping hand, major,' said Ruscin, smiling darkly. 'Wrap this up before any of these other buggers make planetfall, or die trying first. Got that?'

Geiss returned the colonel's grin and saluted again before leaving the room.

A strike force of his own, an unknown and possibly deadly scenario. It was all Geiss could do to stop himself grinning inanely in front of the guards as they saluted him out of the palace.

Polk had been authorised by Munez to find new recruits to replace Okre, Blant and Nauk. Although Polk knew he shouldn't differentiate between men of the same rank, who had all served their Emperor equally in life and death, it was the loss of Nauk that he felt the keenest. Nauk had been Polk's age, but had never risen in rank. This was not a bad thing, far from it – men like Nauk, lifetime infantry, were the backbone of the Imperial Guard.

Nauk would be hard to replace. They all would. Good Guardsmen, all.

But replace them he must. Polk already had two existing

Guardsmen transferring to his squad, but he needed two more, and these would have to be fresh.

Polk wandered down to the dusty square between the barracks, which had rather grandiosely been assigned as the parade ground. Twenty or so locals were being drilled by a sergeant of the 114th, locals who would be policing and defending Elisenda after the Mordians had left. These men and women, less than two dozen, had held a key outpost on Elisenda against rebels for two months, with scant supplies and no military training. They would all make good members of the local PDF, but Polk was looking for something more, that extra quality that would make them Guard-worthy.

Polk had stood in the shade as the men and women conducted exercises, with regular pauses for the sergeant to berate them for their many failings.

The Imperial Guard had been brought to this world due to the exceptional nature of the crisis and the complete corruption of the local enforcers and military. As soon as the Elisendans could deal with their own problems, the 114th would move on. Many in the regiment were eager to do so.

While they understood, in abstract at least, that clearing this place of heretics was important, and had no problem dealing with the rebels as they would any other enemy, many of the Mordians regarded the campaign on Elisenda as slightly beneath the dignity of a venerable regiment. It was behind the lines, the Imperium's domestic trouble. Housekeeping. The rebels themselves were mainly deluded civilians – a threat that needed to be put down, but not real warriors, and not a real war.

Instead of crushing these lowlifes, the men of the 114th wanted to be out there on one of the thousands of front lines in the Emperor's endless war against the enemies of mankind.

Polk had seen a couple of promising candidates emerge during the exercises, potential Guardsmen. He had a good eye for those who might be able to live up to the demands of the 114th, and he thought he could see those qualities out in the yard. Yes, he wouldn't have any problem replacing his lost men, much to the chagrin of the planetary defence force who would need to find further locals to fuel their own needs. Tough. The Imperial Guard took precedence.

These recruitment exercises made Polk uneasy. While he took great pride in seeing raw recruits become skilled fighting men, of seeing that nascent potential emerge from civilians, he had also seen too many lie dead before that potential could be even remotely fulfilled, many a decade or two younger than Polk.

Polk wasn't naive about the sacrifices war required, but that didn't stop the individual losses grinding together in his conscience to form a greater unease. It was the duty of every human being to live and die for the God-Emperor, as required. Where humans died doing an honourable duty, those deaths were not in vain.

Polk just wished that he wasn't so involved in directing so many people towards those duties, those deaths.

Nonetheless, it was his duty and he didn't recoil from

it. Polk had approached the sergeant and whispered in his ear, then directly approached his two new recruits to give them the 'good' news. At that stage he had hoped that the two Elisendans could at least be broken into their duties on home soil.

It wasn't going to happen. Polk wished he had more time to integrate the new Guardsmen into his squad, but preparations were already under way for the strike force's departure for Belmos VII. Polk had to use what time he had as best he could.

Back on the same parade ground, Polk watched Hool running through exercises with the four new men in his squad.

One was Rivez, a Guardsman with a good fifteen years' experience who had been transferred to Polk's command by Munez as the lieutenant reorganised his troops to compensate for losses and new recruits. Rivez was an asset, and Polk was glad to have him. He was a good-humoured soul – many Guardsmen of his age would baulk at taking the lead from someone of their own rank, of Hool's age – they would at least push back a little, jostle for status with the younger man. Rivez just went with it, albeit with a certain light-heartedness, going through the motions as they spun their lasrifles and took positions.

Then there was Hervl, one of the other Mordian youths Polk had rounded up at the same time as Hool. Unlike Hool, Hervl had been in a gang, or at least been trying to make a name for himself. Polk hadn't forgotten Hool and Hervl's history together, and knew he needed to keep an eye on them. For the moment, they seemed to be studiously formal

with each other, Hool issuing instructions and Hervl following them mutely.

The other two were new recruits, Elisendans who had
shown promise on the parade ground: Zvindt and Deress.
They seemed to be learning fast. Polk just hoped it was fast
enough. Both were older than Hool, well into adulthood.
They still seemed incredibly young to Polk.

Sergeant Polk was around forty-four years old, although
the variables of different planetary calendars and the time
distortions caused by space travel made it hard to be entirely
sure. Hardly any age at all compared to the legendary Adeptus Astartes with their god-like genetic inheritance, the
tech-priests with their radical augmentations or even the senior officers within the Guard itself, those who could afford
the juvenat treatments to prolong their lives.

But for a low-ranking Guardsman, thrown out onto the
front line in battle after battle, forty-four years was a long
time to live. Since he had joined the regiment as a young
man he had seen dozens of Guardsmen who lasted less than
a decade, sometimes as little as a month. At the Battle of
Rivas he had seen an entire regiment, newly raised on one of
the outer worlds, not a man over twenty years old, slaughtered in ten minutes by a greenskin attack.

His own regiment, the Unbreakable 114th, had turned
over at least four-fifths of its number in his time, maybe
more. Most of the men he recognised from his first years
with the regiment were senior officers, insulated from the
rigours of the front line.

Polk had no such protection. He had only been promoted

as far as sergeant, and that was long enough ago that he knew he wasn't going any further up the chain. He wasn't an exceptional soldier, but he was a good one. He was competent, but that didn't explain his survival.

No, Polk had been *lucky*. For a quarter of a century, that luck had held, and with every battle he fought, Polk felt the odds of his survival getting longer and longer. He didn't resent that fact. When he joined the Guard, he barely expected to last until the end of the week, the troop ship that had taken him away from Mordian on his first tour threatening to shake itself apart as it exited the atmosphere.

Polk's time was coming, he was sure of it. It made him especially sensitive to the fate of his squad, these Guardsmen serving under him. Time was short, and he hoped to pass on what little knowledge he had before he went, to give them the skills that would, with any luck, allow them to survive as long as he had.

Maybe it was just because Hool was the only other survivor from Polk's previous squad, but Polk was starting to pin these hopes mainly on Hool. He thought Hool might make a great soldier, making sergeant or even higher, if he didn't manage to blow his own lungs out before he got chance. The incident with the roof and the rebels was typical Hool. He followed orders well, he had the clear head that made a natural Guardsman, and he was a devil of a shot, but he had a tendency for spectacular carelessness that sometimes required quick action by those around him to stop an error growing into a disaster.

Still, Hool seemed to always survive, even if by the

intervention of his comrades. With the Emperor's blessing he might live as long as Polk or Smoker.

Smoker. Polk had barely seen Essler since the attack on the power complex. Lieutenant Munez had congratulated all three of the survivors of that strike force on their bravery, speaking with the combination of pride and regret that follows a successful mission with heavy losses.

While Hool had been slightly intimidated by a personal congratulation from the lieutenant, and Polk had taken the compliment at face value without giving it any great thought, Smoker had barely paused in acknowledgement before raising the question of replacing his lost men. Polk and Hool had been dismissed by Munez, leaving the lieutenant and Smoker to discuss staffing issues.

That conversation had taken place while the power complex was still being secured. Smoker's previous squad had been dead for a matter of hours.

Although all soldiers needed to move on from any grief quickly and cleanly, Smoker's lack of reaction took pragmatism to disconcerting levels. Maybe it was just the lack of recognisable human features that left Polk with a lingering unease...

No. It was easy enough to blame the augmetics, but there were plenty of men in the regiment who had some form of augmentation. There was something else disconcerting about Smoker, beyond that lack of human features: something in the way he held himself, the way he dealt with his fellow Guardsmen.

If Polk was lucky, then Smoker was almost *too lucky*, like he had used up all his bad luck in the incident that resulted in his augmentation, and was left untouchable, able to walk away unscratched and unruffled from engagements that left bodies piled to waist height.

As Polk thought about him, Smoker walked past in the distance. He was, as ever, alone, a lit lho-stick in the grille of his rebreather.

Polk watched Smoker disappear between two field-tents, a thin trail of smoke hanging in the still air behind him.

Was it luck or design that kept you alive so long, thought Polk, and if the former, was it your good luck that mattered, or the misfortune of those who stood with you in the heat of battle?

It was an unworthy thought, but, turning his attention back to his current men, who seemed relatively fragile as they prepared for the unknown, it was a thought that Polk couldn't quite shake.

The night of their departure for Belmos VII, as the enlisted men and servitors were already loading their equipment into the shuttle that would take them up to the Navy vessel *Seraphim*, Geiss gathered the officers of his strike force to dine with him.

A long field tent next to the barracks did not have the aesthetic standards of the palace requisitioned by Colonel Ruscin, but Geiss had dined in far worse places. The night was hot, as all Elisendan nights were, but there was a breeze in the air that billowed through the tent now and then, carrying with it the jeering and banter of the men as they prepared for departure.

He had spent the day planning and organising, talking tactics with his three lieutenants, poring over what charts, maps and plans were available. They were preparing for the unknown, but preparing nonetheless; strategising for the most common eventualities, as well as preparing fall-back positions that would allow them to respond to the unexpected.

It had been a productive series of discussions, and Geiss felt a secret thrill. He should, according to the expectations of hierarchy, be feeling a weight of responsibility at being handed an entire strike force to go into an unknown threat situation without the support of the rest of the regiment or his superiors.

Instead, he felt in his element, increasingly confident in his abilities to lead these men, eager to test those abilities further in the face of whatever would meet them on Belmos VII.

The planning stage was on hold for now. They would have plenty of time during the transit to go into their battle plans and contingencies in further detail.

Now was a time to step away from those plans, for the officers to enjoy the last moment of certainty before they left Elisenda and ventured into the unknown, to discuss the campaign they had lived through and bond as a command squad.

Geiss looked around the table at the officers of his strike force, who were making small talk as they ate. Servitors stood nearby, ready to refill empty glasses or fetch the next course when required. They were unneeded most of the time: these were good officers, too intelligent to drink quickly or heavily immediately before the potential horrors of a journey through the warp. Instead, they were enjoying their food while they could, and the peace while it lasted.

Geiss approved: the quarters on Elisenda were basic, but might be luxury compared to wherever they next decamped.

Of the three lieutenants under Geiss's command, Lieutenant Hossk was the most conventional Mordian commander, steeped in traditions of order and discipline. Hossk was a solid-looking man with unmemorable features and flat, heavily oiled brown hair. Others might dismiss him as uncharismatic, but Geiss knew that if he ordered Hossk's troops to hold a line, they would do so to the last.

Hossk wasn't saying much – he rarely did. As with most of the officers at the table, he was listening to Lieutenant Munez, who was recounting some anecdote from early in his career. Munez spoke fast and thought fast, and there was something about his ruddy complexion, twinkling dark eyes and thinning, greyish hair that seemed more avuncular than commanding, a quality that inspired loyalty.

If Munez was a little too likable compared to the stern ideal of a Mordian officer, he made up for that with his skills as a strategist. His resolution of the situation at the power complex on Elisenda had been typical: a strategic solution rapidly established with the limited resources available. Such gambits were risky, but Munez's men knew that he took their loyalty and their lives seriously – the orders he gave were complex judgements, and he gave them for good reason.

Lieutenant Deaz, on the other hand, was not a strategic thinker, but compensated with a talent for battlefield

improvisation, and a tendency for the shocking gesture. He
didn't look like a daredevil, and was in fact the shortest man
at the table and virtually bald, but in a bad situation his
strike teams could break an enemy line with fearless aggression, while Deaz himself stayed back and prepared the next
assault.

Geiss had deployed the talents of all three men on Elisenda,
and in campaigns before that. However, on Belmos VII the
unpredictable situation meant they couldn't rely on the situation on the ground being neatly divisible in such a way as
to allow the targeting of a specific officer to the appropriate
problem.

The other man at the table sat between Geiss and the three
lieutenants, ostensibly listening to Munez's anecdote, but
giving little reaction. Occasionally he seemed to be about
to say something, then decided not to bother. Commissar
Tordez appeared to be around the same age as Geiss, slim
with distinguished cheekbones and thick, jet-black hair that
he kept under control with wax and oil.

But this apparent youth was the result of extensive juvenat treatments. Geiss wasn't entirely sure of Tordez's real
age – the Commissariat was not in the habit of providing
information on their commissars to the regiments they were
assigned to – but he was fairly sure it was greater than the
collective ages of all the other men at the table.

Although Tordez was as fit and healthy as his exterior age,
he thought and spoke like an old man, scattering his speech
with references to the many campaigns he had fought in.
From these allusions, Geiss surmised that Tordez had been

commissar to at least half a dozen regiments and had first-hand knowledge of many of the enemies of mankind out in the vast, hostile galaxy.

Of course, a certain amount of this could be deception or exaggeration, and commissars were certainly under no obligation to be truthful with the men they watched over for signs of treachery and weakness – but Geiss didn't think so. Although Tordez was as aloof and demanding as any commissar that Geiss had met, and he was thankful to have only met a couple, he did not seem prone to deceit.

Neither did Tordez's constant references to his own career seem like boasting or bravado, but simply evidence of a mind that kept constantly drifting into the past. Tordez was a good commissar, as far as any member of the Guard was willing to acknowledge the existence of such a thing – vigilant, hard when needed, but not wantonly cruel – and Geiss suspected he had been assigned to the 114th as some form of reward for a long career of service with Catachans and penal legions.

Compared to most regiments, Mordians presented little difficulty for a commissar. Discipline was in their blood – minimal correction was required.

Perhaps that was part of the reason for Tordez's occasional... absence. Perhaps he was just *bored* by life with the 114th, and sought a return to his glory days with more riotous regiments, administering constant field executions for insubordination.

Munez had reached the end of his anecdote, with a punchline involving an enemy communications tower being seeded with explosives, only for a misalignment of the charges to cause the demolished tower to collapse right on top of the men who planted them. There was a polite ripple of laughter around the table, although Geiss noticed that Tordez's humour seemed strained, even by his standards.

Lieutenant Deaz was opening his mouth, presumably because his ego required him to try and top Munez's story, but Geiss tapped the side of his glass to get their attention before another long anecdote began.

The three lieutenants and the commissar turned to him.

'Gentlemen,' Geiss addressed them. 'This last year we have fought well against the heretics, but while they are certainly worthy of death, those rebels may have been spoiled by receiving that death from a regiment of our heritage.' There was a ripple of support from the three lieutenants at this.

'Tomorrow we leave this planet,' Geiss continued. 'We seek enemies unknown, in circumstances unknown. Whatever strikes against us, we are prepared to remain what we always are.' He raised his glass, and the other officers did the same. Even Tordez raised his glass slightly in acknowledgement. 'The Unbreakable 114th!'

The toast was shouted in reply: 'The Unbreakable 114th!'

THREE

The descent through the atmosphere of Belmos VII was rough, the lander taking the strike force down to the surface struggling to compensate. Geiss took a seat on the bridge for the landing, leaving the preparation of the men to his lieutenants. The journey through the warp had gone as well as could be expected, with only a dozen men executed by Tordez in transit, put out of their misery as they succumbed to madness and heretical visions.

Now they were out of the warp, Geiss wanted to get a good look at the planet before he stepped out onto its surface.

Initially, visibility was poor, as they pierced layer after layer of dark, fractious clouds, their charcoal wisps illuminated by outbreaks of lightning in all its forms: rippling sheets as well as grasping, forked tendrils.

Then the shuttle broke through, beneath the cloud cover

and into a stormy sky. Visibility was little better, but through the grey murk the surface could gradually be seen – an unprepossessing mass of brown, alternating between the rippling brown of the sea and the dull brown of the muddy, swampy ground. As they curved down towards their destination, a bleak grey outcrop of industrial structures could be seen on the horizon.

Before that unhappy-looking conurbation, their target could be seen – a flat grey expanse of rockcrete surrounded by a perimeter wall and connected to the factory-city by a long causeway, built as a crude landing area where cargo shuttles could land and take off without danger of sinking into the perilous ground beneath.

As they came in close, Geiss pressed the vox-button on the arm of his chair.

'Geiss here, prepare for landing,' he ordered. 'I'm on my way to lead us out.'

The lander was large enough to allow the entire strike force to get into formation before leaving the ship. The main body of the force were on foot, arranged in straight regimental marching lines, rifles held across their chests or arms straight at their sides. The Sentinels flanked the infantry, and the regimental Chimera troop transports were split between the front and back of the group. Major Geiss's command Chimera was slightly ahead of the others, leading the charge.

The cargo bay doors and ramp were not built for military deployment, and it took an age for the great metal doors to grind upwards, gradually letting in a thin, watery grey light from outside.

Polk's squad were lined behind Lieutenant Munez's Chimera, and Hool found himself at the farthest edge of the formation, a Sentinel looming over him. Hool realised with some discomfort that the two-legged war machine was piloted by Rebek, one of his assailants from the day he had been recruited.

Hool, Rebek and Hervl had studiously avoided each other since that day, as much as the confines of their shared service would allow, and there seemed no desire from any of them to repeat, or even discuss, their pre-conscription conflict. Now Hervl was part of Polk's squad, and on top of that Hool was suddenly disconcerted by the possibility that Rebek could crush him with one 'accidental' step of the Sentinel.

'Men of the 114th,' barked the major's voice, amplified by the vox-caster in his Chimera, his every word echoing around the hold. 'March.'

Geiss's Chimera began to roll forwards, down the slow incline of the load ramp which stretched from one end of the hold to the other. The rest of the force followed, the Chimeras' engines growling as they slowly rolled forwards, the Sentinels' slow, steady footfalls clanking against the floor of the hold, and the infantry marching in unison, each step ringing out as a precise ripple of noise.

Hool's breathing, and seemingly his very heartbeat, were in time with the rhythm of his marching: left, right; in, out; beat, beat. The rattle of the march subsided as the strike force emerged into the great open expanse of the Belmos VII space docks, the noise dissipating into the barren emptiness, taken away by the wind.

Hool kept his eyes front, but with the discipline of his march so deeply ingrained the rest of his mind was free to take in his surroundings. After the controlled, dark environments of Mordian and shipboard life, and the raging heat and squalor of Elisenda, this was a different world again: an utterly empty expanse of rockcrete, grey and damp, stained with fuel and pitted with burns and scars. Around the edge of the spaceport was a basic rockcrete wall, broken with a single gate.

The men had all been briefed on the basics: this exit led to an artificial rockcrete causeway that connected the spaceport to the city-factory proper. Over the top of the gates, some way in the distance, Hool could see the rough outline of towers, a dark mass in the grey. Detail was obscured by a light mist that hung in the air, and the persistent fall of cold droplets of water.

Hool had heard of this, but never experienced it: rain. As he came to a halt with the rest of the force, the raindrops began to run down his face and drip off the brim of his cap. On Elisenda such a thing would have been a blessing, but the air here was crisp and cold, and the touch of water on Hool's skin acted as a further conduit for the creeping chill. Hool noticed that his breath was forming a mist with every exhalation, like the smoke from a lho-stick, but thinner and quicker to dissipate in the air.

As he stood stock still in a line of equally still men, the rain and cold seeping into his clothes, exposed to the elements beneath a grey, cloud-filled sky, Hool began to develop the beginnings of a very real dislike for Belmos VII.

At the front of the strike force, Major Geiss sat in his command Chimera, looking over the driver's shoulder at the bleak landscape ahead.

'Anything I should know?' asked Geiss.

'No signs of unusual energy signals or other unexpected readings,' said Adept Gilham. By the standards of his brotherhood, Gilham was relatively humanoid, with only two mechadendrites emerging from beneath his red cloak. However, no human flesh was visible on any part of his body: his head had been augmented with a rebreather and complex optic array, while his limbs were covered with a combination of heavy-duty protective leather and metallic plating. Currently a series of thin, luminous cables ran from within the hood of his cloak to connect to a control panel. 'All normal, major.'

'All public and official vox-channels clear, no sign of activity,' added Hillman, Geiss's chief vox-operator.

Geiss rubbed the first two fingers of his right hand against the thumb, an obsessive gesture he had developed over the years. It was a sign he was making a decision.

'No indications of anything, but equally none of the normal niceties. There should be some vox-chatter or power trace in a city this size,' Geiss said, largely to himself. He clicked his fingers. 'Very well, we proceed as planned. Hillman, relay the order. Apart from the men assigned to guard the shuttle, proceed across the causeway as planned. Standard march, slow but steady.'

Commissar Tordez had elected to stay with the shuttle and monitor morale over the vox. Geiss had just nodded at this announcement, unsure whether this was a positive indication of Tordez's attitude to his leadership or not.

Geiss leaned forwards, staring out of the Chimera's narrow, armoured windscreen, trying to catch some sign of what waited ahead.

'Let's roll out and see what's out there,' Geiss said.

The city-factory loomed ahead at the causeway's end, the sloping rockcrete walls that marked its perimeter emerging from the muddy ground like a weather-beaten memorial, a battered row of linked tombstones that curved into the distance.

The wall was high, but the buildings within the perimeter towered over it: blunt habs and admin blocks near the edge, and a mass of towers and smokestacks at the centre, most of which seemed to be inactive with only thin wisps of visible smoke or steam. Crooked fingers of lightning flickered around the tops of the tallest as they reached for the heavy clouds above.

Tension built in the Guard ranks as they marched towards the gate of the city-factory. Such a direct approach was high-risk, but almost unavoidable – any other route would be equally exposed, across treacherous ground, and require a scaling of the city walls.

No, even in the case of a direct confrontation or an attack from within the city, breaching those gates remained the easiest way in. The knowledge that this was the best strategy didn't make it feel any less exposed as they marched towards an unknown enemy.

'Hillman, give me all vox-channels and external amplification,' said Geiss, leaning forwards in his chair as his Chimera rolled to a halt just short of the city-factory gates. The gates were built for function rather than defence – twice the height of a Sentinel, they were made up of several overlaid sections of plasteel that retracted into alcoves either side of the wall.

Geiss took the handheld vox-caster passed to him by Hillman, and cleared his throat before depressing the stud on the side and speaking into it:

'This is Major Geiss of the 114th Mordian Iron Guard regiment. Open the gates in the name of the God-Emperor,' said Geiss, keeping his voice firm but level. He paused, releasing the stud on the vox-caster but keeping it close to his face, the plastic hot in his palm.

As Geiss's voice rang out from the Chimera vox, Hool stood to attention, in line with the rest of the men, eyes forward. They watched, and waited, for any sign of movement ahead or above, of the first indication of attack or surrender.

While their orders included the possibility of a retreat to a defensive position in the case of a bombardment from within the city walls, Hool was fully aware that any assault could take out dozens of Guardsmen before they had time to react.

In the case of such an attack, whether it be from snipers or mortars or even some crude deterrent dropped from above, the first few lines of Guardsmen, including Polk's squad, would surge forwards to aid the withdrawal of those behind, a necessary sacrifice to allow a cohesive counter-attack. It would probably be suicide, but it needed to be done.

Hool felt his palms sweating within his gloves, and restlessly adjusted his grip on his lasrifle, ready to strike if needed.

For the moment, they waited.

Geiss looked across at Hillman, who had a vox-set to his ear. Hillman shook his head – no response. Geiss took a sterner tone when he spoke again:

'I repeat, we are Imperial Guard, open the gates and allow us access.'

Another pause, while Geiss kept his gaze fixed at the view ahead, at the points from which any attack would come. No response. No sign of movement above or around the gates.

'Fine,' said Geiss, switching the vox to his command channel. 'Munez – send your men in and get that gate open.'

'Well,' said Polk under his breath. 'You open one big door against the odds, and this is what you get. Another bloody door to open.'

'Remind me never to be good at anything again, sir,' replied Hool.

They stood back as Rivez fired a grapple launcher at the top of the gates. The hook sailed over the top of the gate, a long, reinforced cord trailing behind it. Rivez hit the switch to slowly draw the grapple back, retracting his end of the cord back into the launcher until the hook found purchase. A wet scraping sound could be heard as the hook dragged its way up the other side of the gate before locking into place.

On the basis of Polk's success in letting Munez's troops into the power complex on Elisenda, his squad had been chosen by the lieutenant to get over the wall and let the strike force into the city-factory.

Zvindt and Deress both seemed unfazed by the prospect of scaling the gates, which Polk put down partially to the precarious climbs the Elisendans must have made across the slums and derelict industrial sites of their home world, and partially due to combat inexperience.

Hool seemed more reticent, understandable considering his tendency to fall.

Rivez had fixed one climbing line to his satisfaction, and launched another hook from the grapple, a slight distance to the right. Two men would go up first, each on a separate rope, and hit the top simultaneously. If there was a threat, single file would be suicide.

'You a good climber, Deress?' asked Polk.

Deress nodded sharply. He was a broad man in his late twenties, a former factory worker, and though he wasn't a Mordian he had taken to the regiment's discipline like a natural.

'Used to climb the transmitter spire at Inaxa for fun, sir,' said Deress.

Polk had no idea where that was, but he got the idea. 'You're up first with me then, Deress. Hool and Zvindt can hold the ropes steady then follow. Rivez, you're up last, the rest of you stay down here until we get the door open. This is hardly a ten-man job.' He turned back to Deress. 'This isn't a race, though. You reach the top first, you stop and hold until I'm with you. We go over the top together.'

Deress nodded again: 'Understood, sir.'

'Right then,' said Polk, and in unison he and Deress gripped their respective ropes, and began the climb up the gate.

As sergeant, Polk had considered it his duty to lead from the front, especially with most of the regiment ranked and watching as he climbed the gate. That didn't make the experience any more comfortable. Pulling himself up, hand over hand, boots carefully finding purchase on the rain-slicked metal surface of the gate, his back twinged at the unnatural angle it was bent into, and a deep ache set into the back of his thighs. The angle of the climb allowed the rain to fall under the peak of his cap and straight into his eyes, and he had to blink water away to see properly.

He was definitely feeling his age. Deress was keeping pace with Polk, probably by slowing himself down and matching his sergeant's movements.

It was a painful climb, but only a short one. At the top, nodding to Deress to follow his lead, Polk held on to the top of the gate with one hand, twisting the rope securely around that arm, and used his free hand to secure a lower part of the rope to the safety loop on his belt. With both hands now free, Polk hung from the rope, feet placed firmly on the surface of the gate, and hauled up his combat shotgun from where it was hanging on a shoulder strap.

Polk glanced across at Deress, who had his lasrifle similarly raised. Polk placed his left hand on the ledge of the gate, and Deress did the same. Polk took a deep breath, then silently mouthed a countdown to Deress: three, two…

…one. Polk and Deress pulled themselves up in unison, careful not to slip straight off the wet surface. The top of the gate was just wide enough to stand on, and at the top Polk perched on one knee, gun raised as he scanned from side to side, checking the area.

Nothing. No signs of life, never mind sources of attack. That didn't mean they were entirely safe, but there was certainly no immediate danger.

Polk leaned back over the gate, and whistled for the others to follow.

Within minutes Polk's men were over the gate, providing cover for each other as they moved quickly to the side, searching for the entry controls.

Hool kept his lasrifle raised, sweeping back and forth for any sign of movement.

It was a large area to keep covered. Immediately behind the gates the rockcrete surface expanded into a wide-open area, the pitted surface covered in tyre-tracks, oil patches and other markings that indicated great numbers of vehicles stopping to load and unload.

This central area led out into three access roads that wound away into the city-factory, disappearing behind the bulky, featureless warehouse buildings that crowded around the gates, ready to send and receive cargo.

Hool looked up at the nearest warehouse. Although mostly blank, the wall had a few isolated windows or airvents, each a potential sniping position.

Even now that they were inside the city-factory, Hool didn't feel any less exposed.

Someone had located the controls. The twin gates began to grind open, age-old gears dragging the segments back into slots either side of the entry way.

The deep rumble of those gears broke the oppressive silence of the dead city-factory, but didn't do anything to lift Hool's sense of unease.

With the entire strike force through the gates of the city-factory, and sentries covering every approach, Major Geiss summoned his lieutenants for a briefing.

Dropping from the Chimera to the rockcrete, Geiss felt a jolt of pain up his right leg as his heel hit the hard surface with his entire body weight behind it. Rolling open a strategic map of the city-factory, he compared it with the three roads ahead.

The central road ran due north to the heart of the city-factory, where the mine's control centre overhung the central shaft. The road to Geiss's left ran north-west through the dirty maze of the refineries, and the map indicated that workers' habs were stacked against the west wall. The road to the right ran north-east to the opposite end of Belmos VII's social strata, winding through the vehicle depots, administrative areas, and opening out into Emperor's Square, where more luxurious hab-towers housed the planetary elite.

Comparing the map with the view ahead, Geiss could make out a silvery monolith to the north-east, presumably in Emperor's Square, while a mass of crane rigs straight ahead seemed to tally with the centre of the mining activity being to the north.

Munez, Hossk and Deaz had gathered at a discreet distance while Geiss was reviewing the map, and he rolled the map and used it as a baton to illustrate his commands as he spoke.

'No signs of life, and we only have a few hours of daylight left, so we deploy as planned and move quickly. Lieutenant Hossk, move north-west, slow and steady through the refineries. Set lasguns to low-charge only. Apparently these places use large quantities of chamazian in the refinement process, and we don't want to ignite the whole place. Good wide spread, let's check as many corners as we can, and if you find anything at all vox me immediately. It's going to be slow going, so you'd better get started.'

Hossk snapped a salute and walked away. Geiss continued.

'Lieutenant Munez, you get the easy part. Secure Emperor's Square. Find and protect any worthies in that tower. Don't endanger the mission in the process, but if possible we want to keep them intact. The square will be our fall-back position in the case of problems, so make it tight.'

Geiss didn't wait for Munez to go before turning to Deaz. 'Lieutenant, you're with me – we're going straight to the centre.'

As Geiss had suggested, the progress of Hossk's platoon was slow. With only one support Chimera and no Sentinels,

Hossk's men moved mostly on foot, and Hossk himself opted to leave his Chimera and walk, laspistol drawn. A vox-bead kept him in contact with Geiss's command channel. They had dropped out of formal march but moved decisively, marksmen covering every angle of attack, scouts moving ahead of the ranks, holding to cover and ready to give warning of problems ahead.

While the Chimera slowly rolled down the main road, Hossk's sergeants sent squads out into the buildings on either side, breaking down doors, cutting through fences, spreading out either side of the road to explore the refinery. They were under orders to keep relatively close and maintain pace with the main group – the refinery buildings were elaborate mazes of oily pipework held in place by girders thicker than a Chimera. Even in daylight, they seemed dark and impenetrable, quiet except for the constant sound of water on metal as the rain flowed from one surface to another.

Hossk walked past a loading area stacked with barrels, each covered in warning signs. They contained chamazian, an extraordinarily volatile and flammable chemical used in heavy industrial facilities such as these. On Elisenda, Hossk had seen a group of cornered rebels kill themselves by firing into a barrel of the stuff. Not only had the rebels been obliterated, but the walls of the store building they had retreated to were blown out, three Guardsmen were rushed to the medicae with seventy-seven per cent burns, and patches of flaming, tarrish liquid chamazian burned where they fell for the following three days.

Hossk voxed a reminder to keep las-fire to a minimum.

There was a high, human whistle from ahead, a signal from one of the scouts. It was a cautionary signal but not alert, meaning the scout had discovered something of interest, and that the rest of the group should hold, but that there was no immediate threat.

Hossk raised his laspistol and nodded to one of his most trusted sergeants, Weir. With Weir and his men in support, Hossk ran past the Chimera, the ranks of Guardsmen stepping aside to let them through.

Reaching the scout, Hossk didn't need to ask what had been found: the scout was kneeling by a dark dried patch underneath an overhanging canopy on the side of one of the refinery buildings. If it had been exposed to the constant rain it would have doubtless washed away, but sheltered where it was the stain was unmistakably that of dried human blood: a great quantity of it as well, pooled on the ground as well as sprayed across a nearby wall. There were signs that a scuffle had spread the blood further, but no clear footprints could be made out.

'Major Geiss,' Hossk said into his vox. 'First sign of disruption located.'

On the other side of the city-factory, Munez's platoon were making similar discoveries.

The central Administratum building was a statement of power, great gilded columns framing brass doors moulded with images of the achievements of the Imperium, all set in a scrubbed white stone that set the whole building apart from the grubbier blocks around it.

The grandeur of the effect was slightly diluted by the wreckage of the entrance. One of the doors lay stretched across the access road, and the other was buckled inwards.

The marbled floor of the great reception hall was encrusted with blood. Chunks had been knocked out of the walls, statues overturned. The bloodstains streaked off in all directions, but petered out with no signs of any bodies, dead or alive.

Smoker voxed his report to Munez without emotion, looking down at the unholy mess before him. Stained-glass windows over the entrance let a trickle of multi-coloured light down into the hallway, mottling the bloodstains in different shades of green and blue.

After Smoker gave his report, Munez ordered him back to rejoin the body of the platoon. The sergeant shrugged impassively, and gestured for his men to follow as he strolled away from the carnage.

In his command Chimera, Geiss received similar reports from across the city, from the platoon with him as well as those led by Munez and Hossk. There was variation in the signs of struggle – occasionally signs of weapons discharge and varying levels of damage to the surrounding area – but otherwise there was a certain consistency.

Blood had been shed, but no bodies left behind. No sign of the assailants or survivors, but equally no evidence of any attempted clean-up.

Geiss had heard of colonies that had been found devoid of life, with no explanation ever found for the deaths or disappearance of those who had lived there. But those 'ghost planets' had been out of Imperial contact for decades, even centuries, not a couple of *weeks*.

Somewhere in the city-factory, there were answers, Geiss was sure of it.

He would start at the centre. Geiss's group reached the perimeter of the mine at the heart of the city-factory. A fence surrounded the mine complex, behind which a cluster of towers and cranes could be seen, the mechanisms that took men and materials up and down the central mineshaft.

The perimeter fence was flattened, corrugated metal. Geiss ordered his driver to advance straight through it, with Deaz's men to follow in a standard attack pattern. The time for timidity was over.

The fence crumpled under the weight of the Chimera, which bounced slightly as its wheels rolled over the obstruction but barely slowed down. The transport pulled up outside the rear of the mining control centre, skidding slightly on the rain-slicked road surface, and Geiss stepped out as Deaz's vehicle came to a halt behind. Further back, Guardsmen were pouring through the breach, their sergeants ordering them to spread out and secure the facility.

Geiss looked up at the mine's control centre. From his point of view it was a squat building, only a few storeys high, but Geiss knew that it went much deeper, with many below-ground levels running down the wall of the main pit, culminating in a gallery overlooking the main works.

'Lieutenant Deaz,' Geiss said, pointing to the building. 'Time for your strike teams to show me their worth. I want a secure route to the control gallery within the hour.'

Deaz gave his superior a crooked smile. 'If there's a carpet in there I'll have them roll it all the way down for you, major.'

Deaz turned away, bellowing orders. The first team went in within a couple of minutes, kicking down a door and disappearing within the building, while a second team ran around the side to take a separate entrance.

Another minute or two passed, then there was a low thump from inside the building.

Geiss and Deaz exchanged glances, and Deaz tapped the vox-bead in his collar.

'Sergeant, talk to me,' Deaz snapped. 'What was that?' He listened, nodding a couple of times, then reported back to Geiss.

'Someone blockaded the stairwell down to the first belowground level, sir,' said Deaz. 'Team cleared it with an explosive charge, and are now proceeding to–'

Deaz suddenly broke off in mid-sentence, glancing at the ground as another message was relayed into his ear. He looked up at Geiss, clearly surprised.

'Sir, we've found a survivor. A civilian.'

It was only as Major Geiss felt a cold rush of shock that he realised he'd grown to expect everyone on the planet to be dead.

'Tell the rest of your men to keep moving, but to leave a couple of Guardsmen with the civilian and hold their position. I'm coming down to interview them myself.'

* * *

'Found him asleep, sir,' said the Guardsman who led Geiss into the oblong store room. The power was out, as it had been across the city, but the thin daylight seeped in through windows overlooking the mine, towering machinery casting cog-shaped shadows across the room.

'Bit surprising, considering we'd just blown through a barrier two rooms from him,' continued the Guardsman. He didn't seem intimidated by Geiss's rank – Deaz's men didn't stand much on ceremony. 'We had to shake him awake.'

'He doesn't look too lively now,' replied Geiss, looking at the man sitting on a box before him, who seemed to be suppressing a yawn. The civilian hadn't looked up as Geiss had entered the room, and was instead staring blankly at the floor.

He wasn't much to look at: short, probably fifty or sixty years old, white-grey hair cut into no particular style, as if hacked down for pure convenience. He either wore a thin beard, or just hadn't shaved for a while, his lined face covered in a mess of stubble. His watery green eyes stared out from behind cheap vision-enhancers, the right lens cracked. His whole demeanour was crumpled and worn, as was the basic light blue bodyglove he was wearing.

Even in the patchy light, Geiss could see dark stains on the man's clothes, although he showed no sign of having been injured.

Geiss cleared his throat. No reaction. So he leaned forwards, speaking right into the man's face.

'I am Major Halvern Geiss of the 114th Mordian Iron Guard,' he said firmly. 'What's your name?'

The man looked up, a placid confusion in his eyes. He didn't seem distressed or traumatised, just detached.

'Your name, citizen,' repeated Geiss, letting more authority into his voice this time.

The man opened his mouth, as if re-learning how to use it, and after a few seconds of deliberation spoke:

'Krick,' he said, his speech slow and quiet. 'My name is Krick.'

'Well, that's a start,' said Geiss, trying not to sound too exasperated. For the first time he wished he had a psyker on his staff, someone capable of pushing through whatever mental problem Krick was having. Even Tordez would have been useful at this point, or an intelligence man, someone familiar with conducting interrogations.

Geiss was a soldier. Getting information out of bewildered civilians wasn't his area of expertise.

'Mr Krick,' he said sharply, deciding to push the conversation along. 'I'm going to presume that you work here in some capacity. Am I right?'

Krick nodded slowly.

'Thank you,' said Geiss. 'Now, please concentrate, Mr Krick. I need to know what happened here?'

'Happened?' Krick repeated blankly.

'Yes, what happened?' Geiss repeated, unused to having to give an instruction more than once. 'Where are the people, Mr Krick? Why is no one working?' Geiss realised that bombarding a confused man with more than one question was counterproductive, but he was losing his temper and couldn't stop himself. 'What has happened to this place, Mr Krick?'

'Something,' said Krick, his expression sharpening a little, as he reached for a distant memory. 'Something did happen. It was…'

Geiss waited expectantly for Krick to continue.

'It was loud,' said Krick eventually. 'There was noise, and blood, and light, and it was so *fast*. Then most everyone was gone.'

'Gone where?' asked Geiss. Krick's expression and tone of voice hadn't changed even as he struggled through his vague recollection of events, but had remained flat throughout.

'I don't know,' said Krick, his gaze returning to the middle distance. 'They're just gone.' He looked up at Geiss. 'Does it matter?'

Within the hour, Deaz's men had cleared a route through to the main control gallery. Along the way they had found half a dozen more civilians, a couple wearing similar bodygloves to Krick, a woman in the neatly pressed formal clothing of a Munitorum official, and three miners. All were in a similar state to Krick – bewildered, dirty, but uninjured and apparently not distressed by their experience.

Geiss had them all confined to a recreational area one floor above the main control gallery. He ensured they were given food from Guard rations, and access to washing and toilet facilities.

Attempts to question them gained little more than Geiss had managed to squeeze out of Krick – vague memories of chaos, but a lack of concern for the details. When left to their own devices, all of them found a bench to lie on and went to sleep.

A more focused interrogation might produce better results. Geiss considered calling in Tordez to conduct it, but put the thought aside.

Until the city-factory was thoroughly explored and secure, there was little point in pursuing a potentially fruitless line of enquiry. There was also the question of power. Something had happened to the city-wide power supply. The city-factory was built around the mine, with an on-site generatorium that relayed power to the rest of the city. Deaz's men were assisting Gilham and his servitors in getting the power online so that at least they'd have light after nightfall.

Night. According to the recording of Gellwood Jenk's final words, he couldn't 'tell in the daylight'. Tell what? Perhaps night would bring answers, but Geiss preferred to have them brought to him first, on his own terms.

Maybe there wouldn't be any answers. Geiss's orders were to re-secure the city-factory and get it working again. If there was never any answer to why the place had ground to a halt in the first place, then Geiss would have to live with that.

It didn't sit easily with him, though. Even as he gave commands and received reports, ostensibly fully in control of the situation, that lack of strategic knowledge itched away at the back of his mind.

While Major Geiss fortified his position, the other platoons continued their missions elsewhere.

It was late afternoon by the time Hossk's platoon rolled out from the farthest edge of the refineries and towards the main habs. The workers' hab-blocks had been clustered in a relatively small area of the city-factory, a patch of land between the outer wall and the more productive, industrialised parts of the city.

There were half a dozen towering habs, brown-grey, rotten-tooth towers linked by teetering sky-bridges, awnings and cable rigs. The towers seemed to bend towards each other, sagging under the number of workers crammed into each block. Meagre, black little windows dotted each tower, with the odd flash of colour visible within – gang colours probably, thought Hossk, recollecting a previous campaign where a conflict between hive gangs had resulted in a full-scale uprising, the 114th having been brought in to quell the rebellion.

Belmos VII was one of the least populated worlds Hossk had ever had the displeasure to visit: one small city-factory around the mine on the entire planet, with a small population of workers and administrators. But even here, with a whole empty world, humanity had found a way to cram itself into a squalid, miserable place like this. Hossk had spent time in trenches on swamp worlds he'd rather live in than these habs.

It was while approaching the habs that Hossk heard the first noises. He'd had the command update from Geiss regarding survivors, so it wasn't entirely unexpected. But after a morning travelling through desolate industrial spaces where the only sounds other than those made by the guards were the whistles created by the wind flowing through corridors and pipes and the constant background patter of rainwater, the sound of a distant, muffled human voice came as a shock.

In spite of the bloodstains and evidence of violence, the emptiness they had experienced so far had had a lulling effect on the men. As the first distant voice rang out – whether it was a scream, a cry, or just normal speech, Hossk couldn't tell – he saw many of his men unconsciously adjusting their grips on their weapons, their shoulders spreading and backs straightening as they tensed themselves for potential trouble.

The workers who lived here had no use for private transport, and the road which ran through the refineries led to the uninhabited sub-levels of the habs, presumably for the purpose of delivery vehicles and maintenance. The workers would rarely come down here, instead trudging up and down the walkways into and out of their habs. Those who lived within an hour of their workstation would keep walking, while others would file into box-like train cars that would rattle them across the city-factory to their place of labour.

Two routes to the habs above were visible as Hossk's platoon approached. The vehicle route led directly ahead, through a darkened underpass between the bases of the hab-towers, while grimy stairwells led up to connect with the walkways that connected the habs with the rest of the city-factory.

Hossk had a choice – to continue moving into the habs via the underpass, moving as a platoon with the Chimera, or to hold the vehicle back and instead access the habs via the pedestrian levels above.

Going in from below would leave them exposed to whoever may be above, and there was no guarantee of a workable route to get to the upper levels from below the blocks themselves. However, taking the stairwells involved splitting the platoon and potentially leaving individual squads more vulnerable.

Hossk made his decision and called the platoon to a halt. These were habs, hives of potentially discontented humanity. Rolling into an open area with hab-blocks overlooking it was suicide. Any confrontation would need to be on a human scale, face to face. There was little use in maintaining the pretence of an orderly battlefield by marching in lines.

Hossk ordered the Chimera and a couple of squads to return to the edge of the refineries and find a secure position, while his sergeants drew their squads together and began to move towards the stairwells. Hossk took command of one squad, sending their best marksman to take point as they approached the stairwell.

Even in broad daylight it was a gloomy prospect. The stairwell was little more than a tube of rockcrete with weathered steps within, open to the air from waist height. Even with the wind blowing through it and the rain to wash it clean, the stench of human waste hit Hossk's nostrils, and the steps were coated in damp scraps and rubbish.

Rifles aimed upwards, Hossk's squad ran up the stairs, covering the angles with every turn, shouts of 'clear!' echoing down the stairwell as they checked the route ahead.

Within a couple of minutes they were at the walkway level. The walkway was itself nothing but a channel for directing a flow of humanity from their place of living to their place of work. Although it was covered, the walkway was open to the windows of the nearest hab-block. Hossk's men stayed low, hugging close to the shoulder-height walls, moving as fast as they could towards the entrance to the main-hab. The doors had been torn out of the wall, leaving an open target for the Guardsmen to run towards.

The first man through made a textbook entrance, dropping low as he reached the doorway and leaning around the corner, lasrifle raised, to find any potential threat.

He did everything right, but it didn't do him any good. A mass of scrap metal on a chain swung down and slammed into the young Guardsman before he could fire off a shot.

Hossk, who was some distance behind on the walkway, saw it happen, the Guardsman's body knocked sideways with tremendous force, hitting the hard edge of the door frame with a crunch and falling, broken, to the ground.

Traps. Every army in the galaxy laid mines and tripwires sometimes, but the practice sat badly with Hossk, who believed that war was best fought face to face, a show of discipline and courage as much as force and ingenuity.

To their credit, the men ahead responded to the trap perfectly, holding back outside the door while a corporal extended a polished mirror on a thin rod around the door frame. The corporal hunched low, sliding the mirror underneath the mass of welded scrap that still swung from side to side in the doorframe.

'Well?' asked Hossk.

'Stairs ascending to the right, sir,' said the corporal, adjusting the rod back and forth to get a good view. 'Looks like this was rigged on the next landing, manually swung down into Arto. They must have heard or seen us coming, sir.' He squinted. 'Some movement on the landing. I think they're just tucked out of sight behind the wall. It's dark up there, no way of telling how many. Can't see any further traps rigged, but that's not saying much.'

Hossk nodded. Although he couldn't see around the corner, the room just through the doorway was empty enough, a functional hallway bare of any ornamentation, but free of any traps. Stairs running down were visible at the far side of the room. The only threat was from above.

'Fair enough, corporal, keep an eye on it.' He turned to the rest of the men. 'Right, I need a fast mover with a good overarm throw.'

One of the Guardsmen raised a hand. He looked the right type – young, wiry.

'Good man,' Hossk nodded. 'Sergeant, a smoke grenade.' He took the proffered munition and passed it straight to the young Guardsman. 'I want this pitched right up those stairs. Let the corporal here give you a look at what you're aiming at.' Hossk turned his attention to the rest of the men. 'The second that grenade pops, we move in. Suppressing fire up those stairs, secure that hallway, then we move up.'

Hossk turned back to the Guardsman with the smoke grenade. 'Ready?'

The Guardsman nodded.

'Good, go.'

The young Guardsman backed down the walkway to give himself a run up, and pulled the pin. He then charged forwards, a thin trail of smoke already seeping out of the grenade, leaping past the hunk of scrap that had killed his fellow Guardsman. As he leapt he tossed the grenade, which spiralled out of Hossk's field of vision.

'Now!' Hossk bellowed, and the rest of the men charged into the hallway, firing to their right. Hossk moved in with the pack, looking up to see a barrage of las-fire disappearing into a cloud of smoke at the top of the stairs.

In the hallway, the Guard took position, lasrifle barrels sweeping the lines of approach.

'Secure, sir.' Someone was helping the young Guardsman who had tossed the grenade, while another was checking the Guard who had sprung the trap in the doorway. The corporal checking the body shook his head at Hossk.

Hossk nodded in unhappy acknowledgement, and returned his attention to the top of the stairs.

'Hold,' he hissed as smoke began to clear, and the las-fire ceased. Half a dozen men held their position, searching for any target in the clearing smoke.

'Get me some light,' Hossk snapped, and lamp-packs flickered to life.

There was the recognisable form of a man at the top of the stairs, collapsed on the floor in a position that no one would choose, face down with an arm bent behind him.

'Get me the next two landings,' barked Hossk, sending three Guardsmen racing up the stairs. 'And vox the other teams. I want to know whether they've met similar resistance.'

As his men went to work, Hossk climbed the stairs slowly to where the man who had killed one of his platoon lay. A spluttering cough revealed he was still alive, although the blood he drooled onto the floor indicated he wouldn't be for long.

Hossk unceremoniously pushed the man onto his back with a boot toe.

The dying man was in a rough condition, unshaven and with tears and dirt all over his bodyglove. His eyes were wild and unfocused, his breathing broken and ragged. The man looked up at Hossk, and between choking gasps managed to squeeze a few words out:

'Why... in the day?'

'What day?' asked Hossk, but the man was dead. He shrugged and walked away. He had little time for the ramblings of rebels and lunatics, especially when they had taken the life of an Imperial Guardsman.

Crude traps and manic citizens. Maybe this was just another tawdry uprising after all.

Hossk tapped the vox-bead at his collar.

'Get me a channel to Major Geiss,' he told the vox-operator. There was a pause before Geiss responded.

'Major,' Hossk said. 'We've met some resistance.'

Hossk looked between the bodies of the two men: the dead Guardsman and his killer.

'No, sir,' Hossk told Geiss. 'We've taken one casualty, but I don't think the threat is too serious. Looks like just another planet with rebellious locals.'

FOUR

It was a single shot, but it rang out across Emperor's Square. The echo made it impossible to tell from where the shot had come. The shot hadn't found a target.

Munez's men responded smoothly: those near cover took it, while those in exposed areas dropped to one knee, reducing their size as a target. All around the square, weapons were raised, eyes looking through gun sights, tracking every window and alcove on the buildings around, systematically sweeping their fields of vision to find the source of the shot, or at least to catch the muzzle flare when the next shot came, betraying the position of the shooter.

Until that second shot came – and even those who had found cover could not be sure that the shooter's line of sight didn't cut straight past their defensive shelter, that the next shot might not be directed at them – the possibility of finding the shooter's location was remote. Emperor's Square was an open area tiled with polished white stone, the centrepiece of which was a gigantic statue of the Emperor Himself, sculpted in the most extravagant high style. Smaller statues, monuments and plaques littered the square, commemorating notable people and events from across the Imperium as well as Belmos VII.

The square was overlooked by lavishly gilded buildings, each of which could house a dozen snipers. The Adeptus Mechanicus had a squat cathedra at one end of the square which was adorned with weatherbeaten statuary and gargoyles, as was the Ecclesiarchy's temple.

From the perspective of the Guardsmen, blue-coated figures against a pure white background, the next shot could come from any one of those windows or balconies or nooks behind statues. It was an environment bristling with threat.

Across the square, they waited for the next shot to come.

Lieutenant Munez, although safely ensconced within the armoured shell of his Chimera, was no less tense for that relative security. Within seconds of the shot being heard he was on the vox, checking for casualties, demanding confirmation.

He received little satisfaction from the replies: almost everyone was certain the shot was from some kind of lasweapon, not just a similar percussive noise. Munez trusted this judgment – if there was anything soldiers learned over their careers, it was to distinguish the discharge of various weapons from sound alone.

'If the shooter is located, report back immediately,' said Munez over the command vox. 'If they hit one of us and a clear retaliatory shot is available, take it. Otherwise, identify the shooter and hold position. I repeat, hold, do not fire until my mark.'

It was the kind of order that would cause discontent in a less disciplined regiment, and not one Munez took any pleasure in giving, but he trusted the men under his command to follow it within reason.

Although he had a good reputation among the rank-and-file, and considered the welfare of his men more than others of his rank, Munez was still an officer and a strategist, and would not hesitate to risk or sacrifice the lives of ordinary Guardsmen for a strategic need.

Munez was also considerably more of a political animal than anyone above or below him in the chain of command gave him credit for. So far the nature of the crisis on Belmos VII was ambiguous: the major had found some survivors, while Hossk had reported a few rebellious slum dwellers throwing crude traps around. With the situation unclear, Munez wasn't going to allow his men to fire at every damn shadow they saw, especially if that shadow turned out to be the kind of local bigwig it would be very impolite to kill.

The square itself suggested that any such bigwigs around might be very big indeed.

Emperor's Square was an exercise in Imperial monumentalism, an urban statement of the importance of Belmos VII's resources to the might of the Imperium, or at least the inflated self-importance of the administrative and industrial elite of the planet. Away from the dirt and industry of the rest of the city-factory, and the squalid conditions of the workers' habs, the city's elite could promenade around the marbled square, drifting from boutique to salon, attended by servitor courtiers, underlings and indentured labourers, a life of luxury for those who ran and bankrolled the dirty, important but highly profitable work of the mines.

At one end of the square the main hab-tower pierced the sky, deliberately placed clear of any buildings remotely as tall. A vast gold aquila spread its wings across the facade, catching the late afternoon light, and statues of long-forgotten, but no doubt wealthy, men and women occupied key positions on ledges and in alcoves. The more functional buildings crammed either side of the tower looked burned-out and battle-scarred, but the main hab-tower was still disconcertingly immaculate.

While the Imperial Guard command structure was theoretically completely separate from the machinations of the Imperium's great civil institutions, influence could always be brought. There was military authority, and then there was practicality.

In practical terms, Munez didn't want to be responsible for one of his men mistakenly shooting the spouse or heir of someone who lived in this kind of luxury. That kind of error would do the career of a low-born lieutenant no good at all.

When the second shot rang out, the Guard were ready for it, instincts tracking the source of the noise, many pairs of highly trained eyes searching for the shooter.

The second shot came nearest to hitting Hool, but that wasn't very near. A las-beam flashed, leaving a sizzling patch on the wet pavement a few metres away from him.

Hool tracked the trajectory of the shot up to the fifth floor of the elite hab. He saw the slightest hint of movement at a narrow window.

'Got it, sir,' shouted Hool. 'Fifth floor, third window from the left.'

Munez was out of his Chimera, and beckoned the two soldiers across to him as Polk and Hool ran, heads low, towards him. He wasn't surprised it was these two – Polk and the gangly youth – who had identified the shooter's location. Munez wasn't a hugely superstitious man, but he had seen how some squads or soldiers could have runs of good or bad luck.

He was too good an officer to let jinxes influence his decisions, but equally didn't push against these streaks when it suited him to work with the flow of fortune. A little of the Emperor's touch didn't do a mission any harm.

The two Guardsmen snapped neatly to attention. They were both typical of their type. The Guard was full of men like Polk, men who rose to the rank of corporal or sergeant and stayed there, the benefit of their experience permeating the ranks. Solid men, reliable.

The young Guardsman was also of a type: one of the billions of infantry across the galaxy who were recruited, given a gun and pointed in the direction of humanity's enemies. Most would die within a couple of years, their first mistakes their last. In spite of his recent run of luck, it was too early to tell whether this young man would be one of the fortunate few who lived longer. Fate would show its hand soon enough.

'At ease,' Munez said, then rolled straight into his questions.

'How far wide of any target was this shot, Guardsman?'

'A few metres, sir.'

'And the shot came from the fifth floor, with a clear line of sight?'

'Yes, sir.'

'And the blast mark from the shot, did it chip the stone?

'Sir…?'

'Did it take a chunk out of the ground, did it leave a crater, however small?'

The Guardsman thought about this for a few seconds before answering:

'No, sir. Just a black burn mark, a bit of smoke and steam.'

Munez nodded. 'Very good.' He turned to Polk. 'Sergeant, no sniper would have failed to hit a target with both of those shots, and they'd certainly have known better than to try and take the shot with a short-range lasgun that only scorches its target at that range. Our shooter is probably a jumpy local, in that place likely some Administratum high-up. The major wants us to avoid trashing the precious fixtures and fittings of this wretched planet, and as far as I'm concerned that includes the local gentry.

'Gather the rest of your squad, and go in via the building on the left there. The top floor should be directly adjacent to the fifth floor of that hab-tower. Blast your way through the adjoining wall. Some gentle suppressing fire will provide a distraction from down here, so they shouldn't hear you coming until it's too late.

'If there's serious resistance, don't hesitate to take them down, but if possible I want our shooter bagged alive. Try not to kill them, but don't feel you need to be gentle. I want whoever is up there talkative. If we can get the major some answers while we're here, all the better.'

On the other side of the city-factory, Lieutenant Hossk had no such reservations. Hossk ordered his men to shoot to kill at the first sign of resistance, no hesitation. His Guardsmen swept through the habs, kicking in doors and searching communal areas.

As the men moved through the hab-slums the occasional barrage of las-fire was heard, always followed very shortly by a vox-report telling of some slum-dweller who had burst out wielding a crude weapon or making some other threatening movement. They provided little challenge to trained Guardsmen, and their bodies were left where they fell. Further reports were voxed in of crude traps of the kind Hossk had seen earlier. These were dismantled with little effort, and the afternoon wore on without further Guard casualties.

Hossk eventually returned to his Chimera at the edge of the underpass, content to allow his sergeants to lead the securing of the habs. They didn't need his direct command to mop up this hive scum. This was grunt work, simple stuff.

At this rate, Hossk thought, they'd have Belmos VII pacified by nightfall. It was barely worth them being there.

* * *

It was the most luxurious building Hool had ever been in, even after some previous conflict had torn through, trashing the fittings, shooting holes in the walls and burning furnishings. Even after all that, it was still an elegant place, the glamour more disconcerting to Hool than the evidence of past violence.

Hool and Rivez took point, covering each other at every turn and corner, while Polk and the rest of the squad followed. They had been supplied with extra explosives for blasting their way through into the next building, and these were in the care of Midj and Hervl in the heavy packs they nervously carried on their backs, divided into pouches of heavy and light explosives.

Without the charges fitted, sealed from the atmosphere and sheathed in thick protective material, most explosives were theoretically inert, with a freak shot required to cause any kind of unintended reaction. Even so, Hool still wouldn't have liked to be one of the men who carried such a quantity close to their person.

Midj's knowledge of explosives was well-known while Hervl had also, by various accounts, proven to be a highly able man with explosives. Hool tried to take the odd complimentary story he had heard about Hervl in his stride – anything before the Guard was a different life, after all – but he couldn't shake the memory of that metal spur about to be brought down into his face, of the other young man's venomous, taunting eyes as he attempted to end Hool's life.

Hool had been in far more life-threatening situations many, many times since being conscripted to the 114th, but

Hervl and Rebek had made the first attempt on his life, and they had done it gleefully, enjoying his fear as they hunted him down like an animal.

Even though regimental loyalty and the needs of the mission overrode all other issues on the battlefield, part of Hool couldn't, wouldn't forget. Since Hervl had joined Polk's squad his presence was an itch in his back, an awareness that someone who had intended him great harm was walking a few steps behind him.

Hool wanted to turn around and shoot Hervl right through the throat. Not a clean kill, but one where Hervl would die slowly, bleeding out on the dirty floor. Part of Hool wanted to see Hervl suffer.

Instead, Hool choked down his rage and concentrated on his surroundings, keeping an eye open for any sign of movement as he and Rivez led the way. On the ground floor they had passed through a grand foyer panelled with a black-green wood polished to a near-reflective shine, then through into some kind of boutique, where elaborately sculpted items of indeterminate purpose, crafted from gleaming metal and set with glittering jewels, were displayed in ornate cases set on velvet-draped plinths. Hool didn't know what any of the stuff was for, but he knew it was expensive.

They moved quickly and quietly, Hool stepping around patches of scattered, broken glass from smashed cases. It looked accidental, a side effect of some other disturbance, or just plain vandalism, but a scattering of fragile, noisy fragments could equally be a crude alarm set by someone hidden nearby.

At the back of the room, a gilded, winding staircase led up, with filigreed banisters and polished marble steps. Hool looked up – it seemed to run right to the top of the building.

The first few steps were covered in dried blood, a wide streak that disappeared into the deep red of the carpet laid at the bottom.

Hool ignored it and looked back to Polk, who gestured for them to continue up. Hool and Rivez took the stairs carefully, as the 360-degree openness of the stairway required wide arcs of cover. They took the stairs in step with each other, almost back to back.

They passed through the next three floors of the building without incident, Hool taking in rooms full of decadent splendour: a restaurant where the tables had been overturned and once-extravagant feasts rotted on the floor; the tiled entranceway to an elaborate bathhouse, echoing with a mordant, slow drip from somewhere within; a floor where embroidered, ceiling-to-floor tapestries depicted scenes of the kind that Guardsmen traded a week's lho-sticks for, the tapestries separating alcoves where presumably such scenes were reenacted; and finally a gambling floor where card tables had been smashed to pieces and the lurid, multicoloured lights on the walls were just burnt-out tangles of dead glass tubing.

On the fifth floor, they worked their way through the ruined gaming spaces, with chips worth fortunes scattered on the floor, and through a door into the working areas of the building.

Beyond that door, the luxuries of the front of the house ended, replaced with drab utility: grimy kitchens, drab store rooms, racks of stained servants' uniforms. In a small side room the staff had set up a card game of their own, the battered cards and tiny piles of small-denomination coins a parody of the high-stakes games being played a short distance away.

When they reached the wall adjoining the hab-block, Midj tapped the surface a couple of times. Satisfied, he found a broken-off chair leg and smacked it into the plaster, dragging it away in lumps. He then gouged the rest off with his gloved fingers, revealing a stone patch underneath.

'Thought so,' Midj said to Polk. 'This place was built right up against the exterior wall. No air between, not even a proper outer wall on this side. This–'

Midj tapped the stone wall beneath the plaster.

'–is the outer wall of the hab.' He shook his head. 'The flashier these places look on the surface, the cheaper they are when you peel that away.'

'Makes our lives easier though,' said Polk. 'Blow it.'

Midj and Hervl worked quickly, the older man instructing the younger on where to set the charges, and how much to use. The other guards retreated to a safe distance.

'No point in being stealthy once that lot goes off,' said Polk. 'So let's go in fast, make a lot of noise, and hit them hard.'

When the wall exploded, Polk led the charge himself. Midj had, as usual, set exactly the right quantity of explosives, and the wall exploded outwards, neatly blasted away into a shower of bricks and plaster. As it did so, dust blew out in a wave, and Polk felt the familiar rush that came from charging into the unknown, running into the cloud of thick, white brickdust, holding his breath and blinking quickly to clear the debris from his eyes.

As he emerged from the dust, Polk took in the scene: a wide room, long windows to the right. A handful of men, one crouched at a window, holding a gun with the barrel resting on a window ledge. The sniper.

Polk raised his combat shotgun, keeping the sniper covered, and bellowed at them to drop their weapons and raise their hands. Polk wasn't aware of the detail of what he was saying, just a stream of the worst expletives he knew.

The men in the room did as they were told, the sniper recoiling from his own gun as if it were threatening him. No one else appeared to be armed. Hands stretched up to the ceiling, blind panic in the eyes.

Civilians, as Munez had predicted. Scared, untrained civilians in expensive clothes, meekly surrendering to the force of will of the Guardsmen flooding into their home.

Civilians who had shot at the Emperor's Imperial Guard, Polk remembered. He grabbed the sniper by the collar and threw him roughly to the floor, then kicked him over onto his back.

'Why did you fire at us?' bellowed Polk, jamming the fat barrel of his shotgun into the sniper's solar plexus. A shot at this close range would probably blast the man's heart through the floor. 'Why?'

'We thought you were them,' babbled the sniper. 'We didn't know you were you!'

'Who?' demanded Polk. 'Who did you think we were?'

'Them,' said the sniper, as if desperate to form the words but finding it hard to describe. 'The others, the ones who changed.'

'Changed? What changed? How did they change?'

The sniper was hyperventilating, scrabbling for the words, his eyes wide and pupils dilated in panic. 'It's hard to explain. They become... more.' He paused to take a couple of ragged breaths. 'It happens at night, we only see them in the dark.'

At that, the man looked away from Polk, his eyes suddenly drawn to the window.

Keeping the combat shotgun firmly pressed to his captive's chest, Polk followed his gaze.

Outside, the sun was beginning to set over Emperor's Square.

Night was falling.

FIVE

The day was drawing to a close by the time Gilham, assisted by his servitors and a group of Deaz's men, restored power to the city, reactivating the power plant at one edge of the mining compound. The adept voxed Geiss to tell him the news.

Geiss, sat in the main gallery of the mine, already knew. The lumens in the ceiling had flickered and then ignited into life, flooding the control room with light, obscuring the smaller, flickering coloured glows sparking on the control panels that ran around the room. The slow background hum of technology began to rise, and Geiss realised how quiet it had been before, an industrial facility with nothing but human noise as a background.

Geiss thanked Gilham and ordered him back to base. He then ordered his vox-operator to connect him to one of the sentries out at the periphery of the complex. The surprised

119

sentry, unused to being addressed by a senior officer, reported that lights were slowly coming on across the city-factory.

'Good job, sir,' said the sentry jovially. 'It's starting to get dark out here.'

Geiss doled out an officerly platitude and cut the line. He walked over to the gallery windows that looked out over the mine, at the tangle of ramps and elevators that plunged into the pit below.

The answer would be down there – how could it not be? A team would need to descend into the mine sooner rather than later and, with power restored, Gilham would no doubt have those elevators up and working in no time. It would be possible to send a squad down there tonight, but leaning forwards to look up at the slivers of darkening sky visible between the hulking mining equipment, Geiss wondered whether it would be better to leave that until the next day. An expeditionary force would perform better if well rested. Perhaps he should let the men make camp for the night, and leave the next stage of the operation until the daylight.

The problem was one of uncertainty. Geiss still didn't know what he was dealing with. Hossk and Munez had both reported minor resistance, possibly rebels of some kind, but no force so efficient and comprehensive as to cause the disappearance of almost everyone in an entire city-factory in a couple of weeks. One sniper and a few traps did not wipe out an entire population. Something else was at work here on Belmos VII, or at least had been.

Even if it was now gone, it must have left traces, some explanation Geiss could present to his superiors. He needed answers, or at least an indication of what questions to start asking. Even if he waited until the next day, any force he sent down that mine would be blundering into the dark with no idea of what they were facing.

It wasn't good enough. He needed more to go on, and he only had one line of enquiry, even if it had so far proven frustrating and fruitless: he needed to re-interrogate Krick and the other civilians. If more forceful techniques were required to sharpen their memories, then he would just have to use them.

The lights were beginning to crawl up the two hab-slums as the power was restored to the city-factory, but in the under-pass beneath those towers the gloom thickened with the end of the day. As his men secured the towers above, Hossk had rolled his Chimera closer, without entering the potential hot zone between the two.

A light rain had begun to fall, the droplets of water glowing in the Chimera's headlights. As the sun faded, the tem-perature outside the Chimera dropped, and the men looked restless, pacing around, patrolling more frequently just to keep warm.

'Halt!' shouted one near the base of the towers, and Hossk, who had been sitting just inside his Chimera, dropped to the ground, reaching for his laspistol.

'We have civilians!' shouted the patrolling Guardsman. Walking away from the Chimera and towards the Guards-man's voice, Hossk found his eyes began to adjust to the thickening gloom. He could make out the shape of a

Guardsman, lasrifle semi-raised, and further away a group of figures, haloed by light from one of the hab-towers' atria.

'Tell them to hold,' shouted Hossk. Accompanied by half a dozen Guardsmen, he walked briskly into the shadows.

'At ease,' Hossk told the Guardsman as he walked up alongside him, then turned to the group of civilians. There were eight of them, and even with the light from the airwell above, it was hard to make out much detail in the gloom. Three men, five women, all wearing neutral workclothes, all relatively tall. Their body language was unthreatening, relaxed, completely different to the twitchy aggression of the rabid hab-scum that Hossk's men had been dealing with in the blocks above. Although Hossk couldn't make out every detail of their faces, he could see the whites of their eyes in the darkness.

'Where did you come from?' Hossk asked.

'We sleep through the day,' one of the women said. 'It's only safe for us after dark.'

'We'll put an end to that,' said Hossk. 'There won't be any no-go areas or curfews now this city is under Guard control. We're reclaiming the habs from the rebels now.'

'The rebels?' said one of the men, his head tilting upwards to look at the habs. As he did so, distant gunfire could be heard above. 'Yes, I suppose you could call them that. They have been a problem.'

There was a ripple of laughter through the group. For civilians in fear of their lives, living somewhere beneath the hab-blocks, they didn't seem too concerned to Hossk.

'We're so glad you soldiers are here,' said the woman who had previously spoken. 'We were running out of food.'

Geiss had voxed Gilham while on his way to the recreation area where the civilians were being kept under guard, ordering the adept to meet him there as soon as possible. While all the Adeptus Mechanicus were bodily augmented in one way or another, Adept Gilham had an intense interest in mechanically adapting the human body that bordered on a hobby, if an adept could be considered to have such a thing.

Gilham knew more about the functioning of the human form, and its capacity for augmentation, than many medicae, and his eagerness to put this knowledge into practice occasionally came in useful, although the adept treated working on human bodies as a purely mechanical problem. He had seen Gilham perform elaborate battlefield augmentations on crippled men, cleaving through flesh and bone with inhuman precision, but without restraint or, often, anaesthetic. Those men had been sent back to the front as if nothing untoward had happened, but Geiss could tell they were changed, and not just physically; Gilham had saved their lives, but taken away part of their humanity.

Geiss was certain that Gilham's knowledge could be turned to his current purpose, that the adept would find a way to induce compliance in these civilians.

Before Gilham got there, Geiss intended to have one final attempt to get a straight answer without coercion. He entered the room, the guards parting to let him through, expecting it to be a struggle to get the civilians awake, never mind talking.

Instead, he found Krick and the others on their feet, pacing the room.

Geiss didn't let his shaken expectations show, instead marching straight towards the shorter man.

'Mr Krick,' he said briskly. 'I see you're more awake than before. I hope this means you're willing to be more talkative.'

Krick stopped his pacing and snapped his head around to examine Geiss. His watery eyes seemed sharper, more intelligent than they had before. The whites of Krick's eyes were unmarked by a single burst bloodvessel or other sign of exhaustion, almost glowing. And there was... something else, some extra edge in Krick's gaze that Geiss couldn't quite identify.

'Of course... Major Geiss,' said Krick, as if remembering something from long ago. 'I apologise for being uncooperative earlier, I assure you it was not intentional. I'm afraid that none of us are at our best in the daytime any more. Please, sit down, I will happily answer any of your questions.'

Geiss shook his head, instead pacing around Krick, facing him directly. He couldn't remember whether Krick had been standing at any point in their earlier interview, but he could swear the old man was taller than he had been. Obviously an illusion of better posture – the old man had been slumped during the day, barely sitting up straight. Now he was straight-backed, alert.

They all were. Geiss registered that all the other civilians – the miners in their workclothes, the bodygloved administrators – were standing straight and still, watching Krick and Geiss's conversation intently.

No, not quite. They were all watching Geiss. Not making eye contact, but looking straight at him.

Geiss ignored them. He was a major in the Imperial Guard, one of the Unbreakable 114th. He wasn't a man to be intimidated by a handful of civilians.

Nonetheless, he found his hand instinctively going to the pommel of his chainsword, the other brushing the top of his holstered laspistol. Both were exactly where he expected.

'Perhaps you could start by telling me what you do here, Mr Krick?' Geiss asked. Start with an innocuous question and build from there, Geiss had once been told.

'I'm an auditor,' replied Krick, speaking quickly. His voice had lost any aged croak, and he spoke youthfully and fluently. 'This facility mines several key minerals, but the amounts of each are inconsistent dependent on the seams being worked at any one time. I monitor the varying outputs of each, and depending on the balance I propose alterations to the mining schedule to try and ensure our relative quotas of each substance are met.'

'Fascinating,' lied Geiss. 'And how has the situation been recently?'

'Well, the mine has been out of action for a week or so, as I'm sure you're aware,' said Krick, rocking back on his heels, making an expansive, *look at all this* gesture that didn't quite conceal that he was rolling his shoulders under his clothes.

Krick smiled at Geiss, taking off his spectacles to look at the major, folding them away and sliding them into an outer pocket.

'I say a week or so,' added Krick. 'It could be less time, or maybe more. The days are a blur to us now. And the nights, the nights have distractions of their own, Major Geiss.'

'Really?' said Geiss. He chose his next question carefully, and was surprised to find himself not asking what had happened to the rest of the city-factory, or how whatever had happened had started. Geiss realised he had a more pressing question, considering his current circumstances.

'Why were you sealed in here, Mr Krick?' Geiss asked.

Krick spread his arms widely again. He smiled, revealing sharp, perfectly white teeth.

'Isn't that obvious, Major Geiss?' said Krick. He leaned forwards, and whispered, 'To stop us from getting out.'

Geiss grasped the handle of his chain-blade, but Krick was fast, incredibly fast, bringing one palm around in a wide slap. The old man caught the major on the shoulder with a blow that flung Geiss sideways. The blow had the force of a wrecking ball, and Geiss was taken off his feet, hitting the wall a couple of metres away. His hand was knocked away from the chain-blade, the blow to his shoulder numbing that arm.

Geiss hit the wall as best he could, landing on his feet, his other hand reaching for his laspistol. As he drew the gun he took in the scene around him – he would get no help from the two guards on the door, who were only now raising their lasrifles as the other civilians charged across the room, heads low, moving at unbelievable speed.

Not that Geiss had any time to worry about his men. Krick was striding towards him, and Geiss suddenly realised what that hard-to-identify look in the old man's gaze had been.

It had been *predatory*, the way a hawk looks at a rodent.

Geiss was no one's prey. He lifted the laspistol, aimed at the centre of Krick's forehead and fired. Geiss was a good shot, and took aim confidently in one smooth motion. The kickback jolted his arm as the shot crossed the short gap between Geiss and Krick...

...where it missed. Either Krick saw some 'tell' in Geiss's movements and was capable of moving out of the way before the shot was taken, or he was even more inhumanly fast than Geiss thought. Krick had bent his upper body back and to the side, the shot burning a hole in the other wall of the windowless room.

The effort of dodging the shot had at least stopped Krick in his tracks, buying Geiss a few seconds.

Geiss knew how to take a lesson in humility when one was given to him. Headshots were difficult, even at short range, and most Guardsmen were ordered not to try and take them unless they were exceptionally good shots and there was a sound reason to do so.

His lesson learnt, Geiss dropped the laspistol lower, aiming for Krick's chest as he snapped back into a standing position, Krick's forward motion pushing him, step by step, closer to Geiss.

Geiss fired five times in close succession. The first shot was aimed directly at Krick's solar plexus, the second to the right, the third to the left, the fourth back and up slightly, the last down a little: a cluster formation, as practised on the firing range.

The rapid fire shook Geiss's arm, even with his other hand

gripping the wrist for support, but the fire pattern did the job. Krick weaved past the first shot, the second went wide, but in dodging that Krick walked into the third, which tore through his left shoulder, causing the old man to reel back with a cry of agony, a cry that had barely begun as the fourth shot caught him high in the chest, cutting off his breath and flipping him over.

Krick collapsed backwards, smashing through a utility table and hitting the floor with a graceless thud.

Geiss didn't know whether the last shot had hit and he didn't care. His bloodlust up, he let the laspistol drop to his side, hanging from the looped gold cord tied to his belt, and reached for his chainsword again.

The chainsword thrummed hungrily to life as Geiss stepped over to where Krick lay. The major swung the chainsword back with both hands, and then brought it down in an arc which would plunge the blade right into Krick's heart.

The chainsword was blocked before it could reach its target. Although Krick's left arm was limp by his side, crippled by the shot to his shoulder, and blood was gushing out of the chest wound made by the other shot, his right arm was still good – the old man had a metal chair leg in his right hand, and was holding it rigid to block the chainsword's descent.

Geiss grimaced and pushed down. To block the chainsword one-handed was an amazing feat of strength, but ultimately futile: the chainsword was already digging through the obstruction, chips of soft metal rolling off the blade. Geiss would need to be careful not to fall onto his own blade when the table leg gave way and the chainsword plunged down. He adjusted his footing to compensate.

Geiss's eyes locked with Krick's as they struggled. Even coughing up blood from the chest wound, gore crawling out of the corner of his mouth, he seemed younger than earlier that day. His hair was darker, his skin smoother, and the whites of his eyes were now so clear and bright as to seem incandescent, his pupils reduced to shadows.

Krick's mouth crawled into a bloody grin, a gurgling laugh taunting Geiss.

The chainsword broke through the table leg and swept down towards Krick, but yet again Geiss was denied – as the major leaned forwards to deliver the killing blow, one of Krick's feet shot forwards, beneath the reach of the blade, catching Geiss low in the torso and smacking into his hip. The blow sent Geiss reeling, but he kept hold of his chainsword, not letting it go for a second.

Down on one knee, about to lift the chainsword for another go, Geiss turned to see a grinning Krick on his feet, swinging a broken half of table-leg towards Geiss's face. It was a ragged, nasty chunk of cheap metal, but it would do the job, and with Geiss's merely human reflexes, he didn't stand a chance.

Before the crude weapon could reach Geiss, its wielder was knocked off his feet, an ornate pneumatic hammer piledriving into the side of his head, snapping his neck to one side.

It could have been a killing blow, but Geiss wasn't taking any chances. He brought the chainsword around in an arc and caught Krick in the waist, between the hard bone of the ribs and hips. With only the vertebrae to block its path the chainsword tore right through the man, cutting him neatly in half. A vile stench filled the room as Krick's guts spilled out onto the floor, a rank smell of hot bile.

The two halves of Krick's body fell to the floor, lifeless. One dead eye stared out of a skull caved in by the hammer blow. Geiss thought he saw a hint of that unnatural whiteness shimmering in the eyeball, but then it faded, the light dying as surely as Krick.

Geiss looked up at the hammer's owner. Gilham had already returned the weapon/tool to wherever he kept it in his voluminous red robes, one of his mechadendrites snaking it beneath the folds of scarlet cloth. The adept's hood was thrown back, his head a copper-coloured helmet of dark metal, his rebreather and optics giving his face a fierce, skull-like aspect.

'Major Geiss,' said Gilham, offering his superior officer a hand. 'I apologise for not arriving sooner.'

'You're forgiven,' said Geiss, gratefully taking Gilham's hand. Through the rough leather work glove he could feel an unnatural strength pulling him to his feet, the result of countless augmentations beneath those red robes. 'Just in time will do for me.'

'Sadly, I was not in time to help the others,' Gilham said. His voice was a deep rumbling bass sound, coming from vox-casters built into his face.

Geiss looked past Gilham to the doorway and swore. The other civilians had torn through the Guardsmen in their eagerness to escape, near-decapitating one man while punching straight through the other's chest. The two young guards had barely moved from their station before dying, their bodies lying on either side of the doorframe.

'You know augmentations, have you ever seen anything like…?' Geiss began the question then cut himself off, silencing any response from Gilham with a raised hand. 'Forget I asked, we don't have time.'

Geiss tapped his vox-bead: 'This is Major Geiss to all stations, we have six hostiles loose in the mining complex. Hostiles resemble human civilians, but have greatly enhanced speed and strength. They're fast enough to dodge fire from a single man, so keep in formation and hit them with wide volleys. I want patrols on that perimeter fence now – these things must not get away. Geiss out.'

Geiss silenced the vox before anyone could reply. He needed to take a minute to get his breath back and restore his composure before he followed up to ensure his orders were carried out. He closed his eyes, breathing deeply, letting his pulse settle. A shaken officer was a bad leader.

He opened his eyes to see Gilham standing exactly where he had been before. The adept seemed to have little sense of time, and virtually no capacity for impatience.

'Right,' said Geiss. 'Let's catch these bastards.' He led the way out of the room, Gilham sweeping silently into step behind him.

'Thank the Emperor there aren't more of them,' Geiss added under his breath.

'What do you mean it happens at night?' Polk said. The barrel of the sergeant's gun was digging down into the sniper's chest, and even from across the room Hool could see that it would take the slightest movement or surprise for Polk to jerk his finger back on the trigger, a point-blank shot that would kill the sniper instantly.

Hool shouldn't have been concerned as to whether Polk fired or not, especially as he had been targeted by the sniper, albeit badly. Hool had seen men die for far less than firing on the Guard, but he felt a strange reservation nonetheless: there was something in the sniper's youth, his lack of training and blind panic that made him uneasy, as if he were looking at himself, having taken a different path in life.

The sniper was blustering in reply to Polk, seemingly unable to form a coherent response, and Hool was about to suggest his sergeant go easy on the man, but he was pre-empted by the man who entered the room.

He walked in slowly, non-aggressively, making sure his footsteps were clearly heard, and he kept his hands raised and open so that the Guardsmen covering him as he entered could see he was unarmed. He was shorter than most of the Guard, bulky but not fat, with slicked-back hair and a grey-green uniform with gold trim that seemed to have suffered a lot of recent tears and scrapes. His wide brown eyes had an expression of desperate calm.

'I can answer all your questions,' he said. 'Please let Plymton go. He shouldn't have shot at you – it was a mistake.'

'A mistake?' echoed Polk incredulously, not moving the barrel of his combat shotgun. Hool and Zvindt had the newcomer covered.

The newcomer winced, realising 'mistake' was an

unfortunately mild term if you were the ones who had been shot at.

'A mistake, a serious error, a crime,' the man said. 'Call it what you like but please listen to me: the people Plymton mistook you for will be here soon, and we need to warn your men in the square.'

Polk placed his boot on the sniper's chest and swung his gun around to point at the newcomer's face.

'You've seen how we deal with "people". What makes you think these will be any more of a problem than you have been?' snapped Polk.

'Because they were exposed,' said the man. 'And no, I don't know to what exactly, but it changed them. They used to be miners but now they're killers, faster and stronger than anything I've ever seen, and while your force out there may be armed, they are not expecting what's coming, trust me.'

'Trust you?' said Polk. 'I don't even know who you are, and you're expecting me to report some rambling story about murderous miners to my lieutenant on your word?'

'My name is Calway,' said the man. 'I was head of security at this tower, and I've been helping the people in this building to stay alive through night after night of attacks from people who used to be friends and family, so please, please let me help you too. Warn your lieutenant.'

Polk finally nodded, and lowered his gun slightly. 'Fine.' He cocked the barrel towards the other civilians, and stepped off the sniper's chest. 'All of you, in the corner. I'm voxing this in to Lieutenant Munez.'

'Sergeant Polk on the vox, sir,' said the vox-operator.

'Luck holding up, then,' said Munez under his breath, before accepting the vox. 'Sergeant Polk, you have the sniper?'

'Yes, sir,' said Polk, his voice distant over the vox. 'Few other civilians as well, sir. Turns out they thought we were someone else and, well, they want me to warn you about them.'

'Them, sergeant?'

'Mine workers, mainly, exposed to something. Made them killers. As far as I can tell, they come out at night. This lot are scared witless.'

Munez chuckled. 'Sounds like a bit of local terror to me, probably rebellious workers. Tell the men in their big tower to put down their guns and let us deal with this. Night's falling, we'll rally round and deal with this soon enough.'

'Yes, sir.' Polk sounded dubious.

'Don't tell me you think there's something in this, sergeant?'

Polk seemed about to answer, when Munez heard a shout from outside the Chimera. Someone had been sighted.

Hossk owed his life to the boredom of his men. Those not on specific duties had gradually drifted towards the conversation between Hossk and the civilians beneath the hab-towers. As boring as it might be, it was the best show on offer.

So when one of the women moved forwards and grabbed Hossk by the throat, there were plenty of witnesses.

Hossk didn't see what happened next – he was too busy

choking as an iron grip tightened around his neck, looking down into the face of a woman who must have been little more than a girl, young enough to be Hossk's own daughter. As she squeezed his windpipe his vision began to blur, lack of oxygen starving his brain, and the last thing he saw was a pitiless, white-hot gaze looking up at him as she shook him like a doll, two bright points staring at him as everything else faded into shadow.

The men acted with the exemplary discipline that Hossk would expect. When their lieutenant was attacked they dropped from a loose gathering into tight formation, rifles raised and searching for a target. The moment they had a clear shot past Hossk's dangling body, they fired as one, half a dozen las-shots streaking through the air, most hitting their target.

The las-fire didn't kill her, but it did make her drop Hossk. He hit the ground hard, knocking the last stale air out of his lungs, then raggedly inhaled. The sound of las-fire filled his ears, and he felt strong arms pulling him to his feet and dragging him backwards.

Someone was shouting for backup.

They were stumbling back out from the underpass, back towards the Chimera, a tight knot of half a dozen men around Hossk maintaining suppressing fire. Hossk's legs felt weak beneath him and his vision was still swimming, a side-effect of his brief oxygen deprivation. He shook his head, trying to shake some sense into himself. Twisting his arm around the grip of one of the men hurrying him along, Hossk pressed the vox-bead on his collar.

Nothing. It must have been crushed in the stranglehold.

Hossk looked back to where he had been attacked. There was no one in the light from the atrium, and as the sun had now set the rest of the underpass was in near-total darkness.

Something moved to his left, terrifyingly fast, and one of his men was gone, a truncated scream and a hideous crack in the darkness indicating his fate.

Then again from the right – something pulled another Guardsman into the darkness, with barely a shout of protest.

Seconds later a burst of las-fire emerged from the dark, bringing down a couple more men. One of the guards surrounding Hossk fell on to him, knocking the lieutenant off his feet, dead weight threatening to pin him to the ground.

Hossk pushed the dead man off him and drew his own pistol. The last surviving Guardsmen were sweeping the darkness of the underpass with torches, searching for any sign of their attackers.

Nothing, not even the body of the Guardsman who had been pulled away.

Of the two Guardsmen felled by las-fire, the one who had fallen across Hossk was dead, a dirty burnmark scorching through his blue coat. The other was still alive, but had gone into shock – a high-intensity blast had cut right through his midriff, and he was bleeding out, a dark stain slowly spreading down his clothes, his breath hurried and broken. Hossk tried to get his attention, nudging the man's shoulder with his boot, but his pupils were dilated and flickering.

Whatever the Guardsman was seeing, it wasn't anything in the real world.

'Get him up,' Hossk ordered one of the two standing survivors. 'Leave the body, we'll come back for it.'

Hossk began to back slowly away, matching pace with the Guardsman carrying the injured man. Hossk swept a lamp-pack back and forth through the dark to their left, as the Guardsman to the right did the same in the other direction.

Something heavy was thrown out of the dark, hitting the other armed Guardsman in the face. He was knocked backwards, barrelling into the trooper carrying the wounded man, who in turn was pushed towards Hossk. The flailing Guardsman's lamp-pack swung up towards the rockcrete underside of the tower above, illuminating a mess of pipes and scaffold, while whatever missile had struck him skidded across the ground and back into the dark.

Hossk fired in the direction he thought the missile must have come from, laying down a suppressing barrage of lasfire over the heads of the fallen Guardsmen.

Hossk stopped firing, and was about to berate the floored men to get back on their feet when a hand clamped down on his shoulder. In one fluid movement, Hossk was thrown off his feet and cast several metres away from the rest of the group. He tried to land as well as he could, but cracked the side of his head against the ground as he rolled three, four times before coming to a halt flat on his back.

The blow to the head had left Hossk nauseated, waves of disorientation spreading from his head injury and into his limbs. He knew that adrenaline was keeping him conscious and holding back the pain, which he could feel welling within him. Hossk couldn't feel his legs, or at least couldn't get them to move properly, so he used his elbows to roll himself in the direction from which he had been thrown, to try and get a better view of what was going on.

He looked back to where his men, who had defended him and tried to get him to safety, had last been. The lamp-packs pointed in several directions, but all had been dropped. His vision was swimming, blurred around the edges, but he could see tall figures moving between the low lights, and Hossk heard involuntary cries from the men on the ground, and the breaking of glass as each light was smashed but one.

Hossk tried to pull himself to his feet, but every movement caused his head to swim, the pain building and threatening to cause him to black out. He lay on the wet rockcrete and watched as the last lamp was picked up and pointed in his direction, then began to move leisurely towards him.

A distant light provided some brief illumination and Hossk could see the female civilian who had spoken earlier walking towards him.

'Now, where were we?' she asked, lifting the torch so that it pointed straight into Hossk's eyes, the intense light both blinding him and aggravating the pain in his skull.

Then the light became even stronger, accompanied by a roar of engines. Hossk saw the woman disappear beneath the tracks of his Chimera as it thundered past, and felt a cold spray as those tracks threw up filthy water. The Chimera skidded in a wide arc and Guardsmen moved out, surrounding Hossk and lifting him up. They were asking him how he was, making concerned noises, but for some reason Hossk couldn't make out their exact words.

The pain, momentarily suppressed by Hossk's fight-or-flight instinct as he was under attack, hit him like a tidal wave now that the crisis was over and he was safe again. He tried to hang on, to keep his senses sharp, but failed.

Hossk lost consciousness as they carried him into the Chimera.

They were first spotted on the rooftops around Emperor's Square – humanoid figures, silhouetted against the clear night sky. Shouts came in from west, east and south of movement high above, of heads seen above parapets, of barely visible figures darting between the statuary and orna-mentation.

Munez didn't get a chance to give the order to shoot or not – none of the men had a bead on these targets long enough to take a shot. They were shadows, distinct enough to not be mistaken for a trick of the fading light, but too fast, too fleeting, to be targeted.

Then, as the night deepened they were seen in the win-dows, or moving across balconies. Munez, stepping away from the searchlight of his Chimera so he could adjust his vision to the dark, thought he saw one himself, a long-legged figure jumping from one balcony to another, only to disap-pear into the next window.

Maybe Polk's civilian was on to something after all.

Sergeant Essler was down on one knee, an elbow resting on his raised knee to steady his hellgun as he swept it left and right, up and down, one artificial eye pressed to the sights. Low squeaks were coming from the vox-caster in his mask.

Munez realised that Essler was counting.

'How many?' Munez asked.

Smoker didn't take his eye away from the sights. 'Visibility poor, hard to tell. May be double counting. Raw sightings? Seventeen in the last three minutes.' He paused. 'Sorry, eighteen.'

'Spread the word,' Munez told Essler. 'If there's a shot to be taken, take it. We are the 114th, the Unbreakables, and we will not be played with.'

'Yes, sir,' replied Essler, standing up without entirely lowering his gun, moving away to spread the order, his gaze still sweeping the buildings around the square.

A vox-operator ran over to Munez, a hand over one ear.

'Message from the major, sir,' said the vox-operator. 'There's been some kind of attack in the mining complex. Civilians, but somehow augmented with strength and speed. Major Geiss is locking down the mining complex to try and keep them contained.'

'How many?' asked Munez.

'Four or five, sir.'

'Four or five?' Munez repeated. He caught sight of something moving at the edge of the square, ducking between shadows to stay out of firing range. In the distance, he could hear whistling: not a melody, but single high-pitched whistles ringing out from different sides of the square, a signal spreading between the people in the shadows.

Munez turned back to the vox-operator. 'Vox Major Geiss immediately, priority channel, in my name. Tell him containment is no longer an issue. They're everywhere.'

SIX

Emperor's Square was surrounded by ornamental lamp-posts, wrought metal poles like twisted limbs gripping high-powered lumen globes that, theoretically, would cast pools of light creating an elegant ambience for the high-class citizens of Belmos VII after dark.

At least, that was Munez's guess. Now, they were just more shapes looming in the darkness. They had all been broken, creating pools of deep shadow around the edge of the square. Some light trickled out of the windows of surrounding buildings, but very little. The fall of night turned the square into a maze of overlapping shadows, the outlines of statues and street furniture becoming indistinct and sinister. The temperature had dropped and collars were turned up against the icy wetness in the air.

'Form a perimeter,' Munez ordered. 'You get a shot, take it.

Don't fall back or move unless ordered. Let's keep this line tight.'

The men did as they were told, dropping back to form a fifty-metre-wide circle with his command Chimera at the centre. Lamp packs created a wider area of light, the beam interlocking as each Guardsman covered an area ahead, with no angle left uncovered.

When they came, it was in force. Munez turned at the sound of shots from the west, and saw half a dozen of his men concentrating their las-fire into a crowd of men and women running across the square directly towards them. There had to be at least fifty, with more visible behind, running out of doorways and jumping from windows one or two floors up.

Las-fire tore into the front line of unarmed civilians, burning through their flesh and killing many, but the tumble of broken, twisted bodies did nothing to impede the mass of civilians surging forwards. Munez saw one or two roll with the shots as they hit them, tumbling out of the way of the mass of the crowd, while others were either thrown aside or trodden underfoot.

In spite of casualties, the civilians closed the space between them and the Guard perimeter in a matter of seconds from being first sighted.

One woman broke the line of the civilians, seemingly dancing between beams of las-fire as she ran. She was slight, with long red hair, unremarkable apart from her running speed – probably little more than a teenager.

She broke the line by running straight into a rifleman of

middle years, a big man as much due to muscle as fat. When the young girl hit him he was knocked to the ground, the girl on top of him, her fists pounding down into his face, a rough, animalistic cry tearing out of her mouth.

The men on either side didn't let their comrade's plight break their discipline, continuing to fire into the crowd as, seconds later, they too were knocked over. One was thrown, tossed aside several metres, knocking over more Guardsmen, while another was hit in the side of the face so hard his neck snapped, his head hanging at an unnatural angle as his body fell to the ground.

The line was broken.

For Hervl, joining the Guard had given him a purpose. While he didn't regret any of his previous life, up to and including hunting down Hool and trying to beat the hell out of him, that life now seemed distant, colourless. He could no longer remember *why* he had done any of the things he had as a boy growing up in the Mordian hives – the petty crimes, the fights, the deals – only that it had all seemed important at the time.

It didn't any more. The 114th had given Hervl something he lacked in the chaos of gang life – clear objectives, and a way of fulfilling them. Having spent so much of his youth looking up to the gangers with their illicit guns, hoping to one day fire one of them, Hervl had rapidly discovered that he wasn't any kind of shot. In active service on Elisenda, he had successfully shot an enemy with his lasrifle perhaps three times.

Explosives were another matter. Hervl had demonstrated the nerve, patience, steady hand and, to his own surprise, precision to handle and deploy explosives in the field. When the las-fire was flying, Hervl managed to maintain focus on the job at hand, setting complex charges and laying explosives that wouldn't bear mishandling.

Hervl could live with the danger – it was the long, dull periods in between he liked less. In the short time since he and Midj had blasted a way into the tower for Polk and his squad, Hervl had zoned out as the sergeant had shouting matches with a couple of locals, talked into his vox for a bit, then continued his discussion with the older local.

They were still at it. Polk was calm now, while the local was getting increasingly heated. Hervl wasn't really bothering to follow the conversation. Sooner or later someone would ask him to blow something up, and then he would make an effort to pay attention.

As if on cue, the local suddenly looked past where Hervl was standing. Hervl lazily followed the man's gaze.

There was nothing to see, just the hole that Midj and Hervl had blown in the wall.

'Ah,' said the local. 'That's how you got in. I heard the explosion but didn't realise you'd made quite that big a hole.' He seemed nervous, aware that his encounter with the Guard hadn't been going too well so far, and that he might not be in a position to push his luck. 'You may want to consider closing that up.'

'Close that up?' replied Polk. 'Calway, it was only by coming in that way that we took your boy here down without killing him or his mates. We could easily have just launched a mortar from the ground and blown the lot of them to pieces, so don't push your bloody luck by expecting us to redecorate.'

'Sergeant Polk,' said Calway, visibly suppressing his temper, 'all of you. While there's an easy point of access to this building not only are we in danger, but the hundred or so innocents who have managed to stay safe here will also be under threat.'

'Threat?' asked Polk. 'You haven't even explained what your bloody threat is supposed to–'

He was cut off in mid-sentence by the sound of ferocious las-fire from outside.

'Our lads are under attack,' reported Hool, who was closest to the window. 'Hard to tell who by, but they don't seem to be armed. They're tearing into us, though.'

Polk and Calway's eyes locked briefly, then Polk turned to Midj and Hervl.

'You two, think you can seal that hole?'

Midj was already ahead of the conversation and had already scoped out the options: 'If we knock out this supporting beam, we should have a controlled collapse. I wouldn't want to be in the room above, though.'

'With your permission, sergeant, I'll send someone up to clear it,' said Calway. Polk nodded, and Calway sent the sniper and his friends off to clear the room above.

Midj slapped Hervl on the arm, and they started setting charges on the supporting beam that braced one end of the room. As Hervl began to lay thin strips of explosive putty, the conversation in the room receded to a dim background hum that Hervl was only faintly aware of.

'How many of you can handle yourselves?' Polk was asking.

'Excluding the children and elderly, only about forty men and women,' said Calway. 'Our main problem is weapons. We never got near the armouries before the PDF – and our access – was wiped out, so we've scavenged what we can, but most of these people have never fired a lasgun for practice, never mind in anger.'

'It's getting bad out there,' shouted Hool. Hervl concentrated on his work, and resisted any urge to wonder what Hool had seen.

'We need to give them support, maybe even open this place up as a defensive position,' said Polk. 'Calway, what kind of–'

'Incoming!' snapped Deress, and Hervl felt the air around him warm as las-fire flew past him.

He glanced down the corridor of the building they had come from, and saw two men running towards him, hands outstretched like talons.

'Midj, Hervl, down!' bellowed Polk, and Hervl dropped to the floor, getting a face full of dust from the wall he'd helped destroy earlier, a fat chunk of plaster gouging a scrape in his cheek.

'Concentrate fire!' ordered Polk, and the las-fire intensified.

Hervl felt a string of sharp pains in the back of his neck, of fingernails pressing into his skin, before another barrage of las-fire streaked overhead and the pressure was suddenly removed.

Someone pulled him to the side, rolling him onto his back. Hervl instinctively closed his hand into a fist, but looked up to see Midj, face covered with dust and splattered with blood, looking down on him.

'Let's get this done,' said the older man, grabbing Hervl around the forearm and pulling him to his feet.

The entirety of Polk's squad were advancing in tight formation, firing past Hervl and Midj, who were off to one side of the hole in the wall. Hervl glanced through the hole – the bodies of a couple of civilians were sprawled close to where they stood, one twisted backwards, sharpened fingernails reaching out towards nothing.

Another one came running forwards at unbelievable speed, dropping into a roll to duck under the first wave of las-fire, then dodging out of sight into another room.

'Hold fire,' shouted Midj, and when he was sure the Mordians had stopped he dashed across the gap to the other side.

The feral civilian took the opportunity to take a run at them, and Midj had barely got across when Polk's men launched another assault. The civilian almost got through the gap before being struck in the right leg, the wound from the las-fire causing him to crumple to one knee. Several shots to the chest finished him off.

'Three-second charge,' shouted Midj, who was setting a timer into a clump of explosive on his side of the gap. Hervl nodded acknowledgement, scrabbling to remove a similar charge from one of the pouches on his belt. He reached up to press the charge into the nearest end of a strip of explosive material running across the support beam – he and Midj had not had time to set a continuous load, but the chain reaction between the different spots of explosive should be enough.

'Fall back,' Midj shouted to Polk.

'Hool, stay with me,' Polk said. 'Everyone else out.' Hervl looked back to see the two Guardsmen maintaining their fire as the civilians, and the rest of Polk's squad, cleared the room. They alternated fire, each shooting while the other's lasrifle had a few seconds to cool, trying to maintain continuous fire with only two men.

'Give us a sign, Midj,' said Polk.

'Three seconds, sergeant,' said Midj, as he and Hervl both took hold of the charge switches. 'Starting… now!'

Hervl and Midj both clicked the detonators and turned on their heels, running around Polk and Hool, who were still providing covering fire.

Getting into the tower had been quick and clean, a simple demolition of a partition wall. Sealing that breach would be messier.

Hervl and Midj virtually crashed into each other in the doorway as they rushed out into a wood-panelled corridor. Hervl looked back as Polk and Hool followed them, and looked past to see half a dozen civilians on their tails, virtually through into the tower–

The charges went off, and the blast threw Hool in Hervl's direction, knocking them both over. The air was slammed out of Hervl's lungs as Hool fell on top of him, and he felt a rib crack as he hit the floor, pain crunching through his side.

A tide of dust and smoke swept through the room they had just left, billowing through the open door and out into the corridor, a choking mass of debris that blinded them all.

Someone slammed the door shut, and the dust began to settle. Polk was on his feet already, as were the men who had got out well before the explosion.

Hool sprung back upright, and Hervl involuntarily cried out from his broken rib.

Hool looked down at him, a look of concern and guilt sweeping over his boyish features. Then that expression stiffened, Hool's jaw tightening, as he remembered who he was looking at, and how they had met.

Some things couldn't be forgotten easily, thought Hervl, suppressing the wave of nausea caused by the intense pain in his side. He didn't feel any guilt over nearly killing Hool – that had been *then*, and although he couldn't relate to what he had done, there was little point regretting it – but neither did he expect any sympathy.

'Just a rib,' grunted Hervl, pushing himself into a sitting position against the wall, while digging for a pack of battlefield pain meds in his webbing. He popped three of the meds into his palm, and swallowed them dry, harder than usual with a throat coated with brickdust. Eventually they went down, and a warm, numb feeling began to alleviate the pain in his side.

'You should get a medicae to look at that properly,' said Hool dispassionately, and Hervl just grunted again.

Polk had his hand on the door handle, his squad ready to re-enter the room they had just left. The sergeant mimed a countdown, then threw the door open, charging in first with his combat shotgun raised.

There was no need. Even from back in the corridor it was clear the explosion had collapsed the ceiling as planned, a drift of rubble closing the hole through which they had entered the building. No one was getting in that way now.

'Good work,' snapped Polk, eyes darting between Midj and Hervl before Polk turned his attention to Calway.

'Now your back door's closed again,' said Polk. 'Let's see if we can get your front door open. I think the lieutenant may need it.'

Hossk regained consciousness suddenly, painkillers and stimulants flooding his system. The medicae treating him stepped back smoothly as Hossk jerked forwards in the command seat of his Chimera, taking a deep intake of breath.

'You've been out for less than ten minutes,' said the medicae, who had served under Hossk for many years and knew exactly what the lieutenant would want to know. 'Your head took quite a jolt and you're seriously concussed. I don't think there's any permanent damage, but I would strongly advise against attempting movement. Medically, I would advise that you leave this seat as little as possible.'

Hossk just nodded – he didn't quite have the will yet to speak. He gestured to his vox-operator for a field update.

'Major Geiss voxed a report of a group of citizens loose in the mining complex, amped up with enhanced strength and speed,' said the vox-operator. 'Does that tally with the lot who attacked you, sir?'

Hossk nodded. He took a deep breath through his nose, suppressing the queasy sensation from the meds flowing through his system, and forced his mouth open. He spoke in a low hiss, a few pained words at a time:

'The towers?' he asked.

'No reports as yet,' replied the operator.

Hossk nodded a little too aggressively, and the tide of nausea welled up again. He closed his eyes, trying to ride the discomfort. He needed to be clear in his thinking, to provide leadership.

'Send out a general order,' he rasped. 'All squads to find the closest securable position they can until further notice. If there are other squads nearby, join forces for greater numbers. Hostiles are extremely fast, extremely strong. Hit them with everything you have on first sight.'

Hossk rolled back in his seat, his head lolling back.

'Sir?' the vox-operator asked. 'Is that the full message?'

'No, no,' added Hossk, not opening his eyes. 'Hostiles seem to only come out at night. We need to keep them back through the night. Tell them to form a line and hold it, the Mordian way. Give the order.'

Hossk heard his message being relayed, but only the first few words, as he sank into a shallow, drug-fuelled unconsciousness.

Out in Emperor's Square, Munez's men were under constant attack. Where their defensive line had broken, the attackers pressed the advantage. Only three men went down in the first breach, but more followed as the civilians pushed past the line and then outwards, assaulting the Guardsmen either side of the breach.

Shouting for backup, Munez stepped forwards to defend the breach and seal the gap in the line.

The red-headed girl who had first breached the line dragged a Guardsman back with one hand, pulling the rifle out of his grasp with her free hand and tossing it away without a thought. The Guardsman fell flat on his back, unarmed, and his assailant pounced on him, clawed hands raining blows down on his face and upper body. In spite of the formal appearance of their blue uniforms, each jacket had a layer of flak armour sewn into it, protecting the chest area, but that didn't stop human fingers clawing at an exposed neck.

Munez shot her with his laspistol. He had a clear shot but the pistol was better at a closer range, and the shot hit her high in the chest, too high for the lungs or heart. It was nonetheless a shot that should have left her crippled, at least temporarily.

Instead she sprung from her present victim and ran for Munez. Unfazed, he took another shot, this time for the head, taking advantage of the close range as his target closed the gap between them. The shot went wide, but the las-beam cut close enough to her face as it streaked past to burn the side of her head, an ugly red welt flaring up on her cheek and a strip of hair disappearing in a burst of smouldering black ashes.

She didn't stop, but screamed in rage as she closed the last couple of metres between her and Munez, swinging her arm into his hand, knocking the pistol aside.

Then she was on him, straddling his lower torso and slashing at his face with her fingernails, tearing out chunks of skin then moving down, ripping through the fabric of his jacket, exposing a layer of armour beneath. Behind the hands tearing at him Munez could just see the glowing whites of her eyes, staring down at him with savage intensity.

Munez tried to swing his arms back up to strike his attacker, but she slapped them aside with near-wrist-breaking force. Her clawed hands began to tug at the layers of armour, threatening to rip the stitching apart. If she could pull away even a strip of armour, clawing fingers would soon be digging into the flesh over his ribcage.

She was going to tear his heart out.

With a burst of strength, Munez brought his knee up hard while pushing back onto his shoulders, throwing the girl off him, over his head. He rolled back onto his front, the rough stone scraping his cheek, and reached for the only other weapon he had, a short blade kept at his belt.

It was an old blade, reputed to have been worn and used by generations of Mordians in the 114th. It had once been a bayonet, but was now fitted with a more ornate handle. Munez carefully kept the blade sharp and polished, but had never used it in anger. He didn't know whether it would just snap on impact.

Now he would find out. As Munez dragged himself to his knees, the knife in one hand, the girl had already landed on her back and flipped onto all fours, poised to strike again.

As she lunged for Munez he brought the knife up, dangerously close to his own face but pointing outwards. As the girl rammed into him, hands squeezing his shoulders and pushing him back, he thrust the blade forwards, letting his assailant's own speed and strength push her into the path of the weapon, her body weight pressing her down on to the blade's tip.

There was a moment of resistance before the blade sank into her neck, the sharpened point meeting tauter skin and stronger tendons than in any normal human, but the girl's own inhuman strength pushed the knife in. The girl's ferocious gaze held in her pale green eyes as she continued to struggle with Munez for a few seconds, staring uncomprehendingly as her grip involuntarily loosened, and her legs gave way beneath her.

Munez pushed her away, pulling his knife free from the girl's neck, a further gush of blood spilling as the blade withdrew. He looked up to see three more civilians running towards him in wide strides, almost bent over on all fours as they pounced.

His pistol still lost somewhere on the ground, Munez raised his little knife as best he could.

A volley of concentrated las-fire came from Munez's right, slicing through the air in front of him, forming a cage of las-beams around the three civilians for a split-second so that their every evasive move walked them into another shot. One, an overweight man, caught a shot in the stomach and reeled backwards, more shots to the chest bringing him down. An old woman with long, silver hair sprung over one las-shot only to receive a shot to the head on her descent. The third jerked back and forth as las-fire tore into him in five places across his body, still twitching as he hit the ground, lifeless.

Smoker and his squad held their fire as the bodies dropped, gun barrels steaming. They had formed a rigid cluster of fire, half the men on their knees and half standing.

'Lieutenant,' acknowledged Smoker, picking something from the ground and tossing it to Munez.

Munez caught his own pistol from the air. Smoker and his men were already opening fire on their next set of targets.

'Well,' said Polk, slightly breathless from running down five flights of stairs. 'That doesn't look good.'

The reception foyer of the hab-tower on Emperor's Square was completely blockaded, the doors welded shut with crisscrossing metal bars.

'We don't go out on foot,' Calway explained. 'We use a separate exit.'

Polk paused by the blockaded doors. Through the gaps in the bars, Polk could see out in the square, where a tight group of his own regiment were firing their guns at wave after wave of enemies – a battle he couldn't get to. Polk wanted to be out there, contributing to the fight, not locked in.

'How is this even an obstruction, if they are so strong?' Polk asked Calway. 'Surely they can just ram it down?'

Calway shook his head. 'They don't seem to think like that. Give them a barrier they can overturn or jump over in one go, and they'll do it; anything which requires any more focus and they'll get frustrated and try and find another route in.' Calway tapped his temple with a finger. 'Something in their animal brains. They're intelligent in a fight, but so eager to chase down their prey they can't make themselves pay the attention necessary to think laterally. Intelligent, in some cases more so than before this all started, but no ability to concentrate on a task.'

'Sounds like the opposite of Hervl,' said Midj, to a grunt of protest from the younger Guardsman, who was still nursing his broken rib, and had taken twice the time to get down the stairs as anyone else because of it.

'What are these things?' asked Polk.

It was a rhetorical question, but Calway tried to answer it anyway:

'They were us, or at least people like us,' he said. 'Whatever happened to them, it changed them absolutely. Sometimes instantly, in other cases it took a while for the change to take effect. But eventually they all succumbed.'

'Great,' said Polk, stepping back from the shutters. 'Enough chat. Calway – I want to get out there.'

'Follow me,' said Calway. 'I want to show you something that might help.'

The career of Infantryman Muumisk divided neatly into two halves: the decade before he was shot in the head, and the decade since. While he had been lucky to survive such a serious head injury, the medicaes had discovered long-term side effects: Muumisk's sense of balance had been badly compromised. He could not run, or target a weapon: if he moved his head too much while walking, he became nauseated and, after only a minute, would pass out.

It was an injury that the medicaes could not resolve with their injections and pills, and nor could Gilham with his experimental augmetics. At only thirty-three years old, Muumisk was suddenly deprived of his entire life and the capacity to serve the regiment he had come to think of as a family, a brotherhood.

After that, he had been assigned to various non-combat duties: weapons maintenance, assisting the regimental quartermaster, and ensuring the servitors assigned the even more mundane tasks did not break down while laundering uniforms or cleaning floors.

Muumisk had been transferred from one rage-inducingly tedious assignment to another, each task steadily chipping away at his morale, for years. While always maintaining discipline and never warranting censure in the exercising of these menial duties, Muumisk's low-level resentment created friction in every role he was given, resulting in him being moved on to the next one. And the next one.

No role stuck for long until Commissar Tordez was attached to the 114th, without a Commissariat-assigned second. By some accounts, Tordez did not consider the 114th a suitably robust environment for a trainee commissar to learn their work, and so had refused to bring one with him. According to other, more cynical voices, he had ejected his original assistant from an airlock while travelling to Mordian to join the 114th, presumably for some minor infraction.

Either way, Tordez had required an adjutant. Muumisk was duly appointed, perhaps in the expectation that he, too, would earn the ire of the commissar and find himself introduced to an oxygen-free environment en route to the next sphere of battle.

But Muumisk had risen to the challenge, shadowing the old commissar ever since, following his orders exactly, acting as his mouthpiece and agent throughout the regiment. Tordez's demanding discipline, and the tension with Muumisk's fellow Guardsmen that his role created, pulled Muumisk from his post-injury depression. It gave him purpose, and structure, and added a bracing tension to his day-to-day life he had missed since ceasing active service.

The first day on Belmos VII had been atypical but uneventful. With Tordez left in command of the troops left to guard the shuttle, what could have been a long day of card games punctuated by intermittent patrols was instead a succession of exercises and inspections.

Not that Tordez had been exceptionally active himself: following the departure of the main body of the strike force across the causeway and into the city-factory, Tordez had issued a set of brisk orders to the men, setting a cycle of patrols, drills and rest breaks hour-by-hour that would cover the rest of the day.

His orders given, Tordez had instructed Muumisk to bring a folding camp chair from the supplies. Muumisk had done so, setting the chair up at the bottom of the ramp that led to the *Seraphim*'s storage bay, with a small field table alongside it on which he left a flask of hot caffeine.

Tordez had then spent most of the day sitting silently, long leather coat buttoned up, watching the orders he had been given fulfilled to the letter. Between errands, Muumisk had stood by Tordez's side, watching the infantry patrol and march back and forth across the wide-open rockcrete of the spaceport.

Alongside the foot soldiers the towering, two-legged Sentinels patrolled in wider arcs, clomping around in circles, each hefty metal step echoing across the empty space, gears grinding and squealing as their knee joints bent. Each Sentinel's heavy gun swept back and forth as they walked, but there were no targets for the human pilots to take aim at. The pilots themselves seemed distant up there, the thin drizzle of rain in the air blurring the space between them and the men on the ground.

So went most of the day. Muumisk was long used to Tordez's company, the way that the commissar's stillness gave no clue as to whether he was keenly observing the routines before him, or just staring into space, absorbed in his own thoughts and memories. Occasionally, Tordez would seem so still and unblinking, his breathing so low and steady, that anyone else might presume that he had fallen asleep with his eyes open.

Muumisk knew better, and was no longer surprised when Tordez would suddenly make a precise observation or issue a specific order, proving that he had been entirely cogent all along.

As the end of the day approached, Tordez had the men set up tripod-mounted lumens around the ship, with a trail of them crossing the spaceport to the beginning of the causeway.

As night fell, the lights began to blink on, the wet rockcrete glistening beneath. Night brought a deeper chill to the air, and Tordez got to his feet, rubbing his gloved hands together. He passed Muumisk a vox-bead.

'Check the sentries, then join me in the hold,' he said, his words slow and deliberate. 'The major has encountered some hostility.' It was typical of Tordez not to mention a development like this until it suited him. 'I'll order the servitors to prepare something hot.'

As Tordez disappeared up the ramp, Muumisk walked between the two rows of lights, where a small sentry outpost had been established to look out over the causeway. Muumisk walked carefully and deliberately, eyes straight ahead, the way the medicaes had taught him to move without losing his fragile balance.

As he approached the sentry point, Muumisk saw that the Sentinel had lowered its cockpit down, legs folded up, and the sentries were gathered around talking to the pilot. There was a whiff of lho-sticks in the air, and Muumisk presumed that, being out of the commissar's sight, the men had been smoking and playing cards. Exactly as Muumisk would expect on a long boring sentry duty, and he had to suppress a smile at memories of similar pastimes, back before his injury.

'Anything out there?' Muumisk asked as they turned to greet him, pretending that they hadn't seen him approach. He noted that Sergeant Frittsch, who was supposed to be in charge of this motley lot, was nowhere to be seen.

'Nothing, Muum,' said one of the infantrymen. Although Muumisk had some secondhand cachet from assisting the commissar, the men of his own rank always made sure to talk to him casually, a constant reminder that he was still just a common Guardsman. If it was meant to irritate Muumisk, it failed – he found the reminder that he was still a soldier comforting.

'Then what's that?' he asked.

Out on the causeway, figures were running, shadows in the moonlit night. There seemed to be more than a dozen, spread out across the causeway but all bounding directly towards the sentry position.

As the Sentinel pilot cranked the walker back up to its full height and the sentries scurried to deploy themselves across the entry to the spaceport, Muumisk activated the vox-bead.

'Commissar Tordez,' Muumisk said. 'We have incoming.'

SEVEN

Krick's fellow civilians didn't make it difficult for Geiss and Gilham to follow them – the trail of bodies and dirty, bloody footprints between each scene of slaughter formed a path that was, if anything, too easy to follow.

'They really don't care if we find them,' said the major after the third time they found one of his men splayed across the corridor floor, casually ripped apart. 'They might as well be leaving a deliberate trail.'

Gilham found this an odd statement: his augmented vision stretched well beyond the human range, so to him any recently occupied room was crisscrossed with heat signatures, floating traces of exhaled breath, residues from hand and footprints and the like, trailing off in all directions with no clear path.

The adept temporarily cycled through infrared, ultraviolet

and all the other modes of vision of which he was capable, and looked at the grey murk that his optical implants showed him. There didn't seem to be anything special apart from the body.

Then, remembering the human eye registered colour, Gilham re-adjusted his optical sensors accordingly, taking away layer after layer of information. The last to go was infrared, and a light thermal trace could be seen stretching from hot pools around the dead Guardsmen to fainter, cooling smears stretching down the corridor. Then he reduced his sight to optical only, and the bright red stains on the floor, pittering away down the corridor ahead, bloomed in his visual cortex, clearer and more vivid than anything else in view.

It was too much, too stark. Gilham restored the full range of his senses, subsuming that bloodstain beneath overlay after overlay of other environmental data.

'I see what you mean,' he told Geiss. 'They don't care whether we follow.'

'Perhaps with good reason,' replied Geiss. 'You killed one of them easily enough, but only because he was preoccupied with me. Maybe in normal circumstances they wouldn't consider the two of us to be threats.'

Gilham didn't reply. While he was entirely capable of combat, he was no strategist. Warfare was an extension of mathematics to him, each shot from his pistol or swing of his hammer a matter of calculating the physics, of the trajectory between weapon and target. Those combat decisions he could make.

Strategic decisions, when to attack and when to withdraw,

what numbers to deploy – these were matters of judgement for an officer like Geiss.

'Let's level the playing field,' Geiss said, hitting his vox-bead. 'This is Major Geiss to all Guard within the facility, you are to move to the following points and regroup...'

The runners on the causeway were approaching the sentry position at the spaceport with great speed. Muumisk could make out more of them further away, and wondered exactly how many there might be. A hundred? More?

'Halt!' shouted Sergeant Frittsch, using a vox-caster to boost his voice. He had come running out of the dark at the sound of a disturbance, and Muumisk suspected he had been asleep in a quiet spot. 'Halt right there.'

'They don't look armed,' Frittsch said, and shrugged. Muumisk spotted the corner of the sergeant's eye twitching oddly. Was he intoxicated? 'Might be locals running from something. Let's slow them down a little with warning shots.'

One of the sentries fired over the heads of the approaching figures. The las-fire lit up the causeway, and Muumisk could see that the runners were human, dressed in a mixture of shabby workclothes and civilian outfits.

'They're not taking the hint, are they?' said Frittsch. He seemed distracted, unconcerned. 'Take down the first couple. Settings low, let's give them at least a chance of survival.'

More shots cut through the rapidly decreasing space between the sentry post and the lead runners.

The group of runners parted around the las-fire, ducking and rolling to evade both shots.

The sentries exchanged looks, unsure how to react, or even if they had actually seen what they thought they had seen.

'What are you waiting for?' shouted Tordez. 'Open fire!'

Muumisk turned to see the commissar marching towards the sentry post, two infantry squads marching in step behind him. Further across the spaceport, the other Sentinel was also approaching.

The sentries still seemed frozen in indecision.

Tordez drew his own pistol, aimed it straight at Frittsch's head. The commissar's grip on the pistol was rock-steady, the aim not wavering as he circled the sergeant to end up level with him at the edge of the spaceport.

'Was that order unclear?' snapped Tordez, addressing the wider body of men. The barrel of his pistol was virtually touching Frittsch's forehead. 'These people have ignored an order to halt, they deserve no more warnings or mercies. Take aim and open fire!'

Tordez swung the pistol away from the sergeant's head, down the causeway, and fired at the first runner. The figure dodged the shot with inhuman reflexes, but was caught by a shot fired by one of the sentries, and fell to the ground. The runners behind him just jumped over the wounded man, continuing the charge.

They met a steady blaze of las-fire. The sentries had followed Tordez's lead, forming a line and firing ahead. Muumisk stepped out of the way as the men who had followed Tordez moved forwards, forming ranks and adding further fire.

Tordez swung his pistol around to place the end of the

barrel once more against Frittsch's forehead. The man hadn't moved in the seconds since Tordez had taken the gun away, and sweat trailed down his temple. The twitch in his eye was getting worse.

'As for you, sergeant, I have been watching you closely for some time. I knew you were a weak link.' Tordez's grip on his gun didn't waver.

'But I–'

Frittsch didn't get to finish his sentence. Tordez pulled the trigger, shooting him in the head. The body dropped to the wet rockcrete. Tordez holstered his pistol and turned to the rest of the men. 'Ignore this dead failure and concentrate your fire,' he ordered, shouting over the constant rattle of las-fire. 'I want an alternating pattern, cover the man next to you as they switch powercells, keep on the pressure. Let Sergeant Frittsch be a lesson to you: never blunt your hostility with mercy or hesitation, do not pollute your senses with anything that might soften your view of the enemy. You are a weapon of the Emperor; to hold your fire when fire is needed is an insult to Him.'

Muumisk looked down the causeway. Bodies were scattered across the full length of the causeway, some within a short distance of the firing squad. None had broken the line. The men seemed possessed by Tordez's words, or at least the threat of his pistol, and fought on with an aggression Muumisk would have thought unthinkable in the men he had seen slumping at their duty earlier.

Still, the runners kept coming. Illuminated by the las-fire, Muumisk could see the tautness of their bodies, the fierce look of determination as they charged forwards, trying to find a break in the welcome Tordez had organised.

'Sentinels,' said Tordez, standing rigid with his arms behind his back, the very picture of a leader refusing to countenance that the line of men between him and the enemy could ever break. 'Lay down suppressing fire. Repetitive bursts, midway down the causeway. Break up this rabble.'

There were a couple of muffled, but enthusiastic, responses from the cockpits of the two Sentinels, which stood at either end of the line of infantrymen. Then both opened fire, their multi-lasers firing over the heads of the infantrymen, rapid bursts of las-fire streaking into the distance and hitting the rockcrete of the causeway like comets, consuming everything in their path.

Muumisk couldn't see what was happening that far back, but the runners ahead of the target of the Sentinels' assault began to thin out, the horde behind them broken and scattered. Their charge lost its momentum, their numbers were less, and they were more easily picked off by the riflemen as they approached.

'Sentinels, again!' barked Tordez, and another fiery barrage hammered down the causeway.

Those few runners in sight began to turn, retreating from the wall of las-fire, only to run back into the assault from the Sentinels' multi-lasers.

'Keep up the pressure,' ordered Tordez. 'Drive them back.'

Soon, there were no living figures visible on the causeway.

'Cease fire,' ordered Tordez, and the monstrous noise ended, apart from the quick breath of the men and the mechanical whine of the Sentinels' multi-lasers as they cooled down.

The sudden silence felt odd in Muumisk's ears, like a cold breeze after a heatwave.

Bodies littered the causeway, smoke rising from las-burns. Further along, the entire surface of the causeway glowed from the heat of the Sentinels' multi-lasers.

There was no sign of any further assault.

'That is how men of the Imperial Guard respond to an incursion,' snapped Tordez. 'An unbreakable line, uncompromising resistance. No mercy, no quarter given until the enemy is routed. You may have believed that Frittsch's slack leadership was a boon, but it was a burden that cursed you all. The only freedom worth anything is the freedom that allows you to serve better.'

All eyes were on the commissar, every man standing rigidly to attention. For the commissar's part, his unflinching gaze swept over all of them.

'I leave this line for you all to hold,' Tordez said, beginning to walk back towards the shuttle.

'Commissar Tordez,' asked one young Guardsman. 'Who were they?'

Tordez paused, looking back down the causeway at the scattered bodies.

'I'm sure we will find out in the morning. For now, it doesn't matter.'

Then he turned on his heels and walked away, Muumisk following close behind.

* * *

'What is it?' Polk asked, looking up at the looming vehicle before him. He was standing in an anonymous loading bay at the back of the hab-tower.

'It's a cleaning vehicle, been in use since the original construction of the city-factory,' said Calway. 'It was used to keep the square in a respectable state, while now...'

Calway trailed off.

'Now, you've converted it again,' said Polk, before turning to his squad. 'Dall, get over here. Think you can drive this thing?'

Hossk was roused from a drug-induced slumber by the urgency in the voice blasting out of the vox-console in his Chimera. His head swam as he sat up too fast, and he pressed his right hand to his forehead, breathing deeply and steadily until his balance settled. When he took his hand away, his palm was slick with sweat.

'Report,' he said evenly.

'Contact across the towers,' said the vox-operator, failing to keep the surprise that Hossk was even awake out of his voice. 'Variable levels of resistance. We have a secure perimeter around this Chimera, but some of the more scattered squads are having difficulties.'

'What was that last vox about?' Hossk asked. The urgency of the message had stayed with him, even though his semi-conscious state prevented him from recalling any details.

'Sergeant Weir, sir,' replied the vox-operator. 'Got himself into a bit of a situation in Hab C, besieged in the seventh-floor refectory with considerable opposition.'

Weir was one of Hossk's best men. If he felt the situation was serious, it was. Hossk would hate to lose him.

A medicae was leaning into Hossk's field of vision, pointing a small torch into his eyes. Hossk batted him away.

'How far are we from C?' he shouted to the driver, taking the fact that he barely winced at his own raised voice as a good sign for his recovery.

'A couple of minutes,' said the driver. 'Four or five on foot.'

Hossk turned to the medicae. 'I want to be on my feet for the next couple of hours, damn the long-term consequences. Give me what I need to do that.'

'Get a squad together,' he told the nearest corporal. 'We're going to give Weir his backup.'

Geiss had ordered every man on the lower floors of the mining complex to retreat to the gallery, where Geiss and Gilham were forming a hunting party, and anyone above that level to withdraw to ground level and assist Deaz in preventing any of the rogue civilians from escaping.

While waiting to gather as many men as he could, Geiss received an update from his vox-operator at ground level. All parts of his strike force were under attack by these ferocious civilians. Hossk's men were fighting them in the corridors and walkways of the workers' habs. Munez was surrounded in Emperor's Square. The most significant report was from Tordez, who had routed an attempt to take the spaceport.

Geiss voxed through to the commissar directly and requested a full report. Tordez went through the events on the causeway once, then again, filling in details as Geiss asked questions

about the battle. Geiss thanked Tordez and cut the line, then
tried to vox Munez to get corroboration on some of the details
of the ongoing battle in Emperor's Square. All he received was
a screech of feedback which caused him to tear the vox-bead
out of his ear.

He sat the vox-bead on the control desk in front of him,
and rubbed his temple thoughtfully, trying to work the echo
of white noise out of his mind.

In the open, Hossk and Munez had run into trouble with
these civilians, as far as Geiss could tell from the reports he
had received. Tordez, however, had managed to rout the
enemy utterly on the causeway.

Geiss chewed his bottom lip. It wasn't much to go on, and
he really needed more information, but there was a hint of
a pattern forming, of an enemy that was ruthlessly effective
in an open combat situation, but with little capability of
learning or strategising ahead. If that were the case, and Geiss
was aware that he was dealing in nothing but hypotheticals,
then these civilians, whatever had happened to them, could
be dealt with. It was a matter of containment, of driving
them into a position where their agility and ferocity were of
limited use.

It would be like shooting fish in a barrel. The problem was
getting the fish into the barrel in the first place.

Eight Guardsmen had made it alive to the gallery, and were
watching the doors, ready for any attack. Eight Guardsmen,
plus Gilham and Geiss himself.

Geiss was in command of an entire strike force, but for
now he had only ten men at his disposal, including himself.

It would have to do.

'This is what we are going to do,' he told the men. 'We sweep each floor, shoulder to shoulder, every corridor, every room. First sight of a target, we hit them with everything – not precision firing, but a wall of pain, covering as much space as we can. Leave them no room to escape.

'Let's clean this place out.'

Just as Munez began to think that the tide of battle had turned in his favour, the enemy started to fire back with the Guard's own weapons.

He had seen several men being dragged away by the civilians in the course of the battle, disappearing into the shadows. Munez had also seen the enemy use their enhanced strength to toss the bodies of both Guard and enemy casualties across the square. He hadn't had time to worry about what the enemy were doing to the dead, as he was too busy rallying the living.

At a glance, two-thirds of Munez's platoon were still on their feet, forming a tight circle around his command Chimera. The remaining third had either disappeared into the darkness or were lying dead or wounded in the square.

The ebb and flow of battle had begun to find a primitive rhythm, with the civilians either rushing to physically attack the Guard, or holding back at the edges of the square and bombarding them with crude projectiles before charging again. There was no finesse to these attacks, but there was speed and, in the case of the projectiles, accuracy.

Munez's men had developed a routine of shielding their

heads when the projectiles came, then having their weapons levelled as quickly as possible when the rain of bricks and other debris ceased and the rush-attacks began again. Supported by powerful bursts from the Chimera's multi-laser, they had kept their attackers at bay, increasing the number of dead civilians scattered across Emperor's Square.

Then the first las-fire came from the edge of the square, aimed at the Guard. The civilians had clearly stripped the corpses of Munez's men, and turned the looted weapons to their own uses.

Initially, this turn of events favoured the Guard. Most of the shots from the civilians went wide, as the wielders of the lasrifles knew how to pull a trigger, but not how to aim properly. Although a few lucky shots found targets, these victories for the enemy were balanced out by the fact that they now provided a much easier target for the Guard, who instinctively aimed for the source of the las-fire and returned fire.

For a few moments, it seemed like picking up arms would destroy the enemy offensive, as Smoker and his squad picked off the sources of the enemy fire, but the enemy seemed to withdraw out of range, into the darkness around the square, moving too fast for the Chimera's searchlight to keep a bead on them, bursts of las-fire coming from random directions.

'I'm getting sick of this,' Munez muttered under his breath. There was a loose pattern to the movement of the enemy. They were orbiting the Chimera at a distance, unleashing haphazard bursts of fire towards the centre of the square. That pattern could be used against them, no matter how fast they moved.

Munez grabbed two Guardsmen and gave a hurried series of orders. Just as he'd finished speaking, a cry came from within the Chimera.

'Overheated, sir,' came the shout. 'Going to take a couple of minutes to cool down.'

Munez looked to the top of the Chimera, where the multi-laser was glowing in the dark, the barrels red-hot. The smell of oil filled the air.

Before the enemy could take advantage of this brief respite, the Guardsmen Munez had given orders to started to follow them, throwing grenades into the darkness of the square. They threw them in an even and wide spread, covering as much ground as they could. Munez's idea was to create a trap of multiple explosions – these civilians were fast, but it would do them no good if they dodged one explosion and ran straight into another.

As each grenade went off, the explosion cast a brief, fiery light on a small area of the square, showing the enemy in motion. The first showed a scatter of civilians, moving with inhuman speed to dodge the blast. The second and third blasts caught a few, smoking bodies propelled through the air, killed as they tried to escape.

There was a sound of howling indignation from around the square, and Munez thought he almost had a rout after five or six grenades. He couldn't move quickly enough to see every explosion – if he could, then they'd be easier to avoid and that would defy the point of the exercise – but he was looking in the right direction when one grenade fell in the same spot that the Chimera's searchlight happened to fall upon.

It happened so fast Munez barely had time to react. The searchlight cast a glare upon a small group of civilians advancing on the Chimera, unarmed but with their arms clawing forwards. They recoiled briefly from the light, and the thrown grenade hit the slabs at their feet, shining in reflected light as it bounced on impact.

At this point one of the civilians plucked it out of the air with inhuman speed and, without hesitation or anything other than animal instinct, threw it overarm the way it had come.

It was as the grenade was in mid-air, sailing towards the open door of Munez's command Chimera, that Munez realised what was about to happen.

'Fire in the hole!' screamed Munez, breaking into a run to get away from his own command vehicle. He didn't look to see whether anyone followed his order, as he was too busy hunching forwards as he ran, closing his eyes and pulling his arms over his head.

The blast threw Munez off his feet, a rush of hot air rolling over his covered head, scorching the hairs from the exposed patches of wrist between his gloves and sleeves as he fell forwards. He tumbled as the force of the blast pushed him forwards, a wave of pressure driving straight into his back. He hit the stone tiles of the square with his right forearm and let the momentum carry him head over heels, rolling sideways a few times before the motion worked itself out and he came to a halt on his hands and knees.

Munez dragged himself to his feet. He drew his pistol from where he had hastily tucked it in his armpit, and looked back at the wreckage of the Chimera. The vehicle was a blackened frame burning red-hot against the night sky. The familiar, temporary deafness that followed an explosion rendered the scene silent, the flames mutely licking the sky. The silhouettes of Guardsmen staggered around the wreckage in disarray.

The strength of the fire illuminated most of the square for the first time since nightfall. Munez tightened his grip on his pistol as tall, predatory figures began to move in on the scattered Guardsmen, confident of easy prey.

Hossk didn't know quite what the medicae had injected into his system, but it had taken away the crippling pain and nausea of his concussion, leaving a lightness in its place. He took the stairs three at a time as he led some of the 114th's toughest close-quarters fighters into Hab C.

One of the civilians leapt out at Hossk on the third-floor landing, and Hossk shot him through the chest with his laspistol, not even pausing for breath as the civilian's body slammed back into the graffiti-covered rockcrete wall. Hossk was already halfway up the next flight of stairs before the body slid to the floor.

He was dimly aware that his current heightened state would come with a physical cost later. The medicae had warned him as much. Hossk didn't care. What mattered was victory *now*. Hossk may have been wrong about the situation on Belmos VII being a simple workers' uprising, but the fact remained that these were unarmed savages they were fighting, and no Mordian should fall to such lowlife. Hossk was determined to beat them back into whichever hole they had crawled out from.

The refectory was a large, low-slung space on the seventh floor, with long, closely spaced tables where the workers would be served their morning rations. Every surface seemed to be carved out of the same bland material, a scratched and stained light blue plascrete. Only every third light was functioning, and the room was divided into pools of light and dark.

As Hossk barrelled into the room, he could hardly miss the position of Weir's squad, even though they were not directly visible – a horde of rabid workers were converging on one end of the refectory, wielding and throwing furniture and tools.

The squad fanned out as they entered the room, forming a tight line, guns raised. They had the advantage of surprise, and with Weir's men still maintaining fire, the civilians found themselves trapped in a pincer movement between two groups of Guardsmen.

As the last few fell, Hossk found himself shoulder to shoulder with Weir. As one of the last workers lunged at Hossk the lieutenant dodged and grabbed him by the collar, swinging him face first into the bayonet attached to Weir's raised hellgun. Weir shook the body free from the bayonet, and gave Hossk a loose salute.

'Thank you, sir,' said Weir. 'Much appreciated.'

Hossk returned the salute, and pointed towards the pile of upturned tables.

'Don't know why I bothered, sergeant,' he said. 'You seemed quite cosy in there.'

Weir took the comment with good humour, responding with equal levity in spite of his bloody and torn uniform.

'Wasn't by choice, sir,' Weir replied mock-apologetically. 'We were doing fine until we were overwhelmed by a second wave charging in.'

Their light conversation was interrupted by the noise of a considerable number of feet stamping on a nearby stairwell, a rising roar of unfocussed anger: the unmistakable sound of an approaching mob.

'A wave like that?' Hossk asked, before turning to the rest of the men. 'Out, now!' he shouted, and both squads ran for one of the refectory's exits, heading in the opposite direction to the unseen, approaching crowd.

As he shoulder-slammed the door open, Hossk briefly wondered exactly how long the meds he was dosed with would last for, and whether he would survive to feel the ill effects when they wore off.

'Major Geiss, we found something.'

Geiss's squad were sweeping the lowest level of the mining complex's control centre, moving as a pack to check each room. It was a tense, tedious business, but as they were moving towards the building's single stairwell, and all sub-corridors ran off a single main corridor that covered the length of the control centre, a systematic sweep left no room for error. The enemy would either run into them, or be driven out.

Most rooms were dull, functional places, drab spaces lined with cogitator consoles and banks of monitoring equipment.

Only the signs of struggle and splashes of dried blood indicated anything awry.

Geiss had been called to a narrow storeroom tucked away at the back of the control centre. Behind stacks of anonymous boxes, a home of sorts had been made – sleeping materials were arranged on the floor. It was a rank, airless space, with a foul stench in the air. The floor and walls were streaked with unpleasant stains.

And, in the far corner, there was a pile of discarded items. It was quite a large pile, and the Guardsman who called Geiss over prodded it with the end of his lasrifle, not wanting to touch.

Geiss dropped down into a squat. The store room was lit by a solitary, flickering light, so Geiss used his own torch to get a closer look.

It was a pile of junk and scraps, mostly metal or other synthetic materials, most recognisable as personal items – chronometers, passcards, vox-beads, crushed pairs of corrective lenses, even whole artificial eyes, wires trailing from where they would have connected to the optic nerve.

Geiss gingerly picked a squat piece of tubing with grilles at both ends from the pile. It was an artificial rebreather of the kind fitted into the throat in an emergency, a basic surgical augmetic that, if fitted quickly, could rectify a potentially fatal injury.

This one was brass, and was covered in scratches and bent at the edges.

'Guardsman,' said Geiss. 'Does this look *chewed* to you?'

The Guardsman didn't reply. He was a hardened soldier,

his face crisscrossed with scars, a man who had seen countless battlefields on a dozen worlds. But this made him
uncomfortable.

'I need you to assist in covering that corridor,' ordered
Geiss, cocking his head towards the door. 'And ask Adept
Gilham to come to me while you're out there.'

When Gilham saw the pile, and closely examined a couple
of items, he took the same view as Geiss:

'Teethmarks, definitely,' he said. 'Human, but slightly over-
sized. There's also sign of digestive corrosion.'

'The indigestible parts of a human meal,' said Geiss. The
idea was distasteful, but unavoidable.

Gilham nodded. 'It would seem so.'

'Leave it for now,' said Geiss. 'Tomorrow, I want this pile
sifted for any further clues. Right now, I want these cannibals
dead.'

Pursued through the stairwells and corridors of Hab C,
Hossk and his men searched for a fortifiable position to
make a stand against the mob on their heels. There was little
shelter to find: the corridors were too open to fortify, and the
tiny living quarters were dead-ends where the Guardsmen
would be cornered and slaughtered.

In the daylight hours, the lower levels of Hab C had been
gutted on Hossk's orders, the doors of the hab's tiny living
spaces kicked in, the residents slaughtered. Hossk's men had
been thorough in their sweep, and the bleak living spaces
of the hab were rendered bleaker by the scorch marks and
blood on the walls.

Occasionally they would glance back to see a tidal wave of workers pursuing them, eyes aglow in the semi-lit spaces of the hab, malevolent spots of light in a washed-out environment.

Hossk's men made their stand on the stairwell between floors ten and eleven, not due to some strategic insight on the part of their lieutenant, but due to the barricade that blocked the way to the next floor. Sheets of battered metal had been welded wall-to-wall, stopping the Guardsmen in their tracks.

There was no way back, but Hossk didn't panic. It was a less-than-ideal position to face off against their pursuers, a windowless dead-end with no possible route of escape, but it had some merits: there was only one way in, and the enemy would need to approach from below.

Hossk didn't need to issue any commands to Weir or the others. They spread across the width of the stairwell, some ducking low, others aiming over their heads. The civilians would be met with a relentless wall of firepower as they rounded the corner.

In the echoing rockcrete space of the stairwell the noise of the approaching horde reverberated as they got closer, shrieks and howls merging into one voice, one shout of uncontrolled aggression. The Guardsmen kept their weapons steady, directed towards the killzone at the turn of the landing, the corner around which the first of the enemy would come.

With the horde only seconds away, Hossk heard a violent metallic scrape behind him, and a voice speaking close to his ear.

'Who are you?'

One eye still on the stairwell, Hossk turned to see a panel opened in the barrier behind him and eyes peering out.

'Lieutenant Hossk of the 114th Mordian Iron Guard,' Hossk replied. 'And if this thing opens I demand you open it at once.' He slammed the butt of his laspistol against the barrier for emphasis.

'You killed my men,' said the man behind the barrier. 'You have been killing our people all day, shooting up the habs.' His voice was rough, uneducated, thick with some unrecognisable local accent.

'My men walked into your traps,' replied Hossk. 'Imperial Guardsmen, servants of the Emperor, killed by traps set by *you*. Whole populations have been scourged for less. Now you can try and correct that sin or you can leave us out here, but don't expect any greater mercy from the next force that is sent here.'

There was a brief pause, and the barrier opened up, folding in ways Hossk wouldn't have thought possible. Standing further up the stairs were a number of men and women in workers' overalls. The man who had spoken through the barrier was a huge, broad man with tight black hair and a scar on his bottom lip, holding some kind of industrial nail gun.

'They're coming,' said the man. 'Make room.'

The workers took position next to the Guardsmen. Hossk noticed that these workers didn't have the glow in the eyes that the others did – they were calm, determined.

Then the horde of civilians turned the corner of the stairwell, and there was nothing to be done but fight. The civilians came in their dozens, clawing over each other to get to the uninfected workers and Guardsmen, a seemingly endless wave of human bodies reaching out with clawed hands and bared teeth, seething up the stairs.

Hossk's men, and the workers beside them, met this torrent with gunfire and converted tools, battering back the stream of feral humanity. Bodies slumped across the steps as the civilians fell, some reaching up towards the Guard even in death, others thrown backwards, leaving them broken against the far wall.

The sound of gunfire was deafening in the confined space of the stairwell, smoke from hot gun barrels and scorched exit wounds fogging the air.

In the haze, some of the civilians got lucky. One of Weir's men was grabbed by the collar and dragged down the stairs and away, the tide of savage civilians closing the gap before anyone could rescue him. Another pounced upon one of the workers, and managed to tear a deep wound into her chest before being smashed back with a wrench.

But eventually, the tide turned, and Guardsmen and workers alike could retreat behind the barrier as it closed once more, the rush of enemies defeated.

The man who had spoken to Hossk through the barrier turned to him now, apparently sizing him up.

'I am Stellin,' said the tall worker. 'This corner of Hab C is one of the few safe places on the entirety of Belmos VII. If there are any more survivors, we haven't seen them.'

'Hurry up,' shouted Polk. 'The lieutenant needs backup, now.'

The loading bay had opened out into a narrow alley that wound its way from the back of the hab-tower to Emperor's Square. The vehicle they were in had bounced up the ramp with surprising speed, but the alley was too narrow to drive fast, and it was taking time to negotiate its twists and turns.

'This is the best we can do, sergeant,' Dall told Polk, shouting back from the driver's cabin.

The entire squad was packed into an articulated vehicle running on a dozen wheels, with a narrow interior in which a crew could control mounted spray cannons placed around the side. This unlikely vehicle, previously used for blast-cleaning the monolithic exteriors of Emperor's Square, had been upgraded with crude armour plating and spikes along the sides, so that any attacker who got past the high-pressure streams would be unable to scale the vehicle. The cannon themselves had been modified to produce a blast of water powerful enough to knock anyone off their feet, and filled with a mixture of water and corrosive chemicals to scar and blind the enemy.

Polk had started to think of it as 'the Cleaner'.

He turned to Hool and the others as they moved into position. Each water cannon required two operators, one to aim and one to control the jet. Calway was running up and down the length of the Cleaner, explaining which button did what. He didn't seem happy to be tagging along for this expedition.

'You lot get ready,' Polk said as the Cleaner rounded a corner. 'We're nearly in the square.'

* * *

Geiss's group progressed unimpeded through the lower two levels of the control centre. Geiss kept his vox-link to Deaz open, so that he would know if any of the feral civilians, these cannibals as he now thought of them, reached the ground and made a break for freedom.

Nothing. All was clear from Deaz's perspective.

On the third floor up, just as the room-by-room sweep was becoming routine, Geiss's group was attacked. It was at a point where doors either side of the main corridor opened up into siderooms, almost immediately before a sub-corridor cut across.

Four angles to attack from, and the cannibals came from two of them. As one Guardsman covered the door to the left, another pushed open the door to the right, while the rest of the group covered the corridors in all directions. This was how they had swept through the other floors – the first Guardsman would enter that room, they would sweep it, then do the room opposite.

This time, the door had barely opened a crack when a hand shot out from within, grabbing the barrel of the lasrifle and dragging the hapless Guardsman inside.

At the same time, the portal on the opposite side of the corridor was kicked open, hard, slamming into the Guardsman who was keeping it covered. The feeble interior door that shattered into pieces, spraying debris everywhere as it was torn off its hinges by the blow.

The rest of the Mordians didn't need an order. They reacted, splitting into two groups and charging both rooms. Geiss was marginally to the left, so he stepped over the downed

Guardsman and through the broken door with three of his men, two crouching low to allow Geiss and another man to fire over their heads.

The woman who had kicked the door off its hinges had dropped back a short distance from the doorway, and all four men fired on her at once. She tried to duck, to make herself less of a target, but she couldn't get low enough to avoid the wide bursts of las-fire which burned through her upper body. She slumped to the floor face down, limbs bent and twitching.

Geiss levelled his laspistol, determined to put a shot through her forehead just to be sure.

Before he could fire he was pushed sideways as another civilian rammed into the group with a table, roaring abuse. All four men were pushed into the wall, virtually falling over each other.

Geiss had his back to the flat surface of the table. He jammed the pistol under his arm, placing the barrel against the table, and fired straight into it.

Thankfully, the table wasn't made of anything las-resistant, and the shots tore through flimsy wood-substitute. The pressure from the other side of the table gave way and Geiss pushed it aside, wincing from where the discharge from his bolt pistol had burned through his coat and shirt, scorching the skin beneath.

The table fell to the ground. It was a long workbench; the room they had charged into was a lab of some kind.

A middle-aged man, face twisted with anger and hatred, had staggered back, smouldering burn marks on his chest.

Before the rest of the men could even take a shot, Geiss had
dropped his pistol and put both hands on the pommel of his
chainsword, powering it up as he took three steps forwards,
thrusting it into the the remains of the man's chest. The
chainsword tore through flesh and bone, digging deep into
the man's ribcage, blood spraying from the wound.

Geiss looked the once-human creature in the eyes as he
pressed the blow home, driving the chainsword right through
his body. The savagery that had illuminated his eyes only
seconds before had faded to a numb surprise, then nothing.

'What are you waiting for?' shouted Geiss to the three
Guardsmen, who had only just got to their feet. 'Support the
others.'

They ran out into the corridor, and once Geiss had levered
the corpse from the blade of his chainsword, he followed.
His entire upper body was rattling with the exertion of having forced the vibrating, roaring blade through layers of
enhanced flesh and bone, his muscles aching from the effort.

In the next room he found Gilham and the rest of the
Guardsmen. One was dead, but so were three more of the
cannibals.

Six down, including Krick. Everyone they had secured in
the rec room. That should have been all of them, but Geiss
wanted to be sure.

He switched his vox to transmit. 'Deaz, this is Geiss. Send
your teams in from above. Room-to-room sweep, kill anything that moves. I think we've got them all, but I'm damned
if I'm calling this place clear until I'm absolutely certain.'

* * *

Munez had been bitten by animals in the past. A trained warhound on Brecasta had taken a bite out of his thigh, a gushing wound that would have finished him through blood loss if it hadn't been for a quick-thinking medicae; camped out on the jungle world of Stont, he had been woken by the agonising sting of a small carnivorous lizard sinking fangs into his ear, the punctures from which had taken weeks to heal over.

However, he had never been bitten by a human being before today. He had seen the occasional bar fight between the lower ranks end in biting, but those were usually quick, vicious bites, a desperate last feral strike against another man.

This bite was not like those. Munez and some of his men had regrouped, and were defending themselves as best they could against the attacking civilians.

It was futile. A few shots had found a mark, but nothing that even slowed down their attackers. The group of Guardsmen were swamped by the civilians, who pushed the group apart, pushing them over, throwing them aside, breaking them up so that they were easier prey.

Munez had raised his right arm defensively as one man moved in to strike him, only to find those hands not punching or slapping his arm away, but instead gripping his forearm by the elbow and wrist. The gripping fingers were as strong and unyielding as clamps in a workshop, tightening around his flesh like metal bands.

Then Munez's attacker bit, sinking his teeth into the lieutenant's forearm, tearing through the thick cloth of his

Mordian-blue jacket and the thinner cloth of his undershirt, pressing down into the meat and muscle of his forearm.

As waves of agony sparked up his arm, the pain of torn flesh overriding the numbness from the grip constricting the arm, Munez tried to shake free. Both he and his attacker were still standing, and the lieutenant threw his own body weight backwards, trying to use gravity against his attacker. His pistol was on the ground, dropped during the fight, and if he could topple them over, Munez might be able to reach the weapon.

Instead of releasing their grip, the biting teeth shifted, digging in deeper, hungrily gnawing at Munez's arm. His attacker's feet didn't shift from their stance, rooted as solidly as any statue as the lieutenant tried to pull him over.

Munez drew his knife with his left hand, and desperately tried to stab the man in the head or arms. An elbow jabbed up to deflect the lieutenant's strike, knocking the knife free. It fell to the ground, uselessly out of reach.

In the fire from the burning Chimera, Munez could see the dark stain spreading across the arm of his coat, dripping down the pale workclothes of his attacker. Munez began to feel the first dizzying tug of blood loss, the agony in his arm fading as all physical sensation became distant. He brought his left fist down on one of the arms gripping his: it was a futile gesture, but he wanted the pain in his bruised knuckles to keep him sharp, to stop the disorientation which threatened to overwhelm him.

Munez was snapped back to full consciousness by las-fire breaking out all around him. The jaws clamped around his arm let go as three las-rounds were pumped into the body of his attacker. The lieutenant found the man collapsing forwards, eyes rolling back in his skull and mouth loosely drooling into the bite wound as he breathed his last. Munez scrabbled to pull the dead man's fingers loose from his forearm, and pushed the body away.

He found himself being pulled up and almost dragged away by two Guardsmen he didn't recognise. Weren't they in Polk's squad? Weren't they supposed to be in the tower? And why were they manhandling a senior officer? That was a shooting offence.

'Clear!' one of them shouted.

Munez jumped at the noise. He realised foggily that something was wrong. He had spent his entire adult life in warzones, and now he was jumping at a shout. He noticed absently that he was near some kind of vehicle, an elongated, heavy-wheeled thing that had jets of water firing from the sides. The lieutenant was vaguely aware of screams in the distance.

Was that good? Were the screams from his side? Who were his side?

Munez was lifted into the back of the vehicle, which began to move. He found his eyes closing, heavily.

Polk watched Gobu and Treston bring Lieutenant Munez on board the Cleaner. Powerful blasts of corrosive liquid were driving back the savage civilians, and helping to turn the tide in Emperor's Square. The troops were beginning to rally, although the Cleaner had stopped firing to allow Gobu and Treston to extract Munez from a mob of assailants.

As the rest of the men resumed firing, swivelling the water cannons to spray as wide an area as possible, Polk turned to Munez. The lieutenant had his eyes closed, and the two Guardsmen who had brought him on board seemed baffled as to what to do next.

'Out of my way,' said Polk, batting them aside. He pulled off one of his gloves and lifted Munez's face by the chin.

'Lieutenant Munez?' Polk said, trying to bring his superior round. 'Lieutenant?'

The lieutenant's mouth began to move, a trickle of drool in the corner, but his eyes stayed closed and he made no coherent response.

'Sir?' Munez said. 'Don't try and speak, we'll try and find a medicae and–'

'Has he been bitten?'

The question came from Calway. Polk turned, his temper rising. This wasn't a matter for a civilian, no matter how useful.

'Sorry, but I need to know,' said Calway, pushing forwards past the Guardsmen surrounding Munez.

Polk quickly inspected Munez. It didn't take long to find the wound on his arm, the teeth marks in the flesh.

'I'm sorry, sergeant,' said Calway. 'Their bite is venomous. There's nothing we can do for him.'

Polk didn't want to believe it, but he knew Calway was right. Munez's breathing was slowing, faint. He would be dead very soon.

But there were men in the square who were still alive. As

Munez lost his grip on life, Polk was on his feet, issuing orders to his men, to drive back the enemy, and to secure a route to safety for the remains of their platoon. Polk was damned if any more good men were going to die while he could stop it.

EIGHT

The old man was lost, bewildered. The mid-morning sun was unusually bright, and he raised a gnarled hand to his forehead, shading his eyes as he looked around.

He didn't recognise anything, but then again, very little pulled at his memory these days. Every now and then he would have a brief surge of recollection, an image of someone he once knew, a sensation of familiarity. These moments quickly faded into the general fog of his days: the search for somewhere to rest and shelter. His waking hours were sparse, as far as he could recall, and ended when he found some dark, dry place where he could lie down to sleep, hoping that the uncomfortable fullness in his stomach would fade by the next day.

It never did. Each morning he found himself burdened by the same stretched pains in his stomach muscles, the same weight pressing down on his lower organs, straining his hips and knees.

As for the nights, he didn't remember those at all.

He would never have been tall, but in his later years the old man had become stooped, his back bent by a life of industrial work, the same life that had left long-healed scars across his hands.

He struck a forlorn figure on this sunny morning, not that he knew it. Shuffling across polished stone, dimly aware of the buildings he was painfully walking towards, only knowing that he wanted to be inside, preferably away from windows and doors.

Somewhere dark, somewhere quiet. Then he could rest.

The morning sun glinted on something in the old man's peripheral vision. He turned, looking up to see what gleamed so brightly.

It was a statue, a golden statue leafed with silver detail, of a god-like figure, armoured and robed.

No, not *god-like*, the old man corrected himself, some deeply taught knowledge reasserting itself through the fog of his broken mind, learning imposed many years ago through rote and ritual. Not god-like, but a god.

The God-Emperor. That was who the statue was of, the God-Emperor.

He was in Emperor's Square, and this was the statue of the Emperor, looking down benevolently on the Ecclesiarchy.

Pleased with this sudden rush of memory, of having retrieved this knowledge and achieved some measure of clarity, the old man smiled, holding this awareness at the forefront of his mind, like a trophy.

The thought, the memory, the feeling of pride – all were suddenly, rudely ended when a las-round struck the old man squarely in the head, burning straight through his skull and brain.

He collapsed, smoke pouring from neat holes on either side of his head, the innocent smile still stretched across his wrinkled features.

Hool watched the old man fall through the sight of his own rifle, but the shot wasn't his. At the next window, Smoker reset his hellgun in one smooth, cranking motion, resting the barrel back on the sill, already on the lookout for his next target.

As one of the better shots among the men who had survived the previous night's battle in Emperor's Square, Hool had been seconded to Smoker on the fourth floor of the luxury hab-tower. Theoretically, Hool was to provide supporting fire, taking out other targets when Smoker was already in mid-shot.

In practice, Sergeant Essler did not leave any scraps for Hool to pick up. In the hour they had been sitting at those windows, aiming down into the full breadth of the square, Hool had not needed to take a single shot. Something moved, Smoker was on it, taking multiple shots in sequence if necessary. Hool just watched the bodies drop.

Smoker didn't speak much, or encourage anyone else to. The only noise between shots and recharges was the mechanical, constant hum of Smoker's augmented breathing.

The order to eliminate any and all civilians on sight was given by Major Geiss in the early hours, following a vox-conference with his surviving lieutenants and, in the absence of the late Lieutenant Munez, Smoker. The presumption was that any non-Guard human had to be presumed to be suffering from whatever contagion, heresy or disorder had turned the other citizens into ravenous killers during the hours of night, and that containment was not a reasonable option considering the small size of the strike force and the already troubling level of casualties.

Any civilian, no matter how harmless-looking during the day, had the potential to be a serious threat by nightfall. They were time bombs, to be defused by fatal means before they had chance to go off.

The only exceptions to this order were civilians who had been witnessed by a member of the Iron Guard during the night, and could be vouched for as unafflicted.

Reports indicated that, aside from Calway's people, there were only a few more confirmed 'clean' civilians – a group in the workers' habs who, in spite of having gone near-mad themselves through the pressures of fighting off their friends and colleagues, had come to the assistance of Hossk's men.

Other than those few, everyone was a target. Hool did not question the order, and understood the reasoning behind it, but the acts themselves did not sit well. He felt unease, a queasiness, at the sight of unarmed civilians gunned down in the street. He was relieved that Smoker was so mercilessly taking each shot without giving Hool any opportunity to participate.

Smoker fired again, and Hool flinched.

'Guardsman Hool,' said Smoker, not looking up from the sights of his hellgun. 'Did I startle you?'

'Sorry, sergeant,' replied Hool, as crisply as he could. 'I didn't see the target before you fired.'

'Attention wandering, huh?' said Smoker, the 'huh' a metallic grunt. 'I apologise if I have hogged the targets, Guardsman, leaving your mind room to wander. Perhaps you would like to take the next few shots, while I merely provide backup?'

Smoker had taken his hands off his hellgun now, and was sat back on one of the antique chairs they had requisitioned. He looked directly at Hool, and obviously registered Hool's reticence, his rebreather rattling with a low chuckle.

'I thought not,' said Smoker, returning his attention to his gunsight. 'You see shooting targets who are not an obvious threat as dishonourable, yes? Certainly compared to last night's manoeuvres, defending your comrades against overwhelming odds in the square?'

Hool didn't say anything. Smoker didn't look up from his gunsight as he continued:

'You are young, Guardsman Hool, and I can see that Sergeant Polk is teaching you well in terms of fighting shoulder-to-shoulder with your fellow Guardsmen, defending yourselves and each other. That will get you far.

'But only so far, Hool. There are limits to defence, and even to controlled, restrained offence. Sometimes a merciless attack is required. Any of these people–' Smoker tapped a finger against the window his hellgun was slotted under, indicating the dead in the square. '–would tear you limb from limb in their heightened state. There is a risk that they might not, but is that an acceptable risk? Is your sense of honour worth your life, or worse?'

Hool remained silent.

'You do not have an answer,' said Smoker. 'I didn't expect one. Think on this: the life expectancy of a new recruit to the Imperial Guard is fifteen hours. You are already well on your way to surviving fifteen months, but so far the enemies you have faced have been weak. The enemies of man are many and strong, while you are human, vulnerable. The ideals that have kept you alive so far may not help you survive the battles to come.'

Smoker turned to Hool again, fixing him with his blank, camera gaze.

'Your duty is to fight to your last breath to attain victory, Hool,' said Smoker. 'To do this, you may have to forego the luxury of sustaining the lives of those around you. Survival. Victory. Nothing else.'

Smoker returned to his target practice, his speech over.

A silence fell on the room once more. Although Smoker didn't seem concerned by Hool's lack of response, Hool was very glad when a vox-operator entered with a message for Smoker – Major Geiss wished to speak to him immediately.

Gilham was doing ten things at once. This wasn't an exaggeration or hyperbole – there was no one to boast to, and Gilham was hardly inclined to self-promotion – but a simple matter of fact.

While resolving the power situation the previous day, Gilham had noted the signs indicating an Adeptus Mechanicus laboratorium within the mining complex. Now, the presence of that lab had proven useful.

The lab was a place for the ritualised assembly of machinery in a sterile, controlled environment. Tech-priests could officiate over the rituals from a sealed observation pulpit overlooking a room of polished slabs, where the work could be carried out either by servants, servitors or via the robotic arms that were cranked around the ceiling on a series of automated winches and pulleys. Each set of arms was fully equipped with cutting tools and optics, and bristled with blades and probes of various kinds.

Gilham sat in the observation pulpit, his back turned to the reinforced window looking out over the lab, one of his mechadendrites connecting his consciousness to the control console. For the purposes of this work, he was the laboratory, looking down on every slab at once, manipulating every mechanical probe and tool as if they were his own limbs.

To all intents and purposes, they were.

On three of the slabs lay the bodies of Krick and two of the other civilians killed in the control centre, and on two other slabs were spread the detritus from their 'lair', as Geiss had referred to it. Gilham was simultaneously autopsying the three corpses and sorting through the fragments, while another set of automated limbs crisscrossed the room, taking samples back and forth to a bank of equipment at one side of the lab for testing.

It was not conventional work for an adept, but Gilham had requested that he examine the bodies rather than the medi-caes. There was something about the idea of these civilians with their enhanced capabilities, of augmentation without surgery, that fascinated him. Of course, any alteration to the human body caused by drug or disease could never match the elegance of welding machinery to human flesh, but nev-ertheless Gilham wished to identify the exact cause.

Gilham directed a buzzsaw to cut through the front of Krick's ribcage, then used long, finger-like probes to open up the chest cavity. What he saw through the optics intrigued him – the lungs were curiously discoloured and swollen.

'Fascinating,' said Gilham to himself, speaking in his native binaric. He extended a long syringe attachment, and prodded into one of Krick's lungs. The syringe withdrew a measure of tarrish, red-purple gloop from within the lung, which stickily lapped the inside of a glass vial.

As a robotic arm carried the vial across to the other side of the lab for testing, Gilham shifted the core of his atten-tion back to the chewed scraps from the lair. Major Geiss had received fractured reports of similar hoards found else-where around the city-factory, piles of discarded augmetics and other indigestible personal items. It suggested that the altered civilians and workers had chewed their way through much of the population, and possibly each other.

A scattering of items from the pile attracted Gilham's atten-tion as he sorted them. One was a sub-dermal tag implanted in Munitorum auditors. Gilham accessed the data in the tag, which identified its wearer as Recorder Gellwood Jenk, resolving one of Major Geiss's mission objectives, albeit unhappily.

Gilham discarded the tag. It was not his concern.

Also in the pile were remains of some sophisticated augmetics, of the kind reserved for the Adeptus Mechanicus themselves. It seemed that the adepts of this sacred laboratory had not fared any better than the common workers.

Among the augmetics was a datacore. Gilham set it aside for further examination.

The first barrage of test results on the liquid extracted from Krick's lungs were available: the sample wasn't any natural product of a human body, even taking into account the possibility of a lung infection. It seemed to have some form of independent existence outside the host lungs.

Gilham's human fingers began to drum the arm of his chair unconsciously, furtively, as his mind began to try and put the pieces together.

Major Geiss wanted to debrief Calway personally, to interrogate him about everything that had happened in the city-factory prior to the arrival of the 114th. Smoker was assigned to assemble a team to escort Calway to the mining complex, and ensure nothing untoward happened to him. While the change in civilians occurred at night, Geiss didn't want Calway shot dead by accident before he could talk to the man.

So Smoker, along with both his and Polk's squads, were crammed into the Cleaner as the narrow vehicle rolled through the wrecked streets, its fat wheels allowing it to grind its way over most obstacles.

Geiss had devised a simple identification system for known 'clean' civilians – a strip of Mordian-blue fabric, tied around the right arm. After the previous night's losses, strips of cloth were in plentiful supply, to be taken from the coats of fallen Guardsmen.

With a characteristic lack of sentimentality, Smoker had gone first, entering the room where the retrieved bodies of the fallen Guard had been laid out, removing Lieutenant Munez's coat, and tearing off a long strip of fabric and handing it to Calway.

Hool had tensed as Smoker began to tear the bloodied jacket into strips, but found as the fabric was rended, a strange relief washed over him.

Munez was dead, but his men kept fighting, using what they needed without sentimentality and remorse. They would rebuild and go on.

As they sat in the Cleaner, Hool occasionally glanced across at Smoker, wondering how much of that gesture came from the sergeant's ice-cold pragmatism, and whether or not he had, in his way, torn Munez's jacket apart to help Munez's men to survive, to move on.

Was he trying to help them?

Hossk didn't realise he was even falling asleep until he woke up. Watery morning light roused him from a dreamless sleep. He was sat at a crude utility table, and the cramps in his back and neck matched the thudding pain in the side of his head. At some point he must have sat down, and a combination of fading adrenaline and the drugs in his system wearing off had conspired to cast him into unconsciousness.

It must have happened fast, as he had no memory of entering the room he was now sat in, a functional kitchen area lined with conspicuously empty shelves. Supplies were running low.

Hossk did remember the hour or so after he passed the barrier into the corner of Hab C fortified by Stellin and the other workers. He had been grudgingly impressed by the way that the mine workers had created a sanctuary against what remained of the rest of the population, and had established a relatively orderly community even under such a pressurised and grief-stricken situation.

Although non-combatants, the rigours and dangers of a life down the mines had left these workers with a strong sense of discipline and honour, qualities Hossk admired above all else, and they had applied these qualities to setting up and running a besieged community.

While most survivors lived behind the barricades, some had insisted on staying in their own rooms on other floors of the hab, and Stellin's people had maintained a network of supply runs and defensive points throughout the hab, setting up the traps Hossk's men had walked into the previous day. There was a limit to how far even the boldest patrols would go – the ground and sub-levels were where the enemy slept, and even in the safe daylight hours few people would risk venturing into the dark.

Beyond the mechanics of maintaining such a community, what struck Hossk was the low number of survivors – fewer than fifty people in the entire hab. Even if other such communities were scattered across the city-factory, out of contact with each other, that amounted to only a few hundred people at most.

The mathematics were alarming. Between the killers and their victims, the population of Belmos VII had been reduced by over ninety per cent in a matter of weeks. Whatever the cause of the murderous behaviour that had engulfed the population, if it could be spread to one of the busier hive worlds, one where billions lived in close proximity, the results could be even more catastrophic.

As Hossk was piecing together what he had learned, one hand rubbing his aching neck, Weir entered the room.

'How long have I been out?' Hossk asked. His mouth was dry, and the words came out with more of a croak than he intended.

'Only a few hours, sir,' Weir replied. 'Didn't see any sense in disturbing you, nothing much happening out here.'

'Reports from the other squads?' Hossk asked.

'Most voxed in,' said Weir. 'Serious casualties, but most managed to find a defensible position for the night.'

Hossk nodded, then regretted the motion as his head swam. He closed his eyes, and focussed on the situation rather than the pain. Casualties, forces scattered.

'Vox all squads, tell them to reconvene at the base of Hab B,' said Hossk. 'Tell Stellin to get his forces together to do the same.'

'Got a plan, sir?' Weir asked.

'Something like that,' said Hossk. 'If these people sleep in the day, then that's when they're vulnerable.' He opened his eyes, blinking a couple of times to adjust to the light, and looked Weir straight in the eye. 'So all we need to do is find the most likely sleeping places, and torch them.'

Geiss's interview with the man Calway proved disappointing.

Calway himself impressed Geiss, by civilian standards. Although he had no military experience, the man seemed to have rallied his people in the face of an entirely unexpected situation, and with no backup since the fall of the PDF. Calway's report of the events he had witnessed, and of what he had been told by others, was concise and focussed on the significant details – all entirely laudable qualities that Geiss appreciated in a man, enlisted or not.

Calway's description of the attributes, limitations and behaviour of those who had changed confirmed some of Geiss's observations, while adding some further details. The strength and speed were self-evident, and that they ate their prey came as no surprise after recent discoveries, but that their bite was poisonous did.

Geiss was most interested in the limits of these people's intelligence – while far from stupid, and capable of conversation and rational thinking in their enhanced night-time state, their ferociously violent mindset seemed to override any ability for medium-term planning. A useful weakness to know.

However, Calway's testimony lacked the crucial details Geiss required to complete his mission. Neither Calway, nor anyone he had spoken to, had any idea of the source of the problem. Everything had been normal until night fell one day, at which point a large proportion of the population had turned on their fellow workers and citizens. Calway and his fellow survivors had been defending themselves against nocturnal attacks ever since. There were no clues to the source of the changes, or how they might be stopped.

Geiss was certain the source was in the mine: where else could it come from on an empty dirtball like this? But the mine was huge, and Geiss had no idea what he was looking for – a virus to be purged with fire, a pollutant that could be cleansed?

He needed more information.

Gilham arrived towards the end of Geiss's interrogation of Calway, and sought an audience with the major at the first convenient opportunity. Geiss took the adept to one side.

'Tell me you have something useful,' said Geiss.

If Gilham took offence at Geiss's tone, he didn't show it.

'Perhaps,' Gilham replied, showing Geiss the datacore.

Geiss gave Gilham a questioning look.

'This is an Adeptus Mechanicus datacore, probably augmetically attached to a servant tasked with official observation,' Gilham explained. 'I retrieved it from the hoard of chewed objects we discovered.'

'Have you accessed the data?' Geiss asked.

'Not yet,' said Gilham. 'I wished to consult you first. The core is designed to allow the user to access their own recorded observations, and then replay or transmit them to another means of recording. It is not designed to be accessed by a third party. I can attempt to do so, but I will need to do so carefully to avoid corrupting the memories with my own consciousness.'

'Meaning?' Geiss asked.

'Meaning I will need to shut down all other thought functions while I access the core, and allow the personality imprint to override my own. I will be unavailable for any other duties until I have completed this task. There is also some risk.'

'Risk?'

'That the host personality should override mine entirely, or that my own personality is corrupted into madness. You may wish to post guards on me while I do this.'

'How great a risk?'

Gilham calculated the odds. 'Approximately zero point seven per cent.'

Geiss took a breath. He didn't want to lose the adept, but then he was running low on options. 'I'm happy with those odds if you are.'

'Very well,' said Gilham. 'Shall I start?' One of his slimmer mechadendrites slid out, a probe hanging over the datacore, waiting to connect.

Geiss raised his hand for Gilham to wait, and called over a couple of guards. As Geiss explained the situation, Gilham cleared the furniture from a corner of the gallery, then sat on the floor. He placed the datacore on the floor in front of him.

'Major Geiss, can I begin?'

The major nodded. The Guardsmen on either side of him shifted their lasrifles, ready for whatever Gilham might do next.

Gilham made the connection.

NINE

Remember everything. Heinrik had to remember everything. It was his job, no *his duty*. That the man who had assigned him that duty, his lord and master, was rocking back and forwards on the floor, and would soon become a threat to Heinrik, did not relieve him of that duty.

In honour of the Machine-God, Heinrik opened up his augmetics, allowing the data to flow.

He needed to record, to recount what had happened, the demise of Belmos VII, the fall of his lifelong home, before he died.

But, as he faced his own death and that of his home planet, as the sound of screams and tearing machinery rattled down every corridor, as his master gurgled and giggled, Heinrik found his focus shifting not to the present, not to the last days, but to the day he had learned what death meant, then deeper still, going back into memories that had been augmented not by technology but by the changing effect of Heinrik's own repeated remembrances, as his adult mind had turned each childhood recollection over and over, holding them close but also rewriting them with his adult awareness.

As they were brought forth one last time, Heinrik's thoughts of those early, hard-to-recall days were burnt to the record, sealed in the datacore, inaccuracies and dreams included.

Heinrik's parents died on the ninety-seventh day of the flood. He was six years old.

That was the day he first understood the finality of death, the meaning of change, when his childhood world was overturned. But that was not how it had started.

It started with the rains.

The rainy season started earlier that year, the rains more ferocious than any Heinrik had known in his short life to date.

Heinrik and his parents lived high in the workers' habs, their small home facing out over the rest of the city-factory. The day the rains started, Heinrik looked out to find he could no longer see the city-factory spreading out below, but instead an endless grey murk stretched out, blurred by the splatters of water hitting the window.

For the first few days, it was a novelty, and even holding his thin pillow over his head to try and block out the sound of water impacting glass held a strange excitement for Heinrik.

After two weeks of the relentless rains hammering against

the windows, the sky blackened so that day was indistin-
guishable from night, even Heinrik knew something was
wrong.

Heinrik's parents worked for someone called the Munitorum, somewhere down the mine. Every morning Heinrik's
mother walked him down the stairwell and across a walkway to the other hab-tower, where he would spend all day
in a long, narrow room where children sat at lines of rickety
desks, as a voice from the front of the room slowly intoned
each lesson. They learnt to write and read, and of the glory
of the God-Emperor.

As they learned each lesson through constant, numbing repetition they were supervised by the servitors, the
half-metal dead-men, who walked up and down each line,
lashing out at any child who moved when they shouldn't.
The servitors were dull, stupid creatures, and would frequently misinterpret a child's actions, thrashing one who
had done nothing wrong or delivering a more severe beating
than was required.

One morning, a month after the floods began, Heinrik
looked through a barred opening on the walkway, down
into the underpass, the well beneath the two hab-towers.
Even with the rains, the walkway was low enough that Heinrik should have been able to see through the gloom to catch
sight of people moving below.

On this day, there was nothing but a surface of water at the
base of the tower.

'The underpass has been flooded,' Heinrik's mother said,
as she tugged his arm, ushering him across the walkway.

'Special walls have been put up around the underpass, and the water is being kept there to stop the refineries from flooding, because the refineries are very important.'

Heinrik asked about the people who lived in the underpass, the people that children like Heinrik were sternly warned against becoming, the people who lived down there because even the habs would not have them.

His mother didn't answer, and instead tugged his arm again, dragging him away.

The floods continued in the weeks that followed. Heinrik was increasingly aware that his parents were somehow involved in the attempts to deal with the rain, although he understood little of their talk of defensive barriers and drainage.

What Heinrik did understand was the tension written in his parents' faces, as they collected him late from the servitors, later even than the children who found that they were not picked up by their parents, but instead by grey-uniformed officials.

The older children whispered about those men and women in their grey uniforms, that they came for the children whose parents had died in the flood, and took the children away.

Where, they didn't know.

The person who came for Heinrik in place of his mother wasn't one of the grey-uniforms, but a tall, red-robed woman carrying a wrought-iron staff from which intricately patterned brass-on-green charms jangled. Beneath the hood of her robe, a mass of clockwork replaced her face, and beneath the robes came the noise of shifting, chittering mechanisms. She spoke with the servitors, then crossed the room to speak with Heinrik.

With every step, the staff hit the floor with a dull *thunk*, and the charms tinkled against the shaft of the staff. As the woman stood over Heinrik, her head covered by a red hood, he could see that the hand that held the staff was skeletal, an open machine that weeped oil from the knuckles.

Heinrik knew why the woman was here for him. He was too upset to be afraid, and too afraid to feel the fear.

Instead he felt a welling tension within him as the woman leaned down to place her other hand, this one entirely human, on his shoulder and tell him what he already knew. As he was led away he felt the tension building, threatening to well over.

He didn't know whether what was rising inside him would come out as tears or laughter.

The woman, Adept Tilfur, was elegantly thin, a twisted stick of a being wrapped in red fabric, but her master was the opposite, a bloated spider of a man, metallic tentacles and limbs spreading out from beneath his robes, a mass of other augmentations writhing beneath the fabric.

Now, ushered into this being's presence, Heinrik finally felt something, a terrified awe and fascination that numbed the darker emotions he had felt since Tilfur told him of his parents' deaths. As Heinrik was ushered into his presence, High Tech-Priest Mankell, Chief Adept of Belmos VII, was lighting candles in the Mechanicus cathedral on Emperor's Square.

The ever-present sound of rain on the stained-glass windows echoed around the arched chamber as Mankell glided across the floor, wielding half a dozen long, burning sticks, touching the flames against candles in ornate holders.

A child of workers, Heinrik had never left the hab-towers. The square, the cathedral, the great altar of a brass cog before which Mankell stood, all of these sights reinforced the importance of the Chief Adept.

'This is the boy, Chief Adept,' Tilfur said, nudging Heinrik's shoulder. He stumbled forwards, his feet dragging on the deep carpet that ran towards the altar, bisecting a hundred rows of benches.

Mankell shifted his mass towards Heinrik, not turning as a single entity but shuffling his many mechanical parts towards the boy. The Adeptus Mechanicus were the opposite of the servitors, those dead men with grey, cold skin, recognisable features and mechanically amended limbs. Where servitors were machines with human faces, the Adeptus Mechanicus were living beings that lived as machinery. Mankell's face was an elaborate mechanism that only crudely corresponded to a face at all, an elaborate mechanism that took in Heinrik with a cluster of compound optics, each shining in the reflected candlelight as Mankell leaned in close.

'Heinrik,' said Mankell, his voice echoing around the vast space of the cathedral. 'Adept Tilfur has told you about your parents?'

Heinrik nodded.

'Your parents are dead. They died in the flood while serving the Imperium and the Munitorum,' said Mankell. 'Now it is your duty to serve. The Munitorum has no use for you, but the Adeptus Mechanicus may.'

Mankell leaned in close to Heinrik. His oily exhalations felt like hot smoke, leaving an acrid scent in the air.

'This is how it must be,' said Mankell. 'But how will you serve the Adeptus Mechanicus? You are too slight to become a servitor.'

Heinrik shuddered at the prospect.

Mankell peered at Heinrik curiously. 'You recoil? Do you think I honour orphans with an audience every day? Most would be left to die alone in the hab slums.' He paused, examining Heinrik. 'You are more fortunate, Heinrik. I have a use for you. You will be blessed to serve me.'

Heinrik did not feel fortunate, or blessed, at all.

And so began the second, longer phase of Heinrik's short life. He lived, and he served, in the manner the Chief Adept required of him. It was his task to observe, to recall details, to record.

Heinrik did this first with data-slates, but as he grew older, and reached the age where his growth slowed down enough to make long-term bodily augmentation possible, he underwent the procedures to make him a living chronicler of events around him. New optical arrays were implanted in his skull, the relays and datacores weighing down his shoulders.

Clothed in dark, rough robes, he silently followed Mankell around, observing most of his work, recording what the Chief Adept considered most significant.

Mankell considered much of what he did significant. Heinrik might have, in another life, have been in a position to understand the disparity between Mankell's impression of his own significance and the reality, but Heinrik's servitude was so intensely ingrained from a youth within the Chief Adept's household that he had no perspective at all.

Mankell was the centre of his existence, his importance too central to question. It was Heinrik's duty to record this greatness.

The request for Mankell to visit Galton, the Munitorum's chief official on Belmos VII, was not taken well. Mankell considered any meeting not initiated by himself as an imposition. As his bearers carried him through the city streets, he complained loudly in binaric of his treatment.

Heinrik had been to Galton's office many times before, observing and recording Mankell's many important visits as the Adeptus Mechanicus's highest representative on a Munitorum world, but this time was different. The lavish furnishings of the office were in disarray, the surfaces were covered in plans and picts, and Galton himself was not the formal figure Heinrik had seen before: his brocaded jacket was open, a crumpled shirtfront visible beneath. Heinrik, ever observant, caught sight of a caffeine stain on the shirt.

'We have made a discovery,' Galton told Mankell in hushed, urgent tones, his eyes darting nervously towards Heinrik.

Heinrik was used to this kind of reticence from others, for many people did not wish to be observed and recorded.

However, Galton was not usually one of them.

'A discovery,' echoed Mankell, drawing Galton's full attention back to him.

'B379,' said Galton. 'The workers were following a weak seam, and broke through to an existing tunnel system. It's very old, and seems to have been artificially carved from the rock. I thought, from our previous discussions, that you might be interested.'

Mankell had been hostile as he entered the room, resentful of the implied summons, but his mood had now shifted. He was examining the picts taken in the mines with interest.

'You were very wise to summon me,' said Mankell, mechadendrites shifting excitedly beneath his robes. 'Potentially heretical knowledge and technology needs to be... dealt with responsibly. We would not want to incite panic among the workers. It takes a refined mind of the kind possessed by you or I to appreciate the significance of a discovery like this.'

Heinrik knew well that Mankell did not consider Galton an equal mind at all.

'Thank you,' said Galton, bowing slightly.

'Of course, it would be unhelpful at this stage for any discovery to be subject to outside interference from minds less attuned to the sensitivities of the situation, you understand...' Mankell trailed off.

'Recorder Jenk is, I believe, auditing activity in the refineries for most of today,' said Galton. 'Would you like to access the site now, without interference?'

'Immediately,' replied Mankell. 'If there is lost technology down there, we need to ensure it is dealt with correctly.'

'Destroyed?' asked Galton.

'Of course,' said Mankell. Only Heinrik's heightened senses detected Mankell's hesitation. Formally, all lost technology was potentially heretical and had to be scourged. Unofficially, the Adeptus Mechanicus were always seeking lost knowledge. Finding some could repair Mankell's standing and secure him a more prestigious position.

'Access to the area has been restricted,' said Galton. 'But I will grant entry to whomsoever you wish to send down to inspect the site.'

'I will take a team down there myself,' said Mankell.

'Very well,' said Galton. 'In that case I will accompany you.'

'Of course,' replied Mankell smoothly.

Heinrik had watched exchanges between these two before, the endless politicking as each man politely but firmly asserted their influence. If one was interested in the discovery in the mine, the other would shadow him, determined to not lose traction.

'We will proceed at once,' said Mankell.

As Galton prepared himself, Mankell turned to Heinrik:

'Boy, I need you to make arrangements while I am away...'

Heinrik was not present for Mankell's descent to the discovery at B379, instead ferrying secure messages from Mankell to members of the Adeptus Mechanicus.

As Heinrik returned from delivering his last message, he found the streets unusually bustling. The stoop caused by his augmetics made Heinrik shorter than most people, and he was jostled by the hectic, angry crowds. He caught murmurs of conversation between various workers, that the mine had been partially evacuated mid-shift, only for the workers to be called back within the hour and then required to work through their breaks to make up time.

Heinrik returned to find that Mankell had returned. He bowed his head before his master, and reported that the messages had been delivered.

'Very good, very good,' said Mankell, one of his many augmetics grinding beneath his robes. Then his vox-caster unleashed a burst of static, then another.

'My lord?' asked Heinrik. Mankell could communicate on many levels beyond those that Heinrik could comprehend. Perhaps this was one of them.

'It is nothing,' said Mankell, the words slightly distorted. 'There was a… gas leakage in the mine. It thickened the air, but caused no lasting harm. Some particles must still be in my respiratory system. No matter, the filters will self-correct.'

Mankell dismissed Heinrik to go about his duties.

'As a senior auditor, I am used to having to make great efforts to discover evidence of incompetence, corruption of dereliction of duty,' said Recorder Gellwood Jenk. 'Most facilities I visit are at least competent enough to organise a cover-up and put their best face forwards, at least for the duration of my audit.'

Jenk had the floor, and he knew it. A room full of Belmos VII's most illustrious citizens, and none dared speak in the long pause as Jenk sipped amasec from a wide, round glass. He sloshed the liquid from side to side before speaking again.

Still silence. Heinrik, stood a respectable distance behind Mankell, observed.

'So,' continued Jenk, at his own pace. 'When a major work outage occurs during the course of a short audit, I have to seriously question the competence of the local authorities, and how unstoppably ruinous that incompetence may be.'

Jenk was a wide man, his manner of dress austere but his girth and the precision fold of his ostensibly basic tunic indicative of extreme wealth. He sat at one end of a long, lacquered table in the main conference chamber of the mine's control centre. The late afternoon sun caught the bowl of Jenk's glass, the glare periodically blinding Heinrik's optics as Jenk rolled the glass in his hand.

After an uneasy silence, Galton coughed and then spoke.

'That you are aware of this minor stoppage should be an indication of our transparency, Recorder Jenk,' said Galton. He spoke tentatively, prepared to reverse any statement should it receive an unfavourable response. He coughed again, rubbing the bridge of his nose.

Heinrik's keen senses noted the sheen of sweat on Galton's face and the lack of focus when he tried to catch Jenk's eye.

'We have no systemic failures to hide, and the matter was resolved quickly with no delays to workload,' said Galton, before holding a silk handkerchief over his face and trying to stifle a loud coughing fit, unsuccessfully.

Jenk raised a sneering eyebrow, then turned to Mankell.

'Perhaps, Chief Adept, you can provide me with some detail regarding this "matter" that caused the temporary evacuation of a large section of the mine? I understand that you were there, along with the Governor.'

'Need I remind you, recorder, that the Adeptus Mechanicus are not a resource of the Munitorum,' said Mankell. 'We are not subject to your authority.'

'Of course,' said Jenk, smiling thinly. 'I merely ask for the benefit of your knowledge of the technologies used in this planet's industries, and as a respected scientific witness.'

'Very well,' said Mankell. 'It was a gas leak, caused by the breach of an enclosed pocket in the lower levels of the mine. A pressurised leakage that spread quickly, but which dispersed without any damage. A common risk in deep mining.'

Jenk smiled wider.

'A common risk, a common risk, of course,' said Jenk, leaning forwards across the table, tracing circles on the varnished surface with his little finger. 'A common risk, just another day in the mine. So tell me, anyone, exactly what was so important about this ordinary drilling day that it required the most senior representative of the Machine Cult of Mars to descend into the dirt to witness it?'

Jenk sat back, letting the question lie there. Heinrik could see Mankell's patience thinning, the tension expressed through the shifts of his mechadendrites.

Galton, on the other hand, seemed oblivious. As the daylight faded outside, and servitors began to raise the lights in the room, he was almost doubled up in his chair, a forlorn figure.

The meeting broke up unsatisfactorily. Jenk had not received the answers he wished from either Mankell or Galton, and so stormed off, flanked by his personal bodyguards, to consult whatever records he considered necessary. Galton himself did not respond as Mankell, the other officials and their various attendants withdrew.

Heinrik followed Mankell as he withdrew through the levels of the control centre. They were stopped on their way out.

'Sorry, sir,' said the guard, bowing to Mankell. 'There's been a disturbance. Some of the workers who had their shift extended are rioting at the gate. The way should be clear soon.'

The sound of gunfire echoed in the distance.

Mankell bowed theatrically. 'Please inform us when this matter has been resolved. We will be in the main gallery.'

They descended back into the depths of the control centre. As they turned a corner, there was the sound of gunfire. A bloodied Jenk ran across their path, one of his bodyguards at his heels, firing back down the corridor.

Mankell looked down at Heinrik.

'Perhaps we should find a secure place for the time being,' he said drily.

Mankell took seconds to override the security cogitator in the small monitor room he had barricaded himself and Heinrik into. From there, he could observe feeds from across the mine complex, and monitor vox-chatter. He hunched over the cogitator, his back to Heinrik, mechadendrites slipping out from beneath his robe to adjust controls and manipulate settings.

'Observe,' Mankell commanded, not turning around to face Heinrik. 'This must be recorded.'

'Yes, Chief Adept,' said Heinrik.

'Disturbances have broken out across the city, beginning sharply after nightfall,' Mankell dictated. 'Reports have become significantly less coherent after the initial attacks, but cross-referencing the more precise statements lodged with work schedules indicates a one-to-one correlation between the perpetrators and those either on duty, or otherwise present, during this morning's gas leak.'

Heinrik stood silently, taking in Mankell's testimony.

'This facility works on a rotation of three shifts, and ninety-seven per cent of the population of this city-factory are indentured mine workers. In effect, a third of the population were exposed to the gas.'

Mankell turned to face Heinrik. His optics tightened, examining Heinrik on a microscopic level.

'This is an unfortunate accident, and we must hope that any violent effect is not universal, or is at least short-term. I myself was exposed, but do not yet feel any ill effects. We shall wait for the current crisis to pass.'

A short while later, Mankell began to feel ill effects. The crisis had not yet passed, the vox-chatter Mankell had been monitoring becoming ever more hectic.

Twice someone outside had tried to batter through the door, screaming obscenities and thrashing against it. Mankell had braced himself against the door, blocking it.

Heinrik had stood and observed, as he was told. Now, his task was renewed, with new purpose.

'It seems that my presumption of immunity was

exaggerated,' said Mankell, sliding down the door to rest on the floor. As his body slumped, his mechadendrites began to dance, throwing the ceremonial robes away and waving back and forth playfully.

'My augmentations seem to have slowed the process, that is all,' said Mankell. 'But the changes of the flesh cannot be denied. I can *feel* my organic components changing. You must observe it, Heinrik! This is your last duty, to record the change, to witness what happens to me.'

Heinrik watched. Physically, he did not move, but even as Mankell rambled on, Heinrik found his attention wandering. He knew death was coming, but that didn't bring a sense of urgency to the moment, instead it sent his mind darting into the past, even as he stood, fulfilling his duty.

Heinrik remembered looking down from the walkway, seeing the floodwaters below, and being aware that the people who lived down below had been swept away. That first taste of finality, of things gone never to be returned.

'I feel a hunger,' ranted Mankell, his movements increasingly frenetic. 'A desire to tear and rend and devour. It disgusts me, that after a life of trying to transcend organic weakness I should succumb to it. I hate that I, I should fall to this.'

Heinrik remembered the day Tilfur brought news of his parents' death, of the wrought staff she carried with the cog sign atop, the jangle of the circuit-charms dangling from the shaft. The news she brought, the absolute change.

The waters lapping below. His mother's hand drawing him away.

'I am Chief Adept Mankell,' snarled Mankell. 'I am augmented man, perfected man, vessel of the Machine-God. I will not be broken by this contagion of the flesh, this filthy, feral condition. I will overcome it.'

Even as he spoke, Mankell was edging across the floor towards Heinrik.

Heinrik stood and watched as Mankell approached. Observing, remembering.

Heinrik looked down into the waters of the flooded underpass, his mother's hand pulling him away. The dark, deep waters, washing lives away.

'Observe, boy, observe as I resist, as I fight off this urge.'

Mankell's mechadendrites arched as he approached, the tip of each angling towards Heinrik, a dozen metallic snakeheads with Heinrik in their sights.

Heinrik watched Tilfur crossing the room, bringing death, her staff tapping the floor. The waters had taken his parents, the dark tide taking them too.

Mankell lunged forwards, pouncing upon Heinrik with fearsome, augmented speed, the mechadendrites piercing Heinrik's body in a dozen places. Tiny, fierce embers of pain, drowned out by the dark tide that rose within Heinrik, consuming his observations, his memories, the jumble of present and past breaking up within his flickering, fading consciousness.

The waters below. The staff, tapping the floor.

The tide rising. Heinrik sinking.

Heinrik died.

Heinrik was dead.

Dead.

No, alive, aware.

Heinrik, alive?

No, Heinrik was dead. Poor Heinrik, dead and devoured, his memories locked in a box, memories of his last moments and of his parents and of the slow, grey waters below.

It was Gilham who was alive.

He was Gilham and he was alive and–

TEN

'B379,' said Major Geiss, one gloved finger tapping the location on a map of the mine. He had gathered Lieutenant Deaz, Sergeant Essler and Gilham in the Gallery, which had been converted into a temporary war room, maps and charts laid out on a table in the centre of the room.

'It all began there, with a breakthrough into some kind of existing tunnel system,' Geiss continued. 'Some time after the wall was breached, some form of gas was released. Unfortunately we still have no idea what the original source of the gas was, but we can presume that it is somewhere past B379, in the newly opened area. We can guess from the interest shown by various parties that ancient technology, perhaps alien or even heretical, was involved.'

Geiss glanced across the table to Gilham as he spoke. The adept's journey through this Heinrik's memories had, externally, taken only a few minutes and left no visible ill effects after Gilham snapped back to consciousness, but Geiss had seen psykers break down through their connection to the minds of others, and was watching for any sign that Gilham's sanity had been damaged. Tech-adepts were not front-line warriors, but their augmentations gave them physical strength that made them dangerous, and Geiss could do without one cracking up behind his lines.

'That is a reasonable supposition,' said Gilham.

Geiss continued to watch Gilham closely. Lord Brassfell had sought to brief Gilham before the strike force left Elisenda. The Adeptus Mechanicus's internal politics were, strictly speaking, none of Geiss's business, but if there was a potential conflict between Geiss's leadership and the Adeptus Mechanicus's intentions, Geiss's next order would draw it out.

'I want the source of this infection located and destroyed,' Geiss said, leaving no pause for rebuttal. 'Whatever interest the authorities on this planet may have had in... whatever is down there... are overridden by the threat it causes to Belmos VII's contribution to the Imperium.'

Gilham held Geiss's gaze, then slowly nodded, almost bowing before the major.

'I assure you, major, I have been given no instruction or guidance to undermine the objectives of this mission,' said Gilham, taking Geiss aback with his frankness. 'Our primary objective here is to restore supplies to our forge world. Any secondary interests are irrelevant if they compromise the supply lines.'

Geiss returned the nod. He hadn't expected Gilham to address the potential of Adeptus Mechanicus intrigue so directly, and there was something about the adept that made Geiss want to trust him, in spite of the absence of normal human expressions and body language that Geiss would usually rely on to assess a man's character.

'Sergeant Essler,' Geiss said. 'I am field-promoting you to lieutenant immediately. By all accounts you demonstrated great initiative last night, and your augmentations make you the best man to lead a platoon in what will be uncertain conditions. Lieutenant Deaz will provide his best men, and Adept Gilham will accompany you to help identify whatever is the source of this gas. Find it, and destroy it by whatever means necessary.'

Essler snapped to attention, giving a brisk and respectful salute.

'Thank you, sir,' Essler said, holding the salute. 'I won't let you down.'

'Don't thank me yet,' said Geiss, looking between both Essler and Gilham. 'I want every man in your platoon with their rebreathers on before they descend into that mine, but if there's gas down there, there's no guarantee those men will be protected. You two have the best chance of filtering the gas, but this Mankell was fully augmented, and he couldn't resist.'

Geiss checked the clock. 'You have eight hours until nightfall. Access to the mine has been re-opened, and the elevators are operational. Assemble your men and deploy as soon as you can.'

When Smoker and Gilham had left the room to make their preparations, Geiss addressed Deaz.

'Once they're down in the mine, I want an equivalent force stationed at the mine entrance for if they return. If they arrive before nightfall and appear normal, quarantine them in the warehouses. If they show any suspicious signs, do not hesitate to terminate them. If they're not back before nightfall, we seal them in until daytime.'

'I'll make the arrangements,' said Deaz. If he had any distaste for his assignment, he didn't show it.

Deaz was almost at the door when Geiss stopped him.

'I'm trusting your men to show good judgement in this, lieutenant,' Geiss cautioned. 'Don't fire in haste, but if they need to fire – don't hesitate. These men may be comrades-in-arms, and they deserve a chance to prove themselves, but if they become a threat...'

'I understand entirely, sir,' said Deaz. He saluted and left.

Geiss stared blankly at the maps before him. He had sent men into one danger, then ordered their possible deaths before they had even set out. It was all necessary, but it didn't make giving the orders any more pleasant.

Infected or not, this planet threatened to make monsters of them all.

Polk wasn't surprised to discover that Smoker had been promoted following Munez's death, but that didn't mean he had to like it. Munez hadn't been perfect – he was an officer, and even the good ones gambled with the lives of common Guardsmen for reasons that were little comfort to the men who died because of those orders – but he hadn't been cruel or careerist, at least from Polk's lowly perspective. All officers were bastards, more or less, but Munez was less of a bastard than most.

Even if his charm had all been a front to keep the men happy, Munez's personality had kept morale up, and Emperor knows there had been times when the men had needed it.

Polk was hard pushed to see Smoker doing the same. Essler was a good soldier, even a good leader of sorts. But Polk still couldn't shake the suspicion that Smoker's decisions meant survival for Smoker and death for those around him.

Not that Polk's opinion mattered. He would serve 'Lieutenant' Essler as he had every lieutenant before him, regardless of how skilled or sadistic or useless.

Follow your command, till you die or they do. That was the Mordian way. Discipline above all.

One aspect of the Mordian way that was rapidly falling by the wayside was their uniform. In preparation for their descent into the mine, Polk and the rest of Smoker's platoon – forty or so men, mainly cleaved from Deaz's platoon – were amending their traditional blue coats with layers of protective clothing. Tape was being applied to cuffs and boot-tops, sealing off gaps for contamination, while protective black cowls were to be worn around rebreather masks. Caps were then perched back on top of heads masked by grilles and wide protective lenses.

By the time the platoon was suited up, they would all look like Smoker, struck in their officer's image.

Polk pulled on his own cowl, the thick protective fabric covering his whole head except for an oval gap for his face. Then he slid on the rebreather. Looking out through the lenses of the mask, his ears covered by the cowl, he felt detached from everything around him – a dangerous illusion for a soldier to be under.

'Test, test, test.' Smoker's voice rang in Polk's skull as if the newly minted lieutenant was barking directly into his ear. In a manner of speaking he was, every man in the platoon issued with vox-beads.

'How is this?' said Smoker at a more reasonable level, obviously prompted by the reaction of someone in his eye-range. 'Good. Men, complete your preparations. In five minutes, we descend.'

Although they were all dressed the same, masked by their rebreathers, Hool could pick out familiar figures easily enough as the platoon marched into the crew elevator that would lower them into the depths of the mine. Even if he hadn't been following the man in formation, Hool would have recognised Polk standing in front of him. There was a certain poise to the way he held his combat shotgun, disciplined but comfortable in his role, the posture learned through decades of military life.

Smoker's platoon took up a small section of the elevator, which was nothing more than a large metal platform edged with a low railing. On shift handovers, the entire elevator would be crammed with up to two hundred and fifty workers, jammed in either on their way to or from their workshift.

Smoker had rapidly briefed his new platoon over the vox as they marched to the elevator. It would descend to the bottom of the shaft, horizontally level with the target area. From there they would need to proceed through a series of tunnels to a location identified as B379, an area of exploratory mining.

It was in this area that the mine workings had broken through into some other, as yet unidentified, underground structure. From that point, it was anyone's guess what lay ahead.

The ground shifted beneath Hool's feet alarmingly. The lights above flickered as the elevator powered up, then the platform began to descend. The sound of great machinery grinding was loud even through the layers of material over Hool's ears, a deep bass rumbling that complemented the rattle of the elevator beneath his feet.

'We have seven hours and ten minutes until nightfall,' said Smoker, his voxed voice cutting right through the background noise. 'The countdown begins. Let's make it quick.'

Calway found himself press-ganged into the Imperial Guard and temporarily promoted within the space of a minute. He would have doubted this was conventional military advancement anyway, and Lieutenant Deaz made absolutely clear to him how fragile his new-found rank was.

'We need you to lead your people, Calway, and to them you'll be a corporal,' Deaz had said. 'But to my men, even the lowliest infantryman, you'll still be a common Guardsman – understood?'

Calway had nodded, making his best effort to stand to attention, something he had never needed to do before.

His recruitment surprised Calway, and he found it hard to mentally process that he was suddenly part of a military machine, a hierarchy, the discipline now required of him. It was a change to his life that he would never have sought or expected, and would have alarmed him a few short weeks ago. He had never wanted to pick up a gun, see combat, be put in a situation where the lives of others were in his hands, and where his life was constantly at risk.

In his old life, the prospect of becoming a Guardsman, submitting to military discipline and risking his life on the orders of others would have appalled him. But that life had gone before the Guard arrived on Belmos VII; he would never get it back regardless of whether Major Geiss and his men resolved the crisis and restored order.

Calway's previous existence had been destroyed, his certainties overthrown, and he had been surviving and adapting as best he could. Becoming a Guardsman, putting on a uniform, were just the next changes along. If joining the 114th allowed him to help save his home planet, even if he then had to leave with the regiment, that was fine by him. Better than fighting defensively night after night, waiting for the slip-up that let the monsters in to kill him.

His first orders, as assigned by Deaz, were to find a uniform and report to his sergeant, who would then lead a squad back to Calway's hab-tower, where the Guard planned to make one of their stands when night fell again. Calway would recruit and lead the best of his own people as part of the regiment, replacing those who had fallen.

But first, there was the matter of uniform. New equipment was not easily available, so Deaz had ordered Calway to retrieve a suitable uniform from the bodies of Guardsmen killed in the night. The bodies had been laid out in a make-shift mortuary in one of the storage buildings in the mine complex, lined up on the floor and covered with whatever sheets or tarpaulins came to hand.

Clean boots in the right size were easy enough to find, as were a belt, a cap, and other accessories. Calway pulled those off the bodies as gently as he could, piling them to one side.

Jacket and trousers were harder to find, especially in good condition.

Calway walked between the bodies, looking under the sheets and mentally measuring each man up, comparing them to himself.

He quickly moved along from those corpses with clothes that had been badly stained or torn, which was most of them: if it was even possible to 'die well', then these men certainly hadn't. Most had received severe injuries that had damaged their uniforms beyond repair, dying in pain and indignity, torn apart with bare hands, their lifeblood leaking out from gouged wounds.

Hours after their deaths, their clothes were black with dried blood.

Eventually Calway found a dead man of approximately his height and weight, whose death had not too badly stained his uniform: his neck had been snapped, and even laid out his head lolled back at an unnatural angle. There had been no open wound, though, and his uniform was pristine apart from a scattering of dust.

Calway rolled the sheet back, then carefully began to take off the man's boots and belt. Squatting over the corpse, Calway rolled the trousers down over his legs, unhooking them from the feet.

Then came the difficult bit: the body had stiffened with rigor mortis, and this man had clearly been heavy in life. Kneeling on the dusty floor, Calway unbuttoned the dead man's clothes, then rolled the body onto one side, shuffling the jacket off one rigid arm. He then rolled the body towards him, the corpse resting against Calway's knees, and rolled the second sleeve off its arm.

Finally, Calway rolled the body off him, laying it out as respectfully as he could. Thankfully the man had been wearing a couple of layers of thermal padding under his uniform, which left Calway feeling a little better about wearing it fresh-off-the-corpse, and also preserved the dead man's dignity, as much as that was possible.

Calway covered the body with the cream tarp that had been used as a shroud. It was all he could do. Last night this man had died doing his duty, and Calway had been called to take his place. Calway wondered how long it would be before he, too, was lying dead on some cold stretch of floor, his uniform and weapons to be stripped and passed to the next new recruit.

Calway picked up the pieces of his new uniform, and left the storehouse. His new life awaited him, however short it might be.

* * *

Hossk too had donned a rebreather, although as a precaution against more mundane gases. As he led a party of his troops and Stellin's workers into the sewers beneath the habs, both Mordians and miners alike wore rebreathers.

Stellin had explained that his own rebreather had served him through an entire career down the mines, a necessary precaution that had its filters changed regularly. He maintained it with a loving delicacy that Hossk associated with firearms, each component obsessively checked and cleaned.

For those who did not have their own rebreathers, a store room was raided.

Once down in the sewers, Hossk was very glad of the precaution. The sewers were adapted from an existing cave system, vast natural tunnels beneath the city that had been pierced with pipes from above then retrofitted with access gantries and lighting rigs. Although the walkways they walked along were high above the filth that flowed below, the air was thick with a dense miasma floating up from the vile flow.

One of Stellin's fellow workers, a man called Ganch, had suggested the sewers as a possible hiding place for the infected during the daylight hours. Unlike most of the surviving workers, Ganch wasn't a miner but a serf, apparently assigned to work the sewers due to some previous crime. He was a wiry man with a slight stoop, which seemed entirely gratuitous to Hossk as the vaulted ceiling of the sewer was higher than most of those above ground.

Ganch led the way as they walked in single file. The walkway rattled beneath their feet, the spindly supporting beams

disappearing into the murky liquid below. Hossk didn't like
to think of what would happen if one of the legs gave way.

'I'm surprised there's so much… stuff down here,' Hossk
said, looking down warily. 'I would have thought there
wasn't much… you know, going in any more.'

'Only flows out when the levels rise,' said Ganch, without
turning around. 'Fills up like a reservoir, only spills out when
there's enough crap and piss, or the rains come down and
sluice it all out. Otherwise, it just sits here, steaming.'

'Charming,' replied Hossk, wishing he had never started
this conversation. 'And where does "it" go to, when it
overflows?'

'Out into the sea near the spaceport,' said Ganch. 'When
they built this city-factory, there was no expense spent: crap
into a hole, let the rains wash it out to sea. Any of your men
at the spaceport?'

'A small force with the ship,' said Hossk.

'Hope they don't try swimming out there,' said Ganch. 'Or
fishing.'

Hossk wouldn't have minded seeing Tordez do either, but
the image was too bizarre for him to even contemplate.

'Here we go,' said Ganch. 'Sewer control, warm and dark.'

The structure they approached resembled a vast, rusty
wheel hanging from the ceiling of the cavern, a circular structure of corroded metal. Hundreds of pipes fed into the top of
sewer control, and a tangled trunk of piping stretched down
from its centre. The walkway on which they stood led to a
small doorway in the side of the wheel.

'No point us charging in full force through that bottleneck,' said Hossk. 'Ganch, lead the way. Weir, follow me. Everyone else hang back. If we're not out in five minutes, follow us in, sooner if it sounds like we need it.'

Ganch opened the door, which swung inwards with a rusty squeak, and he, Hossk and Weir stepped into the dark of sewer control. Hossk's finger stroked the trigger of his laspistol as he aimed it into the gloom.

The interior of sewer control was incredibly hot, and Hossk felt himself sweating into his coat within seconds of entering. As his eyes adjusted, Hossk could see that the room was dimly lit by the glow of control panels and displays around the room: the interior walls of the wheel were covered with pressure gauges and other meters, and the central hub was a cylindrical mass of control banks.

It wasn't the equipment that drew Hossk's eye, but what lay between – the rough grated floor of the room was covered in a mass of sleeping human bodies. They lay sprawled with barely a gap between them, barely stirring beyond the steady breathing of a deep, dreamless sleep.

Weir seemed inclined to back straight out of the room again, an instinct for which Hossk hardly blamed him, but Hossk gave a hand gesture to indicate they should hold their position. Hossk stepped forwards, and gave the nearest sleeper a nudge with the toe of his boot. The woman rolled onto her back with Hossk's kick, but didn't rouse, her mouth hanging open as a rasping snore emerged.

'Dead to the world,' said Hossk, turning to his nervous companions.

Ganch removed his rebreather and rubbed his greasy hair.

'The air is good in here,' said Ganch, in response to Hossk and Weir's stares.

While Weir kept his rebreather on, Hossk took the opportunity to remove his mask. His skin felt irritable and hot where the seal of the rebreather had dug into his neck and the side of his face. Taking a breath, he disagreed with Ganch's assessment of the air as 'good': there was a kitchen stench of rotting meat which made Hossk nearly gag, no doubt the exhalations of the sleepers.

'How many do you make this?' Hossk asked Weir, looking over the room. 'A hundred? More?' The curve of the room made it hard to estimate exact numbers, but it was a wide room and the sleepers were packed in tight.

Weir shrugged, but Ganch answered:

'Closer to two hundred,' said the wiry man. 'Probably around one hundred and seventy-five.'

Hossk stared at him.

'So?' said Ganch defensively. 'Just because I work down here doesn't mean I'm not good with numbers.'

'How many other places like this are there?' asked Hossk, moving the conversation on.

'None this big,' said Ganch. 'But there are numerous sub-stations and store rooms under the entire city.'

Hossk looked around at the sleepers. In their slumber they seemed harmless, and Hossk could almost have mistaken them for innocents hiding down here, were it not for the dark stains on their clothing, and that foul stench of digesting human flesh.

'Let's return to the others,' Hossk said, replacing his rebreather.

They returned to the walkway outside, Ganch resealing the door behind them.

'Prepare several incendiary charges,' Hossk told his best explosives man.

'This is a sewer – methane everywhere,' protested Ganch. 'Fire down here will spread through the entire system. We'll be burned alive.'

'Then we'll put long timers on the charges to give ourselves time to get out,' snapped Hossk. 'I want this entire system purged.'

'Not purged, wrecked,' said Ganch, one filthy hand grabbing Hossk's jacket. 'The explosion will destroy the system, entire city's infrastructure and water supply.'

'Lieutenant, is this necessary?' asked Stellin. 'If we cut off the water supply to the city we won't–'

Hossk pulled Ganch's hand away from his jacket, twisting the wrist so the little man moaned with pain, recoiling. Hossk's other hand had raised his pistol, silencing Stellin mid-sentence.

'Do I have to have both of you shot?' hissed Hossk, his voice muffled through the rebreather. 'You need to understand: this city is finished. All there is left to do is destroy the threat, whatever the damage. The Munitorum wants the mine reopened, they'll raze this place to the ground and build another one where it stood. The place will be as good as new, eventually, and none of the workers who live here will know you lot were here before them.'

Hossk holstered his gun, and removed a small white packet from his belt, waving it in front of the two civilians' faces.

'As for water, we have plenty of field purification tablets,' he said, his tone mollifying slightly. 'We boil and purify the rain. Emperor knows, there's enough of that to go around.'

Stellin and Ganch said nothing, the latter still holding his bruised wrist.

'Are we done? Good,' said Hossk, turning back to his own men. 'Set the charges.'

The elevator platform gave no warning when it was about to stop – it just stopped, pitching slightly to one side as it settled on the uneven surface at the bottom of a shaft carved through solid layers of rock. The platform was lit by tiny lights built into the cage of the elevator, so Smoker's platoon hadn't registered the change from the dark, imposing walls of rock to the total dark of a cavern as the elevator emerged into empty space before making contact with the floor.

Smoker gave the order for scouts to find and activate the nearest light source. Within a couple of minutes the loud putter of a crude generator was followed by a steady glow emerging from lights strung around the cavern, strings of bulbs that ran down the tunnels spreading off in all directions.

Still on the platform, waiting for orders with the other men, Hool looked around.

It was a man-made cavern. The exploratory tunnels that fanned out from this central space were perfectly round. Hool didn't know much about mining – he was perfectly aware he knew very little about anything, bar the inside of a hab and the life of a young Guardsman – but he guessed the initial boreholes were made with some kind of automated machinery.

It was in Hool's nature to ask questions, but he had realised pretty quickly after his recruitment by Polk that an inquisitive nature wasn't considered a good quality for an infantryman to have. He'd learned to clam up, saving his most pressing questions for when he was off-duty.

If he got the chance to talk to one of the miners, he'd want to know why the hell they bothered. To Hool, it looked like a lot of effort to make a big damn hole.

As the lights reached full power they illuminated stacks of equipment around the cavern, and a thin layer of detritus on the floor.

'Move out,' said Smoker over the vox. 'Guard up.'

Polk's squad were on the left of the group as they moved off the elevator platform and out onto the cavern floor. At close range, the scattering of objects across the floor revealed themselves to be more sinister than just industrial waste – Hool saw scraps of bloodied fabric, shattered pieces of glass and what looked like bone fragments.

Hool raised his lasrifle, training it around the curved wall of the cavern. He felt a rush of satisfaction to see that, among the equipment stored in the cavern, there sat a large piece of machinery with tracks, a driver's cabin and a drill-bit nose exactly the size of the tunnels.

Sitting down, in charge of powerful machinery, drilling a hole. In a saner life, it was what Hool might have wished for himself.

There was a movement behind the drilling machine, a dark

shape shifting in the shadow of the machinery. Sure that his eyes weren't deceiving him, Hool tapped Polk on the arm, and pointed two fingers at the machine.

Polk primed his shotgun as he spoke into the open vox-channel: 'We have movement, ten o'clock.'

The entire group began to shift their attention in the direction Polk had indicated.

'Steady,' snapped Smoker. 'Keep all angles covered. Polk, your squad, take the lead. The rest of you, hold back. No overkill. It's still the day – even the infected will be dormant.'

'Yes, sir,' said Polk, stepping forwards. With his shotgun semi-raised, he activated the external vox-caster on his rebreather.

'You there,' Polk addressed the shadows. 'Step into the light.'

The darkness coalesced into a bundle of dark robes as something huge shifted into the light. It walked on a dozen metallic legs, trailing mechadendrites behind it. Its once-red robes were black with filth, and ripped in places to reveal patches of pallid, scarred flesh, the last remnants of a once-organic human being. Once-polished augmentations were dulled and scratched, pistons creaking lazily in and out of its body.

'Chief Adept?' said Gilham, pushing through the Guardsmen to approach the creature. Polk stepped by to let him pass.

'You know this… person?' said Polk.

Hool shared Polk's disbelief. The hulking creature had fewer humanoid parts than a servitor, and seemed both monstrous and pathetic as it staggered into view. Most of the watching Guardsmen had instinctively lowered their guns – this thing looked more like a broken piece of equipment, a mining tool with human components, than any kind of threat, never mind a thinking entity.

'Only by way of someone else's memories,' said the adept, a phrase that meant less than nothing to Hool. 'This is Chief Adept Mankell of the Adeptus Mechanicus, my priesthood's most senior member here.'

There was an odd tone to Gilham's voice. Something melancholy. An unusual depth of feeling to hear through the synthesised vox-caster.

'Is he infected?' asked Smoker. No traces of sympathy there.

Gilham seemed reluctant to answer. He didn't have to.

'The infection, as you call it, only takes hold at night,' said Mankell. His voice was discordant and industrial, redolent of stuck gears and wheezing machinery. 'Even down here, we feel the transition.'

Mankell pointed upwards. 'I feel it every night, the transition of the moon. Its gravity tugs at the poison in my chest, exciting it, encouraging its spread to every fibre of my being.'

As he spoke, the Chief Adept stretched his many limbs to indicate the spread of the infection, the torn cloak hanging off him in tattered strips.

'I am the only one who ever remembers it happening. The others, they forget, in the day,' said Mankell, retracting his limbs again.

'Others?' asked Smoker. 'There are other infected down here?'

Mankell tilted his head towards Smoker, who had steadily approached the Chief Adept.

'Your face seems familiar,' said Mankell, examining Smoker's augmented head at close range. Then his head snapped back to where it had started. 'Others? There were others. I killed them in the day. We ran together at night, but began to consume each other. They were never any threat to me, even at the height of their carnivorous fervour. But I killed them anyway. It seemed kinder, to kill them while they slept, lost in their own ignorance.'

'But you were not lost, Chief Adept?' said Gilham. 'You have held on to yourself.'

'Oh, I am lost,' replied Mankell. 'The infection may only rise at night, but the madness never leaves me.'

Gilham seemed about to respond to Mankell's words when the Chief Adept thrashed out a mechadendrite, a tentacle-like metallic protuberance that whipped forwards like a loose cable, hitting Gilham in the chest. The adept was thrown clean off his feet, and Polk and Hool had to throw themselves out of the way as Gilham flew in their direction.

Hool rolled onto one knee, lasrifle up and pointing at Mankell.

'Take him!' shouted Smoker, just before he was knocked over by another of Mankell's limbs, an articulated, spiny leg that thrashed out and kicked the lieutenant in the face. Smoker's cap was flicked off and he reeled backwards, a silvery scratch gouged out of the polished black metal of his face.

Hool didn't need to be told twice, and was already firing.

Single bursts of las-fire seemed to have limited effect on the giant tech-priest, as most of his body was effectively armour, but as further las-fire cracked over Hool's head, he concentrated on targeting the areas where he had seen pale human flesh.

Whether it was Hool who managed to target a vulnerable spot on Mankell, or one of the other Guardsmen, it was impossible to tell, but a shot found a sensitive area, because the Chief Adept reared up on his many legs, bellowing in pain and rage.

'Press the advantage,' hissed Smoker across the vox. Hool glanced across the cavern to see the lieutenant crawling on all fours, gradually dragging himself up after Mankell's knockout blow.

Hool looked back to Mankell just in time to throw himself out of the way as the Chief Adept charged forwards, barrelling into the body of Guardsmen. Those who were furthest away, and had the quickest reactions, managed to spread out beyond the reach of the Chief Adept, running out of his grasp while firing in Mankell's direction with lasrifles, shotguns and the odd meltagun. The smaller gunfire seemed to just bounce off Mankell, while he ducked and dodged around the heavier firepower.

Those directly in the Chief Adept's path were trampled, slammed into the floor with a dozen spidery metal legs, or slapped across the cavern by his mechadendrites. Hool saw one man lay broken and motionless, blood spouting from where one of Mankell's legs had pierced his chest, stepping straight through him like his ribcage was nothing but wet earth. Others were flung aside great distances, tossed like dolls and hitting cavern walls with a bone-crunching impact, their bodies rolling down to the floor and disappearing out of sight.

Those Guardsmen still standing maintained the pressure, circling Mankell and repeatedly firing at him as he lashed out at anyone within reach, knocking them down or aside. A Guardsman with a flamer managed to catch the Chief Adept with a super-heated blast, and although Mankell managed to knock the Guardsman aside the tattered remains of Mankell's robes were left aflame. This conflagration only seemed to enrage Mankell further and his metallic howling echoed around the cavern.

Temporarily encircled by the Moridans, Mankell broke away again, smashing through the line and charging towards the far end of the cavern, where he jumped up onto a stack of mining equipment and storage crates. He then proceeded to drive back his attackers by throwing boxes across the cavern, six at a time, his mechadendrites reaching out, grasping anything nearby and flinging them across the cavern. Some of the boxes hit Guardsmen, while others hit the cavern floor and shattered, sending tools and component parts ricocheting around the cavern, filling the air with sharp metal items.

Before the Guardsmen could respond to this, Mankell was off again, grabbing the lighting rigging that ran around the cavern wall and running along it. His weight was far too much for the rigging to hold, and as he ran the cables came free from the wall and the lights fell to the floor, but Mankell's scurrying momentum was such that he managed to get halfway around the cavern this way before jumping across to the elevator platform, swinging off one of the support cables, and jumping across to where Hool had first spotted him hiding behind the drilling machinery.

Hool was still frantically firing, tracking Mankell as fast as he could and trying to cluster shots in the tech-priest's upper body. It was like trying to take down a tank with a laspistol – Mankell was a mess of burning machinery, but one with no clear weak spot. He just kept going, lashing out at anyone within range.

Mankell had begun to pull apart the operator's cabin of the drilling machine, stripping away barbed lengths of twisted metal to throw at any Guardsman who stayed still long enough to be a target. Hool saw Polk tumble backwards as he threw himself out of the way of a nasty-looking chunk of shrapnel. Hool heard the sergeant curse as he landed flat on his back, and began to scrabble back to his feet.

Mankell turned his attention to Hool, who was still maintaining fire. The Chief Adept began to tear off the entire hood of the drilling machine, a sheet of ragged metal with serrated edges where the pins holding it in place were torn out.

Hool's lasrifle began to fail. In the heat of the firefight he had been firing too fast, and the shots dampened to a weak splutter as the rifle's powercell began to overheat. The stream of las-fire from the weapon spluttered and died, leaving Hool repeatedly pulling back the trigger to no avail.

Mankell pulled at the sheet of metal, trying to flick it across at Hool. It was stuck, the front edge jammed beneath the rounded edge of the drillhead, the lip of which held it firmly in place. Mankell screeched and added a couple more mechadendrites to his effort, tugging at the metal to try and pull it free. The back of the drilling machine was almost skeletal now, Mankell's mechadendrites having torn away the metal shielding to reveal the inner workings. The Guard circled in closer as Mankell wrestled with the wrecked machinery, maintaining a barrage of las-fire. It didn't seem to distract the Chief Adept from his task.

Hool looked down at his lasrifle, swearing to himself. The powercell built into the body of the rifle was steaming, overheated to the point of meltdown.

'Back,' Hool snapped into the vox. 'Everyone, get back.'

Then Hool was running forwards, squeezing down on the trigger of the lasrifle. Nothing emerged from the barrel of the weapon, but Hool could feel an intense heat under his arm as the powercell overloaded.

Mankell tugged the metal cowl off the drilling machine, a sheet of razor-edged plasteel that he could wield like an axe, cutting through every layer of protection worn by the Guardsmen attacking him.

Hool threw his overheating lasrifle past Mankell, towards the exposed guts of the drilling machine. He knew very little about mining, or machinery, or any of these technical matters – but he knew that a power core contained behind a thick layer of protective plasteel probably shouldn't have an overloading powercell thrown into it.

As Mankell swung the sharpened sheet of plasteel at Hool, the Guardsman fell forwards, beneath the sweep of Mankell's reach, closing his eyes and pressing his arms over his head, his elbows down to absorb the impact as he hit the ground.

Hool landed just as the powercell of his weapon over-loaded, detonating the power core and onboard fuel cells of the drilling machine. A discharge of fiery energy rolled over his head as it consumed Mankell. The noise was horrific, a deafening blast that shook the walls of the cavern.

Hool's elbows and knees took the impact as he hit the cavern floor. He felt multiple stabs of pain through his limbs, but he kept his head down.

He stayed down for a few seconds, until the heat that he felt on his back subsided. Then he pushed himself up onto his knees.

One side of the cavern was a blackened mess, a smouldering mass of twisted machinery. The giant drill-bit remained intact, albeit scorched and tipped over to one side, but the machine that had driven it through the solid rock had been torn to pieces.

Unbelievably, at the heart of the wreckage, something still twitched. Its limbs had been blasted off, every vestigial scrap of human flesh had been burned from its mechanical skeleton, but still the bulky torso and head of Chief Adept Mankell jerked and thrashed in the wreckage, its body fused with parts of the drilling machine in the heat of the explosion.

As Hool slowly got to his feet, shaking his head to shift the ringing in his ears, Sergeant Polk walked past him, combat shotgun raised.

Polk levelled the shotgun at Mankell's head, and pulled the trigger at point-blank range. While shotguns had proven ineffectual at a distance, at close range the blast annihilated the Chief Adept's head, burning skull fragments spraying through the air in a black dust of scorched particles.

Hool looked around. The cavern was chaos. Stunned, injured and dead Guardsmen lay scattered across the entire chamber. Those still standing looked shell-shocked and twitchy.

Smoker's voice broke the stunned silence.

'Tend to the injured, confirm the dead,' said Lieutenant Essler over the vox. Hool looked across to see Smoker adjusting his cap, as if the last few minutes were a minor inconvenience.

'Ten minutes, then we move out,' said Smoker. 'Remember this, we have yet to even approach our main objective. Our day has barely begun.'

Above ground, Hossk checked his chronometer. The incendiaries should have gone off already. He was about to chastise someone for this error when the ground shook, and a nearby drain cover flipped high into the air.

The disc of thick metal flew upwards on a column of smoke and steam, Guardsmen running out of the way as it clattered to the ground nearby. Nearby vents and gutters were steaming, and Hossk could hear the muffled *crump* of secondary explosives in the distance.

Hossk had already voxed Major Geiss and the other officers to warn them about the forthcoming explosion, and to stay well away from any drains. While Geiss had not commended Hossk as such, he hadn't made any suggestion that Hossk's solution was the wrong one.

To others, what Hossk had done might be considered an extreme, even reckless solution that endangered civilians.

As far as Hossk was concerned, he had provided a simple solution to a simple problem, and if any uninfected civilians had been harmed, that was acceptable collateral damages.

What mattered was that a threat had been found and eliminated. No matter the cost to innocents, the Mordians were safer than they had been. Their mission was one step closer to being accomplished.

ELEVEN

They were first seen out at sea.

Rather than allowing the men to relax after a tense night, Tordez had ordered regular, looping patrols in addition to the sentry posts established at key points on the spaceport. The men were on alternating shifts between sentry duty, perimeter patrols and brief rest breaks.

If the men had complaints about the relentless duties, and the brevity of the time left to catch up with sleep or food, they didn't voice them.

The patrols worked their way around the top of the continuous wall that circled the spaceport. Like the rest of the facility there were no niceties, just functional rockcrete, and up on the wall there was only a waist-high barrier to protect the men from the elements. The sections of wall facing out to sea were constantly battered by waves breaking against them, spray blasting over the top, leaving the patrols soaked to the skin by the time they went off duty, doomed to waste precious downtime drying out their uniforms.

It was one such patrol that spotted them: shadows flitting over the turbulent sea, visible as much from the way their anti-gravity fields cut white-foam wakes through the surface as for their outlines, barely visible in the mist that hung over the water.

They were dark shapes in the fog, moving incredibly fast, disappearing in and out of view.

Below ground, Smoker's platoon counted the cost of their confrontation with the deranged Chief Adept Mankell.

Four men dead, three injured including the unfortunate Hervl, who now had a broken arm to go with his broken rib.

Hervl was aware he was the lucky one. The other injuries were serious. One trooper was conscious and burbling in agony from three shattered limbs, while the other couldn't be roused at all, comatose after hitting the cavern wall head-first.

Hervl, at least, was well enough to self-medicate. He'd shot pain meds into his broken arm and crudely splinted it up himself.

The platoon took a moment to lay out the dead, as a medicae tended to the seriously injured. It was a solemn moment, only broken by the wailing of the man who was awake.

Smoker, having decided they had honoured the dead enough, turned to his medicae for a report.

'Guardsman Hervl needs no further treatment as you can

see, but these two need urgent assistance,' said Avrim, the medicae. He nodded towards the elevator platform. 'Could we send them to the surface, sir? Hervl could accompany them so that we don't spare an uninjured man.'

Smoker shook his head. 'We need that platform accessible for a quick withdrawal, and I have duties for Guardsman Hervl down here. It goes up with all of us or not at all. Make these men comfortable.'

'Yes, sir,' said Avrim, turning his attention back to his patient. He applied a pain shot to the neck of the incoherent man.

'Hervl,' said Smoker, beckoning him out of earshot of the others. 'Can you still set charges?'

Hervl nodded. 'I've still got some use of my hand. Provided I have enough time, I can set anything you like.'

'Time isn't a problem,' said Smoker. 'Stay with the injured men. When we have gone, set charges on the elevator. I want you to be ready to destroy all access to the surface if you have to.'

'Why would I have to?' asked Hervl. Even in a room full of men wearing blank rebreathers and speaking through their vox-links, Smoker seemed inscrutable.

'If anything comes through those tunnels that isn't us, able and sane, blow the platform,' said Smoker.

Hervl started to protest, an impulsive reaction at what was pure suicide. Smoker cut him off before he could begin.

'Guardsman Hervl, I assure you that the major will have plans in place should we return to the surface infected,' said Smoker, speaking faster and in more detail than Hervl had ever heard. 'He will have to, for the safety of the rest of the regiment, and to ensure the completion of this mission. But I will not allow my platoon to put other Mordians in the position of having to fire on us. If we will die down here, it will be by our own hand. Do you understand, Hervl?'

Smoker mimed pressing a detonator with his thumb.

'Yes, sir,' said Hervl.

'Good,' said Smoker. 'This is between us, understand.'

Then he turned back to the rest of the platoon and started throwing out orders over the open vox:

'We move out now,' snapped Smoker. 'Hervl, stay with the injured. Avrim, leave them with Hervl. Hool, have you retrieved a lasrifle? Good, don't lose this one…'

Above, at the spaceport, the patrol voxed in a report of the shapes seen out at sea. Wary of the fate that had befallen Sergeant Frittsch, the patrol were already firing out to sea at the slightest movement and a nearby sentry point was doing the same, autocannon firing into the gloom. It was hard to tell if they were hitting anything at all, but at least the aggression of their response would not be found wanting by the commissar.

Tordez himself spent most of his time in the shuttle, which sat squatly where it had landed, a windowless hunk of ugly metal that would have seemed inert were it not for the low hum of its powercells.

The vox was received by Muumisk, Commissar Tordez's assistant, who was manning a vox-relay on the shuttle. Tordez himself was out checking on the status of the sentries at the entrance to the causeway, but had heard the echo of autocannon fire from high up on the wall.

Muumisk voxed Tordez, and passed on the details of the sighting, such as there were, and the request for further instruction.

Tordez listened to Muumisk's report while standing by the sentry point, his back to the causeway. The rain was blowing in from the opening in the wall, and running down the back of Tordez's long leather coat. He had the collar up and his cap down, keeping himself relatively insulated from the weather, as opposed to the miserable-looking Guardsmen before him – only the trooper tucked away in the Sentinel's cockpit looked protected from the downpour.

The men couldn't hear Muumisk speaking over the vox. To them, Tordez had just frozen in mid-sentence to stare into the middle distance. This suited Tordez. It didn't pay for the men to understand his every action. A good soldier was predictable, reliable. A good commissar was often the opposite, an enigma who could not be second-guessed by the men who might require his discipline.

Although seemingly calm, Tordez's mind was racing, comparing Muumisk's secondhand description to memories of battles from the recent and distant past. Tordez had been a commissar for countless decades, and there was little he hadn't seen on the battlefield. But such a long life created a deep well of memories; to try and explore them for a single salient image or moment was to sink deeper and deeper, further away from the surface of the present, not knowing when he would find what he needed.

A couple of possibilities seemed most likely to Tordez. He opened his mouth to vox a few questions to Muumisk, questions which would narrow down the possibilities.

Before he spoke, the shuttle exploded.

He didn't see where the missiles came from, or who or what launched them. There was a brief moment where lines of fire and smoke streaked the sodden sky, all intersecting where the shuttle sat at the centre of the spaceport. Where each missile hit, an explosion, a gout of flame and erupting energy ruptured the hull, tearing inwards into the ship's fabric while spilling outwards, unimpeded, into the surrounding air. These smaller explosions reached out to each other with tendrils of destruction as the hull cracked and tore and–

The entire shuttle exploded, the collective damage of the smaller explosions bringing about the destruction of the whole. A wall of flame spread downwards and out, blackening the nearest parts of the perimeter wall, incinerating any unfortunate Guardsmen or crew in its wake. Debris was thrown up and outwards with tremendous force.

Tordez was outside the immediate bloom of the explosion, but not the reach of the shockwave or rush of debris. He was hit by the hot rush of air, the jolt through the rockcrete beneath his feet. A stray chunk of hull smashed through one leg of the nearby Sentinel, causing it to topple over, the infantry sentries scattering as the cockpit smashed into the rockcrete surface.

After the explosion came silence, the temporary deafness after the blast, the white-hot after-image streaked into the vision.

Around Tordez, around all of those who still stood on that spaceport, the rain still fell in the silence, accompanied by a different shower, a gentle fall of charred black fragments tumbling back to the ground.

The tunnel leading to B379 was on a low incline, descending steadily from the main cavern to even further beneath ground level. As Smoker led the way, his platoon passed frequent evidence of exploratory digging, varying from shallow, manual scrapes in the wall to smaller tunnels leading off to who-knew-where. Some of these tunnels were lit by the same chains of bulbs that illuminated most of the mine workings, while others had been totally abandoned.

As he passed these darkened tunnels, Hool directed his torch into the darkness, searching for signs of movement, but he didn't find anything but the shadows cast by abandoned equipment and the beams bracing the less-stable tunnels.

The tunnel wasn't entirely straight, and Hool felt increasingly distant from the open cavern they had left behind, the hard stone pressing in from all directions, the light both uncomfortably dim and harsh to the eyes. Time seemed to stretch below ground, and when Smoker voxed for the platoon to halt, Hool could have been walking for an hour.

'We're here,' voxed Smoker.

From his position towards the back of the group, Hool couldn't see where the hell they were supposed to be, beyond another stretch of identical tunnel.

'On my mark, we breach and secure the immediate area,'

said Smoker. His harshly artificial voice sounded disturbingly intimate in the confines of Hool's cowled, rebreather-covered head. 'I want flares in every corner. Light it up.'

There was a brief pause. Then Smoker gave the order:

'With me. Now.'

Hool was just one man among many, following the flow. He followed Polk's back as they turned the curve of the tunnel, and then they were passing through a breach in the wall, stepping up on to a higher level.

Then they were through. Flares were being thrown out in all directions, lighting the space beyond with a fierce, flickering red light, and all around the Guard were spreading out, securing the area. Hool dropped into position with the rest of Polk's squad, fanning out into a great open space.

It was a vast area entirely unlike the tunnels of the mine. Whereas the tunnels were curved, here the floors and walls were harshly flat, and in place of the rough grey stone that the mines had been hewn from, this cavern was built from polished black stone. The light from the flares showed flickering traces of elaborate patterns carved into every surface.

Hool looked back. The hole they had walked through to get into the cavern had broken straight through a solid wall. Otherwise, the room seemed featureless, as far as the flare-light showed it, empty of furnishings or decoration. The light of the flare didn't reach high enough to show a ceiling, so Hool had no idea how high up the chamber went.

What he did have, from taking in this blank, jet-black space, was a sensation of unyielding harshness, of a brutal architecture that made the High Gothic melodrama of the

Ecclesiarchy seem relatively soft and friendly. There was something in the barbed loops of the designs carved into the walls, and the hard black stone, which made Hool feel uncomfortable.

It didn't feel like a place that *people* would build. It didn't feel human.

'Sir, we have a door,' said a voice over the vox.

'Very well,' replied Smoker. 'Let's go.'

Since detonating the sewers, Hossk had not rested, instead directing his men via vox as they explored every dark corner of the hab-towers, searching for further infected to eliminate in their dormant daytime state.

Hossk would have burned the habs to the ground if he'd had his way, doused the lower floors with chamazian and retreated to a safe distance as the inferno consumed any survivors. Unfortunately, such action required Geiss's agreement, and Geiss had vetoed the proposal, considering the destruction of the sewer system infrastructure damage enough for one day.

They were there to save Belmos VII, not destroy it, at least according to Geiss. Hossk couldn't see the conflict – as far as he was concerned the existing colony was done. Raze the city-factory and build a new mine later. It was the easiest way.

While coordinating the teams led by Weir and the other sergeants, Hossk paced irritably around the base of operations he had set up near the hab-towers, on the border of the refineries. Once the hab-hives were clear, he would send men back into the refinery. Such a place had far too many dark corners to hide the enemy.

He looked across at the hab-towers in utter contempt, just as a series of floating blurs swept overhead, indistinct shapes cutting through the wet air and heading straight for the base of the hab-towers.

Hossk could do little but watch as the indistinct vehicles fired into the side of the first couple of hab-towers, then disappeared between the buildings, out of Hossk's vision.

Although he no longer had line of sight, Hossk could still hear explosions in the distance.

Torches sweeping the darkness, Smoker's platoon moved out of the chamber, through a sharply curved archway and out into what seemed to be another dark, empty space. Some of the torchbeams caught further flat, dark walls at various junctures, but it was hard to make out the extent of the space they were in.

'Someone pass me a flaregun,' said Smoker. 'Then you can see what I see.'

Hool had forgotten the extent of Smoker's augmented senses. With the rest of the Guardsmen blinkered by the goggles of their rebreather masks, Smoker must have had an even greater advantage over the rest of them in terms of sight.

Smoker fired a flaregun. Rather than firing it out, he launched the flare directly upwards.

The red ball of flame shot up, and up... and up.

And as it rose, it cast light.

At its peak, before it began to fall again, the flare showed the curve of a domed ceiling, one which curved into the distance ahead of the Guard's position, and was well beyond the reach of a flare – by the looks of it, they were at the near-edge of a vast domed structure.

And beneath the dome was a small city. In the red glare, Hool could see that they were standing in a street between buildings, including the one they had broken into. Some were towers so tall they doubled as support columns, reaching to the domed ceiling, while others were lower-slung buildings, about five or six storeys in human terms. All were built from the same jet-black stone, their outer surface punctuated by sharp ridges and jagged ornamental spikes.

It was an entire alien city, deserted, kilometres beneath the ground of Belmos VII, an ancient city in a domed artificial cavern buried so deep that it had taken centuries for a deep-core mining operation to stumble upon it by mistake.

As the flare fell to the ground its light became too much, and Hool dropped his eyes to the floor beneath their feet.

It was then that he saw the lines of red and gold embedded in the black polished stone beneath their feet. They curved off to the left and right, parallel with the walls of the chamber, two lines, one within another.

Hool pointed his lamp down an alleyway slightly ahead. Further lines could be seen cutting across the path between buildings, disappearing beneath the walls.

Concentric circles covered the entire chamber. Hool wondered whether these were purely decorative, and if not – what lay within the innermost circle?

* * *

Calway had barely returned to Emperor's Square when the
first strike came. He had entered the lobby of the main hab-
tower with a number of Deaz's men, ready to induct the best
of his own people into the Guard and begin the process of
fortification, when a tremendous explosion came from the
square, blowing out the few windows that had survived previous assaults.

Looking out onto the square from the shelter of the
lobby, Calway could see the wreckage but not the cause: the
statue of the Emperor at the centre of the square had been
blasted to rubble, and the smaller statues around it had
been similarly flattened. Chunks of metal and stone were
strewn across the entire square, while nearby buildings had
smoking, broken facades from where hot wreckage had
blasted into them.

If this wasn't distraction enough, the conscript Plymton
came running down the stairs to find Calway, stumbling
and nearly falling down the last few steps in his eagerness
to reach him.

The urgency with which Plymton approached suddenly
stalled as the boy saw Calway's Guard uniform, and didn't
seem to know what to say.

'Spit it out,' snapped Calway. 'This better be important.'

'We're losing people, Mr Calway,' said Plymton.

'Has the tower been hit?' Calway asked.

'No, not losing people like that,' said Plymton. 'They're disappearing from inside the building. There's shouts and then
they're gone. Desap thought he saw a shadow drag away
McGurty, but they just vanished.'

Calway blinked at Plymton a couple of times. The boy wasn't the brightest spark, but he was no liar or fantasist.

What the hell was going on?

The reports came in from around the city-factory, from Hossk and Calway and others, but at the centre, where Major Geiss received these voxed reports, all was quiet.

Looking out over the mine from the main gallery, Geiss saw no sign of activity at all – he had watched the lift with Smoker's platoon descend beneath the ground, the great chains grinding through the towering, skeletal machinery that plunged deep beneath.

Since then, not a movement, just the sound of orders being barked to Guardsmen, of preparations being made for the assault that the night would bring.

Then the reports came in. Explosions. Disappearances.

Anyone exposed, out on the streets, was in danger of attack from above.

Anyone indoors was in danger of being snatched by… who knew what.

No one had yet seen their attackers. It wasn't consistent with the capabilities or attack patterns of the altered, infected, *whatever* humans. The reports didn't fit with anything that had happened on Belmos VII so far.

It was at the exact point where Major Geiss thought things couldn't get any worse that Tordez's voice broke through onto the command vox-channel.

* * *

Tordez and the survivors from the spaceport, of whom there were less than a dozen, were running down the causeway towards the city-factory gates. They were under no illusions that they were successfully escaping trouble – over the city walls, fires and smoke could be seen pluming from the city-factory's towers as they fell under attack – but knew that there was no point remaining at the spaceport.

At best, there would be nothing left for the Guard there, and they would achieve nothing.

At worst, the attackers who had destroyed the shuttle would come back to finish any stragglers.

So they ran, Tordez in the lead, towards the city-factory. So far, there was no sign of pursuit as they ran down the thick strip of rockcrete, but that didn't encourage them to slow down.

As he ran, Tordez repeatedly tried the vox command channel. With the relay on the shuttle destroyed, his range was limited, and they were halfway across the causeway when he got a weak, broken signal. He didn't hesitate to communicate his message, as clearly as he could:

'Tordez to Major Geiss, Tordez to Major Geiss,' said the commissar through shallow, ragged breaths. 'Shuttle destroyed, repeat the shuttle has been destroyed by unknown attackers. Withdrawing to city-factory now.'

Tordez took a couple of deep breaths before speaking again. The vox was silent.

'Major Geiss, please confirm message received,' Tordez said.

'Message received, commissar,' said Geiss. His voice

sounded weak and distant. That could have been the strength of the vox-signal, but Tordez wasn't so sure.

Some would say that Geiss was right to take the news as a blow. Geiss's strike force were under attack from forces unknown, their numbers dwindling by the hour. They had many hours of the day to go, at which point the night would bring fresh attacks from their known, but equally dangerous, foes.

It was a doomed situation, getting ever worse. Stronger officers than Geiss would have cracked by now, fallen to despair.

Tordez, for his part, was just getting interested. He had seen hundreds of battles in his time, to the extent that they blurred into each other. But the current situation had novelty.

Running from a flaming wreck towards a warzone, from one devastating threat to another, Commissar Tordez was almost beginning to enjoy himself.

The air was full of light.

As Smoker's platoon moved through the streets of the underground city, they steadily realised that the torches they carried were becoming increasingly unnecessary, in spite of a thickening mist in the air. There was a light being cast, but the source was hard to identify.

It was Gilham who made the connection.

'The light is in the air,' he told Smoker. 'There's a steady flow of particulates in the air, and they're emitting a low level of light.'

'Flow?' said Smoker. 'Where from?'

Gilham pointed towards the centre of the chamber. The buildings were getting lower as they moved closer to the centre, and as the platoon switched off their torches, an eerie glow could be seen haloing the buildings. It wasn't a white light, but one of indeterminate, shifting colour.

Hool waved a gloved hand in front of his face. Even through his rebreather lenses, he could see a trail of light behind his hand as the particles were disturbed.

'There's the source of our infection, I'll bet,' said Polk as he watched Hool playing with thin air. 'Not something you'd want to breathe in.'

'The carrier, perhaps, sergeant,' said Gilham. Hool and Polk hadn't realised they were on open vox-channel still. 'But not the source. That, I expect, lies ahead.'

'Let's find it, then,' said Smoker impatiently.

As they moved closer to the centre, the thickening mist was accompanied by a noise. At first, Hool thought it was his own breath echoing within his rebreather, or one of the other men breathing into the open vox-channel. Slowly, he realised the noise was muffled, but steadily rising, a rhythmic noise in the cavern itself, stirring the air back and forth, the glowing particulates in the mist pulling away and then pushing back.

A tide rolling in and out. Hadn't Mankell mentioned something about the moon and the tides?

The thought was curtailed as they turned the final corner, and saw what was at the centre of the city underground, the heart of the cavern. The source itself.

At the centre of the chamber, where the buildings and

structures stopped, the concentric circles on the floor began to tighten, each a short distance above the outer circle, forming a raised dais in the centre of the cavern. On this central raised platform sat the source, towering over the tiny Guardsmen below, sprawling out in all directions.

It was a *mass*, of some sort. A shifting, pulsing, breathing thing, parts of which seemed metallic or glass, others seemed meaty and fleshy, flushed with the red of mammalian tissue, while other parts seemed to have the thick, inert green-brown matter of a plant or tree. It had gills that hissed out the glowing mist; pulsing, beating protuberances, transparent tubes and flat surfaces. It was rooted, tendrilled and huge, huge beyond the size of not only any living thing that Hool had seen, but anything he could imagine.

The Guardsmen of Smoker's platoon spread out around the bottom step that led to the dais, guns half-raised, not sure what to do. There was a wide enough area for them to move out into, so they fanned out, transfixed, looking up at the *thing*.

Was it a creature, a machine, or some heretic or alien's demented idea of a god?

Hool tore his eyes off the thing, and saw that even Smoker and Gilham seemed stunned into silence.

It was Polk who broke the silence with the pertinent question of the moment.

'How do we kill *that*?'

The shuttle destroyed. Diminishing troop numbers. Invisible enemies firing death from above, stealing people in the shadows. A noose tightening around the city-factory, encircling the mine at the heart of the city but not yet squeezing in.

Major Geiss needed to stop, to focus. He was, so far, not under attack. The action was elsewhere, but his command centre was quiet. He needed to use this advantage, to take stock.

There had been no sign of activity outside the city-factory when the *Seraphim* entered Belmos VII's orbit, and any enemy landing since then would have been detected by the ship. This raised a disturbing possibility.

The vox-caster in the gallery was sufficiently powerful to reach the *Seraphim*. Geiss ordered the vox-operator to contact the ship. There was no response. It was possible that atmospheric interference was disrupting communications, but equally that the *Seraphim* had already been destroyed without anyone on the world below even noticing.

No ship, no escape. That seemed to be the scenario, and there was no use speculating any further. Geiss needed to take charge. To lead his men from afar.

This is what he had trained for. This was what he had *wanted*, the chance to prove his leadership abilities.

An unseen enemy, an unpredictable scenario. It was in such circumstances that great leaders emerged. If he was to become the man he wanted to be, Geiss had to seize this moment.

He closed his eyes, raising the vox-caster to his lips, his thumb hovering over the stud that, when pressed, would transmit his voice to his troops across the city-factory. His lips were dry. He ran his tongue over them, breathing deeply.

He thought back to the plans of the city-factory he had first looked at when planning this operation, then in his mind he overlaid this flat, stable image with the reality of the planet as he had found it, and then added onto that the various details of the emerging situation: abductions in the hab-towers, the burning shuttle.

He opened his eyes, pressed down the vox-stud and spoke quickly:

'This is Major Geiss to all men of the 114th. I want everyone off the streets, now. Those of you already indoors, gather together, provide cover for those retreating from the streets, join into as large a group as you can, move from building to building. Cover the windows, cover the dark corners. Observe, report, and if you get a clear shot, *destroy*. I want heavy weapons in key spots looking for these fliers, and I want teams turning over the interiors until they find these lurkers.

'Whoever is attacking, they have the element of surprise, they want us in chaos, but we will not let them break our line. We are unbreakable, and we will meet their cowardly attacks with an unflinching gaze and iron discipline. It is they who will fail, they who will reveal themselves and they who will be eliminated.

'You are men of the 114th Mordian Iron Guard, the Unbreakable Regiment. No enemy has broken us yet, and no enemy ever will, not any day and certainly not today. Geiss out.'

Geiss released the vox-stud. The strategy was sound. He

had faith in his men to carry out his orders, to regroup and strike back.

He hoped it would be enough.

Tordez heard Geiss's message over the command vox, and approved. It was a sound strategy, and the men needed to hold their nerve.

The great gates of the city-factory were still open, and as Tordez reached the end of the causeway he ran straight through, a dozen men on his heels. He skidded to a halt on the wet rockcrete, and began to bark orders at the men before they were even through the gates.

'Find the locking mechanism, I want these gates closed. You, get to the nearest sentry point, watch the spaceport. If anything lands on that pad I want to know about it.'

He tossed out a few more orders, all to the end of securing the city-factory gates and keeping the spaceport under guard. The men ran off in various directions to fulfil these orders, some still wheezing from the sprint across the causeway, all of them determined to do whatever was needed of them.

Tordez needed that determination from them now. He didn't believe that destroying the lander was just a shock tactic, or a way of cutting off the Guard's route off Belmos VII. No, Tordez was certain that the spaceport was needed, that it had been cleared to allow another vehicle to land.

Tordez remembered another world and enemies in the dark. A population in chains, a desperate attempt to prevent those souls being lost. An attempt which had failed, the enemy vanishing in shadows, their captives damned, spirited away, the cruel laughter of their inhuman captors ringing in the ears of the defeated Imperial forces.

Tordez would be damned himself before he let that happen again here.

The clouds broke above the centre of the city-factory.

In the main gallery of the mining complex, Major Geiss stopped his pacing, distracted by the sudden bright shafts of sunlight over the mine. He looked out of the windows, up through the crisscrossing scaffolding of the mining machinery, but all he could see was the glare of a rarely-seen sun.

Major Geiss hoped this was a good portent, that it signalled a change in the fortunes of his strike force. Then, in that moment, his thoughts were on the success of the mission, of the survival of his men.

What Geiss couldn't see from down below was the vast shape that had scattered the clouds, a ship like none mankind had ever constructed. It was a city in the sky, barbed with bristling towers and spires, its form twisting into cruel spikes, its surfaces black and unyielding. It would have been a graceful vehicle if its creators had minds less encumbered with unremitting cruelty.

On the bridge of the vessel, under high-vaulted ceilings, the ship's commander sat on a throne of twisted silver, one tapered forefinger rubbing the corner of his thin, cruel mouth, while his other hand lolled idly over the arm of his throne, swishing through the air in a gesture of studied, long-practiced boredom.

'Archon,' said a masked and robed figure standing a respectful distance behind the throne. 'The charge is ready.'

'Will this work, Zekov?' asked the creature on the throne. His voice was musical, but discordant.

'This is the area of least obstruction, archon,' said Zekov, flexing his knuckles within gauntlets covered in blunt barbs. 'A single charge should clear a descent lateral to the Lung. From there we–'

The noble dismissed Zekov's elaborations with a careless flick of his wrist. His underling's explanations irritated his tender senses.

'I am fully aware of the strategy,' said the archon. 'Did I not devise it myself? Dispatch the charge. Let us be done with this.'

Zekov nodded respectfully, even though he was out of his archon's line of sight, and relayed the orders.

'Charge fired,' said one technician.

A single shot was fired from the alien ship, a ball of light that rolled from the underside of the vessel, hurtling straight down, gravity carrying it to a precise spot at the centre of the mining complex.

White-hot tendrils tore through everything in its path, disintegrating all around it. It landed directly on the main mineshaft, spiralling as it fell, a wake of destruction spinning outwards.

The structures built over the mineshaft just disappeared, as did the buildings surrounding the mine. Major Geiss, stood in the main gallery, was consumed in an instant, blasted to atoms, his thoughts still consumed with the threats to his men, unaware that he himself was even under threat. He and everyone in the control centre died, instantly and cleanly. Where the blast radius stopped, it stopped, with no outward shockwave, buildings that crossed the edge sliced clean through, the outer sections intact.

Lieutenant Deaz and the majority of his men were out of range of the blast. They could do nothing but shield their eyes as the sphere of energy tore down through the centre of the complex.

The ball of energy didn't stop at ground level, but kept descending, following the path of mineshaft B371 but creating a wider, smoother hole, consuming all human constructions in its path as it dug, deep down into the solid rock of Belmos VII.

On the bridge of the alien ship, a report was whispered into the ear of Zekov, who tilted a withered head surrounded by bony protuberances as he listened. He whispered further instructions, then stepped back towards the throne, his extended spine flexing as he silently shifted across the floor.

'My archon,' said Zekov. 'The charge was successful. We are moving to the landing site now.'

'Very well,' said the archon, stirring from his throne and getting to his feet. 'Have my armour prepared, and ready my Raider for planetfall.'

At these words, servants withdrew into the darkness of the ship.

Archon Kulkavar, scourge of a thousand worlds, the

damnation of a billion human souls, let a cruel smile pass across his thin lips.

'Let us seize this treasure from the mon-keigh, so ignorant of the glory hidden beneath their feet,' he said to Zekov, his haemonculus. 'Then we will unleash its power on their Imperium, and see the worlds of man stripped of their souls for our pleasure.'

TWELVE

As Smoker had instructed, Hervl was setting a series of small explosive charges on the elevator. It was painful, slow work with only one fully working arm, with Hervl fumbling to connect remote-controlled detonators to each charge, then stick the charge where it was required. As he went about setting charges on weak spots in the chains supporting the elevator platform, Hervl's work was initially accompanied by the background noise of an injured Guardsman wailing in his delirium.

Eventually the noise ceased. Hervl didn't stop to check why the Guardsman had gone quiet. There was nothing he could do for the man.

When the last charge, which Hervl had fixed to the elevator's main control panel, was set, he walked back to the front of the platform and sat down, staring at the tunnel down which the rest of the platoon had marched. The platform was almost exactly thick enough for Hervl's legs to dangle comfortably a little distance off the cavern floor, so he sat there with the remote detonator in his hand, the trigger covered by a safety cap. All it would take would be to flick back the cap and press a button, and the elevator would be scuttled, detached from the chains that lifted it and its control panel wrecked.

Hervl hoped it wasn't going to be necessary. He wasn't a man to think about things much, but he knew he didn't want to doom himself in the depths of the mine. He would rather the decision were taken out of his hands.

His wish was granted. Hervl had the barest awareness of a light from above, and a crackling in the air tickling his scalp, before the ball of energy ploughed down into the cavern, consuming everything in one last burst before dissipating. Hervl, the injured Guardsmen, the body of Mankell and everything else in the cavern disintegrated as the infernal sphere burnt itself out.

Then there was silence in the expanded cavern, only broken by the trickle of debris tumbling down the vertical, open shaft that the dark eldar weapon had gouged through the dirt of Belmos VII.

On the surface, Lieutenant Deaz and a handful of his men approached the edge of the crater. The mining complex was in ruins. With a hole blasted through the machinery that had clustered over the mineshaft, the sections of those structures that had survived the blast were left unstable, twisting and rocking. Many had already collapsed. Where the blast had sliced through buildings and structures, the sutured edges were white-hot, and the rim of the crater glowed with lava even in the daylight. The air was filled with steam as a thin drizzle of rain made contact with the burning ruins, evaporating instantly.

Deaz felt a vertiginous swirl as he looked down into the endless hole before him. He shook the feeling out of his head and tried the command vox-channel, but it was consumed with interference. Reporting Geiss's death to the other officers would have to wait. Deaz had better luck with the local vox for his platoon, getting a static-filled, but usable, signal.

'All survivors to the main compound gates,' shouted Deaz over the vox-static. 'We're withdrawing to Emperor's Square.'

Geiss was gone, but his strategy still held. They would make a stand in Emperor's Square.

As for Smoker and his platoon, hopefully they would destroy whatever had caused this mess in the first place. Either way, there was no need for Deaz and his men to wait for their return.

There was no way back to the surface for that platoon now. Infected or not, those men would die down there, and there was nothing Deaz could do to either help or hinder them.

Tordez swore. It was a rare indulgence of externalised emotion for the impassive commissar, and he nearly swore again in self-disgust.

From the walls of the city-factory, Tordez had direct line of

sight to the spaceport. He had produced a pair of field bin-
oculars from one of the many inner pockets of his regulation
leather coat, and even with a thin fall of rain obscuring the
view he could see what was going on out there.

He had thought that the black, twisted shape of the craft
that landed in the scoured patch left by the destruction of
the shuttle was of a familiar aesthetic sense, but had hoped
that he might be wrong. When a landing ramp lowered and
the first honour guard of slim, chitinously armoured figures
marched out, all doubt was dismissed.

Dark eldar. It was confirmation of their presence that had
produced a rare curse from the old commissar, who had
encountered these creatures before. A branch of the eldar
race, they combined the heightened senses of their species
with the cruelty and malice of Chaos. Pirates, sadists and
slavers, they sought the souls of others to prolong their lives
and defer their own damnation.

Most of the enemies of man would only kill you once. The
dark eldar were not so kind, consuming their captives' souls,
a destruction that went beyond the mere death of mortal
flesh.

The vox was nothing but static, presumably a result of
the flash Tordez had seen as the dark eldar ship flew over
the centre of the city-factory. All he could do was watch the
enemy, and hope for some sign of their intent, some clue as
to their objectives and how they might be defeated.

Kulkavar stepped out onto the surface of Belmos VII in his
full armour. Curved black shoulder pads edged with gold

jutted out, tapering to wicked points. A half-cloak of deep blue covered his right side, while at the opposite hip hung a great barbed blade. His right hand, his sword hand, was covered in the same chitinous black armour as the rest of his body, articulated at every knuckle so as to not impede his sword grip. The armour was so deeply polished it had a deep blue glow.

On his left hand Kulkavar wore a ceremonial hellglaive, a powered glove with bladed fingers that would tear apart any opponent who dared step within range of the dark eldar noble. A thick cable slunk from Kulkavar's left elbow to a powercell in the back of his armour, tucked beneath the half-cloak.

It was part of Kulkavar's personal vanity, the aura of fearlessness he sought to create, that he went into battle bare-faced, with a maskless helmet that tapered to a red plume and which was held in place by gilded cheek guards that joined at the neck.

Kulkavar turned his face to the sky. A billion drops of moisture fell above him, and he took in every one. Each drop that touched his face was an unwelcome sensation, scraping his heightened eldar senses as if each drop were sharpened, but he suffered the sensation, and that suffering gave him a dark pleasure.

A billion raindrops falling, one for every human soul that the Lung would bring him.

A billion? A conservative estimate. A billion would be the beginning.

The haemonculus Zekov followed Kulkavar at a respectful

distance, as he always did. Zekov was waiting for his archon to dismiss the honour guard who had lined the spaceport to greet their kabal leader, three dozen dark eldar warriors in their seamless black armour, weapons respectfully raised.

Kulkavar hadn't noticed their presence until Zekov's reticence drew his attention to them. Their gesture of respect and submission broke his moment of self-contemplation. Kulkavar waved them away dismissively, and they broke ranks and began preparations for the attack.

Zekov finally stepped into his master's presence. His armour was tighter and less ornate than Kulkavar's, part battle gear and part protective coverall, the bloodstained workclothes of a master torturer. Beneath his clothing he was thin, almost skeletal, and over his face he wore a sculpted deathmask, the mouth contorted in torment.

'Zekov, what progress?' Kulkavar asked.

'The advance landing party have had great success, my archon,' Zekov reported. 'The Raiders have driven most of the humans into hiding, while the soulsnatchers have already gathered many slaves. The Lung's effects appear to have reduced the human population considerably, so it should take little time to gather the survivors and acquire the Lung itself.'

'Very good,' said Kulkavar, his tone indicating that Zekov's performance in this respect was, at best, adequate. 'You have the Ear?'

'Of course,' said Zekov, bowing slightly as he produced a small wooden box from his robes. The gnarled limbs that emerged from his spine flexed with tension as he held the box.

Kulkavar looked down at the box. It was crude, chipped at the edges and lacking elegance, but its significance…

'My glory rests in your hands,' Kulkavar told Zekov. 'Take Veldrax's warriors, and bring me the Lung. I will oversee the subjugation of these vermin personally.'

'Very well, my archon,' said Zekov, bowing again.

While the two dark eldar had discussed their battle plans, further ordnance and troops had been deployed onto the scorched rockcrete of the spaceport.

A Raider transport hovered bulkily nearby, the sybarite Veldrax and his black and red-armoured troops already on board. Veldrax himself stood at the prow of the anti-grav vehicle, a gold streak on his helmet indicating his status, his dark lance resting on the vehicle's railing. Veldrax saluted Kulkavar as Zekov boarded the Raider, and then the vehicle rose, hovering for a few seconds before moving away in a blur of motion, its anti-grav engines utterly silent.

With Zekov and Veldrax dispatched on their mission, and his own command Raider nearly prepared for departure, Lord Kulkavar looked into the grey sky once more, and idly wondered whether they had been pursued to Belmos VII.

No matter. Kulkavar's objective was in his sights. Any obstructions would be swept aside without mercy, and made to suffer for their impertinence in the process.

Gilham wasn't surprised when, in spite of the best efforts to amplify vox range, Smoker's vox-operator had no success in making contact with the surface. Gilham's augmented vision had allowed him to watch his own connection to

Major Geiss's command channel fade and cut out as they descended through the many levels of the mine.

Following the confrontation with Chief Adept Mankell, it had not occurred to Gilham to check any vox-channels beyond the limited loop of Smoker's platoon. He had been absorbed in his own thoughts, disturbed that psychosis had taken possession of such a senior member of his own priesthood.

On Elisenda, Lord Brassfell had requested in private audience that Gilham act as courier for any confidential communication Mankell wished to transfer to his superiors within the Adeptus Mechanicus. Gilham had no idea what such communication might have been, but felt a bitter regret that he would not be able to fulfil Lord Brassfell's request. Instead, he would bear bad news.

These concerns had blunted Gilham's ability to observe his surroundings, as had the sight of the alien city and the... thing at its centre. If he had paid more attention, stretched his abilities to observe his environment on multiple spectra and frequencies, he might have noticed *it* earlier, rather than having to be told by an unaugmented vox-operator.

'There's a signal cancelling out any long-range communications, sir,' the vox-operator told Lieutenant Essler, after much effort to connect to Major Geiss on the surface.

And once he had mentioned it, Gilham could not fail to hear it – it was everywhere, undetectable by human hearing, but a broad-range signal of incredible power, an unidentifiable alien pattern transmitted in a loop. He could not decipher the message it transmitted – some form of encryption far beyond Gilham's understanding had been applied – but its brevity suggested something simple.

A beacon, calling out into space, requesting help or announcing its position.

'Can you not hear it, Lieutenant Essler?' Gilham asked.

Essler looked at Gilham but didn't reply.

'Your augmentations should allow you to tune in to the signal,' said Gilham, still speaking on the audible vox-spectrum. 'Here, I will connect you.'

It was a simple matter for Gilham to relay the alien signal to the augmented sensory array built into Lieutenant Essler's skull, the implants that Gilham had placed there himself when he augmented the injured Essler, saving his life.

Gilham was surprised when Essler not only rejected the relayed transmission, but strode towards Gilham, pushing aside Guardsmen standing between them.

'Do not get into my head, adept,' said Essler, his synthetic voice rippling with distortion and feedback. The lieutenant shook his head as if trying to shake something off his scalp. Essler looked straight at Gilham. 'I am not like you. I did not choose… *this*.' He waved his free hand around his head in an expansive gesture.

There had been limited contact between Gilham and Essler since the adept had saved the Guardsman's life all those years ago. This was not a matter of evasion, at least not on Gilham's part, it was simply that their roles within the regiment rarely came into contact. Gilham had barely considered the augmentations he had made to Essler that day, but when he did it was with a certain pride – they were complex augmentations, and Gilham had relished their intricacy, and he had done all this while saving a man's life.

It was only now, watching Lieutenant Essler turn on his heel and redirect his ire towards the Guardsmen who were failing to provide a solution to the destruction of the alien artefact before them, that Gilham realised that the augmentation of the flesh, the sacred enhancements of blessed machinery elevating the weak human body, might not be considered such a gift by those outside the priesthood.

Following Geiss's last orders, Calway had brought together as many of his people as he could, along with the Guardsmen in the hab-tower, and gathered them on the fifth floor. The slim, well-lit apartments of that floor were eminently defensible, providing the enemy did not mimic Polk's squad and come crashing through the walls from an adjacent building.

If they did, Calway's people would at least hear them coming, and whoever these attackers were, a loud assault did not seem like their style. Instead, they attacked from the shadows, silently taking people away. The only sign of their presence was an absence – a paradox that Calway found unnerving, especially after weeks dealing with an enemy that attacked with feral, direct force.

A rough headcount suggested that perhaps three dozen people had gone missing during the day. The people in the hab-tower had become used to counting each other in and out at the start and end of the day, and Calway saw no reason to doubt these numbers as they were reported to him. They had also become used to living in smaller and smaller sections of the great hab-tower as their numbers dwindled, and so there was no shortage of unused rooms where the enemy might be lying in wait or dumping the bodies of their victims.

That's if there were bodies to be buried. If the infected citizens had mutated or evolved in some way, allowing them to operate in the daylight hours and with greater intelligence, then they might just be picking off uninfected citizens one-by-one and consuming them whole. Another thought to make Calway unhappy.

Calway was soon called over to a window by Plymton, where he found out that his presumptions and guesses were all wrong, but the truth made him no happier.

At first, Calway wasn't sure what he was looking at. From this elevation, all he could see was a line of his own people shuffling out into the square, although they did not seem to be coming from any door to the tower. Looking closer, he could see that they were connected with some kind of chain, a black thread linking each man or woman to the next, neck-to-neck. They looked dejected, heads bowed, the odd limb twitching as if the owner were recovering from some unknown trauma.

Then Calway saw their captors. They had hidden in the shadows before, but were now out in the open. The rain had thickened to a steady shower, obscuring the details, but Calway could make out lithe, inhumanly thin figures wearing black body armour. They had tapered helmets and curved weaponry, rifles of a kind Calway had never seen and twisted blades.

Their movements, the way they walked, made Calway feel ill: while strangely graceful, these creatures moved differently from humans, their body language entirely alien. Their camouflage removed, they looked fearlessly out across the square, aloof to even the possibility that any humans might threaten them.

'Shall I take the shot, sir?' asked Plymton, who had taken his old sniping position by the window. The lad had taken to referring to Calway as 'sir' since he discovered Calway had been inducted into the Guard, even though Calway hadn't made any move towards recruiting Plymton into the ranks.

'Hold your fire,' said Calway sharply, remembering the last time Plymton had fired on an unknown enemy. 'We don't even know what these things are.'

It wasn't long before Calway found out. He was trying vainly to vox Major Geiss and report the sighting when Tordez answered instead.

'Take cover!' Tordez shouted, running down the staircase leading to the city-factory walls three steps at a time. 'Back from the gate, take cover. Prepare to fire on my command!'

As he reached ground level, the men were already scurrying into position behind refuelling posts, a squat guard station and the other functional structures that clustered around the city-factory's main gates. Tordez had shouted the order the moment he saw the dark eldar anti-grav vehicles rolling out onto the spaceport – an assault couldn't be long in coming. He had seen those things move before, and knew they were fast.

Tordez took position behind the staircase, pointing his pistol at the gates, his gun-arm resting on the wet metal step. Ice-cold rainwater began to seep through the gap between his sleeve and glove, chilling his skin, but Tordez ignored it. He was banking on his presumption that the dark eldar, having flagrantly landed their ship in the most obvious place, would make no attempt to breach the city-factory's walls from an unexpected angle, but would take the direct route across the causeway and through the gates.

In this, Tordez was entirely correct. The gates exploded in a plume of dark matter, colourless energy tearing through the metal and twisting the shredded remains back on themselves, a hot shower of fragments blowing back into the city-factory.

Tordez briefly ducked his head down, protecting his eyes and face from the blast, then quickly raised his gaze again, hand tightening on his pistol, waiting for the attack.

Instead, the dark eldar vehicle that swept through the ruins of the gate tore past, heading straight down the central access road to the heart of the city-factory. If the crew even noticed Tordez and the other Mordians gathered around the gates, they did not stop to open fire or take any interest at all.

The vehicle moved so quickly that it was out of range before any of them could think of squeezing a trigger.

Through the gap between the metal steps, Tordez could see the men breathing sighs of relief, unclenching from their firing positions. Tordez remained concerned. The dark eldar were greedy, cruel enemies who descended on the nearest prey without mercy. For them to act with such purpose was very bad news.

The position at the gates was lost – there was no point in trying to hold it further. Tordez ordered the men to follow him, and began the quick-march retreat into the heart of the city-factory, keeping off the main access roads and staying in the shadows as they headed into the darkness of the refinery and Hossk's last known position. They only had a few hours left until nightfall, and the Guard needed to regroup as best they could before facing both enemies at once.

While trying to vox any available officer, Tordez found himself talking to Calway. Tordez didn't recall the name, but then it wasn't his business to know every man in the regiment.

'Put me through to the most senior officer you can find, man,' Tordez ordered the moment he realised that he was speaking to a newly seconded civilian. He had no patience for wet recruits now.

'Sir, with all due respect the most senior man here was Sergeant Allend, and he has been taken captive by the enemy,' said Calway.

'Never mind,' snapped Tordez. 'Why are you on this vox-channel, Calway?'

Calway explained what he was looking at.

'Those things are eldar,' said Tordez. 'Xenos of the most corrupt kind, and they have support transports heading into the city-factory now. You must not let them take those slaves away, Calway.'

'Sir?'

'Free the slaves, Calway, or ensure that they are not taken alive,' said Tordez. 'You must not let the souls of the Emperor's servants fall to the xenos filth, even if you have to obliterate their bodies to do so. Do you understand?'

THIRTEEN

The Raider carrying Veldrax's squad and Zekov swept through the streets of the human city unimpeded. Suspended on an anti-gravity field, the Raider moved with equal speed over flat roads and scattered rubble. A gunner sat behind the dark lance mounted at the vehicle's prow.

Zekov gripped the railing, crouching slightly so as to not break the aerodynamics of the Raider as it moved directly towards the centre of the human city-factory. A handful of blue-jacketed humans leapt out of the way as the Raider reached the perimeter of the mining complex at the heart of the city, but the warriors on board ignored them – others would scoop up these valuable souls. The eldar on board the Raider had another objective.

As the Raider approached the crater surrounding the open hole the dark eldar had burned through the existing mine-workings, the pilot shouted for all on board to hold tight.

Zekov braced himself against the inside of the Raider's armoured carapace. The pilot was the finest in Lord Kulka-var's kabal, entirely capable of the feat of anti-gravity steering he was about to engage in, but that did not mean it would be an easy ride.

As the Raider reached the lip of the crater, the pilot killed the forward anti-grav thrusters, causing the rear of the vehi-cle to suddenly elevate at a forty degree angle. By raising the back of the vehicle well above the level of the front, the pilot ensured that it fell nose-first into the abyss.

The Raider fell straight down, the relentless grip of gravity aiding its descent. As it fell, the Raider drifted close to the sheer rock wall of the shaft, at which point the pilot briefly fired the anti-grav thrusters, causing the Raider to spin away before it made contact. Before it could hit the opposite side of the well, the thrusters fired again.

The friction between the anti-gravity fields and the wall slowed the descent of the Raider as it fell, turning a fatal descent into a controlled ricochet. It was a skilful demonstra-tion of piloting, but not a comfortable ride. Zekov felt like he was being pulled apart, spiralling forces tugging him in many directions at once. The haemonculus and Veldrax's warriors clung to whatever they could to prevent themselves being thrown out of the Raider by the gravitational whirlwind.

Zekov had calibrated the charge that drilled this shaft him-self, and it was precisely calculated to burn itself out at the level required. As the Raider reached the bottom of the shaft the pilot performed another series of quick-fire anti-grav bursts that flipped the Raider the right way up, then slowed their descent to the floor of the cavern below into a gentle drift.

The gravity reversal required to turn a near-freefall into a graceful descent was so severe that it caused an upwards wave of excess anti-gravity force, lifting the dark eldar on board the Raider from the deck. Zekov felt a shuddering wave of lightness tremor up through his body as they came to a halt.

The pilot cut the engines, and the Raider landed fully. Normal gravity re-asserted itself.

They had landed in an artificial cavern, littered with debris. A number of tunnels, far too narrow for the Raider to traverse, branched out in all directions.

Veldrax's warriors had been trained to make planetfall in slim drop-ships from which they were expected to emerge fighting, far rougher descents than they had just experienced. They marched off the Raider the moment it hit the dirt, awaiting the haemonculus's instruction.

Zekov stepped down onto the cavern floor. Warmth drifted up through his thick boots, afterglow from the dissipation of the charge. The haemonculus opened the wooden box that Lord Kulkavar had presented him with. He lifted it close to his face, not just looking under the lid, but listening.

After a few seconds, he snapped the box shut and pointed to a tunnel.

Veldrax nodded, and the warriors moved out.

* * *

At the dark eldar's intended destination, Smoker's platoon had found that while their objective was easy to locate, destroying it was another matter.

The... thing at the centre of the alien city was remarkably hard to damage. Las-fire didn't scratch it. The mist hanging in the air dampened explosives, so that large detonations inflicted minimal damage. Direct physical assaults on the living machine, either from melee weapons or shots from a lasrifle, resulted in injuries which rapidly healed up – a thick yellow fluid pumped out of the wounds, rapidly drying and hardening. By the time that crust was smashed away, having hardened to a rock-like consistency within seconds, the damage underneath had been entirely repaired.

Hool had both watched and participated in the attempts to damage this thing. In line with its hybrid appearance, it seemed to have the unthinking solidity of a machine and the survival instinct of a living thing.

After all the Mordians' attempts, its bulk loomed over them, pulsing, undamaged, an ethereal light shimmering across its surfaces.

Most of the Guardsmen were left to patrol the perimeter of the central platform while Smoker argued with Gilham and his sergeants. Hool took a position not far from where they were 'debating' the options, where he could watch one of the 'alleyways' leading between the 'buildings' of the underground city – although, as most of those buildings didn't have any visible doors, they could have been sculptures or machinery for all Hool knew.

Even through the muffling effect of the protective headwear

the Guardsmen were wearing, Hool could hear Gilham and Smoker's part of the conversation, as they were using their external vox-casters rather than a private vox-channel. That Smoker seemed to be raising the tempo of the conversation in his frustration just made it easier to follow.

Hool could understand the lieutenant's frustration. They were the Unbreakable Regiment, renowned for standing resolute in the face of an onslaught. Here, they found themselves thrown against a seemingly immovable object, something they couldn't shoot or blow up. Hool found himself strangely reassured by the argument, partially because it demonstrated that Smoker had some feelings left, that he was capable of doing something as human as losing his temper. It reassured Hool that the lieutenant wasn't entirely a machine.

The argument, and the uncomfortable need to not react while superiors let their tempers get the better of them, also provided a welcome distraction from thoughts of the thing they had come to destroy. Its presence unnerved Hool. He had spent a year under alien skies, walking alien soil, but always in the presence of human artefacts, of buildings and machinery constructed by humans for their own use. Even if the specifics of the Elisendan factories or the Belmos VII towers were novel to a Mordian hab-rat, the scale of these places was comprehensible to Hool.

This *thing*, this living machine, was of another order of strangeness altogether. Its shape, scale and substance didn't fit with anything in Hool's experience. Its sheer alienness made his skin crawl, and he tried not to look at it.

So he looked away, concentrating on his duties, maintaining line of sight down the 'alleyway' facing him. No one expected them to be disturbed – since the Guard faced off against Mankell they hadn't seen any signs of life, just the odd scrap of debris from the recent human intrusion into the alien city – but the duty in itself was a welcome distraction for Hool, a useful focus for his attention.

It was this level of concentration that allowed him to see it: a flicker of movement in the distance, a shadow darting between one of the alien 'buildings' and another, a brief disruption of the misty air across the alley.

It was a brief flurry of motion, but Hool caught it. He dropped into the cover of the nearest building, leaning around the corner with his lasrifle aimed down the alley.

Others might have doubted their eyes, but Hool knew he had seen something. Not taking his eyes away from where he had last seen movement, he tapped his vox.

'Movement sighted,' Hool hissed.

It was Polk who responded first, running to the other side of the alley and taking a mirror position to Hool.

'Where?' Polk asked, cocking his combat shotgun.

'About one hundred metres,' said Hool. 'It crossed the alley. Not entirely visible.'

Smoker broke in over the vox, transmitting to the entire platoon:

'Possible incoming from the mine,' said Smoker. 'Form a perimeter, keep your eyes open.'

In Hool's peripheral vision he could see Guardsmen dropping into position around the edge of the platform, facing out into the alien city, looking down the alleys and byways, searching for signs of movement.

'Got something…' said a voice over the vox. 'But it's gone again, sir. Whatever it is, it's fast.'

Hool caught another glimpse of movement ahead, closer this time. As it broke through the thicker mist closer to the centre of the city, Hool could make out an outline: a figure too tall and too thin to be human, a spindly, almost insectoid figure reeling with athletic grace through the mist before disappearing behind another building. He felt a rising bile, the same unease he felt while looking at the machine thing on the platform, a revulsion against the unclean, the alien.

'Sighted again,' Hool snapped into the vox. 'Humanoid, but I don't think it's human.'

'Fire at will,' said Smoker.

When the slim figure broke cover again, Hool opened fire with his recently acquired lasrifle. Although it was the same standard manufacture as his previous lasrifle, there were subtle differences in the firing: the previous owner, now deceased, preferred a looser, well-oiled trigger, which made for quicker, but less precise, bursts of las-fire. Hool's first shots went wide and the lasrifle bucked uncomfortably in his grip. His target spiralled behind a wall on Hool's side of the alleyway with precise, graceful movements.

The shots at least lit up the alleyway, and gave Polk a clear view of the intruder: from Polk's position on the other side of the alleyway he had a clearer line of sight to where the intruder was hidden. As Hool hastily adjusted his grip on the new lasrifle, Polk fired a couple of blasts from his combat shotgun in the direction of the intruder. The shotgun fire echoed like thunder in the empty streets of the underground city, then there was a moment of silence.

'Did you hit it?' asked Hool.

'I'm not sure…' said Polk, peering down the alleyway, a haze of gunsmoke further reducing visibility.

If there was any doubt as to the alien creature's intent, it was dispelled by the returned gunfire from its hiding position. There was a sharp crack from down the alley, as the air was sliced by a projectile cutting through the space between the creature and its human assailants.

Polk was mostly in cover, but not quite. Hool watched in horror from the other side of the alleyway as Polk reeled back, collapsing to the ground in a motionless pile.

'My warriors have encountered humans,' said Veldrax. He stated this without alarm, but as a matter of general interest.

'Hardly unexpected,' replied Zekov. He didn't look up from the contents of his wooden box. 'Who else would have disturbed the Lung and activated its signal beacon?'

'They are surrounding the Lung itself and presenting armed resistance,' added Veldrax. The sybarite and the haemonculus were standing close to the perimeter of the underground city, letting Veldrax's warriors scout ahead.

'Destroy them,' said Zekov. Then he thought again, and snapped the wooden box shut. 'No heavy weapons,' he added. 'We cannot afford to damage the Lung. Contain the humans, kill them if you can, but do not risk the Lung. Soon, we will be able to eliminate them at leisure.'

While Veldrax relayed the order, Zekov turned his attention back to his box, opening it to hear the whispering from the object within. It was calling out to its kindred technology, whispering on many different levels: audible, technological, psychic. Zekov listened closely to the communication, letting it guide him. As he did so, a map of the city formed on the surface of his mind, with a number of positions illuminated as markings of variable strength: there was the burning, resonant presence of the Lung at the centre of the city, and the smaller presence of the thing in the box.

Then there was a third presence, dormant, but ready to be woken.

It was closer to the centre of the city, a few streets from the Lung itself. Nodding for Veldrax to follow him, Zekov ran into the depths of the city.

Hool was about to dash across the mouth of the alleyway to check Polk, when his superior stirred, hands idly reaching upwards from where he lay.

Hool had exchanged fire with the shooter a couple more times since Polk went down, neither hitting the other. The enemy's ammunition seemed to be brittle rods of a crystalline material that shattered when they hit a solid surface, spraying razor-sharp fragments.

Two days ago, Hool thought he was getting to grips with life in the Guard. Now, he realised he knew nothing. Rebels and traitors were only the beginning of the threats to mankind.

Hool was about to make a run to help Polk up, when he got a sharply ordered word over the vox.

'Stay where you are, don't break cover,' said Smoker in clipped tones. Hool looked across to see the lieutenant running across to Polk's position.

Another crystal shard narrowly missed Hool's position. He fired another burst from his lasrifle, but the alien had disappeared into cover again. Hool could hear gunfire from across the chamber, and a scatter of reports over the vox – the enemy were approaching from all sides, sneaking between the buildings, edging towards the centre of the city and the alien machine-thing.

Hool looked across to see Smoker examine Polk's head and upper body.

'Glancing blow to shoulder, some shrapnel. Flak took most of the impact, jacket shredded but not reached skin. Knocked over, hit head,' said Smoker, cocking his head. 'Avrim, man down, possible concussion. Be careful with shrapnel, could be poisoned.'

As the medicae came running, head low to try and dodge enemy fire, Smoker raised his hellgun, while still concealed from the enemy's view by the wall he was flat against.

'Hool, draw his fire,' said Smoker.

Hool nodded, and as Avrim leant over the fallen Polk, Hool made a more ostentatious assault on the enemy position, stepping out into the alleyway and launching a wide volley of las-fire down the alley. When he stopped firing, he lingered out of cover for a couple of seconds.

Tempted by the open target, an armoured figure leaned around the corner of the building, a slim, squared-off rifle with a wickedly sharp blade beneath the barrel carried in both hands. The creature's armour was polished black with dashes of red, the curved helmet topped by a plume of long red hair. It had the bladed rifle raised, pointed directly at Hool's head.

Three shots from Smoker's hellgun caught the thing square in the chest and it reeled back, gracelessly keeling face first into the ground.

'Hool, with me,' ordered Smoker, and before Hool knew quite what he was doing he was running behind Lieutenant Essler, who was dashing for the fallen enemy's position. Hool swept his lasrifle around all the possible lines of attack as Smoker dropped to his knees and started tugging at the dead creature's helmet.

'Know your enemy,' muttered Smoker through the vox, and Hool was unsure whether that was advice or just Smoker thinking aloud.

Hool moved his lasrifle back and forth. They were on a crossroads between buildings, with three directions to cover: left, ahead, right. Behind them, the alley led back where they had just been, to where Avrim was trying to revive Polk.

Smoker made an unintelligible synthetic hiss and Hool couldn't help but glance down to see what had raised this reaction. What he saw was the dead creature's head, exposed with the helmet removed.

It had the same basic features as a human: eyes, nose, mouth, even hair in the normal place, but the proportions were *wrong*, the head too long, the mouth too thin. Even in death the dark, glassy eyes disconcerted Hool with the depth of their gaze. In contrast to that darkness the skin was papery white, deathly and fragile.

'Xenos,' said Smoker. 'Eldar.'

'You've fought these before?' asked Hool.

Smoker shook his head. 'No, but have heard–'

He broke off to pull his hellgun to his shoulder and fire past Hool. Hool looked down the side-alley to see a couple more eldar dropping into cover, raising their rifles.

'Back,' said Smoker, pushing Hool in the direction of the platform, encouraging him back towards their earlier position. Hool didn't need further encouragement to get away from the dead eldar and its uncanny stare.

Zekov tried to ignore the repetitive *crack* of splinter fire as he searched for an entrance to the tower. It was a slim, black column of a building that overlaid ring thirteen, only a short distance from the central platform and the Lung. Veldrax's warriors were steadily advancing on the humans' positions around the Lung, while also driving back any humans who ventured away from the platform. At the periphery of Zekov's vision he could see two warriors firing at enemies outside his line of sight.

In spite of the thunderous report of gunfire being exchanged, Zekov's mind was clear, almost meditative, as his fingers traced the carvings on the sheer black wall before him. He found a square section that moved slightly under his touch, and pushed it firmly inwards. There was a click, and a large section of wall slid almost soundlessly into the floor, revealing a darkened stairwell.

'Stay here,' Zekov told Veldrax. 'Do not step outside concentric twenty,' he said, indicating the gold rings that ran around the floor of the cavern. Zekov indulged himself with a cruel thought. 'However, if you can drive the humans beyond that point, do so.'

With that instruction, Zekov left Veldrax below and climbed the stairwell in the tower. The walls began to emit a gentle glow as Zekov ascended the narrow steps, and the haemonculus could feel a growing agitation from the wooden box. The steps were steep and bare, carved from the same black stone as the rest of the tower, each step protruding from a central column that ran up through the entire tower.

The chamber at the top of the tower was square and unfurnished, and dominated by the mechanism emerging from the centre of the floor, a mechanism that extended its tendrils down through the tower's central column and into the ground below. It didn't have any visible controls, but instead splayed out into a series of jagged spurs of machinery linked by blade-sharp wires that crisscrossed the room.

Zekov opened the wooden box, and the wires sang, the outcrops of machinery flexing hungrily. Zekov gently removed the ovoid object from the box.

They called it the Ear because of its capacity to hear its maker's other creations from the farthest distances. It was an egg-shaped device seemingly made of panels of polished crystal, held together with seams of brass and tipped at each end with polished wood. The Ear was far heavier than it initially appeared, and seemed to shift its shape and colour imperceptibly.

Zekov had – on the occasions when Lord Kulkavar let it out of his possession – studied the Ear intently, but still knew little of its purposes, or how it worked. He had, however, seen it *squirm*, bulging and twisting in a way no device of inert matter ever should. With Kulkavar's acquisition of the Lung, Zekov hoped to study the two together, to learn more about both of them.

For now, Zekov needed the Ear for another purpose, to bring the Lung out into the open. Careful not to touch the wires, which vibrated with excitement, he reached between them to hold the Ear at the centre of the mechanism, then carefully lowered it. The spurs of machinery closed inwards, gripping the Ear in a precise embrace.

Zekov let the Ear go, allowing the mechanism to hold it in place. The room was coming to life, the parts of the machine slowly beginning to rotate, the wires cutting across each other in an ever-shifting mesh.

It was ready for instruction.

'Rise,' said Zekov.

A shimmer of activity passed through the mechanism, and vibrated down the central column of the tower, the floor shaking beneath Zekov's feet.

In the distance, he could hear great gears begin to grind.

To Hool's relief, Polk was conscious, slightly wired even due to whatever Avrim had injected into the sergeant to bring him round.

'I'm all right,' protested Polk, his voice muffled and breath-less through the vox. 'Knocked the wind out of me, tap on the head, nothing serious.' He flexed his arm in its socket experimentally. 'Bloody hurts though.'

Hool imagined it did. The shot from the eldar weapon had hit Polk in the shoulder, breaking against the overlap between the seam of the body armour he wore under his coat and the reinforced pack-strap. That accidental armour had prevented the shot seriously wounding Polk, but the impact had been enough to flip him backwards. The slug, or whatever it was, from the eldar rifle had shattered on impact, and fragments of crystal had torn through his coat in a wide radius, thankfully without breaking the skin.

'Wish I could take a proper look,' Avrim told Smoker, flicking his finger between Polk's face and his own to indicate the rebreather masks they were all, Smoker aside, wearing. 'But it seems you were right. Concussion, bruising. He'll be fine.'

There was a cry over the vox as another man went down. Smoker nodded and Avrim ran off to deal with the latest injury.

'Back to work, sergeant,' said Smoker. The lieutenant had been crouched down next to Polk, who was sat up against a wall, and was halfway into a standing position when the ground shook beneath him, causing Smoker to hastily adjust his footing.

Hool, who was down on one knee, was thrown to the side and had to extend a gloved hand to steady himself. As his palm pressed against the stone floor, he could feel a steady vibration transfer through his wrist and up his arm. The jolt twisted his wrist in an uncomfortable direction and he jerked his hand away, shaking his hand straight.

'What now?' said Smoker, voicing Hool's unspoken question. Even boosted by the vox, effectively transmitted straight into their ears, his voice was muted beneath a growing rumble that accompanied the vibration.

Hool got to his feet, carefully to compensate for the constant juddering, and looked around, trying to find any visible source. He could see a rain of displaced powder falling from the cavern ceiling above, but no evidence of heavy machinery, beyond the thing on the platform nearby, and that seemed to be exactly the same as it had been since they got there, with no sign of increased activity.

Then Hool felt his feet moving apart. He looked down and saw that his booted feet were on both sides of one of the gold lines that circled the platform, the concentric rings that worked their way through the city.

Either side of the line, the floor was rotating in different directions. It was a slow movement, but the two sections were definitely moving against each other.

'Sir,' shouted Hool, pointing downwards. Smoker followed his gaze. 'The ground is moving.'

Polk suddenly rolled forwards, away from the wall that Avrim had propped him up against. He scrambled to his feet, staring up at the building he had been leaning on. A shower of black dust was falling down the side of the structure, which was visibly shaking even compared to the shifting floor.

'It's retracting into the ground,' said Polk, his voice dizzy with disbelief. 'It just started pulling downwards.'

Hool looked down to the base of the building, which did indeed seem to be retracting into the floor, a deposit of black dust building around its base as the rock surface retracted.

'No,' said Smoker. 'I don't think it's sinking.'

His head was tilted upwards. Now it was Hool's turn to follow the other man's gaze.

Above them, the curved ceiling of the cavern was getting closer, but also shifting, moving outwards, a space opening in the centre of what had seemed an entirely solid body of rock only minutes before.

The platform at the centre of the city was beginning to move upwards, and the rock above was beginning to part to allow it access.

Hool shook his head. 'No, it can't possibly... We're too far...'

Before Hool could even complete that sentence, a tiny pin-prick of light glittered unfathomably high above them.

Daylight.

As the chamber began to change, Veldrax led his dark eldar warriors on the offensive.

As the platform rose, slowly taking the Lung to the planet's surface, the outer areas of the underground city would collapse, the rest of the cavern falling in on itself as the central section was removed. Veldrax was determined to drive as many of the humans as he could past concentric twenty, the outer limit of the safe area, where they would be crushed to death.

Kulkavar would have his prize, and the humans would be buried.

The humans were in disarray: unlike Veldrax's warriors, they had no doubt been unaware that the city, once a bustling laboratory complex, had such an elaborate capacity for self-destruction.

Now was the time for the warriors to press this advantage. As the central section of the chamber rose above the buildings, those buildings began to crumble, their ancient stone structures falling to pieces. The rational lines of the underground complex were transforming into something else, a rubble-strewn maze of scattered ruins.

Veldrax's warriors moved through this landscape in a pincer movement, intending to drive the humans away from the Lung, back into the depths of the city. Most of the humans would die by splinter fire, while those who did not would be ground to paste.

Either outcome would satisfy Veldrax.

Betrayed by the very ground beneath their feet, Smoker's platoon had drifted into disarray. As the stone floor shifted around them, it had levelled out at the centre: the raised platform which bore the alien machine, and the stepped levels coming down from it, had flattened out to become part of the far larger platform that was rising towards the surface. With the terrain around them changing, the Guard were left reeling from every new change, running from the shadow of a collapsing building, staring at the opening far above.

They had forgotten they were among enemies.

It was Polk who brought them back to their senses, although initially he was more severely disorientated than any of them. A broad patch across his shoulder ached from where he had been shot by the eldar. The back of his head smarted from where it had hit the stone floor, and his senses were dulled by the shot Avrim had injected into Polk to bring him round. His tongue felt fat and heavy in his mouth, the air within his rebreather mask stale and nauseous.

The last thing he needed in such a state was for the entire environment around him to shake and shift. Staring up made Polk feel sicker still, so instead he bowed his head, closing his eyes and letting the rumble of shifting stone fade to a distant rattle, allowing his body to shift in time with the vibrations rather than fight against the motion.

Deep breaths, focus, let the nausea settle. Polk focussed on an imaginary point of calm, a bright, white glow. It was a training exercise he'd been taught many years before. Imagine the endless dark, and the light at the centre, like the darkness of the universe, with the Emperor's light on Terra shining out to guide mankind.

Polk was not a deeply religious man, but the thought gave him comfort. Centred, he opened his eyes, looking straight ahead.

The first thing he saw was the shadow of an eldar warrior creeping out from behind a large block of jet-black stone.

'Incoming!' shouted Polk into the vox, raising his shotgun and letting loose a blast in the direction of the eldar. The creature ducked back out of sight as one corner of its cover was blown away in a shower of fragments.

Rivez and Zvindt were the first to react to Polk's call. They had been separated from Polk and Hool as the platoon spread out in a cordon around the alien machine, but now they came running from the opposite direction as Polk approached the stone block, lasrifles raised, moving in on the same target.

Before they could close in on what Polk hoped was a cornered eldar, a separate attack came from behind Rivez and Zvindt: two eldar warriors emerging from a ruined building, their rifles blazing. Polk could see a couple of unprepared Guardsmen falling to the floor, long splinter rounds piercing their bodies.

Before Rivez and Zvindt could turn around, the older man was shot in the back. Polk could do nothing but watch as a crystalline shard emerged from Rivez's chest.

Zvindt, quicker and younger than Rivez, turned faster, his lasrifle firing, but the eldar who had shot Rivez at near point-blank range ducked lithely under Zvindt's shots, a long leg spinning out to kick Zvindt in the guts. The kick made contact and Zvindt staggered backwards, but by now Polk had the eldar in his sights. He was about fire his combat shotgun when a hand on his shoulder suddenly pulled him backwards.

More toxic crystals narrowly missed Polk's head as he was jerked backwards. Hool, who had dragged Polk out of the line of eldar fire, leaned past him to let off a couple of shots of suppressing fire, his lasrifle shaking and firing wild as Hool lifted it with one hand, the butt tucked under his right arm to keep it steady. The las-fire went as wild as would be expected, but it was enough to keep the eldar back for a couple of seconds. They were emerging from the cover where Polk had just spotted them, firing on any Guard in sight.

The air was thick with las- and splinter-fire as Polk gently shrugged off Hool's grip and stepped into line next to him, firing on the eldar who had killed Rivez and was on the verge of plunging the curved bayonet on the end of his splinter rifle into Zvindt's throat, the young Guardsman having been backed against a wall by the eldar warrior, his lasrifle knocked to the ground. Polk's shotgun blast caught the black-armoured eldar sideways, tearing apart the armour on his right arm and causing the alien to reel away from Zvindt.

Zvindt dropped to the ground and swept up his lasrifle, but the injured eldar had already disappeared into the shadow and another was stepping out, firing at Zvindt. The shots went wide, but only gave Zvindt enough time to retreat to Polk and Hool's position.

Polk, Hool and Zvindt rejoined the rest of the squad as they hurriedly backed away from the incoming eldar, who were intermittently emerging from the broken buildings and rubble to fire on them. They were being driven away from the alien machine, back into the crumbling remains of the alien city.

As his warriors drove the humans away from the Lung, Veldrax moved back to where he had last seen Zekov. Lord Kulkavar would be displeased if Veldrax failed to protect the haemonculus, more so if he didn't protect the little wooden box in Zekov's care.

The entrance to the tower was gone, disappeared beneath the rising floor. Veldrax circled what little remained of the slowly disappearing tower – perhaps two storeys at most remained above the stone floor – but could not find any other door or window.

Veldrax was considering how to explain this when the building crumbled away. It did not collapse into chunks of masonry and stone as the others had, but melted into black dust, as if consumed by some inner force.

Zekov stepped out of the building as it disappeared around him, the box in his hands. Veldrax glimpsed a hint of something behind the haemonculus as he walked through the disappearing walls, a flurry of liquid machinery, but it was gone.

'The humans are being driven back,' said Veldrax. 'The Lung will soon be ours.'

'Then the archon will be pleased,' said Zekov.

FOURTEEN

He fell from the sky without fear.

First there was the starship. It was a small, sleek vessel of white-gold, and it broke the atmosphere of Belmos VII, hiding within thick cloud cover as it flew over the city-factory, avoiding detection by the dark eldar forces below.

The small ship's target was the opening a short distance from the city-factory's walls. On the ship's bridge, the opening ground had created a flurry of readings, as the Lung's distress signal and strange energies became ever more visible as the layers of rock and dirt between it and the surface of the planet parted.

In the ship's landing bay, a single occupant strapped himself into a silver landing capsule. It was a customised device based on salvaged parts, and he hadn't steered such a vehicle before.

However, he was confident he could pilot it successfully, as he was confident in most things. As the bay doors opened, the capsule's occupant flicked a series of runes, and a hololith displayed the terrain below in rough lines of red and green, a crude visualisation of the surface outside the windowless, featureless capsule.

The target area was displayed as a flashing blob, shifting lines indicating the relative position of capsule to target.

When the lines came together to point directly down, the capsule was launched from the ship, a release mechanism propelling the capsule straight out of the bay doors.

The ship itself hit its thrusters as soon as the capsule had dropped far enough to not be incinerated by the blast. Within seconds it had escaped the atmosphere of Belmos VII, retracting to a secure position on the dark side of the planet's moons to await further instructions.

The capsule fell. Below, ancient machinery was clearing the capsule's path, creating an open shaft down which it could fall directly to its target landing zone.

Before it could land, the capsule's occupant needed to avoid being smashed to pieces against the walls of the shaft, or flying wide and burying himself in the muddy ground of Belmos VII.

Thrusters around the edge of the capsule allowed for subtle adjustments in its course. The occupant grasped twin joysticks, rubbing the switches which would activate the thrusters. On the battered pict-screen before him, the shaft below was a target in the centre of the display, a target that shifted as the capsule was buffeted around by the winds of Belmos VII's turbulent atmosphere.

At the corner of the screen, the numbers indicating the distance between capsule and target got smaller and smaller as the rocky ground approached, gravity pulling the capsule inexorably downwards. While the thrusters allowed some adjustment of its descent, the capsule had no capacity for directed flight. There would be no second chances, no opportunity to bank away and take another pass.

The pilot gritted his teeth as he steered the capsule towards its target, a relatively tiny hole in a vast expanse of hard, rocky ground.

Smoker had regrouped his platoon, but they were being steadily worn down, driven back by the eldar assault. There was no opportunity to go back and help any injured or isolated Guardsmen: the eldar had pushed Smoker and his men away from the alien machine and back into the semi-collapsed ruins of the alien city.

They were moving in the opposite direction to the side of the city they had entered, into a graveyard of broken buildings and rubble, and Smoker's men took what cover they could, emerging to exchange fire with the relentlessly advancing eldar. Under Smoker's constant commands they had formed a tight group, trying to hold the line, to step back no further.

Beneath their feet, the floor continued to steadily rise.

Hool was at the forefront of the action, ducked behind a jagged tooth of polished stone. Peering around the corner, he had a clear view of the area surrounding the alien machine. The mists had cleared a little since the ground started shifting, and Hool could see across to the ruins all around the perimeter of that open central area.

The eldar seemed to be everywhere – sniping from the top of a high wall in the distance, or firing close-range shots as they spiralled from one piece of cover to another. They were fast and agile, hard to target. It was near impossible to tell how many there were, but Hool was sure he had seen the same dented eldar helmet appear from different directions a short time apart. It was far too easy to imagine that they were moving swiftly behind cover, firing from different vantage points to exaggerate their numbers.

Hool found himself almost wishing he was fighting the feral humans from the previous night. They were fast and deadly, but at least they were direct.

A shard of crystal struck close to Hool's head, shattering as it hit the edge of his cover. He rolled out of harm's way as fragments ricocheted off the black rock surface, and made a low run for a narrow wall behind which Polk was sheltered. Hool threw himself over the wall as heavier fire smashed chunks out of it, landing in a crouch on the other side.

Steadily, the eldar were driving them back. Crystalline shards impacted all around the surviving Guard, who could barely emerge to take a single shot as their cover was gradually eroded and compromised.

Hool realised that, without some kind of game-changing bit of luck, they were finished.

Within seconds of Hool having that thought, before the horror of that realisation had curdled in his stomach, the silver sphere fell from above.

It was a dance.

In spite of the grip that She Who Thirsts had on his soul, and the souls of all his warriors, Veldrax still had the sensitivities of an eldar. He could see the beauty in the way his warriors weaved between positions, keeping a pressure of constant fire on the humans, emerging from new angles which gave them line of sight on the savages even as they sheltered behind diminishing cover. The warriors weaved a complex pattern through the ruined streets as they moved, like the steps of some elaborate formal dance, moving around each other's positions without colliding.

It was a dance, a beautiful dance of death, and its grace was utterly disrupted by the silver ball that fell from the sky.

The pilot of the capsule had no time to breathe a sigh of relief as his vehicle dropped precisely into the opening shaft. The forces that were carving a path between the cavern deep below and the surface of the planet were still at work, widening the breadth of the passage and holding back countless tonnes of displaced dirt and rock that threatened to fall back in and bury whatever was at the bottom of the pit.

If the capsule hit the sides, those forcefields would rip it to shreds, compressing the slivers into the walls of the shaft itself.

As the capsule fell down the pit, the pilot gently tapped the thrusters nudging the capsule from side to side, constantly recalibrating its trajectory to avoid any contact. All the while the countdown to the bottom of the pit shrank, the distance being reduced both by the capsule's rapid descent and the slow rise of the area at the bottom of the pit.

The numbers spiralled downwards from two hundred to one hundred to fifty...

He hit a release, just as the capsule emerged from the shaft into the cavern below, and felt the entire capsule jerk back as chutes were ejected, slowing the momentum of the capsule in its final descent. The capsule began to spin, spiralling as a rapid descent turned into a slower tailspin.

The capsule's pilot braced himself for impact.

The silver ball dropped into the cavern directly above the Lung, but as silver chutes burst out of the capsule and slowed its descent it curved off course, spiralling down towards the eldar position.

Veldrax cursed, shouting an order to his warriors. Zekov was already running, his frail-looking limbs and twisted body moving with surprising speed. The eldar had been keeping out of sight by moving back and forth behind a long, low stretch of largely undamaged building.

When the silver capsule hit the floor of the cavern it did so at an angle, bouncing slightly and rolling straight into that building, smashing through the wall and sending chunks of black stone flying.

Veldrax and his warriors cautiously withdrew from their

attacks on the humans, hastily finding deeper cover as the silver capsule settled in the rubble. Veldrax found Zekov at his shoulder, the haemonculus staring straight at the silver ball.

'That is not our technology,' said Zekov.

The impact of the silver capsule was felt across the cavern, even over the background vibration of the rising floor. Hool had watched its crash with horror and fascination, unsure as to whether its arrival was good or bad news.

'Cover that thing,' said Smoker over the vox. The lieutenant, at least, was not optimistic.

The occupant of the capsule monitored the life readings in the immediate area with interest, noting the relative positions of the eldar and human groups.

This would require some quick manoeuvring.

The capsule steamed from the heat of atmospheric entry, and crackled with energy from the dents where its internal mechanisms had been damaged on impact. The chutes that had helped its descent had fallen around it, giving the ruined buildings a surreal appearance of elegant sophistication, covered in shining fabrics.

Two dark eldar warriors approached the capsule, keeping themselves largely to cover behind broken walls, but keeping their splinter rifles aimed directly at the capsule. Cautious, stealthy. Nothing would sneak past them.

When the capsule opened, it was not a subtle attempt to evade detection. A square hatch, its outer lines camouflaged in the filigreed surface of the capsule, burst outwards with a colossal outrush of white vapour.

The occupant of the capsule wasn't far behind it. In his pure white robes he seemed to coalesce from the gas rather than simply emerge from it, a tall human male whose floor-length vestments were complemented by several finely crafted, highly polished pieces of golden armour plate: a breastplate, shoulder-pads, greaves and gauntlets. The last of these provided support for his lower arms as he wielded a pair of ornate bolt pistols. His head was covered by a clear-fronted brass rebreather helmet with vent-grilles at the sides of the neck.

His pistols were aimed before he even emerged from the smoke, and spat fire at the two dark eldar warriors before they had time to react. The left-hand bolt pistol fired its payload straight into a dark eldar's head, where the bolt exploded within the alien's skull, scattering fragments of brain matter and shards of armour plate. The bolt pistol in his right hand fired a bolt straight into the other dark eldar's chest, causing him to fall backwards, blood from a cavernous wound trailing through the air as the corpse hit the ground.

Further dark eldar warriors opened fire from safer positions, but the man was already moving, striding backwards while returning fire, circling the crash site of his capsule and heading towards the Mordian position. Eldar fire peppered the ground around him but he weaved from side to side as he moved, providing an unpredictable target.

Continuing to exchange fire with the dark eldar, he broke into a run.

* * *

Hool had never seen anything like the man in gold and white. He moved with the lethal purpose of a killer, and clearly knew how to handle a weapon, but he didn't look or act like a soldier. There was a looseness to his actions that showed no sign of military discipline, of weapon drills and correct postures.

'Hold your fire,' ordered Smoker as the newcomer ran towards their lines.

As the man approached, Hool got a better look at him. His chest plate was engraved with an ornate cross over the body of an aquila, the wings of which spread towards his arms. The clear-faced helmet revealed a narrow hollow-cheeked face, tanned and weathered skin contrasting with ice-blue eyes and short silvery hair. His gaze was impassive, his small mouth set in a near-pout of displeasure.

He holstered one bolt pistol, and while still firing on the eldar position with the other weapon, he used his free hand to produce an amulet from his robes, which he held high for the men to see. The same design displayed on his breastplate was embedded in the amulet in jewels and fine metals, clear enough to be visible from several metres away.

'I am Inquisitor Felip Velasco of the Ordo Xenos,' the man declaimed, sweeping the amulet from side to side so that all could see it. 'The Imperium is gravely threatened, and you will all follow my orders to avert this threat.'

FIFTEEN

––– *From the Inquisitorial record of Felip Velasco
of the Ordo Xenos.* –––

It was as approbator to Inquisitor Montiyf that I first heard, or to be more precise *read* the name Dalson Graath. It would be many years before I truly understood its significance.

As Montiyf's acolyte I engaged in all aspects of inquisitorial duties, but my role as part of Montiyf's retinue was that of translator and linguist, due to an affinity for both written and spoken languages. In between more active engagements I was tasked with translating alien texts, documents and so forth, scouring them for intelligence that might provide a strategic advantage.

The threat we pursued lurked on the fringes of the Pious Worlds, a string of tiny planets orbiting a cold star. The worlds were so named because of the piety of the communities who inhabited them, who led lives of meditation and

331

deprivation, hard work and prayer beneath a thankless, dim sun.

The people of the Pious Worlds used the only resource of any value available to them to create items for trade – the hard, rock-like wood from the scattered trees that managed to survive on these worlds, a pallid, almost translucent substance of great, albeit bleak, beauty.

The wood could only be carved with slivers of rock chipped from the walls of their primitive dwellings, and they spent their days shivering in their caves within the stunted mountain ranges that scarred the Pious Worlds, carving idols of the Emperor and other items of devotion, their gnarled hands scarred from years of gouging cold stone into unyielding wood.

These carvings were then exported off-world to penitents across the Imperium, fetching high prices on distant worlds, very little of which trickled back to the poverty-stricken sculptors, who sold them in bulk for tiny sums to continue their subsistence.

I found their gestures of faith rather feeble. The God-Emperor in His majesty is a fact of the universe, and I very much doubted these crude tokens were of interest to Him, nor the ostentatious humility of their creation. To serve the Emperor of Man is a noble thing, but to do so in symbolic gestures and ritual, rather than through defending the Imperium against its aggressors, seemed to me to be entirely without value.

If the Emperor looked upon these people at all, He did so in agreement with my position, as He did nothing to prevent the dark eldar raids that plagued the Pious Worlds. They struck repeatedly across the system, enslaving whole populations and leaving already barren worlds devoid of human life.

Although the people themselves were of little significance, that xenos could harvest souls from the Imperium repeatedly and with impunity was an offence that could not stand, and so Inquisitor Montiyf sought to cleanse the threat. Montiyf had devoted much of his career to the defeat of the dark eldar, the Chaotically tainted cousins of the effete eldar. Raiders, slavers and pirates, they use their ability to traverse another plane of existence called the webway to take whatever they want in savage raids, usually human slaves or some resource that their spacefaring, parasitic existence fell short of.

The strikes on the Pious Worlds followed the common dark eldar pattern, in that there was no pattern: attacks were without reason, and their mastery of the webway allowed the dark eldar to strike worlds at different ends of the system in close succession. They left no trail to follow, just destruction: corpses shredded by crystalline shards, stone hermitages scorched and devastated by dark-matter weapons.

We picked through the carnage they left behind, scouring the ruins for clues as to our enemy's intent, anything that might allow us to intercept them. On most worlds we found little of use, just the lines of scuffed footprints where slaves had been led away, as well as the aftereffects of the aliens' destruction.

But on some of the Pious Worlds we found

evidence of something else, some other activity preoccupying the dark eldar forces beyond the gathering and sacrifice of souls, signs of unusual action, of digging and excavations outside the human settlements they ravaged. On one world we found that they had located ruins in their search. They had carved into the side of a hill with powerful weaponry, revealing a tomb-like series of chambers beneath. Opened up to the sky, these ruins were slowly filling with snow drifts as I searched from room to room.

It was largely fruitless: if there had been anything of value, the dark eldar had stripped it away. But in one room, hidden in a corner, I found writing on the walls, scratched into the stone and written in the eldar's own language. My grip on the poetic complexities of the eldar tongue is limited, its huge alphabet and complex metaphors tough for the human mind to master, but I could recognise the prefixes used to indicate a proper name, and could break a name into syllables.

One name recurred throughout that scrawled text: *Dalson Graath*.

It was many years until I would see the name Dalson Graath again.

When I did, it was under very changed circumstances. Having risen to become an inquisitor in my own right, I had left the company of my mentor Montiyf and had begun to build a retinue of my own.

It is the privilege of an inquisitor not simply to wield great power but to also have considerable leeway in the manner in which those powers are exercised. Montiyf was the kind of inquisitor who acted almost as a general, imposing his authority to ensure he always had an army at his back. Other inquisitors worked alone, operating within the shadows and concealing their identities, only emerging to task others with the execution of their enemies before vanishing once more into the dark.

These approaches were shaped by the unique skills and abilities each inquisitor brought to their work, whether the blunt instruments of force and intimidation or the subtler insights of the psykers.

I took a different path, one based on deductive reasoning and an intuitive ability to see patterns in the actions of humanity's enemies, to seek out and eliminate xenos threats that no one else was aware of, or even capable of gaining the awareness of. While I did not adopt either austerity or anonymity, I stripped away much of the ritual and pomp of my office, instead forming a close retinue around me, able specialists who would be able to provide technical advice and knowledge.

It was with this small group that I travelled the fringe worlds of the Imperium, seeking out the patterns that would reveal a coalescing xenos threat, determined to head such threats off before they could manifest. It was out there, among the rogues and borderline heretics, that I heard another name, whispered among both turncoats low enough to have dealings with the dark eldar, and the few broken individuals who escaped their slavery.

Kulkavar.

The dark eldar were petty and cruel, raiders and slavers who, from the perspective of beleaguered humanity, acted as a merciless swarm without notable individuals. Kulkavar, however, had somehow gained a reputation above and beyond that, a reputation for sweeping ambitions that threatened humanity beyond the disconnected raids on human settlements.

Lord Kulkavar – an *archon*, in their terminology – wished to improve his position within the aristocracy of the dark eldar, and to do this he required the only currency that counted within that hierarchy: the souls of living creatures, to be offered to the darkness to assuage their own unholy thirst. The Imperium provided a ready supply, but one that was inconsistently obtained due to the scattershot nature of the dark eldar's raiding tactics.

Kulkavar wanted more, to somehow reap human souls on an industrial scale. How, I did not know, only that any such plan would constitute a terrible threat to the Imperium, and that it was my duty as an inquisitor to prevent it. In fact, I considered myself the only possible candidate to save humanity. No one else was looking for the clues that I was – they were too blind or too afraid. It was my calling to look fearlessly where others would or could not.

Through intelligence gathered I began to gain an insight into Kulkavar's actions, and to some extent could anticipate his raiding parties. It was in pursuit of one of Kulkavar's raidships that I and my retinue gave chase through treacherous

systems, where the siren fields disrupted naviga-
tion and wrecked starships on graveyard moons.

It was on one such moon that one of Kulkavar's
raidships crashed, torn in half, leaving the two
ends of the ship just two more promontories on
the rocky surface. All hands and slaves were lost
in the crash, and human and eldar bodies drifted
idly past as we slowly crossed the moon's surface,
every step an exertion in our heavy life-support
suits.

On board the ship Zandt, a tech-priest tasked
to my retinue, instructed servitors to strip out all
the communications equipment. As he did so,
I could hear Zandt chanting over the open vox,
prayers and exorcisms to prevent contagion from
contact with heretical xenos machinery.

Zandt is a genius, of sorts, with a natural apti-
tude for understanding and retrofitting obscure
machinery. I first encountered him on a distant forge world, ruled by an odd sub-sect of
the Adeptus Mechanicus. His brothers found
his talents disturbing, and would surely have
executed him for heresy years ago were it not for
his very vocal, sincere piety, which often borders
on fervour. Needless to say the temple were
glad to honour my request to transfer Zandt to
my retinue, and happy to free him of his other
obligations.

While Zandt was an invaluable asset, his constant prayers often wore on my nerves. I reduced
the volume on my helmet-vox, his entreaties to
the Machine-God reduced to a low background
hum.

While the salvaged equipment would allow

me to monitor Kulkavar's communications in the years that followed, albeit erratically, it was another discovery on board that wreck that provided a deeper insight into the dark eldar lord's plans. In a dank onboard laboratory were papers of varying age, some carefully preserved, others scribbled across and annotated.

They were notes relating to the activities of one Dalson Graath.

The notes were fragmented, written not just in the eldar language but often in code, some of which the previous owner of the papers had only semi-translated. However, from those, and similarly fragmented discoveries since, I managed to piece together most of the story.

And 'story' seemed the best word to describe what was written in these pages, not so much a historical account or series of facts as a narrative assembled from myth and hearsay.

Some facts were established: that Dalson Graath had been a haemonculus, one of the dark eldar's scientist-torturers some thousands of years ago. The accounts were unclear as to which kabal or lord Graath served, and whether he broke away from dark eldar society through choice or by being cast out, but Graath's work had taken him far away from Commorragh, the dark eldar's nightmare city in the webway.

Graath's outcast status appeared to have driven him from remote world to remote world, using the webway to establish underground laboratories where he continued his work – his exile did not seem to hamper the resources at his disposal, and there were largely incomprehensible notes in the margins of several documents suggesting that Graath worked under continued patronage as part of some obscure power struggle between the dark eldar lords of the time.

But it was the nature of Graath's work that made even I, Inquisitor Felip Velasco, who had stood at the side of Montiyf as he destroyed the Carnage Shard, question whether I was reading anything more than a fable.

While most of the haemonculi created weapons of pain for the battlefield or torture chamber, Graath's experiments were on a far grander scale, colossal devices melding alien technologies to subject whole populations to pain, subjugation, and finally the stripping of their very souls for consumption by the dark eldar.

The most notorious of these had become known as the Organs of Torment, and I was shocked to realise that I had heard of some of these before, or at least heard of their effects.

There was the Weeping Heart, whose beat could echo through the stars and cause the inhabitants of a dozen worlds to keel over and die, convulsing in despair.

There was the Blinding Eye, which converted a moon into a machine of enslavement, stripping the will of everyone on the planet below as they passed within its umbra.

Then there was the organ known simply as the Lung, the steady breath of which could drive a human population mad, prone to destabilising savagery during the night, but leaving them meek and malleable during the day.

None of these devices were ever mass-produced or duplicated, as far as I could tell. But their potential even as individual objects was terrifying enough. Whether Graath had been driven out of dark eldar society or left out of choice, it seemed that he had finally been purged for good, his work lost.

Lost, that is, until Kulkavar began to seek out those works, desperate to acquire these mythical devices to fulfil his own ambitions.

Since then I have devoted my not inconsiderable intelligence and abilities to preventing Kulkavar from acquiring the Organs of Torment or any of Graath's artefacts.

The equipment salvaged from the crashed dark eldar ship has allowed my retinue to monitor Kulkavar's communications, and while the dark eldar's access to the webway makes them hard to track, we have kept only a few steps behind them, and have intercepted Kulkavar's forces on a dozen different worlds.

While I have fought and killed Kulkavar's agents and warriors countless times, the dark eldar lord himself has never been present, and remains beyond my reach. He acts and I respond, my actions foiling his plans.

I cannot imagine that the distance between us will remain forever. Soon we must meet on the field of battle.

To date, the only functioning artefact that Kulkavar has managed to retrieve is the one called the Ear. Alas, while harmless within itself, the Ear is said to link to the other Organs, and provide a path to their discovery. My work becomes ever harder.

We have detected considerable activity on Kulka-var's communication channels relating to the Ear lately, and while the cogitators work to translate these messages, it seems almost certain that a discovery has been made.

Of what, we cannot yet tell, but we will pursue every trail and clue, strive to prevent Lord Kulka-var's ambitions and hopefully, very soon, wipe him from this universe for good.

--- *Entry ends* ---

SIXTEEN

Hool had heard of the Inquisition before. He had first been told about them as a child, stories of the Emperor's inquisitors, seeking out and punishing weakness and heresy across the Imperium, able to see the lies and evil in men's hearts and to burn the wicked with their very touch. Described like that, they were a children's story, something to scare you into behaving, mentioned in the same breath as the undercrabs who lived beneath the Mordian hab-pyramids, and the night snatchers who took unruly infants and cast them out of the hab windows, leaving them to fall to their doom on the cold ground below.

Hool had grown up to realise that the undercrabs and the night snatchers were just stories and the inquisitors were real, even if they weren't the creatures of his childish imagination.

However, years later the inquisitors were still bracketed together in Hool's mind with those other fables.

343

Which made the presence of Inquisitor Velasco disconcerting for Hool, especially considering he seemed closer to the kind of inquisitor that Hool might have imagined as a child than anything a cynical Guardsman could conceive of.

Both the conscious, adult part of Hool's mind and the latent, childish part were united in one sentiment: they were glad that Inquisitor Felip Velasco was on their side.

'Now!' ordered the inquisitor, using an external vox-caster to bellow his commands through the air rather than accessing the Guard's vox-channel. 'Hit them with everything.'

He shouted the words with his back to a thin slice of wall, having spun through open space firing his twin pistols at the dark eldar position, a fearless gambit to draw their fire and bring them out of cover. It had worked. Splinter fire was ricocheting off this meagre cover as the inquisitor reloaded his pistols, ready for the next pause in enemy fire, at which point he would doubtless fling himself into danger once more.

Hool had never seen anything like it. In his year of combat he had seen men take risks with their lives to secure an objective, even to rescue or protect fellow Guardsmen, but those were still disciplined manoeuvres undertaken as part of a wider army, moving between the stances and postures drilled into every man of the 114th. Even when engaged in seemingly reckless actions, a Guardsman of Hool's regiment did so correctly, the way he was trained.

Confirming Hool's initial impression, Inquisitor Velasco had no such restraint, running into danger with little more than his reflexes to get him out of trouble. Unbelievably, this was his plan, which he had snapped out to the Mordians in brief sentences. He would make himself a target, drawing the dark eldar out of cover so that the Mordians could get a better aim. With the dark eldar under pressure, the inquisitor and the Guardsmen would drive them back, putting them on the defensive.

Velasco had taken control of Smoker's platoon in minutes, issuing a flurry of orders that included concepts Hool had never even heard before. The inquisitor was clearly aware of the alien device, which he referred to as 'the Lung', and specified that these were 'dark' eldar, whatever that meant. As well as wielding the authority of the Inquisition, Velasco seemed to have a clearer idea of what was going on, and Smoker seemed almost happy about the usurping of his command by this newcomer.

It was a good call. Velasco's plan, mad as it was, was proving effective. Whereas before Velasco's intervention the Mordians were being driven away from the centre of the city, their position was already stronger, while the dark eldar were being driven back, scurrying for cover. Three or four of their number lay dead, or had retreated visibly wounded. The men of the 114th advanced to find better cover for themselves, and as they advanced the air became thicker with bolt-rounds and las-fire than with enemy splinter shots.

Hool glanced sideways to where Polk was firing off a couple of blasts from his combat shotgun before ducking behind a wall. As Polk reloaded, he looked up and caught Hool's eye, and a look was exchanged between them, a shared excitement that the tide was turning, and that these dark eldar could be defeated.

'Hold fire,' hissed Velasco, somehow audible over the din of gunfire. It took a few seconds, but the men of the 114th ceased fire.

Silence. There was no movement or fire from the dark eldar.

'Did we get them all?' asked a voice Hool didn't immediately recognise.

Smoker made a scratchy, electronic coughing sound over the vox.

'No chance,' said Smoker bluntly. 'Just regrouping, waiting.'

'Very good, lieutenant,' said Velasco, with a hint of surprise. He didn't give out compliments often, it seemed. 'We're not their objective, the Lung is.' Velasco tipped his head in the direction of the alien device that loomed over everything else in the chamber. 'When this platform reaches ground level, reinforcements will be waiting. They will secure the platform and prepare the Lung for transportation off-world. Fortunately, this will take some time – time enough for us to stop them. There are more of your regiment here?'

Smoker nodded. 'In the city-factory. Strike force.'

Velasco consulted a data-slate. 'When we reach ground level we'll be one kilometre from the city-factory. We need to withdraw, gather your strike force, and destroy that thing before the dark eldar can get it off-world.'

The inquisitor and the lieutenant continued to discuss the route to the city-factory, but Hool's mind was elsewhere. When the dark eldar had attacked, they had seemed to emerge from the underground city. It hadn't occurred to Hool that they might be on the surface as well.

If the dark eldar were loose on the surface, possibly in greater numbers than below ground, then everything might have changed. What would they find when they returned to the surface?

Looking across Emperor's Square from the shadows of a burnt-out restaurant, Calway realised that there had been far more survivors in the city-factory than he had realised. While Calway had barely encountered a single sane survivor prior to the Guard's arrival, the dark eldar had somehow dug into the city's depths and found tens, if not hundreds of battered and dirty humans. The eldar were gathering these slaves in the square, chaining them in lines in an ostentatious display of superiority. Initially there had just been a few people, dragged out of the buildings at the edge of the square, but since then more and more had been brought.

Eldar warriors arrived in the square either on their floating vehicles or on foot, always dragging hapless citizens in their wake. It was impossible to tell during daylight how many of those were infected, but even if they were Calway couldn't help but feel sympathy for them in this broken state, any resistance thrashed out of them with gauntlets and whips, the blows from which caused the unfortunate victim's entire body to arc and convulse.

The slaves were all kept facing the opposite end of the square, where an elaborately decorated eldar vehicle had just landed, disgorging a lavishly robed figure, clearly the leader of this force. He strode the paved surface of the square, haughtily surveying the humans broken in his honour.

The spectacle sickened Calway, the sight of his home, a great square built in honour of the God-Emperor of Man, defiled so that some filthy xenos could lord it over tormented humans.

In the last hour, the rain had stopped and the interference on the vox had died down. Calway had been in constant communication with Lieutenant Deaz as well as the frankly terrifying Commissar Tordez, and a plan had been hatched.

Two plans, in fact. As the minutes ticked down to the beginning of the first, Calway prayed to the Emperor, whose statue lay broken in the square below, that the second plan wouldn't be necessary.

Around the edge of the square, within the buildings that faced into it, Deaz's men were on the move. Broken into small units, they moved quickly and, as much as possible, quietly, accessing buildings through the rear, then stealthily moving within the buildings themselves, staying as far from the windows and exterior doors as possible.

As the eldar displayed their slaves in the square, the men of the 114th were silently encircling them. It was an ancient approach to urban warfare – never step outside, burrow through the buildings. Plasterwork was rammed through as cleanly as possible, while heavier walls were taken down with discreet explosive charges. Marksmen moved to higher floors, ready to take a vantage point when the signal was given, while the rest of the men stayed at ground level, holding back for the same cue to move into position.

Once in place, they waited in the dark.

Kulkavar looked out across a sea of downtrodden human faces. His warriors had done well, sniffing out vulnerable souls across the city-factory, gathering them for their master. Their spirits broken by the merciless application of agonisers, the revolting animals hunched and slumped on the stone-clad ground.

The sun had emerged, a rare break in the persistent gloom of this planet's atmosphere, to cast a light on Kulkavar's achievement. Its heat displeased him, the change in temperature disturbing his pale eldar skin. He longed for Commorragh's icy darkness, the obsidian corridors that echoed with the screams of the tormented.

This handful of humans were a mere precursor to the souls he would gather with the Lung and, in due course as Zekov's knowledge of the works of Graath expanded, *Lungs*. Whole systems subjugated, billions of souls reaped in the name of Kulkavar.

Then, Kulkavar would return to Commorragh in triumph, and his rivals would fear him as these pathetic primates did.

Though he did not let any sign of his discomfort break his outer grace, impatience for news from Zekov grated, Kulkavar's exquisitely attuned sense of time passing making each second that went by without news of the Lung's retrieval a torment.

Kulkavar forced himself to savour the sensation, the

tension of unfulfilled desire, rare for an eldar born to rule, to have his every whim seen to. Satisfaction would come soon; only the practicalities of retrieving the Lung delayed it.

He decided to enjoy the wait. After all, there was little else to do with the human population already crushed. This far from the Imperium's heaving hive and forge worlds, there was no one, no thing, that could stop Kulkavar from fulfilling his destiny.

Closing his heavily lidded eyes, sliding his thin tongue across the roof of his mouth, Kulkavar could almost taste the victories to come, and the manifold miseries he would inflict on humankind.

A short distance from Emperor's Square, Lieutenant Deaz and a small group of his men sheltered beneath an underpass, watching the skies for any sign of dark eldar attack. So far they had seen the occasional vehicle flick past in the distance, darting between the towers and industrial chimneys of the city-factory, but none had come close to Deaz's position.

It was one thing to conceal a small group of men, and indeed for many such groups to secrete themselves around the square. It was quite another to not draw attention to the vehicle which came to a halt beneath the underpass. It was the vehicle Sergeant Polk had christened 'the Cleaner'. As the loader came to a halt, the driver leaned out of the door and gave the lieutenant a brisk salute.

'No problems?' asked Deaz.

'Handles better than it looks, sir,' replied the driver.

'Handles like a beast, but it's simple enough to drive, even this heavily loaded.'

Deaz nodded. 'How long do you reckon it'll take to roll the rest of the way?'

The driver shrugged. 'Three minutes should do it.'

Deaz sucked in air between his teeth. Three minutes was longer than he'd hoped for. With any luck it wouldn't be necessary, but if it was, they needed a hell of a distraction to ensure the dark eldar didn't take the Cleaner out before it was in position.

'Three minutes it is,' said Deaz. 'Get rolling now and I'll give the order. When you're in position, stay put until I say otherwise. You're just a backup, remember?'

The driver's eyes warily darted back to his cargo as he ducked back into the vehicle's cab. 'I won't forget it, sir,' he said, slamming the hatch shut behind him.

The Cleaner began to roll forwards, and Deaz winced at the loud rumble of its engines. Surely the eldar would hear it coming?

Suppressing his concerns, he tapped his vox-bead and spoke to the rest of his men.

'Plan B is on its way. Begin Plan A,' said Deaz.

Kulkavar's eyes snapped open at the sound of gunfire, a rude awakening indeed. It was not one shot, but many, echoing around the square. Kulkavar's sensitive ears recognised that the shots were not from eldar weapons.

Kulkavar drew a breath, taking in the scene before him. His perception of time slowed with the controlled breath, and he could see the las-fire slicing through the air in a dozen places, shots fired from high windows in the buildings around the square. On the ground, Kulkavar's warriors were the targets. Some fell, shots finding their mark, collapsing with smoking holes in their armour. Others received only light wounds and began to fire back, moving towards cover.

The slaves provided a living shield, and resourceful warriors slipped into the ranks of cowering humans, firing over their heads at the enemy positions.

Kulkavar exhaled, and his perceptions returned to normal. His retinue of guards were encircling his position, and as a paving slab near Kulkavar's feet was scorched by a las-shot, his guards returned a precise salvo of splinter-fire in the direction from which the shot had come.

The ambushers had the benefit of surprise, but it would not get them far. Kulkavar was relaxed in the knowledge that his warriors were more than capable of eliminating a handful of marksmen. Aside from the returned fire tearing into their positions, the humans would soon find shadows moving in on them, agonisers poised to attack.

Soon, the attackers would be enslaved with the others.

As Kulkavar savoured this certainty, the second wave of the attack hit the eldar lines.

Plymton ducked as splinter-fire shattered the window from which he was firing. Crystalline shards cut through the space where Plymton's head had just been. He fell to the floor as chunks of plaster and masonry exploded from the walls and ceiling above and behind them.

Plymton scrabbled forwards on his knees, staying out of sight. The fire from below subsided, and Plymton peered over the windowsill, looking down into the square below to see the dark eldar preoccupied. Small teams of Guardsmen had emerged from around the square, rapidly moving in on the dark eldar, firing on the aliens as they were distracted by the marksmen above.

The dark eldar guarding the slaves were caught between the marksmen above and the heavier fire at ground level, and were thrown into disarray.

Calway was with one of the squads on the ground, emerging from the burnt-out restaurant, running towards the nearest line of human slaves and their eldar guards. He had been with a squad that had blown through wall after wall to get into position within the buildings, but out in the open he had a very different job. Keeping low, he let the trained Guardsmen draw fire from the eldar, and ran straight for the slaves.

As he got close, a dark eldar guard turned in his direction. The xenos was a spindly creature, its tapered helmet and chitinous black armour plates giving it a repulsive, insectoid appearance. Turning to Calway, the creature drew back a long whip, preparing to strike. Ripples of alien energy distorted the area around the whip, and Calway flinched at the sight of it.

The eldar was thrown back by a burst of las-fire cutting into its chest, and fell to the ground, the whip flailing harmlessly backwards as it fell.

Calway didn't look back to see which of the Guardsmen had saved him, but concentrated on his own objectives. He ran to the slave at the end of the line, and began to examine his bonds.

The eldar handcuffs were elaborately wrought rings of black metal, seemingly crude but sophisticated enough to have tightened precisely around the captive's wrists. Too tight for the hands to slip out, they left enough room to allow blood circulation. To discourage attempted removal, the inside of each cuff had an undulating curve to the surface, which peaked in vicious-looking spikes – let the cuffs hang and the spikes would barely graze, but try to remove them and they would dig deep into the flesh.

Hurriedly inspecting the cuffs, which were linked to a chain running down the entire line, Calway couldn't see a lock, clasp or weak point. The cuffs seemed welded solid.

'Did you see how they locked these?' he hurriedly asked the slave, not looking up. 'Is there a key?' If there was, Calway could search the body of the nearest eldar...

He was receiving no reply. Calway looked up, paying attention to the face of the man before him for the first time. He was young, with dirty shoulder-length hair. Slim, pale, blue eyes. Unremarkable, but for his facial expression: his eyes were unfocussed, his jaw slack, but with a twitch at the corner of the mouth and a narrowing of the irises that suggested something other than a comatose state.

Calway repeated his question, holding the man's chin to try and get him to focus. Nothing, just the same vacant stare, and a quiver that suggested that the man was preoccupied by some imaginary threat or struggle.

A shot narrowly missed Calway, hitting the next slave down the line. Calway flinched, turning his attention to the woman who had been hit. She too had the same blank expression, even as she bled out through a throat wound and slumped forwards, blood spurting from her neck. She didn't make even the most basic, instinctive attempt to break her fall, her neck twisting at an unnatural angle as she fell face down on the ground, her eyelids fluttering before she went still.

Her dead weight dragged the slaves either side of her down as the chain tensed, but they didn't react, just twisted.

Back in a crouch, Calway ran down the line of slaves, looking into their eyes, giving them rapid shoves and taps, trying desperately to get any reaction.

Nothing. Whatever the eldar had done to them, they were all broken.

Calway turned and began to run for cover, giving a high whistle to tell any Guard in range to retreat. Similar whistles rang out across the square, faintly audible over the gunfire.

Retreat. Abandon mission. Objective lost.

Somewhere among the chaos, officers would be relaying the whistled message by vox to Lieutenant Deaz, the message that the slaves were lost, broken, beyond saving. Plan B was required.

As he ran for cover, Calway uttered a silent prayer to the Emperor: not for his own survival, or even for the slaves himself, but for forgiveness for what came next.

* * *

The Cleaner was just turning into the square as Deaz received garbled, overlaid reports on the vox regarding the slaves: although the men were talking over each other, the message was clear. The slaves could not be helped.

Deaz, who along with a dozen of his men was jogging alongside the slow-moving loader, switched vox-channels and gave the driver an order.

As the Cleaner moved onto a straight path towards the centre of the square, the cab opened and the driver scrambled out as the Cleaner continued rolling, locked on course.

Deaz looked out into the square. He could see fallen Guardsmen, while survivors were retreating to the edges of the square, fighting off the eldar as they did so. The eldar were still dealing with fire from high windows, and Deaz could see a cluster of heavily armoured eldar near a lavishly decorated alien vehicle, a floating barge of some kind.

Then there were the slaves, still lined up across the square, oblivious to the battle around them.

Painfully slowly, the Cleaner kept moving towards the centre of the square. Deaz hoped that the eldar didn't notice it until it was in position, and if they did, that they reacted as he expected them to.

Enraged, Kulkavar barged through his retinue to personally cut down one of the human warriors with his monomolecular sword. The blade hummed, a pleasing feedback vibrating through the hilt as the sword passed unhindered through the human's body, slicing down through shoulder to waist.

Kulkavar watched with satisfaction as the human fell into two neat pieces, blood soaking into the blue cloth of its jacket at the edges of the divide. As the soul of the dead man left his body, Kulkavar closed his eyes and inhaled, savouring the despair of his last moments.

The consumed human soul momentarily took the edge off the emptiness that forever gnawed at Kulkavar from within, a brief respite from his eternal need. He opened his eyes, his senses blissfully taking in the clamour of gunfire, the smells of blood and burnt flesh.

He felt something else, a disturbance in the air, an unfamiliar vibration in the ground. Sheathing his sword, he turned to see a long, ugly human vehicle slowly moving towards the lines of slaves. A rescue vehicle perhaps? Kulkavar scoffed. Such an attempt was futile.

'Destroy that thing,' he ordered his incubi dismissively, and a wave of dark matter was unleashed upon the vehicle.

In the millisecond after the dark matter struck the vehicle, before there was even any visible sign of a reaction, Kulkavar felt a subtle change in the air. A subtle, but unmistakable, rush of heat…

He turned, all grace and dignity abandoned as he ran for his Raider, screaming an order to the pilot, desperate to stay a precious second ahead of the inferno he could feel approaching.

Deaz couldn't stop a bleak smile passing his lips as the dark eldar fell for the bait, firing on the Cleaner as it approached the slaves. The smile faded quickly with the knowledge of what would come next, as Deaz turned away from the square, ducking his head as he did so, preparing for that inevitable rush of heat.

The Guard all looked away as the Cleaner, stacked with chamazian barrels, exploded under the dark eldar fire. The explosion was tremendous, a vast wall of fire spreading in all directions as the volatile chemical ignited. All the slaves, and the remaining guards, were consumed by fire in an instant.

At the centre of the blast the shell of the Cleaner flipped in the air, a blackened skeleton at the heart of a white-hot explosion.

The eldar, clad in their armour, fled the heat but were mostly unscathed, some emerging from the fires itself, armour smoking but seemingly otherwise unharmed. At the end of the square the large floating eldar vehicle tore away, armoured eldar warriors jumping on board as it moved off, its lavish canopies scorched and covered with little patches of flame as it escaped the worst of the inferno.

The fire burnt itself out as fast as it had started, the flames dissipating to reveal blackened, twisted carnage where the incredible rush of heat had done its terrible work. At the centre of the explosion, a deep crater had been gouged into the ground, shattering paving slabs and digging into the earth itself, and the wreck of the Cleaner fell into the pit, vanishing into the depths of the hole.

Smoke wafted from every surface below. At ground level, the fronts of the buildings around the edge of the square had been scorched, paint blasted away and the few unbroken windows cracked by the sudden temperature. As the smoke cleared, the ground became visible. Ashes drifted like sand dunes across a black-scorched surface, the entirety of the square burnt clean of life.

Strewn across the centre of the square were mounds of charred remains, still roughly in line even as they were thrown back by the blast: the burnt remnants of the slaves, set free in the harshest and most final way from the dark eldar and their cruel, soul-draining tyranny.

Kulkavar, taking the command throne at the rear of his Raider, composed himself. The slaves may have been lost, but they had always been a very secondary objective, a handful of souls compared to the millions Kulkavar would soon gather. The humans had played a clever hand with their firebomb, but Kulkavar's warriors would be ready for any proposed repetition, and prevent it.

Nothing of significance had been lost. However, it would be remiss of Kulkavar not to order his warriors to regroup and return immediately to the scene of the explosion, storming every adjacent building until the perpetrators were captured so that their souls could suffer for the indignity that they had inflicted.

Kulkavar's train of thought was interrupted by an incoming communication from Zekov.

As Kulkavar listened to his haemonculus, a rare smile played at the corner of his mouth, the loss of the human slaves and his undignified retreat from the fireball entirely forgotten. While part of his mind listened to Zekov's words, another part of the archon's consciousness simply rolled a single phrase around, again and again:

The Lung was his. *The Lung was his.*

As the platform carrying the Lung and the struggling dark eldar and human forces finally reached ground level, Inquisitor Velasco and the Guardsmen of the 114th now under his command did not have a plan for how they were to prevent the dark eldar's plans, but they did at least know what they needed to do next: retreat and regroup.

Velasco had calculated on a data-slate their relative position to the city-factory, and where they would need to be on the platform to provide the most direct route back. Avoiding detection by the dark eldar, they had moved under cover around the platform edge.

Velasco's calculations were correct. The platform emerged at the centre of a barren rocky outcrop a kilometre from the city-factory's west wall. Between them and the city-factory was an ugly stretch of rough, muddy moorland pitted with stinking, treacherous bogs. Skeletal trees and huddled bushes littered the route ahead, pitiful signs of life in a desolate landscape.

As soon as they could get off the platform they did, and Hool found his boots sinking in the swampy ground as, Velasco in the lead, they began to run towards the looming mass of the city-factory, its twisted jumble of industrial towers and chimneys silhouetted by the cold light of the late sun.

The sun would begin to slowly set in an hour or so, thought Hool, as he ran with as light a step as he could, trying to avoid sinking. Past nightfall, their problems would double.

Nearby Hool could hear a breathless vox-operator trying to raise a response from Geiss and the other officers. To destroy the Lung and deny Kulkavar his prize would take more than the remnants of Smoker's platoon. Hool wasn't sure what it would take – even with the inquisitor taking the lead, a hostile alien force and a weapon as unearthly as the Lung seemed beyond the capabilities of common Guardsmen.

Hool heard a shout of warning, a semi-audible declaration of something behind them. He turned, lasrifle raised, expecting to see the dark eldar in pursuit. What he saw instead was possibly worse.

Behind them, the Lung stood on the platform surrounded by the crumbling remains of a handful of buildings. Raised from its underground home, the Lung had begun to glow more vibrantly, and seemed to be pulsing with agitation. The alien device was becoming more active, and there was clear, visible evidence of its increased activity. A low bank of pure white mist was beginning to roll out from the platform, a wave of infection expanding across the moor towards the city-factory.

SEVENTEEN

An hour passed in hectic activity.

The survivors of Hossk's platoon, supplemented by Stellin and the other workers from Hab C, were the first to respond to the vox-messages from Smoker's platoon. The dark eldar had abruptly abandoned their slave-raids on the workers' habs, Hossk, his men and the surviving workers rapidly moved out, opening a maintenance gate on the west wall to allow Velasco and the Guardsmen back into the city-factory.

Also answering the call were Tordez and the survivors from the destruction of the ship. Deaz's men were further away in Emperor's Square, but moved out as quickly as they could on Velasco's command, and remained in constant vox-contact.

The remains of the strike force were being reassembled in the west of the city, at the edge of the refinery area. Velasco convened with Geiss's officers, forming a plan of attack.

Resources were gathered, and troops reorganised to compensate for men lost.

News was hastily shared. For those who had accompanied Smoker underground, there was the shock of Geiss's death and the losses inflicted on the 114th by the dark eldar. For those who had lived through those losses, there was the revelation of the existence of the Lung, the source of all Belmos VII's current woes.

Sentries had been posted on the west wall, looking out towards the craggy, raised area where the Lung had reached the surface. The fragmented remains of buildings from the underground city that littered the platform looked like standing stones, ancient monuments built to the glory of the weapon at the centre of the platform.

As the Guard prepared to make their move, the sentries caught sight of dark eldar movement around the Lung, their anti-gravity vehicles moving to and fro as the aliens made preparations of their own.

'My archon,' said Zekov, bowing obsequiously, one arm gesturing towards Kulkavar's prize, as if it were a personal gift from the haemonculus to his master. The archon saw it differently – The haemonculus was merely an agent of destiny, bringing Kulkavar the means to his inevitable ascension, a footnote in the rise of Kulkavar.

As soon as Zekov had informed him that the Lung was real, intact and raised to the surface of the planet, Kulkavar had ordered the pilot of his Raider to take them out of the city-factory and head directly to the haemonculus's position.

They had swept out of the city's main gates, banked off the causeway and rapidly arrived at a rocky island in a dreary sea of mud. Kulkavar had disembarked before the Raider had even landed, casting protocol aside to stride quickly through the broken remains of ancient buildings that, in their chilly blackness, reminded him of Commorragh, the home that the Lung would allow him to return to a champion, his unassailable status bought in souls and conquest.

And here it was, the instrument of his glory, neither machine nor beast, a living weapon rippling with unnatural life. There was poetry in the deep, bass rhythm of its exhalations, a beauty in the shimmering colours that flowed through its undulating skin like liquid. Glowing mist seeped out of its great vents, changing the quality of the air, harmless to an eldar but ruinous to their enemies.

Ignoring Zekov altogether, Kulkavar removed a gauntlet and walked close to the Lung, placing his naked palm against a section of its semi-metallic flesh. It felt warm and cold at the same time, natural and unnatural. The complexity of the sensation thrilled Kulkavar in ways he had not experienced for some time.

'A thing of wonder,' Kulkavar said, stepping away from the Lung and sliding his gauntlet back on. 'Graath truly was a genius, even by the standards of our race, to create such a weapon. To us, a weapon. To the savages it will break, the Lung must seem like a god. A god under my command.'

There was a brief silence, Kulkavar's underlings no doubt taking in the depth of his rhetoric.

'Yes, my archon,' Zekov said after a while.

'Are the preparations for transporting the Lung under way?' Kulkavar asked.

'The anti-gravity rig is almost ready,' said Zekov, waving his arm to indicate the metallic collar that had been fitted around the base of the Lung. 'It will require some tailoring to the current size of the Lung. We will also need to counteract the gravity locks connecting the Lung to the platform.'

Zekov tapped the toe of one boot against the brushed stone surface beneath their feet. Kulkavar held him with a questioning gaze.

'The platform is a gravity device,' explained Zekov, his masked helmet as impassive as ever. 'Most of the energy of the city below will have been expended driving the platform to the surface, but a negligible field remains to keep the Lung in position. Nullifiers will remove the effect.'

'Then proceed with the work,' said Kulkavar.

Tearing his eyes away from the Lung, Kulkavar turned to inspect the rest of the activity on the platform. Warriors had been recalled from attacks and slave-gathering sorties within the human settlement to support and guard the removal of the Lung, Raiders landing around the platform, sybarites giving their forces new orders as they arrived.

Kulkavar had lost any taste for enslaving the inhabitants of this world. An under-populated planet like this was barely worth picking over at the best of times. The Lung was exhaling enough mist to pollute the entire population, and Kulkavar was content to leave the humans to tear themselves to pieces under its influence.

He was savouring this image when Veldrax approached,

discreetly seeking his attention. Kulkavar graciously turned to the sybarite, consenting to be addressed.

'My archon,' reported Veldrax. 'The mon-keigh are approaching from their settlement. They wish to engage us.'

Kulkavar paused to assess this new development. These primitive apes refused to submit to the inevitable, and this defiance was unacceptable.

'I was willing to let these creatures kill each other in their own time,' Kulkavar told Veldrax, sighing ostentatiously. 'But if they wish to confront us, so be it. Assemble all warriors. We will grind these humans into the dirt of their filthy world, and leave no survivors.'

'This is not the time for surprise or stealth,' Velasco had said, standing atop Hossk's Chimera and addressing the gathered men. 'They will be expecting us, and we need to draw them out and away from the primary target. Fire as soon as you are within range, make them meet us out on the ground.'

Hossk's platoon, supported by the workers from the habs, were to strike first. As the west gates of the city-factory slowly ground open and Hossk led his men out onto the muddy moor, he was entirely aware that they had been sent ahead to absorb the brunt of enemy fire. His was the largest surviving part of the strike force, especially when supplemented by the workers.

It was understandable that Velasco saw them as easy cannon fodder. In the case of the workers, Hossk would broadly agree with the inquisitor. Velasco's strategy required that the dark eldar be drawn away from their fortifications to as great an extent as possible, and these civilians, untrained but brutalised from their weeks surviving, were the best candidates. They would fight and die for their Emperor, as would the Guardsmen they fought alongside.

What made less sense to Hossk was his own refusal to take a more strategic role. Velasco had suggested that Hossk might better serve the plan by holding back and forming part of the second wave, to assist in the storming of the platform. Hossk had surprised himself by arguing against this, insisting that his men, and especially the undisciplined mob of workers, needed his leadership out in the field.

In doing so, he had put himself in danger with them.

Hossk was unsure what motive had driven him to do such a thing. He had signed away men's lives without a thought on many occasions, and there would have been no cowardice in holding back. Velasco's plan had little chance of success, and a high chance that every man involved would die today, with the only variable being the opportunity for glory in death. Why had he chosen the less glorious path?

Hossk pushed these questions aside as he led his men out onto the muddy moorland. Cold seeped through his uniform as he took his first steps onto the bleak ground. Ahead, across the barren expanse, stood the cluster of broken buildings atop the eldar platform. As Hossk and his men approached, they would be easy targets for snipers gathered in those ruins.

Hossk looked around at the men he led. The Guardsmen marched in perfect time, but even the workers in their overalls, wielding weapons dropped by fallen Guardsmen or their own adapted tools, stood tall as they walked.

Behind Hossk's platoon came the rest of the men, spreading out and staying low, moving from rocky outcrop to clump of vegetation, trying to stay in cover as much as possible.

Hool was among them. Inquisitor Velasco seemed to have adopted the survivors of the force he had encountered when he landed on Belmos VII, with the majority of Smoker's platoon assigned to follow him.

Ahead, the usually conspicuous figure of Velasco led the way. Velasco had produced a long, green-grey cloak from under his robes, and with it tied around his neck his brass armour and white robes were largely concealed.

Across the moor the Guardsmen marched, advancing on the platform. Behind them, three Chimeras rolled out of the city-factory's west gate, each surrounded by a defensive ring of Guardsmen, moving slowly so as to not prematurely detonate the sensitive barrels of chamazian loaded on board.

Lieutenant Deaz led this odd convoy from a seat next to the driver of one of the Chimeras, painfully aware of the volatile liquid loaded behind him, and the extent to which he would be incinerated in a second if a stray bolt or las-shot hit one of the barrels.

As the Chimera rolled out onto the moorland with a lurching thud, the barrels behind him making a loud *slosh*, Deaz was reminded of the fate of the slaves in Emperor's Square, burned alive in seconds.

It wasn't a comfortable thought, but Deaz knew that getting at least one of these Chimeras to the target was their only hope of eliminating the threat the Lung posed. He just hoped to be well away from the explosion when it happened.

The first assault came as Hossk's platoon came in range of the platform. Splinter-fire tore into the first line of men, as armoured dark eldar warriors emerged from the ruins of buildings to fire on the approaching humans.

Hossk himself was not hit, but a shard hit Weir square in the chest, and the sergeant fell backwards, his coatfront shredded by shrapnel.

As the Mordians fired back at their attackers, las-fire pounding the dark eldar's fragile cover, Hossk dropped to his knee to check his sergeant's condition. The wounds were not deep, but they didn't need to be – Weir was convulsing, muscles taut, and even through the lenses of his rebreather mask his eyes were wide and reddened, pupils unnaturally small: he had been poisoned, the dark eldar venom from the splinter shot destroying his nervous system. The projectile could have lightly grazed him and been just as deadly.

Hossk swore, but couldn't allow himself to be distracted by the death of one man. As he stood up, he shouted to the men around him to rally, to charge the dark eldar on their platform, and to make them pay for every drop of blood spilled on the muddy ground.

* * *

As Hossk's men engaged the first wave of aliens, the rest of the force moved in to provide backup, to fill gaps in the line where Guardsmen and workers had fallen.

As the platform was higher than the surrounding moorland, Smoker's troops had a line of sight over the heads of their comrades, so the more able marksmen could take aim at dark eldar warriors as they appeared at the platform's edge or over the tops of the broken buildings.

Hool managed to get the odd shot in, but his lasrifle was hardly up to the task and he thought most of his shots went wide, although it was hard to tell as the air ahead became crisscrossed with las-fire. Smoker and his squad of grey-jacketed marksmen were more confidently opening fire, Lieutenant Essler pausing to let off a couple of shots from his hellgun before taking a few more steps ahead.

The exchange of long-distance fire was broken as the Imperium forces and the dark eldar met at the edge of the platform, the xenos spilling down onto the ground to attack the Guard with glaives and scythes, the humans rushing forwards to meet them.

Velasco tossed away his concealing cloak to reveal his brass armour, and bellowed an order to charge, to meet the dark eldar face to face.

'Right then!' shouted Polk to his squad. 'Let's show these xenos filth whose planet this is!'

They charged.

Kulkavar strode into the fray with his retinue, monomolecular sword slashing right and left. He aimed to strike cleanly, but not to offer any easy deaths: one human raised a pistol and Kulkavar slashed through the creature's forearm, the hand holding the gun falling to the muddy ground as the mon-keigh reeled away in agony.

Kulkavar ignored the wounded mon-keigh as he fell to his knees, instead turning to pierce the heart of a bulky human in coveralls, who had impertinently swung a large cutting tool in the direction of Kulkavar's head. A follow-up kick pushed the corpse from the end of Kulkavar's blade.

It was an indulgence, stepping out onto the battlefield while the Lung was being secured, but Kulkavar felt the need to deliver a lesson, as well as to treat himself to the pleasure of seeing the humans fall to his sword. It was one thing to order pain on a massive scale, to rain torment upon a planet, but quite another to step in and treasure each individual wound. A smile twisted at the corner of Kulkavar's mouth as he let the fury of battle overtake him.

The roar of battle could be heard across the platform, but Zekov barely noticed.

The Lung was rising, the gravity field around it reversing.

The most difficult part of the process would be guiding the Lung over the rubble of the hazardous, rubble-strewn surface of the platform itself. Once out onto the moorland, it could comfortably hover across land and sea all the way to the spaceport.

Zekov needed to be close to guide it. He ordered a Raider to attend him.

Then, it would just be a matter of slowly leading the Lung back to the ship, like guiding a pet.

A pet that Zekov was eager to dissect, of course. But that had been the fate of everything that came into his care, so why should this be different?

On the moor, carnage.

Closing the gap between the human and dark eldar forces had reduced any advantage the latter had in terms of stealth, preventing them from picking off the human forces from afar with their splinter weapons.

But up close the dark eldar were ferocious killers, acrobatically spinning from one attack to the next, wielding glaives and curved blades in vicious, arcing strikes that severed limbs and ruptured bodies. All of their close combat weapons seemed to be powered or poisoned or both, so that even the most glancing blow could leave a man screaming on the ground or convulsing in agony.

Deress had already fallen, a powered glaive jammed into his back by an eldar warrior. Hool shot the dark eldar where he stood, hand still attached to Deress's back, but it was no help to the Guardsman – the shock from the glaive had already stopped his heart.

Nearby, Hool could see Inquisitor Velasco swinging his chainsword around to slice straight through the nearest eldar, leaving the alien's right arm hanging by a sinew.

As the wounded eldar collapsed, Velasco elbowed him aside, stretching over the falling body to swipe at another, seemingly unaware of the bladed gauntlet an eldar warrior was about to swipe into his armoured back, each bladed finger rippling with pain-inflicting energy.

Mark Clapham

Before Hool could raise his lasrifle to protect Velasco, a shot from Smoker's hellgun sent the gauntleted dark eldar reeling backwards. The inquisitor didn't register the shot, as his chainsword was locked with two monomolecular daggers wielded by an eldar warrior, the fight reduced to a contest of strength as Velasco put his full body weight behind his blade, forcing the eldar's guard down.

'Polk, Hool – cover the inquisitor,' Smoker ordered. 'But don't get too close to that chainsword of his.' Before either Guardsman could respond to the order, Smoker had disappeared into the fray, hellgun barking at some distant target.

Hool and Polk provided covering fire to keep the other eldar back as Velasco, locked in a hand-to-hand struggle, pressed downwards with his chainsword as his opponent continued to try and force him backwards. When the eldar lost the struggle, its arms giving way to gravity and the tremendous force Velasco was exerting, it wasn't Velasco's chainsword that killed it, but the downward descent of the eldar's own blades as they sliced into his upper body.

The inquisitor seemed to be in a near-frenzy, his gaze sweeping in search of another target. A dark eldar swept a scythe-like weapon in the direction of Velasco's head, but the inquisitor just ducked under the blow and batted it aside, swinging his chainsword through the alien's guts.

Hool was so distracted by the inquisitor's performance that he didn't notice a dark eldar heading right for him until Polk shoved him aside, levelling his combat shotgun and firing at almost point-blank range at Hool's assailant. The shotgun blast shattered the dark eldar's helm into fragments, and left a bloody, broken mess where the front half of the alien's head had been.

As Polk helped him to his feet, Hool muttered a thank you, a pleasantry muffled by his rebreather.

Each of the three Chimeras had a data-slate mounted inside, displaying a crude layout of the platform as captured by Inquisitor Velasco. There were two routes between the few buildings left standing large enough for a Chimera to pass through that led to the Lung, but judging by the entry path of dark eldar vehicles landing on the platform, the one at the south end of the platform would be blocked by the Raiders and other vehicles spotted by sentries earlier.

The heavy-tracked vehicles were rolling in single file across the moor, arcing to the north to circumvent the battle and mount the platform. Deaz's Chimera was at the back of the convoy, which allowed him to lead from a secure position but was frustrating as he could not see ahead.

They were halfway to their destination when the vox squawked.

'Halt, immediate halt,' voxed the driver of the first Chimera. 'We've hit quicksand.'

'Can you reverse out?' Deaz asked.

'Afraid not, sir,' said the driver. 'Muddy crust only broke when we were half on, we're nose-down in it and we're not getting out without a tow.'

Deaz switched the vox off and let off a string of imaginative curses, loud enough for the driver sitting next to him to flinch slightly in his seat.

Chimeras could handle most ground, but even they would get stuck if the terrain was rough enough.

One down, two to go. They would need to find their way around the quicksand, and hope the route didn't delay them too much.

Inquisitor Felip Velasco barely noticed the xenos as he fought them. These were footsoldiers, underlings, and he cut through them like thin cloth in pursuit of his real target. Velasco knew Kulkavar must be close by, and any obstruction was a mere distraction to be dashed aside. His real enemy drew him on with a force akin to gravity, a relentless onwards tug.

Everything else was insignificant. Velasco followed his instincts as he weaved through the hectic battlefield, humans and dark eldar alike dying at his feet. When they obstructed his path, he stepped over them without a thought.

Velasco didn't have any difficulty identifying his prey when he saw him. Although he had never seen Lord Kulkavar before, a dark eldar lord was hard to miss, even to the untrained eye of a human: his robes were lavish and, even compared to the naturally imperious nature of the eldar, every movement Kulkavar made dripped with contempt for those around him, for the Guardsmen falling to his blade.

Velasco stepped forwards and issued a challenge.

It was with exquisite boredom that Kulkavar realised a monkeigh was shouting at him, and turned to face the speaker. A human male was approaching, a rather different figure to the others. He was almost as tall as an eldar, and dressed in some gaudy plating that was almost elegant, certainly more so than the bulky armour worn by the hardier human warriors.

The human was wielding a crude cutting tool with rotating teeth, a clumsy weapon if ever there was one, but dangerous enough to have Kulkavar drawing his own, far more graceful, sword.

The whole situation was unutterably tedious and a worthless distraction, especially when Kulkavar was on the verge of triumph, but the dark eldar lord forced himself to mentally translate the human's guttural utterances.

'– that we should meet under such circumstances, after all this time,' it was saying.

'All this time?' repeated Kulkavar, the words rough against his tongue. 'Should I know you, primate?' His monomolecular sword was fully drawn now, and it hummed through the air between the dark eldar and the human.

'I am Inquisitor Felip Velasco,' snapped the human, raising his chain-blade. 'I have thwarted your efforts on a dozen worlds and denied you your prizes every time.'

Kulkavar tilted his head, inspecting Velasco closely, trying to untangle his words. They seemed loaded with significance, but Kulkavar couldn't quite fathom the inquisitor's meaning. Efforts, worlds, prizes…?

'Ah,' said Kulkavar, hissing the exclamation. 'You are the little thing that keeps interfering with my acquisition of Haemonculus Graath's creations? Your efforts have been futile, as you can see, little nuisance. My destiny is at hand.'

'Your destiny?' repeated the affronted Velasco. 'Destiny,

yours or anyone's, has nothing to do with it. It is my duty
to defeat your plans at every turn, and it was inevitable this
would draw us together like this, into battle.'

Kulkavar smirked. He and the human were circling each
other, just a sword-length out of range of each other.

'You think you are of relevance to me?' Kulkavar asked
Velasco. 'You are nothing more than a pest. Nonetheless, if
you want your grand conflict, to fool yourself that you are
worthy to be some kind of nemesis to me, I am happy to
oblige. You have been a sufficient irritant to warrant dying
at my hand.'

Hool and Polk held back as the inquisitor confronted the
dark eldar lord, watching from a distance as the two circled
each other, exchanging taunts.

Hool found the whole experience surreal. A year of war had
taught him to shoot first, because if you didn't the enemy
certainly wouldn't hesitate. It was the lot of the Guardsman
and, he supposed, the common rebel or xenos warrior to be
thrown against the opposing lines, to feel that desperate rush
to kill the enemy before they killed you, a frantic struggle to
survive.

The inquisitor and the eldar lord danced around their
conflict as if it were some aristocratic game, some fancy or
distraction, exchanging fine words and diplomacies before
attacking each other. Even in the heat of battle, eldar and
humans alike were stepping away from them, creating a
duelling space at the centre of the battlefield.

Velasco made the first move, wielding his chainsword in a

low sweep that aimed to cut straight through the dark eldar lord's waist. The alien easily sidestepped this blow, using his own sword to flick Velasco's weapon sideways, the mono-molecular blade briefly engaging with the chainsword's rotating teeth in a shower of sparks.

As Velasco stumbled sideways, Kulkavar brought his blade around and up in a jab for the inquisitor's throat. However Velasco had regained his balance and easily ducked the blow, stepping back to take a fighting stance.

The two blades clashed and the duel continued.

With Kulkavar engaged elsewhere, Veldrax was leading the Kabalite troops. His success in obtaining their archon's prize had ranked him above the other sybarites in the shifting sands of the dark eldar warrior hierarchy, and they followed his suggestions as orders. Veldrax knew this situation wouldn't last – all it would take would be for one of the other sybarites to claim some measure of victory in this battle, and the jostling for position would begin anew – but he used his authority while he could.

The dark eldar fought well, claiming many souls, but the mon-keigh were many and the battle was fierce. Although they were crude creatures, Veldrax was surprised by the directness of the attack, the brazen onslaught.

This suspicion caused Veldrax to look further afield, and it was then that he saw the human vehicles.

It was Ganch, of all people, who spotted the dark eldar officer redirecting his troops in the direction of the two

Chimeras. The former sewer worker had managed to survive the battle while many more experienced fighting men had not, and was clubbing a fallen eldar in the face with the butt of a salvaged lasrifle when he spotted the shift in the tide of alien warriors, and alerted Hossk.

Ganch pointed, and Hossk looked across the field of battle to see a squad of dark eldar breaking away from the main melee, firing in the direction of the Chimera as they approached the platform.

Veldrax's warriors opened fire on the human vehicles, but splinter weapons were no match for armoured vehicles, especially at such a great distance. He called for Keldaz to bring his dark lance to bear.

Keldaz levelled the lance and he was cut down by a torrent of las-fire. As he fell, his back a mass of smoking burns, Veldrax could see a blue-jacketed mob approaching, guns blazing.

Hossk was barely aiming as he ran at the group of dark eldar who had broken away to attack the Chimera – the aliens had made themselves a discrete target by leaving the field, an easy cluster for Hossk and his men to attack.

The dark eldar returned fire, turning their attention to the humans behind them and breaking off their attack on the distant vehicles. Either side of Hossk, Guardsmen were falling in mid-stride, cut down by splinter-fire, but ahead of them the xenos numbers were thinning too, breaking under the onslaught from the Guard.

Hossk hadn't even noticed that he had ceased to think of the workers from the habs as a separate group. As Stellin collapsed into the mud, doubled up by a splinter-shot to the gut, he was as much a comrade to Hossk as any Guardsman. Even Ganch, pierced through the eye by a barbed shard of crystal, struck Hossk as a loss.

All the dark eldar were dead and wounded as Hossk and the last of his men reached their position. Hossk skidded in the mud as he came to a halt, digging one heel into the wet ground.

A wounded eldar rolled over in the mud and raised a long, heavy-barrelled weapon Hossk and his final surviving troops were no more, blasted to pieces in a flurry of dark matter.

Veldrax was dying, but still found enough pleasure to smile as fragments of the humans he had obliterated with the dark lance fell all around him, smoking scraps littering the ground. The sybarite coughed painfully, liquid filling the grille of his helmet. There was a low, numb heat in his chest, a las-wound that had burnt through a lung and who-knew-what else.

Soon, She Who Thirsts would know him. His tainted soul was doomed, there was nothing that could stop that, but Veldrax could cause a little more suffering before he went.

Chest wracked in agony, Veldrax rolled over on the filthy ground, raising Keldaz's dark lance and aiming it at the first of the two Chimeras.

He would not get a chance to fire at the second – as the weapon unleashed a furious burst of dark-matter energy, its kickback caused the entire weapon to buck, slamming into Veldrax's injured chest and crushing his lungs. He slumped across the lance, dead eyes unable to see the carnage he had caused.

The Chimera ahead of Deaz was gone, dark energy tearing through its armour and leaving little but a patch of liquid metal. Deaz instinctively recoiled, but the shot consumed the Chimera's volatile cargo whole, without any wider explosion.

Deaz shouted at his driver to swerve around the smoking wreckage, which somehow he managed to do without igniting any of the chamazian within. They prepared themselves for a further attack, but none came.

A couple of minutes later, Deaz's Chimera rolled onto the platform, heading towards the Lung.

The Imperial and dark eldar forces had both suffered heavy casualties, but their respective leaders still fought on. Hool watched as Velasco and Kulkavar continued to circle each other in what was an increasingly uneven combat: the dark eldar lord had the upper hand, the inquisitor seeming clumsy and exhausted by comparison. Kulkavar was dancing around his opponent, his blade slicing right through Velasco's armour, leaving long, bloody cuts.

The dark eldar lord could have killed Velasco at any time, but instead he was toying with one of the Emperor's inquisitors, torturing him for sport in front of a field of Guardsmen. The insult would not stand, and Hool aimed to end this farce.

He raised his lasrifle to fire at Kulkavar, but Polk lunged over and batted it down again.

'Velasco will shoot you himself if you interfere,' said Polk.

'Then he's insane,' replied Hool. 'That eldar is going to kill him.'

'He's an inquisitor, and our superior,' Polk snapped. 'You can't say he's insane, and if he wants to fight this xenos to the death, we need to let him.'

Hool was about to protest, but was struck by the precision of Polk's words. *You can't say he's insane.* Not *he isn't insane,* but *you can't say he's insane.* Hool looked back to where Velasco and the dark eldar lord were fighting. The inquisitor had rallied, and had pushed his opponent backwards, smacking the flat side of his chainsword's blade into the eldar's lower arm to knock away his sword.

They were insane, but the likes of Polk and Hool weren't allowed to say it. The rational thing to do would be for Hool to intervene on Velasco's behalf, but Polk, a lifelong Guardsman, had stopped him. Because inquisitors, lords and officers had to be given free rein to indulge their madness.

Was this how it was to be a Guardsman, was this the unspoken presumption beneath everything they did? That in spite of all the noble talk of the Emperor's will and the good of mankind, men like Polk and Hool lived and died at the whim of lunatics?

Were all their battles as meaningless as Velasco's grudge duel against an alien he had never met before today, an alien who didn't even know who he was?

Hool felt a cold weight of realisation in his stomach, that

even if this were the case, the Guard was his life now. He would either bend to the insanity as Polk had, or be broken by it.

After much trial and error, Zekov had aligned the gravitational forces involved, and was successfully towing the Lung. He stood at the rear of the Raider's deck, and as the vehicle lifted from the platform the Lung did also, staying at a fixed distance behind.

He ordered the Raider's pilot to rise higher, to bring them above the level of the buildings around them, so that they could guide the Lung off the platform.

Out on the moor, dark eldar and humans alike turned to see the Lung rising above the cluster of blackened buildings on the platform. It seemed even more alive while defying gravity, its corpulent mass glowing from within, as if it were elevating itself.

Kulkavar knocked back an incoming blow from the human Velasco, and took satisfaction in his prize as it was lifted to safety. Some of the humans were attempting to fire on the Lung, but their feeble las-weapons couldn't scratch it.

His victory was complete.

Deaz could hardly miss the Lung as the Chimera rolled into the centre of the ruins on the platform. Deaz ordered the driver to floor the accelerator, but he knew he was too late. The plan had been to drive at least one of the Chimeras to the centre of the platform, abandon it and detonate the chamazian from a safe distance. But it was clear the dark eldar were on the verge of escaping.

The Chimera rolled under the Lung without even scratching the underside, braking over the scuffed section of platform where the Lung had sat for so many centuries.

Deaz craned his neck forwards over the Chimera's dash, staring up at the strange alien device above. Was it even within range?

There was no time to find out. Deaz wished he had time to let the driver get away. He wished he had time to let himself get away. But there was no time left.

Deaz drew his bolt pistol, leaned into the back of the Chimera and fired a bolt-round straight into a barrel of undiluted chamazian.

The Chimera was torn apart by the blast, a white-hot fireball ripping through its armoured shell, casting out fragments of red-hot metal as flame spilled out in all directions. Most of the roof of the vehicle was thrown upwards as a single slab, smashing into the bottom of the Lung as flame enveloped it.

The power of the explosion buffeted Zekov's Raider, and the vehicle carrying the haemonculus spun out of control, reeling over the buildings to crash on the other side of the platform.

At its centre, the surface of the platform was cracked and scorched by the explosion, a crater gouged out of the centre where Deaz's Chimera had been just seconds before. Fault lines began to open up, cracks spreading out from the areas of greatest damage.

The Lung had been unaffected by the initial blast, its uncanny surfaces untouched by burnmarks, but the same could not be said for the gravity rig Zekov had attached to it, which was utterly destroyed. Without it, the Lung's great weight dragged it downwards as the smoke cleared. The Lung hit the ancient stone surface with an impact that could be felt well beyond the platform's edge, that reverberated out into the muddy ground of the surrounding area.

In spite of the force of the impact, the Lung remained undamaged. But the platform itself was not. What had been hairline cracks after the explosion widened as the jolt from the Lung shook the ancient stone, spreading out. Sections of rock began to fall away, revealing the pit below, a sheer well that reached all the way down to the Lung's original underground location.

A central section of the platform began to tilt, freed by deep cracks that ran on either side. As that section tilted, so the Lung began to slide downwards. The weight of it accelerated the tilt of the stone, and the section of platform swung through one hundred and eighty degrees, the Lung unceremoniously falling into the pit below in a shower of smoking stone fragments.

The Lung fell, tumbling into the pit below, hurtling towards the empty cavern where it had sat, neglected, for uncounted years. Where once it had rested on its platform at the heart of Dalson Graath's underground lab, now there was just the dusty rock floor where ancient machinery had detached itself on its rise to the planet's surface.

While Graath had built the Lung to be resilient, even

he could not protect it against the momentum of such a fall. It hit the bottom and shattered on impact. As its shell was breached, the unnatural energies that flowed within it expanded outwards in a rush, a column of gaseous energy spiralling outwards and upwards, searching for release. The flow of sinister energy burst from the hole in the platform, piercing the sky, wraithlike currents churning within it.

For a few seconds, the air for kilometres around was filled with blinding, unnatural light.

Then, as suddenly as it started, the light was gone, leaving nothing but a smoking, frayed hole in the centre of the platform, steam rising from the vertiginous chasm below.

The Lung was destroyed, no trace remaining.

EIGHTEEN

Kulkavar looked away from the pillar of smoke emerging from the platform, to see the human Velasco smirking.

'Everything you try and achieve, I will destroy,' said Velasco, raising his chainsword with visible exertion. 'Now I will kill you, and end this.'

'There is no "this",' replied Kulkavar, sheathing his monomolecular sword. 'This is a setback, and you are an irrelevance unworthy of my attention.'

Kulkavar issued a high whistle as he turned his back on the inquisitor. Responding to their master's signal, Kulkavar's retinue sprang into action, forming a wall between their lord and the human.

Kulkavar walked away, his warriors forming a path for him across the battlefield, some throwing themselves into inevitable death from the humans to do so.

'No!' shouted Velasco, his chainsword meeting the shield of one of Kulkavar's personal guard. 'Come back here!' Guardsmen were running to assist Velasco, firing at the wall of warriors between him and the dark eldar lord, but this support wasn't arriving fast enough. Kulkavar was slowly, impassively walking away.

'No heroic confrontation for you, Velasco,' Kulkavar called back. 'Live or die here, you are beneath my attention.'

As Kulkavar walked away, the screams of his enemy at his back, he maintained a nonchalant external appearance. To deny Velasco his impertinent dreams of significance was the only revenge open to Kulkavar.

Beneath this impassive surface, a storm of rage was boiling. *Denied his victory! Denied by a human!*

Across the battlefield, the dark eldar were retreating, laying down suppressing fire as they withdrew to the remains of the platform. Anti-gravity vehicles began to lift off, swooping away towards the spaceport.

The men of the 114th fought them every centimetre of the way, not letting them retreat without casualties. Commissar Tordez rallied the surviving men, threatening a las-shot to the back of the skull to any man who didn't hound the retreating xenos with fire and fury. Even as the last Raider flew away, Smoker was down on one knee, hellgun spitting at the distant vehicle.

And then they were gone, leaving only a field of dead eldar and humans as evidence that they had been there at all.

* * *

Zekov awoke to disorientation and nausea to find himself slumped against cold metal. Wherever he was, everything was moving. He tried to move, but every part of his body hurt. Under certain circumstances such pain might be appreciated, but not considering the humiliation the haemonculus had just endured.

Opening his eyes, Zekov found that he had been dragged aboard Kulkavar's personal Raider, and he lay slumped on the deck, propped against a railing. Kulkavar was sat on his command throne, eyes looking down at the haemonculus, but unfocused, as if Kulkavar's attention was turned inwards.

Zekov wasn't sure Kulkavar had noticed him wake until his lord spoke. He turned his attention elsewhere, his eyes falling upon Veldrax's corpse lying on the deck of the Raider, glassy eyes staring upwards. The damage to the corpse seemed limited, and although Veldrax was quite dead, Zekov would have the sybarite regenerated without any difficulty, to fight, and possibly die, once more for Kulkavar.

It was the archon's voice that broke Zekov's train of thought.

'Everything lost,' Kulkavar said, his voice low. His posture was almost slumped, and he seemed stripped of his aristocratic bearing. 'To have come so close, but to be denied...' He trailed off, one gauntleted hand grasping through thin air.

'My archon?' Zekov said, his throat hot and raw, the words slurred.

Kulkavar was staring off into the darkening moorland. The sun was beginning to set across the bleak landscape, and the cold air whipped the dark eldar lord's hair behind him.

'This… this…' Kulkavar trailed off, then threw back his head and laughed in a way Zekov had never seen before, each laugh seeming to shake some of Kulkavar's old aristo-cratic bearing back into his shoulders. By the time he tipped his head forwards, a bitter smirk still slashed across his fea-tures, he seemed restored.

'This loss, this rage at denial, is quite the most exquisite misery I have tasted in decades,' said Kulkavar. 'To experi-ence such unique suffering, why, it justifies this venture in and of itself.'

Kulkavar laughed again, his laughter echoing across the causeway as the Raider swept into the spaceport.

As the dark eldar ship took off in the distance, streaking out of Belmos VII's atmosphere, Velasco was already barking orders into his vox, requesting extraction.

With Major Geiss and his three lieutenants dead, Smoker, lieutenant for less than a day, was now the most senior surviving officer on the planet. As such, once the battle was over he shadowed the inquisitor, ready to receive orders. Smoker assigned Hool to follow him, to relay said orders to the troops.

There were none. Velasco barely spoke once the dark eldar had retreated. In spite of having denied Kulkavar the Lung, and having prevented what terror the dark eldar might have inflicted with such a device, the conflict had left him brooding.

Surprisingly, Velasco's landing capsule had survived the

destruction of much of the platform. Scorched but not destroyed, it sat at the end of a jagged outcrop over the still-steaming pit. Either fearless or heedless of the possibility of collapse, Velasco walked across the fragile-looking promontory, and stood on top of the capsule to wait.

The mist had cleared, and Velasco removed his rebreather helmet. Unmasked, his features seemed more ordinary, more human, to Hool. His silver hair and blue eyes were still striking, but he had a weak chin and protruding ears.

'Lieutenant Essler, I suggest you withdraw your men to the city-factory,' Velasco said, looking down from his perch atop the capsule. 'When my shuttle grapples the capsule on board, it will need to hover low. This may cause further structural damage to the area. I would not wish your men to suffer any injury.'

'Thank you, sir,' said Smoker, snapping out a salute.

'I regret that I cannot offer your men transit, or stay to aid you in your mission,' added Velasco. When asked, the inquisitor had described the wreckage of a ship in orbit around Belmos VII, confirming the destruction of the *Seraphim*.

'I must continue my pursuit of Kulkavar, and prevent his next gambit,' said Velasco. 'When opportunity arises I will inform your superiors that you require extraction.'

With another exchange of salutes, Smoker and Hool left the inquisitor standing alone in the ruins. Shortly after his silver shuttle hovered overhead, the roar of its engines temporarily deafening them all as the capsule was hoisted into the ship's cargo bay, the tiny figure of Velasco clinging to the cable as the capsule was winched home.

Then the shuttle was gone, and with it the noise.

The Guardsmen were left to return to the city-factory in silence.

The silence that hung over the surviving Mordians as they trudged across the moor was not just a response to the losses they had incurred, although those had been terrible.

It was the knowledge that night was falling, and the inevitable conflict that would occur.

The numerous battles, explosions, raids and fires of the previous day and night must have reduced the infected population severely, but no one among the Guard could retain enough hope to presume that infected numbers would be minimal, or that the destruction of the Lung might have wiped them out or cured them.

Hool was aware of the threat that faced them once they crossed the city walls, but the day's events had left him with difficulty processing any new danger. In less than a day he had encountered his first xenos, an Imperial inquisitor, and a living weapon capable of incredible destruction. He had been exposed to the terrors of the universe in ways he had not previously thought possible, and had his eyes opened. It was all much, much worse than he could have imagined.

Most of all, Hool couldn't shake the image of Velasco and Kulkavar locked in futile, self-indulgent combat, and how it might be a microcosm for all the struggles across the galaxy. A million battles, each the whim of some commander aiming to make his mark. Billions of lives lost on vanity and miscalculation.

Hool looked furtively across at Polk. These thoughts were not the kind that the sergeant would approve of. Even after the losses they had suffered, Sergeant Polk continued to walk tall, uniform torn, wounds showing, but still the picture of a Mordian Guardsman, disciplined to the last. Unbreakable, as a man of the 114th should be.

Polk might entertain doubts about this or that order, but he would never let them undermine his loyalty to the Guard, his duty to his fellow Guardsmen.

But, past Polk, Hool could see Smoker, striding along, a lho-stick lodged in his grille. Hool couldn't pretend to entirely understand Lieutenant Essler, but he suspected that he was not beset by doubts, not because he had endless faith in the orders passed down to him, but because he simply did not care.

Smoker was a machine for survival. He did not concern himself with the context of his actions – he just continued to survive.

Hool's thoughts remained conflicted, but to an extent he had no conflict at all, as he was too exhausted to do anything but react. Instead he marched, and steeled himself for the night ahead, suppressing the frantic, uncomfortable feeling that he was at the edge of coping, that he was one further crisis away from losing some part of himself altogether.

As they re-entered the city's west gate, Polk was keeping an eye on Hool. The young Guardsman seemed disturbed. Understandable, perhaps, but Polk didn't want to see Hool survive so much only to receive a commissar's bolt in the back of his skull due to a battlefield panic.

The area around the west gate was an anonymous goods yard, equidistant between the workers' habs and the refinery. The ground was greased with tyretracks and spilt oil, and multicoloured barrels were stacked high on all sides.

Polk's instinct was that, having survived so far, Hool would cope with the inevitable battle against the infected, and would continue to persevere. He was a good Guardsman, a survivor, the kind of man the Unbreakable 114th rested upon.

This confidence grew in Polk's chest. He was increasingly certain Hool would be fine. That Polk would be fine.

'We are being watched,' said Gilham.

'I know,' replied Smoker. 'Prepare yourselves. Make no move until they do.'

Polk *felt* fine. Better than fine. In spite of the day's exertions, he felt strong and well. Although night had settled on the goods yard, and lighting was intermittent, he could see the infected on the city walls and jumping across the rows of barrels, their eyes gently glowing with a dull inner light. He could almost smell them, even over the bloodrush of his fellow Guardsmen.

'Here we go,' Hool muttered.

To Polk's sensitive hearing, he might as well have shouted it. Yes, here we go, Hool. Another battle, *ho-hum*, as if the younger man really knew what he was talking about, had lived through real conflict. Who was he, to talk of war, when Polk had decades of experience over him?

'Incoming,' snapped Smoker, raising his hellgun to shoot

an infected out of the sky as he leapt from the top of the barrel stacks. 'Fire at will.'

Polk ignored the order. He was staring at Hool, who had started firing his lasrifle at approaching infected. Polk's bitterness had curdled to rage, that rage tinged with hunger, and his fingers tightened around the barrel of his combat shotgun as he looked at Hool, and saw neither a friend nor ally but prey, coursing blood and tender meat and–

'Sergeant?' asked Hool, turning to Polk. 'Is something wrong?'

When he looked closer, and saw the unnatural glow of the whites of Polk's eyes, Hool knew, knew not just what had happened, but how. He saw in his mind the moment when Polk had fallen near the Lung, deep underground, shot down by a dark eldar. There had been no injury, but Hool remembered how the splinter had shattered on impact, tearing through the front of Polk's jacket.

It would have been an easy thing for any of them to miss, a stray crystal fragment nicking the rebreather mask Polk had been wearing. The tiniest fissure would have let the gas from the Lung into the mask, and Polk would have been breathing it in from that point on.

One breath, and he would have been infected, and it took a similar amount of time for Hool to realise that, and to raise his lasrifle. He heard himself making some entreaty to Polk, but had no idea what he was actually saying. Whatever it was, it did no good – Polk batted Hool's lasrifle aside and piled into him, knocking them both to the ground.

Then Hool was flat on his back, winded, clawing hands digging into him. There was no help from elsewhere – in Hool's peripheral vision he could see Guardsmen fighting off incoming infected. In the chaos, no one had noticed Polk turn on Hool.

Polk's right hand clamped on to Hool's face, the thumb gouging into his cheek, tearing through skin and flesh, as Polk's forefinger pressed into Hool's left eye. Searing pain burned through Hool's optic nerve and he screamed, choking with effort not to black out, as Polk's finger burst his eyeball.

Looking up through his one good eye, his reduced vision blurred further still by a mist of tears, Hool could see Polk was completely rabid, reduced to utter savagery. There would be no reasoning with him. Another wave of pain and nausea wracked Hool's body as Polk's forefinger dug ever deeper within Hool's eye socket, the corresponding thumb scraping bone within the wound it had torn into his face.

Finger and thumb were pushing closer to each other. Hool had the horrific realisation that Polk was going to grip his skull and tear Hool's head off.

With a rush of cold fury Hool brought his knee up into Polk's chest, knocking the older man upwards. The blow didn't loosen the grip of Polk's right hand on Hool's wrecked face, but it did leave the other arm flailing, allowing Hool to bat it aside. As Polk jerked briefly upwards, Hool's hand darted into the narrow space between their two bodies, to where Polk's combat shotgun still hung on a safety strap. Grabbing the barrel, Hool pulled the gun upwards so that as Polk fell flat on top of Hool, the shotgun was jammed between their chests.

The pressure of Polk's body weight pressed the shotgun down into Hool's ribcage, the barrel a solid bar of metal that threatened to crush the air from his chest. Hool had perhaps one lungful of air before he was finished.

His face in agony, pain shooting through his entire body, Hool let go of his grip on Polk's right wrist, removing the resistance to Polk's attack. As Polk used his other hand to push himself upwards, his hand digging further into Hool's face, Hool dropped his free hand down to the trigger of the shotgun, fumbling into the space between them as Polk pushed himself up, preparing to tear Hool's head off.

With both hands gripping the shotgun, Hool exhaled and put every gram of energy in his body into one great upwards thrust pushing the shotgun up into his mentor's chest, the tip of the barrel resting against Polk's chin.

Hool's pain-drowned mind swam with memories and emotion.

Recruitment on Mordian, saving his life and giving it new purpose.

Training him to survive, watching each other's backs.

Side by side on Elisenda and Belmos VII, surviving while all around them fell.

Fighting together against rebels, savage humans, eldar.

Camaraderie, leadership, loyalty.

Hool's mind snapped back to the present, his one surviving eye taking in the now, Polk's merciless, savage gaze, the glow within the whites of his eyes, the mouth twisted in sadistic fury. A monster, the old Polk already gone.

Hool's little finger pressed down on the trigger of the combat shotgun. Polk kept the mechanism well-oiled and easy to use, and it only took a little flick of the finger to fire. The shell that burst into Polk's chin shattered his skull explosively, and the kickback slammed the weapon into Hool's knee, almost shattering the kneecap.

Polk's headless body bucked backwards with the impact of the shot, and the force of Hool jabbing the gun upwards combined with the sudden loss of tension in the lifeless body sent Polk's corpse rolling across the oily ground.

Hool lay there for what could have been seconds, hours, minutes, his entire body wracked with shock, the open wound in his face feeling ever colder. Presently Hool saw a face looking down on him with urgent concern. It was only as Hool instinctively swung the combat shotgun up towards the man looking down at him that Hool realised he was still gripping the weapon with both hands.

Avrim batted Polk's shotgun out of Hool's grip, the gun slipping between his numb fingers. The medicae leaned close over Hool, examining the extent of his wounds, and swore under his breath.

'We need to get you to safety,' said Avrim slowly and precisely, resting a reassuring hand on Hool's shoulder. 'Once we get you clear, I'll give you a shot to put you out, and I'll fix all this before you come round.' Avrim gestured to the mauled side of Hool's head.

'No.' Hool didn't know he was going to protest until he did, but as he spoke cold certainty rose within him. He had suffered so that he could fight on, not retreat from the field. He needed to fight on, it was why he survived. Hool grasped Avrim's upper arm, and the medicae looked surprised at both Hool's sudden strength and his determination.

'Seal this up and give me enough stimms to get through the next hour or so,' Hool told the medicae. 'Everything else can wait.'

Avrim held Hool's gaze for a few seconds, as if weighing up whether Hool was fit to make such a decision.

'Very well,' the medicae said, digging into his kit for the right instrument. 'This is going to hurt a lot.'

It was through the efforts of every man standing that the 114th won the night against overwhelming odds.

Adept Gilham, technically a non-combatant, slaughtered dozens of infected, swinging his pneumatic hammer back and forth, his red robes torn to shreds.

Calway, a civilian the day before, led his group of new recruits in a tight squad, suffering only two losses in a gruelling battle.

Tordez, fighting both the enemy and the danger of a collapse in morale, hectored every last man to fight on in the face of exhaustion and the relentless nature of their enemy, wielding his pistol and his words with equal vigour.

And there was Hool, a young Guardsman, fighting alongside Lieutenant Essler as he led the Mordians to victory.

Everyone who saw Hool, bloodied and one-eyed, fighting that night agreed that he seemed to be unstoppable. When the power cell of one lasrifle gave way with a splutter, Hool tossed it aside and pulled another from the dead hands of a fallen comrade, doing so without hesitation or emotion. With his infected sergeant dead by his own hand, Hool rallied the remnants of his old squad to keep fighting through the night.

It was this level of relentless aggression that won the night, that drove back the few infected who survived, infected who would be hunted down and slaughtered over the coming days, until Belmos VII was clean of the Lung's influence, and all there was to do was wait until extraction arrived.

Throughout, Fernand Hool fought without fear or mercy. Unbreakable.

EPILOGUE

Inquisitor Velasco had proved as good as his word, informing the authorities on the next planet he visited that an Imperial Guard strike force required extraction from Belmos VII. This message had been relayed to the appropriate military authorities, including Colonel Ruscin on Elisenda.

This information had been accompanied by a glowing endorsement of the strike force's military prowess from the inquisitor, for their assistance in – and these were Velasco's exact words – 'the spectacular aversion on my part of a disastrous threat to humanity from a xenos mastermind wielding a weapon of terrible power.'

Thus, when a shuttle from the Imperial Frigate *Iphigenia* landed on Belmos VII, six weeks after the strike force had landed, they not only provided a welcome extraction for a force of men who had killed the last of the infected a number of weeks before, but also news that they had raised their reputation within the Imperial Guard.

No longer would the 114th Mordian Iron Guard be deployed against rabble like the Elisendan traitors – after their victory against the dark eldar, they were considered worthy of a place on the front-line against the enemies of man.

The fringe of the Gothic Sector, where greenskins infested countless worlds, awaited them.

The existing city on Belmos VII was, as the late Lieutenant Hossk had predicted, finished. The few civilian survivors had been press-ganged into the 114th, and left their former home with the regiment. Few looked back as they mounted the ramp of the drop-ship.

Somewhere, the Munitorum had set in motion the process to rebuild and repopulate Belmos VII. Soon, great ships would come, with cargo bays loaded with equipment and supplies. Legions of servitors would go out onto the surface, and repair and rebuild the industrial facilities and living quarters.

In due course, a new population of workers would arrive, shipped in from some other planet due to a change in Imperium priorities. They would be set to work, entirely unaware of what had previously occurred on Belmos VII.

That was for another day. As the troopship lifted off, the city-factory was left empty, the dead lying where they had fallen, the streets deserted, the only movement that of debris tossed around by the icy winds that swept in from the moors.

* * *

On board the *Iphigenia*, the men of the 114th began to recover, to resume training and recuperate from any injuries. For some, limbs were splinted and painkillers were provided. For others, more radical interventions were needed.

'Look at the orange dot,' Gilham said, holding up a data-slate with a glowing circle in the centre of the display. 'Now keep looking at the dot, follow it, but don't move your head.'

Gilham moved the slate through a precise series of manoeuvres: up, down, left, right. Hool sat on a chair, sensors taped to the rim of the optical augmetic Gilham had fitted into his empty eye socket. The augmetic was simple, a red lens fitted into a housing of polished plasteel, and wires trailed from the sensors attaching it to a second data-slate on Gilham's work bench. His tests finished, the adept checked the readings on the second data-slate.

'All seems to be in order,' he told Hool, leaning over to remove the sensors.

Underneath the augmetic, the wound on Hool's face had begun to heal into a livid pink scar, still criss-crossed with the surgical staples Avrim had used on the battlefield. Gilham had consulted with the medicae to ensure Hool's wounds were sufficiently healed to accept the augmentation, and Avrim had mentioned that the staples had been redundant for a week, but Hool refused to have them removed.

Gilham was not a medicae himself. He understood how to augment the human body, but was not equipped to deal with the general health of his subjects, and certainly not their mental health. Nevertheless, Gilham's brush with the repressed anger Lieutenant Essler felt over his augmentations had left the adept with a wish to be more diligent in Hool's case. Lingering trauma was not beneficial to the functioning of the regiment.

'I understand that augmentation cannot entirely compensate for an injury,' Gilham said, attempting to express concern in his synthetic voice. 'It is understandable should you continue to feel some sense of loss–'

'I'm fine,' said Hool, cutting Gilham's rambling speech off in mid-sentence. He pointed at his augmented eye. 'I'm a soldier. Providing I can still fire straight, I'm fine.'

Hool and Gilham stared at each other for a second. Gilham's enhanced senses noted the pure whiteness of Hool's surviving eyeball. It almost seemed to glow, but Gilham had no metrics to assess whether this was actually the case.

Gilham had considered the possibility that the gas emitted by the Lung might have caused multiple levels of infection: that, aside from those transformed rapidly by breathing deeply, that limited exposure to the gas, perhaps via the skin, might cause a slower change, one with a longer incubation period.

It was a possibility, but Gilham had no hard data, certainly nothing to warrant raising it with authorities who might exterminate the survivors of the strike force on a precautionary whim. Gilham would watch and wait. The predicted life expectancy of a Guardsman was fifteen hours: what chance had a slow-incubating infection of actually taking effect?

This entire chain of thought passed through Gilham's cogitator-enhanced brain in a second as he held Hool's gaze.

'The augmetic has welded to the optic nerve well,' Gilham told Hool. 'Your marksmanship should be as good as before, if not marginally better. Please, return to your duties.'

'Thank you,' said Hool, standing up from the examination bench. He had stripped down to his shirt sleeves for the examination, and reached over to a hook on the wall to retrieve his jacket.

As Gilham stood patiently, Hool wordlessly buttoned the charcoal-grey jacket that marked him out as one of Essler's elite marksmen. He had changed squad on Belmos VII, barely resting in the weeks since the destruction of the Lung, as Smoker's squad gunned down the savage infected during the night, and burned down vacant buildings thought to harbour them during the day. Gilham had seen Hool take to this bloody work with cold determination. There was a difference in the man that Gilham didn't have the insight into human behaviour to quite place.

As Hool leaned forwards to put on his cap, for a moment all Gilham could see of the man's face was the red glow of the optical augmetic, and it was like Essler was standing there himself.

Then Hool straightened himself, gave Gilham a clipped salute, and left the room.

With an unplaceable sense of unease, Adept Gilham watched Corporal Hool walk away.

ABOUT THE AUTHOR

Mark Clapham was born and raised in Yorkshire, studied and worked in London for over a decade, and is now an itinerant writer and editor based in Exeter, Devon. His short stories have appeared in the *Fear the Alien* anthology and the monthly magazine *Hammer and Bolter*. *Iron Guard* is his first novel for Black Library.

WARHAMMER
40,000

ANDY HOARE

COMMISSAR

AN IMPERIAL GUARD NOVEL

An extract from Commissar
by Andy Hoare

If the first phase had been rough, the next was hellish. As the drop-ship plummeted through the thermosphere its outer hull grew white hot so that traces of flame whipped across the outer skin of the viewing port. As the ship crossed the Kármán line at one hundred and fifty kilometres above ground level the temperature soared further. Several times Flint blacked out, only to come to what must have been a few seconds later. Several of the provosts had passed out too, and a number had developed fearsome nosebleeds, red liquid splattering about the cabin as the force threatened to shake them all to atoms.

The vessel's regulators cycled to full power in an effort to counter the heat but still the passenger bay felt as hot as a furnace. Flint longed to cast off his heavy leather storm coat but he knew the drop would be over in minutes. Then he saw that the loadmaster had his hand pressed firmly to his earpiece and was shouting loudly into his vox-pickup.

'What?' Flint bellowed at the loadmaster, unable to reach across so powerful were the forces pressing him into his grav-couch. The officer tapped his earpiece and held up three fingers to indicate that Flint should set his vox-bead to channel three.

Clipped and fragmentary conversation burst from Flint's earpiece. '…locked. Repeat, target lock confirmed, over.'

Damn, Flint cursed inwardly as the pitch of the drop-ship's systems changed and he felt the vessel roll. 'Ground defences?' he yelled into the vox.

'Yes, sir,' replied the loadmaster, his voice distorted over the link. 'The rebels have control of one of the ground-to-orbit defence silos.'

Memories of Flint's first drop, the disastrous Gethsemane Landings, came unbidden to his mind, but with an effort of will he quickly dispelled them. There was nothing he could do except trust to the skills of the flight crew, the inexperience of the rebels controlling the defences and, most importantly, the beneficence of the God-Emperor of Mankind.

The drop-ship bucked wildly and the passengers were jolted hard in their restraints. Flint quickly scanned the faces of his staff to gauge their reaction to the situation. They had no idea what was happening and there was no point in telling them. Bukin maintained his steely expression, which Flint knew he felt compelled to do to keep up his position as top dog even though the rank brassard he wore at his shoulder was sure sign of it. The other provosts had their eyes screwed tight shut and their jaws set in a rictus grimace. Flint glanced sideways at his aide and saw that Kohlz was mouthing a silent prayer. Smart lad, thought the commissar.

The drop-ship bucked a second time and Flint felt it slew violently as it plummeted. He cast a look out of the port and saw that the barren wastes of Furia Penitens now completely filled the view. Jagged mountain ranges were visible through churning swirls of dark clouds illuminated from within by pulsating electrical storms. Millions of square kilometres of hard ground rushed upwards as if to swat the drop-ship from existence or smash it to oblivion in an instant.

'Receiving confirmation from intelligence, sir,' the load-master said through the vox-link. 'The rebels have control of a single battery. It's too late to abort; we're going in as planned.'

'There's no other option,' Flint agreed as the drop-ship's descent speed increased still further. To divert the first wave because of a single threat would be unforgivable, even if he himself was in that wave and therefore at risk.

'Incoming!' the loadmaster called over the vox-link. Flint glanced outside, though he knew he had no chance of catching sight of a missile homing in on the drop-ship before it struck and killed them all. A bright explosion blossomed several kilometres fore of the ship. The rebels had fired a cluster warhead.

Lacking the ability to fire a missile with pinpoint accuracy, the rebels must have coerced one of the weapon's crew into launching a weapon that would scatter a wide area with deadly munitions. As the explosion faded dozens of smaller points arced away on thick, black contrails. The fire of the detonation faded to be replaced by a dirty smear of turbulent smoke and the drop-ship was plummeting straight towards it. Flint fought against a sudden sense of overpowering vertigo as the entire vessel powered nose first into the debris cloud. One of the cluster munitions zipped past at hypervelocity and an instant later the drop-ship was out of the remnants of the explosion and the world below resolved once more, the mountains and valleys of the surface now visible in stunning detail.

'What the hell was that?' shouted the provost beside Corporal Bukin, his voice only barely audible over the roar of air against the drop-ship's hull. 'Some bastard shooting at us?'

'Not *us*,' shouted Corporal Bukin, 'just *you*,' before the entire drop-ship shuddered violently and the restraints tightened in response, pinning the passengers hard into their grav-couches. Flint knew instantly that one of the cluster munitions must have clipped the drop-ship.

The vessel's engines screamed like a gargantuan beast in terrible pain and the air pressure in the passenger bay bled out rapidly. With a sudden rush a blast of ice-cold air flooded the compartment and pressure masks dropped down from the bulkheads above each drop-station. The loadmaster reached up and pulled his mask over his face and in a moment Flint had his fitted too. He took a deep breath of the bottled oxygen then looked outside to judge the ship's altitude. The vessel shook violently as the pilot fought to bring its nose up and level with the horizon as a jagged spire surrounded by a halo of chimneys rose in the distance silhouetted against the grey sky. Flint guessed the drop zone was less than a minute away, if only the ship could hold together that long.

Flint lifted his mask and yelled, 'Everyone prepare for rapid disembarkation!'

He couldn't tell if any of the passengers heard him over the roar of the wind both inside and outside of the drop-ship. The sound grew louder still as the ship levelled out. Flint took a ragged breath of the cold air and found that the pressure had equalised enough for him to breathe normally.

As the drop-ship plunged through a rearing cloudbank it shook violently and Flint's ears were assaulted by the deafening sound of a section of the metal hull shearing away. The shaking increased to a continuous, bone-jarring tremor punctuated by subsonic growls and high pitched, metallic wails.

'Ten seconds!' the loadmaster called out. 'Brace for impact!'

Flint knew the drill. He folded his arms across his chest and set his head firmly against the padded headrest. The provosts' training had kicked in too, regardless of their outward brusqueness. But Kohlz had loosened his seat restraint and was attempting to secure his vox-set which was working its way loose of the cargo bin he had stowed it in.

'Leave it!' Flint ordered, grabbing Kohlz'ss wrist hard. At that very moment the drop-ship struck a tall rock spire and the world turned upside down. The illumination inside the passenger bay cut out, a bright spear of sunlight arcing through the small viewport. The vessel dropped what must have been a thousand metres in a second and rolled onto its side. It held its course for several seconds more before the deafeningly loud roar of tearing metal made Flint look left. A massive wound had appeared in the side of the vessel and the thrashing bodies of several passengers had already been sucked through it. There was nothing anyone else could do, either to rescue them, or to avoid a similar fate. The only possible course of action was to pray to the God-Emperor of Mankind, and hold on for dear life.

Seconds later, the drop-ship slammed into the hard ground with bone-jarring force.

Exclusively available
from *blacklibrary.com*